THE SCHOOL OF NIGHT

Also by Karl Ove Knausgaard

A Time for Everything

MY STRUGGLE
A Death in the Family
A Man in Love
Boyhood Island
Dancing in the Dark
Some Rain Must Fall
The End

Home and Away: Writing the Beautiful Game (with Fredrik Ekelund)

SEASONS QUARTET
Autumn (with illustrations by Vanessa Baird)
Winter (with illustrations by Lars Lerin)
Spring (with illustrations by Anna Bjerger)
Summer (with illustrations by Anselm Kiefer)

So Much Longing in So Little Space: The Art of Edvard Munch
In the Land of the Cyclops: Essays

MORNING STAR
The Morning Star
The Wolves of Eternity
The Third Realm

THE SCHOOL OF NIGHT

KARL OVE KNAUSGAARD

Translated from the Norwegian by Martin Aitken

1 3 5 7 9 10 8 6 4 2

Harvill, an imprint of Vintage, is part of the Penguin Random House group of companies

Vintage, Penguin Random House UK, One Embassy Gardens, 8 Viaduct Gardens, London SW11 7BW

penguin.co.uk/vintage
global.penguinrandomhouse.com

First published by Harvill in 2025
First published with the title *Nattskolen* by Forlaget Oktober, Oslo, in 2024

Copyright © Karl Ove Knausgaard 2025
Translation copyright © Martin Aitken 2025

The moral right of the author has been asserted

This translation has been published with the financial support of NORLA

No part of this book may be used or reproduced in any manner for the purpose of training artificial intelligence technologies or systems. In accordance with Article 4(3) of the DSM Directive 2019/790, Penguin Random House expressly reserves this work from the text and data mining exception.

Typeset in 10/15 pt Swift LT Std by Six Red Marbles UK, Thetford, Norfolk
Printed and bound in Great Britain by Clays Ltd, Elcograf S.p.A.

The authorised representative in the EEA is Penguin Random House Ireland, Morrison Chambers, 32 Nassau Street, Dublin D02 YH68

A CIP catalogue record for this book is available from the British Library

HB ISBN 9781787304208
TPB ISBN 9781787304215

Penguin Random House is committed to a sustainable future
for our business, our readers and our planet. This book is made
from Forest Stewardship Council® certified paper.

For my brother, Yngve

The clock will strike

PART ONE

There is no reason to be afraid of death — when we exist, death is not; and when death exists, we are not. This, roughly, is how Epicurus put it a long time ago. I tend to think of it as like sharing a flat with a lodger you never see. The flat has two rooms, and two doors. Whenever you go through one door, the lodger goes out by the other. You might hear him moving about from time to time, but the moment you go in, he'll go out to where you just came from and start moving about there instead. This is how we live our lives, with death on the other side of the wall. The day we meet him in the doorway, it's over. The sly thing is that we never know when it's going to happen, only that sooner or later it will. Of course, if we want to, we're free to take the matter into our own hands and provoke the encounter.

Which is what I'm intending to do.

Perhaps the above sounds like I find there to be something casual about it all — a flat, an encounter with a lodger — but the lightness belongs to the language, not to me. If I could articulate what I'm feeling as I sit here, the despair that night and day rips and tears at me, the bottomless darkness, you would understand. But I can't, for in language there is hope, in language there is light. The night is without language. And language is always directed towards another. To convey loneliness by means of language is therefore impossible. Where there is loneliness, language is not; where there is language, loneliness is not.

In other words, then, I am 'lonely'. And I am going to 'take' my own life.

But first I'm going to write this. Every day, in the weeks to come, I'm going to wake in the room upstairs, come down here, make coffee, and sit down at this desk in front of the window; I'm going to look out on the little harbour, and beyond it to the sea — which at this time of the year is mostly greys and blacks; I'm going to drink my coffee, smoke and work away at this story until it is finished. Why, I'm not entirely sure. Is it to do with how everything that happens just peters away into nothingness, and that this basically makes every event meaningless? The way it's all to no avail? If those events are written down, they at least will exist somewhere. As for whoever may read what I now write, I don't care. Perhaps it will be you, Emil, since you're the owner of this house I have appropriated for the purpose. If so, I hope you can forgive me — I trust at least that I'll have made sure to tidy and clean the place when I've finished with it and that you'll find it in a better state than when you left it. Or perhaps it will be you, Yelena — in which case you need read no further: you know what's coming. Perhaps it will be you, a local policeman, searching the place after my corpse has been found washed up on the shore somewhere close by. Or drifting on the sea, discovered by a fisherman or by the crew of one of the big containers ships that plough back and forth off the coast here and whose passage I follow through the windows every day. I don't know, and I don't care. I'm writing this for myself. Or rather, for 'my self'. The two words that contain everything we ever were, are and will be. Sitting here, at this particular moment, I am just a fraction of all that, perhaps only a few thousandths of it, while the rest, the bulk, lies stored in my cells. Some of it I am able to activate of my own accord — it's called remembering — though most of it comes and goes as it pleases. So it is for all of us, presumably also for cats and dogs. As creatures they are superior to us — not only is much of their sensory apparatus more highly developed than our own, they have also had the nous, in what can only be described as an evolutionary stroke of genius, to halt the advancement of their conscious minds at the ascertainment *I am here*, rather than proceeding, as we have done, to the question of *why*.

Procrastination, this is called. I don't want to think, I don't want to know, I don't want to understand. And yet I must. Must I not?

Yes.

I don't want to write about what happened to me. But then again, I don't want to die before I've done so.

So where do I begin?
At the beginning, perhaps.

*

The first time I came across the name Christopher Marlowe was in August 1985, the summer I moved to London, where, much to my surprise, I'd been offered a place to study photography at an art school. Apart from music, I knew practically nothing about British culture, so one of the first places I visited was Foyles, the bookshop on Charing Cross Road, where I bought ten contemporary British novels in paperback, and then the collected works of Shakespeare, as well as a non-fiction book about creativity. I began with Shakespeare, but his plays were as good as impenetrable to me, so I returned to Foyles a few days later and bought a biography of the man and a book about the age in which he lived, to see if they might become more accessible to me. I dropped the books into my bag and walked towards what I now knew to be the Bloomsbury district, continuing on to Camden Town, where I sat down with a pint outside a pub and began skimming the biography. The very moment I set eyes on the name Christopher Marlowe, I looked up and saw in front of me a big lorry with the words *Marlowe Removals* along the side, green lettering against a white background. As if that wasn't enough, I then read that Marlowe had been killed in Deptford — the same district I'd moved to only a few days earlier. Someone was pointing, but I didn't look. I just closed the book, put it back in my bag and tramped off in a northerly direction, in the gigantic metropolis in which I now lived.

Lectures didn't start until three weeks later. I knew nobody, and so I bought a bicycle and started to familiarise myself with the local area, at the same time as I took loads of photographs, always uncertain as to whether my work would be good enough to meet the school's standards. The bedsit I rented was small and sparsely furnished — a bed settee, a desk, a bookcase — and so I spent as little time in it as possible. The neighbourhood wasn't exactly charming either — the riverside area was run-down industry, disused warehouses, old factory chimneys, broken windows, piles of rubble from buildings that had been demolished and not been replaced. Chugging lorries here, scrap merchants there. And if in places a patch of green had grown up in all the colourless grey, rubbish would seemingly always be dumped on it. The shops in the streets had long since gone to seed. Often, they'd be selling a clutter of different goods, mostly things that I imagined could have been sold in the shops back home in the 1960s, things that looked so outmoded I'd never seen them on sale anywhere before. The signs above the doors of these places all seemed to stem from the previous century, or at least the 1920s or 1930s. There were cafes with handwritten menus and net curtains in the windows; a bakery, a butcher's shop, where those behind the counter wore white, blood-spattered aprons. In this world behind the times, there was a brilliant record shop called Solid Cut, it was only small, but they had really good stuff, and I spent more than a few quid there during the first couple of weeks. There were foreign shops too, I guessed at African — one sold wigs, hair extensions, colourful fabrics, and I photographed the place from the pavement. I wanted to go inside and take pictures there as well, but I held back, unsure of how to go about things yet.

In the evenings I'd sit drinking over a book in the nearby pubs — there was practically one on every corner, the smoke-stained interiors unchanged in decades. The people there laughed a lot more than I was used to at home, and the bar staff called everyone *love*. The England I knew from the *NME* and *Sounds* was nowhere to be seen here — the odd young guy in a long overcoat with a cool haircut might go by once in a while, a group of goths might be sat in a corner one night, and a jukebox would occasionally play the Jam or U2 or the Alarm (I remember hearing 'Into the Valley' by the Skids once, and 'Teenage Kicks' by the Undertones), but that was just the area, Camden and Soho were different altogether.

It's weird — a few nights in a row in the same place and you start recognising people, someone might acknowledge you with a nod, you get talking, and if it happens more than once then all of a sudden you're friends, perhaps even for life, without either of you having intended. That was how, in those first few days in London, I met Hans, a Dutch artist ten years older than me. He wasn't the only artist living in the area, I soon found out — everything was so run-down around there they could afford to rent studios as well as somewhere to live. There were a lot of drugs about compared to what I was used to, and plenty of dreams that came to nothing, or at least were radically scaled back. Even the strongest, most determined of wills could be ground down in the space of a few short years. By what? it might be asked. What forces are powerful enough to wear out a human life? Biologically, it's obvious enough — our physical decline begins in our twenties, it's a process that ticks away in us all. But what of psychological erosion, what governs that? This is fate, of course. All those thousands of chance occurrences that lead you to one place rather than another, to people whose wills and dreams and abilities collide with the prevailing conditions there. That's why artificial intelligence, AI, will never be able to think like us. Even if the machines are self-teaching and able to adapt according to experience, the parameters are still rational, the machines will necessarily and for always be remote to the deep, slow-shifting layers of reality where fate is at work, and therefore they will always be remote to us. Even as simple a thing as coming up with a random number turned out to be far from straightforward for a machine, for in any circumstance there was always a program in the background that first had to define the algorithm, whereby all randomness was cancelled out. The solution was to connect the machines to other, chaotic systems in nature and allow what occurred there to govern the selection. But the issue of chance and fate appears considerably more complex to artificial intelligence than to us, because in the human world chance is often charged with meaning, beyond our control, often beyond our understanding too. How do we give the machines access to something whose nature is unknown to us?

I'm sounding like Hans now. Machines that communicate with each other and interact with the world around them, that was his domain. Of course, I knew nothing about anything like that the first time we spoke. Probably he knew little more — in the late summer of 1985, machines that could think on their own were still basically science fiction. But he was already there, at the interface of biology and technology, with his own particular ideas.

I'd noticed him the night before, a tall, skinny man with big hair the exact colour of which was hard to determine, a chiselled chin and narrow eyes, wearing a pair of faded jeans that looked like they'd once been black and at any rate were too short in the leg, a thin blue knitted jumper with a greenish pattern across the chest. He was a head taller than everyone else in the place, I suppose that might have been why I noticed him, but he was loud too, playing pool with his mates, all of whom were considerably less vocal, and so untidy in his movements. I assumed he'd had a few pints and was a bit drunk, that his mates were just lagging behind. He looked a bit gormless as well. That particular night I was sat reading one of the English novels I'd bought when a voice in front of me suddenly said:

'Did you just move here?'

I looked up and there he was, the lanky rake.

'What makes you think that?'

'Tourists never come here. You can't be visiting someone either, or else you wouldn't be sitting on your own reading. At least not every night. So all in all there's only one possibility. Where are you from?'

'Norway.'

'Yeah? Are you into speed skating?'

When I shrugged rather than actually saying no, he asked if he could buy me a beer. Normally I'd have found a way to get out of it, it wasn't my style to sit and curry favour with people I didn't know, but I hadn't spoken to another person in days and, anyway, I'd tired of my reading, so I reckoned it wouldn't do me any harm, and a minute later he was sitting at my table, his big hands curled around his pint, probing me about my knowledge of Norwegian speed skaters. I'd sat in front of the television watching the skating with my dad on many a winter's afternoon when I was a kid, but I definitely couldn't claim to be an ardent follower. Of course, I knew the four S's, even if I did only remember the names of two of them — Sten Stensen and Kay Stenshjemmet.

'Odd that you remember Stensen of the four,' he said. 'He was the most anonymous, and a long-distance specialist, so he hardly won an all-round title after the others came through. Are you the sort who always roots for the underdog?'

'I don't usually root for anyone.'

'The two others are Jan Egil Storholt and Amund Sjøbrend. Sjøbrend's interesting. Always underestimated. His technique was sublime, far better than the other three's. His angles were near-perfect, no one negotiated the bends like him, and his timing was spot-on, always. He didn't win a lot, though. How come, if his technique was as good as I say?'

He fixed me with an intense gaze.

'No idea,' I said. I was trying to sound as uninterested as I could in the hope he'd take the hint.

'He was unlucky. Some people are, much more than others, you know. Strange as it seems.'

'I see,' I said, and downed a mouthful of the pint he'd put on the table in front of me. The beer was on him, only now it appeared I was being made to pay for it anyway.

'All outdoor sports contain elements of unpredictability, especially winter sports. It's a matter of chance whether it's going to snow when you're out there, what the visibility's going to be like. In speed skating it's not just the weather that's changeable, it's the quality of the ice too. But that's all going to be made a thing of the past. They're already building an indoor arena back home, it's set to open next year. It's going to revolutionise the sport. And then things will get interesting.'

He paused, presumably to allow me to ask in what way.

'Actually, I think skating's a bit boring,' I said. 'It's so monotonous, the same thing all the time.'

'Exactly!' he said. 'And now it's going to be even more so. You must think of speed skating as a closed system, where the decisive factors are the ice, the track, the skates, the skaters and the laws of physics. Previously, the track and the skates were fixed elements, and the laws of physics etched in stone of course, whereas the ice and the weather were variables. Once the sport moves indoors, they too become fixed, which means all of a sudden there's an approachable ideal — think of a speed-skating robot taking all the bends optimally, the perfect balance of speed, gravity and centrifugal forces. The only variable then will be the skater. He's characterised by his biological unmanageableness. That makes every race a contest between the imperfection of biology and the potential perfection of the system. But what is perfection? What does optimal actually mean? Why is there a point where you can go no further? Even more interesting perhaps is that we can build machines that can attain optimal efficiency, whereas we ourselves can't. Speed skating illustrates, no, speed skating *is* that very contest between man and the forces that constrain us. And that, my friend, is neither monotonous nor boring!'

'I get the feeling you've thought a lot about this,' I said. 'There can't be that many people in London you can talk to about speed skating.'

'More than you think,' he said. 'But not many, no.'

'What are you doing over here, anyway?'

'I keep myself busy. How about you?'

'I study photography.'

'Oh!' he said and began immediately to talk about photography as a medium. The pictures didn't interest him, but the technology did. It was one-way conversation; the words came so thick and fast it was impossible to get one of my own in edgeways. By the time he got to his feet a quarter of an hour later, I still knew no more about him than that his name was Hans, he was from the Netherlands, and that he had a theory about speed skating. Of course, I was slightly more enlightened about his personality and realised now that he wasn't nearly as gormless as he looked. He was the type who liked to hold forth, to lecture, to come across as a thinker, albeit, preferably, an unorthodox one. He believed himself to be more interesting than he was — but then who didn't? Did I know anyone who genuinely thought themselves uninteresting?

No. A person who didn't understand much wasn't likely to realise it either, they'd be content with what little they knew, which to them was all there was. That's how people were wired.

I saw Hans a couple more times in the weeks before term started, we said hello and exchanged a few words, I wasn't interested in a new lecture and he didn't embark on any either, and then when autumn came he was gone. Not that I noticed to begin with, he was just a guy I'd spoken to now and again, and anyway I had more than enough to be getting on with in commencing my studies. So it wasn't until I ran into him again in the same pub, it must have been mid-December by then, that I even remembered he existed.

'How's the photography going?' he said.

'Good.'

'Are you going to let me see?'

'See what?'

'Your photos.'

I looked at him in surprise. He smiled faintly and hooked his thumb and index finger around his chin.

'What would you want to see them for?'

He gave a shrug.

'Photography interests me. Where do you keep them?'

'Some are at the school, some at home.'

'Are they big?'

'No . . . no, they're not.'

'Why don't you come over to my studio and bring them with you? You can have a look at what I do while you're there.'

'OK,' I said, taken aback by him going straight to the point, missing out all the steps in between like that. I was surprised, too, that he had a studio and was therefore, apparently, an artist — nothing about him until that point had suggested anything of the kind. Nevertheless, the following Friday I found myself placing a pile of selected photographs carefully in a cardboard box I then wrapped into a carrier bag — it was pouring down outside — before slipping it into my backpack, putting on my rainwear and carrying my bike down the stairs and into the street. His studio was out towards Peckham somewhere, no more than fifteen minutes or so from my place. It was dark, the rain was heavy, the traffic dense. Cars glistened in the headlights of those behind, horns were tooted impatiently, engines revved, red rear lights like lanterns in an inky asphalt sea. It was a joy to be able to slip past them all, feeling the rain as it battered my face, every sound made dull and underwater-like by the protective hood of my anorak.

The place was quite hard to find, he'd said, so we agreed to meet in a cafe opposite the train station. He must have seen me through the window, and came out just as I was about to lock my bike.

'Kristian,' he said. 'Did you bring the photos?'

I nodded, and patted my bag.

'Shall we go, then? Or do you want a coffee first?'

'No, let's go. Is it far?'

'Ten minutes.'

On the way, he told me he'd first arrived in London when he was the same age as I was now. He'd been a 'photographer' too, he said, and put air quotes around the word. He'd only been thinking of staying a few weeks, crashing on the sofa at a friend's place, but the city had enchanted him — that was the expression he used — and so he'd stayed.

'Do you still take pictures?' I asked, wheeling the bike alongside him. I'd pulled my hood down now, so I could hear what he was saying. My hair was sopping wet already.

He shook his head.

'What sort of pictures were they?'

'Pictures.'

'You mean, "pictures" pictures?' I said, repeating his air quotes.

'You get me, I'm glad,' he said with a laugh.

Of course, I'd wondered why he'd asked to see my work, and what he even wanted with me — we weren't exactly friends, far from it, we hardly knew each other — but the fact that he'd been into photography himself and had come to London at the same age as me explained a lot. No doubt there was a sense of commonality too in the fact that we were both from abroad.

We turned down a little side street that broke the near-endless line of brick buildings. Around us now, abandoned industrial premises decayed behind wire fencing, grass and shrubs peeping up wherever they could get a foothold.

'This is it,' he said after a couple of hundred metres, halting outside what looked to be a disused garage. A graffitied metal roll-up door; flaking, white-painted concrete. He gestured dismissively as I made to lock my bike.

'Just bring it in with you.'

He unlocked a door round the side and switched on the strip lighting. Yes, it had been a garage, the grease pit was still there in the middle of the floor. Opposite, some stairs led up to a room where a window looked out onto the main garage space, presumably there'd been an office there once.

'A big place you've got,' I said. 'Is it all yours?'

'I don't own it, if that's what you mean. But yes, I'm the only one who uses it. Do you want a drink?'

'Thanks, I wouldn't mind.'

'Have a seat,' he said with a nod towards a cluster of furniture over by the wall — an old sofa, a coffee table, a chair, next to which three buckets were lined up catching fat drops of water from the ceiling.

While he disappeared through a door over at the other side of the former workshop, I took off my anorak and rain pants and draped them over the bike, then took the parcel of photos from my bag. I was standing there holding it out in front of me when he reappeared with two bottles and a couple of glasses he put down on the table.

'You first or me?' he said, pouring vodka into the glasses — at least I assumed that was what it was, the bottle had no label.

'Makes no difference.'

He topped the drinks up with pink tonic and handed me mine. We chinked glasses. The alcohol was strong and pinched at my throat.

'I make it myself.'

'Seriously? It doesn't taste like home-made.'

'I know. Years of experience. Anyway, let me see what you've got.'

I sat down on the sofa and took the box out of the carrier bag, then removed the lid and the semi-transparent tissue paper.

'Anyone would think it was a holy relic you'd brought,' he said. 'Are your pictures holy to you?'

'Not at all,' I said, and felt myself blush. Until that point, I hadn't cared what he might say about them. Now, I was nervous all of a sudden in case he didn't like them.

I handed him the pile.

'Can I use your toilet?'

'Through the door over there,' he said with a nod.

Why should I care what *he* thought, I told myself as I pissed into the bowl. The actual room was as cramped as a cupboard and there was no towel, so I pulled off a length of toilet roll and used that instead. My photos were good, they weren't going to become bad just by him saying.

They were already stacked on the table again when I went back in.

'Not bad,' he said.

'You think so?'

'Yes. You've got talent.'

He made it sound like an insult. I picked up the pile and started looking through them myself. I'd photographed different people at different times in exactly the same place. For instance, five — in this case Helene, my mum, Filip, Joachim and Elise — were sat in my chair in my old room, five more were naked in my bath, another five were seated at the kitchen table, and so on. All were adopting the same posture, even the clothes were all the same, so everything was identical apart from the faces. This was the series that had got me into the art school.

I straightened the photographs, folded the tissue paper around them again and returned them to their box. Hans was watching me.

'Yes, they're not bad . . .' he said again.

'But?'

'But they're very much the expression of an idea. Once you've grasped the idea, there's nothing else there. The pictures in themselves have no value. They're connected to an idea, instead of the world. You could just as well have written a sentence: "People look different, but their lives are the same", for example.'

'I don't agree. These are photos of people. If that's not connecting with the world, then I don't know what is.'

He smiled, but said nothing.

'What did you want to show *me*?'

'I hope you're not offended? Come on, drink up. I'll show you the studio in a minute.'

He replenished his empty glass. I poured some more tonic into mine. The situation had become awkward, but he didn't seem to mind, he just sat there on the sofa looking like he was absorbed in his own thoughts. His square chin jutted slightly, making him look vaguely like a fish, it was what gave him that gormless look of his, I supposed, and I found myself wondering why, what it was that made the unconscious mind connect a certain kind of jaw with a certain kind of intelligence. Then I started thinking about what kind of an artist he might be. Up until then I'd seen no sign of anything in the way of visual art — nothing on the walls, neither of the workshop space nor the toilet. The place was just green-painted floor, black walls, bare concrete. Maybe he was an 'artist'?

The thought made me smile, which returned him from his thoughts with a slight start. He took a good swallow of his drink, placed a hand on each knee and fixed me once again as he leaned forward.

'We need ideas, don't get me wrong. But even ideas have got to have some form of physical expression, don't you agree? Nothing can exist beyond the physical realm. Your photographs are physical objects. You can hold them in your hands. The people you photographed, they're physical beings. Their transformation, from human being to image, is a physical process. Light photons are physical, they have weight.'

'But not ideas.'

'Oh, but yes! They must exist somewhere, otherwise they couldn't exist to us at all. That's the point! Everything we know and think has to be physically grounded somewhere. Be it Marxism or the belief in eternal life, it has to exist somewhere, in some *physical* form.'

'In the brain, you mean?'

'For example. Thoughts, ideas, conceptions are all encoded in neurons.'

'Obviously.'

'Is it obvious? Well, maybe it is. Only I don't see any of that in your pictures. Those photographs separate everything into different compartments. Photography here, subject here, idea here. It's all right that they're not changing the conversation, because you're only starting out, but you need to think about *why* they're not changing the conversation. If you don't, you might as well start taking photos for your local estate agent. Don't you agree?'

I didn't know what to say. All sorts of feelings were tearing around inside me, and none was of the good kind.

'Of course you don't agree!' he said, and let out a laugh. 'You want to defend your work, as fiercely as you can. But it's not just you. It's our entire image culture — all it is is perpetuation, preservation of the same thing.'

'Which is what?'

'A space! A conceptual space! Haven't you ever thought about it? All photographs possess a certain perspective, which someone, the photographer, has selected. So what you're seeing, in the main, is intention. The photographer's intention is what you see, and the photograph is an image of that intention. How do you get rid of the intention? As a photographer you need to think about that. Yes?'

'I'd like to have seen your own photographs.'

He laughed again. Apparently, this was hilarious.

'My photographs were like yours! Of course they were! But forget about that, I'll show you what I do now.'

He stood up and I followed him into a room out back. Strip lighting flickered a few times, ripping the darkness and allowing glimpses of a room crammed with stuff from floor to ceiling, until the place was flooded with light and details could emerge. The first thing I noticed, unavoidably, was a line of mannequins that were stood up against the back wall with their arms outstretched. They looked like they were waiting to receive infants. The longer walls were lined with shelving. Here was a collection of stuffed fauna, there various rocks and stones, and big seashells too. Further along, a number of animal skulls. Elsewhere, heaps of dried reeds, piles of twigs, ferns. There were two television sets, one whose casing had been removed to reveal the insides, and I counted three computers. A lathe occupied the space underneath the window, while a metal bench ran underneath the shelves along one wall — on it were soldering irons, odds and ends of wiring, and items of electronic equipment. Beside the mannequins, a number of planks were leaned up against the wall, tools hung too, like in a garage, and as well as tubes of oil paints I saw several large tins of what looked to be regular decorating paint.

But there was nothing he appeared to have produced. No pictures, no sculptures.

The rain lashed against the windowpane, which threw back a reflection of the room and the two of us in it.

Hans went over to a wooden crate, maybe two by two metres, that stood on top of a table.

'This is what I call my Rat Run.'

'What is it?'

'It's a labyrinth. Come and have a look.'

I stepped closer. The crate was open. Inside, a number of thin partitions indeed appeared to form a labyrinth.

Then, he took what looked to be a stuffed rat from one of the shelves and put it down inside the labyrinth at one end, before flicking a switch on the side of the crate. A second later, the rat scuttled cautiously forward through one of the narrow corridors. Reaching the end, it stopped with a bump, scuttled back, and tried the next available passage.

It was unsettling. The rat was lifelike, it looked almost to be thinking too. I had to keep telling myself it wasn't alive.

But apart from that, what was the point of it?

It certainly had nothing to do with art.

Every time it came to a dead end, it went all the way back and started again, remembering where it had already been, gradually working its way further and further inside the labyrinth.

When eventually it found its way out, it pressed its nose against a switch. A light flashed and a bell rang.

Hans laughed.

'I can't get tired of it,' he said. 'But tell me, what do you think?'

'Not bad,' I said. 'You've got talent.'

'Oh, come on!' he almost shouted. 'You're not still moping about *that*, are you? Tell me the truth, for fuck's sake!'

'Which would be what?'

'You're deeply impressed, fascinated, and a bit scared!'

He flicked the switch into the off position, picked up the rat and returned it to the shelf, putting it down between a cat and a badger.

'What's it made of?' I said.

'It's not made of anything. It *is* a rat. Stuffed, of course.'

'Sorry, but who cares?'

He looked at me astonished.

'Is it a work of art?' I said.

He shook his head and stared at the floor a moment, as if he couldn't believe I could ask such a stupid question.

Instead of answering me, he lifted his head, looked me in the eye and put a hand on my shoulder, the way a father might have done when sending his son to war.

'Let's have a drink,' he said. 'Then I'll show you my turtles.'

'You've got turtles?'

'I have indeed. What's more, I made them myself.'

Back in the main garage space he filled our glasses again.

'Do you know anything about computers?' he said.

'No, nothing. Do you?'

'Do they interest you? Are you curious about them?'

'Why should I be?'

'No, why indeed?' he replied with sarcasm. His vodka was powerful stuff, it had already smoothed away some of the edges inside me, freeing me up to some extent, but also narrowing my outlook in a way. My eyes followed him as he crossed the floor and went towards the back room again, and for some reason I found myself thinking about my sister, Liv. Nothing deep, or even pertinent, just something I'd seen once and now remembered — she'd gone off to school one day with a puppy inside her coat, and it was that image I suddenly recalled, one body, two faces, hers and the dog's — yet it was enough for my eyes to not really be seeing as they followed Hans's movements. Or rather, my eyes saw him, but my thoughts were detached from them, so what I saw almost didn't seem to be happening at all. A moment later, he was standing in the middle of the room holding something heavy in his hands, which he then put down.

Was it a turtle?

He went away again, and came back with another. Then another.

He beckoned me closer.

'What's this?' I said.

'These are my home-made turtles.'

He kneeled and tipped up the rear of one of them and put his hand in under the shell. He returned it to the floor, and with a hum the turtle began to move forwards. He did the same with the other two, then got to his feet beaming a wide smile. The first turtle reached the grease pit, where it stopped and turned, then continued along the edge. The second one was headed towards the wall, but halted before bumping into it, then likewise spun round to carry on in a different direction.

'Are they a kind of robot?'

'Call them what you like. But now look.'

He killed the ceiling lights and we stood in near-darkness for a few seconds before he switched on a torch. He shone it up into his face, mwahahaha! he said and grinned at me like a demon, then turned the beam to the floor.

'Come on now, my little turtles,' he said. 'Come to Daddy.' And, weirdly, that's what they did. Slowly, all three oriented themselves towards the light, and when he moved the beam, they followed.

'It does look like they're alive,' I said.

'I know! Now look.'

He shone his torch directly on a turtle and immediately it backed away.

He laughed loudly. Switching the lights back on, he then went and sat down while the three turtles trundled slowly around the room like ancient trilobites.

'What do you say now?' he said. 'Still not interested in computers?'

'Not in the slightest,' I said.

He smiled.

'Nice little playthings. I can't say I get why you're wasting your time on them, though.'

'The Romans were familiar with the steam engine. But they just used it as a toy. They couldn't think of any other purpose for it.'

'So you're saying these turtles can be put to better use than just amusement? What would that be, then?'

'This lack of imagination's starting to bring me down. Let's go back to some drinking. A couple more and I'll be as stupid as you!'

When I got home, well drunk, I discovered I'd forgotten to switch my record player off, the LP I'd been listening to was still spinning on the turntable, the stylus clicking endlessly in the run-out groove. I lifted the arm, put the stylus down at the start and turned the volume up. *First and Last and Always*, I could listen to it for the rest of my life without ever getting tired of it. I ate a couple of slices of bread, gulped some water, made my bed up, turned the record over, switched off the lights and lay down. I liked falling asleep to music, the way my thoughts melted into the sonic darkness from which, before long, they could no longer be separated. I didn't care about Hans's criticism. He couldn't go down in my estimation, for the simple reason that I hadn't held him in any esteem to begin with. Besides, it wasn't hard to parry what he'd said about my pictures. He was a nobody. That stupid rat of his, what was that all about? A labyrinth with hidden tracks, something anyone with even the slightest bit of technical know-how could have rigged up.

Nevertheless, what I'd seen at the garage left an impression on me and kept reappearing in my mind during the weeks that followed. I wasn't consciously returning to it, somehow it just wouldn't let go of me, as though my subconscious knew something my conscious mind did not, and now, in annoyance, was trying to make it understand. But the conscious and unconscious minds don't operate on the same wavelength, they're two different systems, mutually impenetrable. So it stopped there, at images from a disused garage. Hans, seated on the sofa in front of me, my photographs in a pile on the coffee table, standing in the back room at his Rat Run, the three scuttling turtles on the floor of the garage space. These images came with a certain mood, December gloom and pouring rain, a glare of strip lights, water dripping into plastic buckets, stuffed animals, mannequins and computers. What kind of a mood was it? It was a sense of something being awry, cross-threaded. But none of this was manifest to me in the form of thoughts, it was all just a feeling — vague and unclear, all of it. That wasn't the case, though, when it came to what he'd said about my photos and what, in his opinion, they were lacking, the thrust to 'change the conversation'. This was something I thought about actively. And what he'd said about perspective, about the photographer's intention being more conspicuous almost than the subject itself, was suddenly at the forefront of my mind whenever I considered visual material. It was distorting my view — *this* was now all I could see. As such, his problem became mine. But only I was tormented by it; he was no longer a photographer.

The Christmas break began early, I had ten days on my own in my bedsit before I was due to fly home, those of my fellow students I hung around with had already left town, and so I thought about giving Hans a ring. He'd given me his number, which I took to be a fairly unambiguous sign that he wanted us to stay in touch. But that was his initiative. As for myself, I was in two minds, if not to say reluctant. Still, I phoned him from the pub one night after a few pints, the beer possibly clouding my judgement. Not that I went around with his number on me. No, I knew it off by heart — I could remember any number, not only his. But he didn't answer, which, when I woke up the next day, I was relieved about.

And then I went home for Christmas. My parents picked me up at Fornebu, were waiting in the arrivals hall when I came through customs with my suitcase. So happy they were to see me! All hugs and beaming faces, the moist eyes of my mother.

'Anyone would think I'd been away twenty years,' I said. 'In China or somewhere.'

Dad resolutely took my case, while Mum, as easily moved as she was domineering, as befuddled as she was stubborn, began with all her questions even before we'd got to the car. It was new, I saw when we halted beside it. No surprise there. Dad liked to have a new one every two years.

'How come you didn't say you'd got a new car?' I said anyway.

'You've not exactly been phoning . . .' Dad said with a smile.

It was how he always criticised — with a smile and a pleasant tone of voice. Only people who knew him well were aware that the main thing was what he said, not the way he said it.

The sky was black and full of stars as we drove north, the landscape covered with snow. I was amazed at how empty it was. In London there were buildings everywhere, mile upon mile in every direction, and people wherever you looked. I hadn't thought about it much while I'd been there, but now, as we drove through the wide-open land, where houses could be kilometres apart, it struck me forcefully. It felt impoverished. London *was* impoverished, it was ugly and run-down, and full of human misery, but the city was rich in people and occurrences. Here was as dead as the grave.

The heater whirred. The radio gave out cosy, low-voiced chat. My parents sat motionless in comfortable silence on the front seats. I leaned my head against the window and slept, waking only as we passed through the gate and climbed the hill to the house. The snow was thicker here. Dad had cleared a gleaming lane with the tractor's snow blade.

I went upstairs and unpacked. My room was good and warm; Mum had obviously turned the radiator on for me that morning, and likely hoovered as well.

I put my boxes of photos on the desk. I'd have plenty of time to myself in the next few days, so I was planning to work on the book I wanted to put together. I hung my shirts up in the wardrobe, put the rest of my clothes in a drawer, then stood at the window and stared out. In the daytime you could see for miles; now, everything was blacked out, apart from the outbuildings, which were all lit up. The outdoor lamps gave the snow beneath them a wash of yellow. A sick colour in the night-time, I'd always thought.

The room felt like a skin I'd sloughed. A snake could surely feel no less for its former skin than I did for my old room.

'Kristian?' my mother called up the stairs. 'Coffee and cake!'

She'd set the table, with a white tablecloth, the good china and cutlery, and lit the advent candle. A fire crackled in the fireplace.

'I always forget you're so traditional,' I said. 'How do you reconcile that with being such a radical, exactly?'

'There's no conflict between wanting things to be cosy and having a sense of justice,' she said.

'How's the school going, anyway?' Dad said. 'Are you liking it?'

'I am, yes. There's a lot to do. A lot of new things to learn.'

'Are you going to show us some of your work? Have you brought anything?'

'I have, as it happens. I'll bring it down later on.'

'Have you made any friends over there yet?' Mum asked.

She used the Danish *yet*, rather than the Norwegian — *endnu*, instead of *ennå*. Although she'd lived in Norway more than thirty years, her Norwegian was still tinged with Danish words, intonations and pronunciations. For the same reason, my friends had never really taken her seriously. Mothers had to speak the mother tongue; if not, they couldn't be proper mums, they must have felt.

'A few, yes. Those on the course, and the odd one or two besides.'

They'd asked if they could come over and see me, they loved to travel, but I'd said no, I needed to settle in a bit more first. I'd nothing against them, in fact I liked them well enough. But if people were houses and could see each other through the windows, and communicate by opening their doors to give out sounds, our own houses were facing each other and wide open at the front, meaning we could tramp in and out of each other's lives at will whenever we were together. I didn't care for that.

When my maternal grandmother died, Mum said that part of the grief was in losing a witness, someone who'd known her all her life and who knew who she was. I was only fifteen at the time, but I remember feeling a reaction, I couldn't understand why anyone would want others to witness the things they went around saying and doing. And who felt like having their ten or twenty-year-old self thrown back at them the rest of their lives?

'How have things been here? Anything new?' I said, and popped a gingerbread biscuit into my mouth. It was baked in the shape of a pig.

'I wouldn't say so, not really,' Mum said. 'We've booked a trip to Jerusalem in February.'

'Jerusalem?'

'Yes. I've always wanted to go there. It is one of the most ancient cities in the world.'

'How about you?' I said to Dad with a smile. The corners of his eyes creased as he smiled back, his head big and unwieldy-looking.

'Oh, yes,' he said.

'The hotel we're staying at is where the Swedish emigrants Selma Lagerlöf wrote about lived in that colony,' said Mum. 'Have you read it? *Jerusalem*?'

I shook my head.

'It's over there on the shelf, if you get the urge.'

'Thanks, maybe I will.'

'We'll fetch the tree tomorrow,' Dad said.

'Of course,' I said. 'Will Helene and Liv be coming?'

'Helene is. We're hoping for Liv,' Mum replied.

She filled my cup with coffee from the jug, which she held aloft, then raised slightly as she tipped, allowing the dark liquid to descend in a plume through the air before putting it down again on the table. The red gemstone of her ring gleamed in the light, as did, when I looked up at her, the matching one she wore around her neck.

'Always good coffee here,' I said.

She smiled at me. It was as if she had two different ages. One young, in her eyes. Another, older, in the rest of her face.

'You must taste the *smultringer*, too. I made them this morning.'

'I'd rather wait until Christmas Eve, if that's all right.'

'Oh, I almost forgot,' she said. 'Vidar rang. I said you'd ring him back once you got home.'

'What if I don't want to?'

'Vidar's a good man,' Dad put in.

'What if he is?' I said. 'I don't need to look up every good man I know, just because I'm home.'

'You can do as you like,' Mum said. 'Only don't say I didn't tell you!'

It wasn't until I went back upstairs that I remembered that Vidar had started at NTNU, the science and technology university in Trondheim, and knew about computers. I wouldn't have minded a beer, now I thought about it. The freezing cold air would be good, too.

I kneeled down in front of the old crates I kept my records in and started looking through them. *Now* I felt at home. I'd spent long hours arranging them in the perfect order so that each one gave something to the next. I could choose between two ways of approaching any selection. First, there was what I called *flow*, where each album had something in common with the next, added something new and pointed ahead to the next after that, meaning that after a while you suddenly found yourself somewhere else entirely in relation to your starting point. For instance, you could follow pathways leading from Bowie's *Lodger* and Talking Heads' *Remain in Light*, both of which were collaborations with Brian Eno and featured Adrian Belew on guitar, moving via Eno to Jon Hassel, who played on one of Eno's ambient albums, then on to David Sylvian, on whose *Brilliant Trees* Hassel played trumpet. From there, you could then pick up on Mick Karn, for example, progressing onwards to Bauhaus, since Karn formed his band Dalis Car with Peter Murphy, or you could follow Karn in a different direction and end up at Ultravox, New Order, PiL, Can and Holger Czukay. Of course, from Bowie and Byrne you could choose to follow Belew instead of Eno, in which case you naturally ended up somewhere different altogether, for instance at Shriekback, XTC or the Police. If you didn't fancy *flowing* like that, you could do the opposite and go for contrast in allowing *very* different records to meet. This was the second option, and the more demanding, for the albums selected still had to *complement* each other in some way — the radical combination still had to feel right, natural even. Regardless of which method you chose, the aim was to constantly breathe new life into the collection, to make it explode with meaning. And it could actually be done, to bump up the standard of even a mediocre record collection containing a number of poor albums. It was all a matter of curation, of selecting the playing order. I'd become rather adept at it. And as a photographer I didn't really come good until I understood how to exploit those same ideas in terms of my pictures too. The principles were the same — pictures could flow, or they could clash surprisingly.

I paused. *Seventeen Seconds* came after *Revolver*, which was all wrong, even if I did remember the thought behind it — the Cure weren't nearly as gloomy and industrial as was normally held, there was a pop group hidden away in their experimental sound, whereas in the case of the Beatles, the experimentalism was folded into the pop, this being abundantly clear in 'Tomorrow Never Knows' — and it was just as incongruous that what followed was Hüsker Dü's *Zen Arcade*. These were glaring errors. What had I been thinking?

Wrong, wrong, wrong.

I flipped through in search of others. The problem, of course, was that I couldn't remove an album without it leaving a hole that would then have to be filled. Ideally, I'd be looking for a straight swap.

I hesitated at *Lodger*. It could possibly slot in before *Seventeen Seconds*, but definitely not after. Well, not even before, once I started thinking about it. I moved on. How about NEU!? No, that would shut things down, not open them up.

But if I went for flow instead?

That would involve massive upheaval and hours of work. But why not? It was Christmas, a succession of long and otherwise uneventful days.

I'd have to give Vidar a ring before it got too late. At the same time, it was hard to tear myself away from my collection like that when now I'd discovered something that so obviously upset the balance.

What about simply having *Faith* and *Pornography* following on, intensifying the depressive aspect, and then proceed to Bauhaus? Then the Birthday Party after that? And *then*, Hüsker Dü could come in! The Birthday Party were both bleak *and* noisy, they'd be the perfect transition from Bauhaus to Hüsker Dü. A bit like the missing link between humans and the apes.

With the idea now in my head, I got to my feet and went downstairs to phone Vidar. He must have been sitting waiting for it to ring, because he answered straight away. We agreed to meet at the Station in half an hour. I went back upstairs and took my old coat from the wardrobe, found one of Dad's scarves on the peg in the hall, and put my shoes on.

'I'm going out,' I called.

'All right,' Mum called back.

The cold hit me as soon as I opened the door. The snow creaked underfoot as I went down the drive to the road. The sky was clear and starry. I wanted my photographs to be like this: cold and crisp, vivid sparkles of light that could never be grasped, only seen.

Conscientiously, my eyes scanned my surroundings as I followed the combined pedestrian and cycle path, for my eye was, if not my weapon, my instrument, and like any other instrument it was essential it be kept in good working order.

The path had been diligently cleared, even though hardly anyone ever used it; the marks left by the snow blade could still be seen. A low bank of snow separated it from the road, muffling the sound of the occasional passing car. I'd divided photographers into two schools: those who photographed the world the way it was, and those who sought to magnify what was in it. Made it monumental, sculpting with light, drawing forth the dramatic in objects, landscapes and people. I'd wavered a bit, but was now increasingly convinced that my future lay in the monumental. Magnifying the world, not dissolving it. For instance, seen in isolation, one of the light poles that lined the road here could take on a strikingly imposing appearance, its gleaming metal perhaps coated with ice, the light it shed suspended as if frozen in the darkness. What would be the point in underlining ordinariness, everyday utility? My series of different people in the same settings leaned in the same direction, the information it conveyed wasn't gathered, cloak-like, around the subject, it was dissipated, and thereby weakened, but it was that very idea that made the images come across so powerfully and unified them as a series. The school's admission committee had seen that. It didn't matter in the slightest that the Dutch quasi-artist hadn't.

When I got to the Station, the cereal farmer's son was already sat waiting. He lit up when he saw me, got to his feet and gave me a hug, even let out what sounded like a laugh.

'Great to see you,' he said.

'Likewise,' I said, unwinding my scarf and stuffing it into the sleeve of my coat, which I then slung over the back of a chair. 'How's things, all right?'

'Good, thanks. Came back yesterday. When did you arrive?'

'Just got here, basically. I need a beer.'

The bar, which had opened in the old railway station building, was about half full. I looked around as the bartender poured my pint. Fortunately, there weren't that many I knew. Some I recognised from my old gymnasium school, then were was a group Helene used to hang around with. At the table behind theirs, three girls were sitting; one, short and pudgy, though with delicate, rather attractive features, met my gaze, and when I sat down next to Vidar and cast another glance in her direction just to check, she did it again. In both cases, she made sure her mates didn't notice, which told me she wouldn't be averse to leaving them on their own.

'How's London?' Vidar said with his usual wide-open expression.

'Good,' I said. 'How's Trondheim?'

'Good, yes.'

She was maybe four or five years older than me.

'Cheers,' he said.

'Cheers,' I said.

We chatted a while about what we'd been up to since the last time we saw each other, while around us people kept trickling in. It turned out he'd moved in with a girl up there, Wenche, her name was, and he produced his wallet to show me a photo of her. A big, round, matronly face, narrow lips, a commanding look in her eyes. She'd take care of him all right, I thought with a smile, and congratulated him on his catch. He smiled at me proudly as he put it back.

'I met this weird guy in London and was wondering,' I said. 'He's some kind of artist, works with computers and stuff. He showed me this labyrinth he'd made, with a rat in it. Would that be something you've heard about?'

'A physical labyrinth?'

'Yes, in a wooden crate. I can draw it for you, if you like.'

I got my notebook out and made a quick sketch.

'That looks like Claude Shannon's maze.'

'Who's he?'

'A computer pioneer. One of the scientists who laid the foundations for digital computers in the thirties and forties. He was actually an electrical engineer for a telephone company. Bell, if you've heard of them?'

'Really?'

'Yes, he constructed something exactly like that. Shannon's rat, it's usually called. He cobbled it together at home using telephone technology, if that's the word.'

'What was the point of it?'

'The point was that the rat possessed memory. It could remember things, and learn from experience. So whenever it went the wrong way, it would go back and try a different route. What he did there was massively important for what's happening today.'

'So why would anyone want to do it again now?'

'No idea. Anyone could, it wouldn't take much.'

'Could you?'

He laughed.

'Of course I could. The principle's really simple.'

'He showed me these little robots too, that could steer their way around obstacles and could follow a beam of light.'

'They're from around the same time. Walter's turtles.'

'So they're a thing, that people know about?'

'Oh yes.'

'So this guy I met is basically just copying what someone else invented decades ago?'

'Yes. It's all classic stuff.'

I could tell that Vidar was pleased with himself at being able to impress me a bit. It didn't happen often, he was very much the quiet, unassuming type, and I don't suppose I'd ever shown that much interest in anything he was good at. It probably went back to when we were kids together. He'd always been so gullible, so easy to deceive — I remember once having told him he'd get big muscles from pushing the soapbox car we played with for a while, especially if it was made heavier by me sitting in it, and so he'd kept pushing me up the hill while I sat there like a king. How old had we been then? Six, maybe, or seven. He believed anything I said. I told him I dreamt the next episode of an ongoing dream every night, and he believed me and would listen avidly as I recounted it to him on the way to school every morning. When we were a bit older, I sent him to the shop one day with a note I'd written in his dad's name saying he was allowed to buy cigarettes for him, and so great was the sway I held over him that he didn't even snitch on me when he got caught. In gymnas, I'd get him to lend me money he'd never see again — all I had to do was keep saying I'd pay him back next week, until at last he decided to forget about it, always shying away from any conflict. Sometimes, of course, I did pay him back, and occasionally I'd let him come with me to a party he otherwise wouldn't have got into, so there was at least a measure of balance in our relationship.

The pudgy girl was standing at the bar.

'Fancy another?' I said to Vidar, and drained my pint.

'I wouldn't say no,' he said.

I went up and stood next to her. She had this little black handbag that dangled from her shoulder, and rummaged around in it, the bartender stepping away a moment to take another order. There were two glasses of red on the counter. She found her money and without looking at me held out a note for him. He took it and handed her the change, which she simply let drop into her bag, and then when she picked up the two glasses and turned to go back to her table, she just couldn't resist, and looked up at me.

Oh my days. Her eyes were dark with longing and a serious intent, it was obvious she meant it. She was looking for adventure. If she wasn't, she'd never have held my gaze those extra three seconds.

Vidar's guileless, fleshy face lit up as I put his pint down on the table. He was the salt of the earth. But how exciting was that? It never took him anywhere, just kept him away from everything that could possibly ignite into something interesting. There was no edge to him, so he never really engaged with anyone. As such, you could say niceness was an egotistical quality, it never lit a spark in the world, and was sufficient unto itself.

'Where's Wenche now, then?' I asked. 'Not here, I take it?'

'No, she's spending Christmas with her family. They live in Kolvereid.'

'Kolvereid?'

'North Trøndelag.'

'She's a Trønder, then?'

'That's right.'

'How do you tackle that? The dialect, I mean. Isn't it a bit of a turn-off?'

'Not at all,' he said, and looked down at his feet.

'You're not telling me you think it's *sexy?*'

He looked up again with a smile.

'You *must* be in love,' I said, and laughed.

We sat and chatted a while, kept a conversation going rather than saying nothing at all — he even asked if we'd put the tree up yet at ours. I went on the vodka, just to inject some life into things, which worked up to a certain point: time stopped flowing and instead started shifting sequentially, while the room we were in, soft human bodies among hard surfaces, the sheeny wall behind the bar, with its mirrors and bottles and gleaming lights, became cut off in its connections to the world outside, and was eventually all there was. It was as if the bar and everyone in it were floating in space. The girl appeared from out of the toilets. I got up and blocked her path. We stood there for a long while, chatting in the middle of the room, until at some point we went and sat down at a table and carried on. I'd forgotten all about Vidar until someone touched my shoulder and I turned to see him standing there in full winter garb, hat, scarf and gloves, saying he was off home now and thanks for a good night out.

'Say hello to Stina before you go,' I said. 'Stina, this is my good friend, Vidar.'

'Hi, Vidar,' she said. 'Haven't see you for ages!'

'You two know each other?'

'I'm friends with Maria. How's she doing, anyway? Is she home?'

'She is, yes,' said Vidar.

'Then say hello from me!'

'I will,' he said, and left.

I wasn't that keen on her knowing Vidar's sister, it connected her to my world in a way I wasn't sure I wanted, but in the broader scope I didn't suppose it mattered that much. Nor, in fact, in the narrower scope, where she and I were now, sitting close together as I ran my hand up and down her thigh under the table. We'd entered the zone where no error could be made — whatever either of us did now it simply fed into our mutual lust.

She was eager, and fast in everything. Speed-talking, a constant flutter of eyelids, she seemed only to want to follow her impulses, even the oddest of them, like when, before we'd even kissed, she suddenly buried her nose into my armpit in an urge to discover my smell. She was five years older than me, as I'd guessed, had lived here all her life, qualified as a nurse from the Høyskole in Elverum, and was now working in the home care services. She said she'd seen me before, quite a few times, and had always liked what she saw. I told her I liked what I was seeing too, and leaned across to kiss her. She responded greedily, curled her hand around my neck, and smoothed my cheek when eventually I drew away.

'Shall we go?' I said softly, stroking her thigh again.

'Yes,' she said. 'I just need to tell the others.'

I looked away as she went over to her mates, drained my vodka, which the melted ice cubes had watered down considerably, and then scanned the other tables to see if any other girls had come in.

'They asked if I'd started cradle-snatching,' she said as we went towards the door.

'What did you tell them?'

'I said you were mature for your age.'

She laughed. Then, noticing that I didn't, she squeezed my hand.

'Had you going there, didn't I?' she said. 'Only joking.'

I felt my excitement drain away. It didn't matter that she hadn't meant anything by it.

We went down the steps outside. The street lamps yellowed the snow.

'Is there something wrong?' she said.

'No,' I said. 'Why, should there be?'

She led me into the entrance of an adjacent building, then lifted her face to look up at me. An air vent hummed in the wall behind her.

'Kiss me.'

Hesitantly, I did.

She opened her eyes.

'Properly.'

She held me tight and pressed her body against mine. This time we kissed the way she wanted. She was intense.

'Where do you live?' I said.

'Nordåsen.'

'Shall we go back to yours?'

'Can't we go to yours instead?'

'You must be joking! I'm staying with my parents, I told you. I can't go bringing women home with me. We'll go to yours. It's not *that* far.'

'Einar's there.'

'Who's Einar?'

'My son.'

'You've got a son?'

'He's two and a half. My mum's babysitting for me while I'm out.'

'She doesn't live there as well, does she?'

'No! No, she doesn't.'

'And she's not going to be staying the night?'

'No, she'll go home again once I get in.'

'Then what's the problem? I'll make sure I'm gone before he wakes up. Come on.'

She pondered a moment, then nodded.

There were still people hanging around outside the Station, the odd car still cruising up and down the two streets that made up the centre of town, music thudding dully from their stereos. She took my hand and kept looking up at me. The flat was in one of the blocks at the top of the hill. Her frosty breath puffed in front of her face as she opened the entrance door in a glare of outdoor lighting. The building was nearly as cold inside as out. She took off her hat in the lift and glanced at herself in the mirror before gripping my coat and pulling me towards her.

We stepped out onto the sixth-floor landing and she gestured to indicate her door. Inside, a kid's sledge cluttered the cramped hallway; coats bulged from the pegs.

I was already wishing I hadn't gone with her.

'Hi, Mum. I've brought someone home with me,' she called out.

The mother had thin, frizzy hair and from the bewildered look on her face when her daughter opened the living-room door and she stared at first her, then me, she must have been asleep where she sat on the sofa.

'This is Kristian,' Stina said.

'Hello there,' I said, smiling as best I could.

There was an empty bottle of wine on the coffee table, another half full next to it. A big ashtray was overflowing with cigarette ends — Prince Mild, if the packet was anything to go by.

Stina removed the bottles and took them out into the kitchen.

'What time did he fall asleep?' she said as she went.

'Eight,' the mother said, teetering a moment on her feet before making towards the door. I stepped aside to let her past. She didn't even bother looking at me. Stina followed her into the hall. I went over to the window, and heard their low voices. A big hideous poster covered the wall above the sofa — a kitten peering up out of a basket. The sofa itself was black imitation leather, while the small coffee table in front of it was on castors. An obtrusive TV cabinet took up the opposite wall.

The front door clicked shut, and Stina came back in. She smiled at me, turned the big light off, fetched a fat candle from the kitchen, lit it.

'Do you want to see Einar?' she said. 'His bedroom's in there.'

'No, it's all right.'

She looked at me quizzically.

'I've seen sleeping kids before.'

It wasn't just the cheap and tacky furnishings, it was the inhospitable feel of the place.

She stepped up and put her arms around me, and reached to kiss me. Her mouth was wet, her tongue as eager as a dog's.

'Let's go to bed,' she said softly. 'I want you.'

I pulled away.

'Actually, I think I'd better go.'

'Go?'

'It doesn't feel right, that's all. Nothing personal.'

I went out into the hall. She stood in the doorway and watched me put my shoes back on. I straightened up and took my coat from the peg, and she stepped up close again.

'Come to bed with me,' she whispered. 'I want to be naked with you.'

'No, thanks,' I said, turned, and opened the door with one hand as I threw my scarf around my neck with the other. Outside again, I waited a few minutes to make sure I wasn't going to bump into her mother. The stars shuddered in their firmament. I gauged the temperature to be around minus fifteen, the freezing air assailed my cheeks, and as I walked home, down the hill, through the town centre, already emptier now, and onwards from there, my skin became more and more numb, the muscles of my face stiffened and lethargic. The long walk nullified the effects of the alcohol and by the time I let myself in I was stone-cold sober. For good measure, I gulped down a couple of glasses of water before going upstairs to bed.

The next morning, Mum had left the breakfast things out for me. She came into the kitchen and sat down while I was still eating.

'Did you have a nice time last night?' she said.

Koselig was the word she used. It was too Norwegian to sound right coming from her.

'I did, yes,' I said. 'It was good. I was with Vidar.'

'How's he doing?'

'He's doing fine. He's moved in with a girl up there.'

'Oh, really?'

I nodded and took my time sipping my coffee in the hope she'd take the hint and realise I couldn't be bothered talking about it.

After breakfast I went up and got my photos to show her. Dad was the one who'd asked, but she was more likely to understand what it was I was trying to do.

I handed them to her one by one and watched her expression as she studied them. Now and then, I directed her attention to what I considered to be an important detail, but apart from that I allowed her to look at them in her own time.

'These are fantastic, Kristian,' she said eventually.

'It's a brand-new series,' I said. 'Hardly anyone's seen them yet. Do you like them, really?'

'I do, really. I think they're outstanding.'

She smiled at me and I took the photos back upstairs with me to my room, where I sat looking at them, trying to gauge what it was that she'd seen in them.

The series explored the idea of the vanishing point. It was all converging diagonals — city streets, tree-lined driveways leading up to country houses, forest paths, rivers, fences, stone walls. High on contrast, low on detail. I'd called it *Vertigo*.

I imagined the Dutchman casting a cursory eye, tossing them back onto the table:

'It's all been done a thousand times before. Is this the best you can come up with?'

Then me, back to the wall already:

'But that's where you're wrong. As a series, this is nothing but original. It's sameness in difference. Patterns that are found everywhere, without our seeing them. But I see them. It's my job. To see the unfamiliar in the familiar, and vice versa.'

'Words, words, words! The truth is you haven't an iota of talent. You're clever on the technical side, but who cares about that?'

'You can talk, you and your stupid rat.'

Downstairs the doorbell rang. From the voices that followed I could hear it was Helene and Ane. I put the photos back in their box and went down to say hello. Helene was already seated, with Ane snuggled up to her, meaning we didn't have to go through the hugging routine.

'Here he is,' Helene said. 'Our Londoner returned. How are you doing?'

'Good,' I said. 'You?'

She smiled and winked.

'Oh, I'm always good, as you know.'

'How about you, Ane?' I said.

'What?' she said.

I sensed she was a bit unsure of me.

'He's asking if you're all right,' Helene said.

Ane nodded. Her upper teeth stuck out, which along with her glasses gave her a rather goofy appearance. It didn't matter now, but in a few years it would.

She let go of her mother, got up off the sofa and slipped past me to go into the kitchen where her grandmother was.

'She's grown,' I said. 'How old is she now?'

'Kristian,' Helene replied with ill-concealed scorn.

'I know approximately, just not exactly. No harm in asking, is there?'

'She'll be nine in April. Anyway, what have you got her?'

I stared at her, confused for a second.

'For Christmas?'

'For Christmas, yes. You're not going tell me you haven't bought her anything?'

'No, of course I've bought her something.'

'What, then?'

'You'll see tomorrow. How's Rickard doing? Haven't you brought him with you?'

'He's working today.'

'I see.'

The shopping centre was open and it was still early, so there was no need to panic yet.

Mum came in with Ane following closely behind her. She handed Helene a cup of coffee and put her own down on the table.

'Do you want a cup, Kristian?'

'No, thanks. Did you get some pop, Ane? Lucky you. What flavour is it?'

She looked at me without answering as she sucked on her straw, determined, so it seemed, to make things hard going for me.

Helene, thickset and sturdy, ruffled the girl's hair. She was the one who resembled Dad the most, physically as well as in mind. The same calmness, the same build, only with womanly curves. The same blue eyes, too. She'd never had ambition of any sort, other than to start her own family. She'd wanted lots of kids, but had only the one and couldn't have any more. Not even that had rattled her, at least not as far as I knew. Liv, four years younger, was her opposite in just about everything. She'd inherited Mum's nervous energy, though not her willpower, which meant she fluttered all over the place. I'd never had much to do with either of them. Liv had been eight when I was born, Helene twelve, so they'd been more like a pair of aunts to me.

Aunt Brown and Aunt Electric Blue.

Through the window I saw Dad come over the yard. A few moments later and he was standing in the living room, his face flushed from the cold.

'Are you ready, Ane?' he said.

She nodded earnestly and went into the hall to put her coat on. Helene and I went after her. I borrowed one of Dad's padded jackets and a thick pair of mittens. I wasn't going to be seen by anyone, so it didn't matter what I looked like. But Helene had a dig at me anyway, not for what I'd borrowed, but for my own woolly hat.

'You look like a condom,' she said with a laugh once Ane and Dad had gone through the door. Annoyingly, I couldn't think of a suitably scathing reply. Stepping out, I bent my head against the wind and went across to the barn, where Sleipner stood harnessed to the old sleigh. We climbed aboard. Helene wrapped a blanket around Ane's legs, then offered me one too — I shook my head. Dad took hold of the reins and with a click of his tongue we pulled slowly away. The sky was grey, still keeping its cold. Tiny, whirling specks of snow swept to prickle our faces. I folded my arms across my chest and slid down on the seat. The cars on the main road slowed as they saw us; their occupants stared shamelessly as they went past. Ane waved at one of them, and they waved back. By the time we swung down the lane of a neighbouring farm I was freezing, but loath as I was to let Helene get one up on me, I left the spare blanket where it was and pretended not to be bothered. Reaching the pond, which was frozen solid, the snow whipping across its surface, we turned onto the forest track and were soon surrounded by rows of spruce, young trees some three or four metres tall, planted when I was still a little boy.

We'd done this every year on the day before Christmas Eve for as long as I could remember. Dad had done the same thing with his father, and, for all I knew, my grandfather likewise with his father too. In those days, they'd have used sleighs anyway, they wouldn't have been the outlandish sight they were now. Now it was all just pretending. We could have used the tractor or the pickup, as Dad would have done if he'd been doing anything else in the forest. The possibility didn't even occur to him. But why couldn't the song of Christmas be one of metal and combustion engines? At the end of the day, Christmas in our time was nothing but a commercial pandemonium entirely revolving around the shopping centre, so using a more modern vehicle such as the tractor would have been far more appropriate and a lot less hypocritical.

All these illusions that governed our lives.

People were so gullible.

Dad drew the sleigh to a halt and jumped down, then took the axe that had been next to him all the while on the driver's seat.

'Can you see any good ones?' he said to Ane as we walked among the rows. 'One a bit taller than me, perhaps?'

'Not yet,' she said, scanning those closest.

'How about that one over there?' I said, pointing a bit further ahead. It was unusually neat, nicely symmetrical, the branches sufficiently close together without the greenery being too dense.

'We'll let Ane choose, eh?' Dad said.

'Yes, of course,' I said. 'She won't find anything better than that, though. What do you think, Ane?'

She shook her head and moved on, laboriously scrutinising each tree in turn. It was all so dispiriting, the whirling snow among the low, bedraggled trees, the bitter cold, Dad and Helene allowing Ane such a free rein.

'This one,' she said at last, halting at a tree almost twice her height. There was no obvious reason for her choosing that particular one rather than any other. It was quite wonky, and the lower branches were vigorous on one side, sparser on the other. But Dad congratulated her on her choice all the same and set about chopping it down as we looked on.

'Doesn't it hurt the tree?' she asked her mother.

'Not in the slightest. It can't feel a thing.'

'But it dies, doesn't it?'

'We'll give it some water when we get home and then it'll be well again.'

There was something wonky and asymmetrical about her too, so maybe she'd identified with it, I thought, and smiled at the idea.

Dad dragged the tree back and dumped it by the side of the sleigh, then poured four mugs of steaming cocoa that we drank standing up. Helene ventured a few childhood memories to lighten the mood, how much she'd been looking forward to this, the sleigh ride into the woods was when Christmas really began for her, she said. Dad was verbally challenged as usual; talking was something he preferred to leave to others, such as Mum and Helene.

Ane kept glancing at me over the top of her mug. The look she gave me seemed hostile, but she was only eight, so it was more likely she just hadn't got the measure of me yet. She was wrapped up in her mother's loving care, everything in her world felt safe and familiar to her, until this uncle of hers turned up from London, representing something else entirely.

When we climbed up onto the sleigh again, I took the extra blanket for my legs, reasoning that Helene wouldn't pick up on it now. Dad laid the tree crosswise in between the seats and we set off home. The blanket didn't help much, the frost was in my bones. Once we were home I went straight upstairs and ran myself a bath while the others put the tree up and began decorating it. Afterwards, I lay on the sofa to read some Shakespeare. It had turned into a project without end: after five months I'd only got as far as 1593 and *The Taming of the Shrew*. My interest was flagging. I'd stopped consulting the dictionary all the time, realising I'd never get finished otherwise, and anyway you didn't have to understand every word to get the gist. A trick I'd discovered was to say the difficult words out loud; somehow, they often seemed to click into place then. The spelling in those days was ridiculous, it was as if the letters were just tossed about. Occasionally, quite often in fact, I'd come across clear, transparently Norwegian words in there too; they were as if in disguise, but if you spoke them out loud, their true identity would be revealed.

The tree, decorated now, stood in its corner, glittering with fairy lights, draped with garlands of little Norwegian and Danish flags, resplendent with shiny baubles and thick, boa-like tinsel of silver and purple, as well as the paper decorations my sisters and I had made at school over the years. Mum had kept everything, there wasn't an exercise book that hadn't been put away for posterity in a box in the attic.

That ninety-nine per cent of it was absolutely worthless, fit only to be binned, was something she refused to listen to. Mum was sentimentality's archivist. What do you want to keep that for? What are you going to do with it? This? Why?

Humans descended like snow through the ages. There were billions of us, we danced this way and that until our flight was abruptly over and we settled on the ground. What happened then? Billions more came falling, descending to smother us. I was one such snowflake, and I was still falling; Mum and Dad, Helene and Ane were too, along with everyone else who was alive now, there were billions of us, all falling at this single moment, and so slow was our flight that our thoughts and the things we owned seemed important to us; but the hordes of people whose descent had just begun, and those whose descent would soon begin, the enormous blizzard of the as-yet unborn, all waiting to descend, would completely smother not only us, but every sign of our lives, which thereby would become less than meaningless, would become nothing, zilch, nada. They would become snow in snow, darkness in darkness. And so would we.

No, nothing cannot *become* anything. If it could, then it would be something.

Nothing isn't even nothing.

I made myself comfy on the sofa with one of the cushions for a pillow, and the woollen blanket, settled back and began to read. The voices of my mum and Helene drifted from the kitchen. Ane I assumed was with my dad, probably in the cowshed, kids loved the cowshed, or maybe in the barn. They liked that too.

The Taming of the Shrew seemed to be a comedy of false and mistaken identities: a nobleman tricks a poor drunk into believing he's a lord, and convinces him that a male servant dressed up as a woman is his wife. It might have been hilarious once, about four hundred years ago, but it wasn't any more. It wasn't even amusing. And apart from that, it was totally irrelevant to anything that was happening in the world of today.

'I'm reading as well,' said Ane all of a sudden. I looked in the direction of her voice and discovered her to be sitting on the floor underneath the window. She was holding a book in her lap.

'So I see,' I said, and carried on reading.

'I'm reading *The Lion, the Witch and the Wardrobe*,' she said.

I didn't want to encourage her into a conversation, so I said nothing.

'Have you read it? It's quite good.'

I nodded without taking my eyes from the page.

'They go into a wardrobe and come out in another world.'

Silence.

'What are you reading?'

I sighed.

'Shakespeare.'

'What's that?'

'He's the person who wrote it.'

'Is it any good?'

'No.'

'Why are you reading it, then?'

'It's *considered* to be good,' I said, and immediately wished I hadn't. I'd have to explain now.

But again there was silence. After a bit I heard her disappear up the stairs. Clearly, she was used to her own company. Outside, someone opened the garage door. I'd been hoping I could borrow the car to go to the shopping centre. Too far to walk in this weather. Still plenty of time, though. I could wait until whoever it was came back. But who was it? Mum? Where was she going?

Out to get something she'd forgotten.

The girl came down the stairs again carrying a big box of Lego she then emptied onto the floor beside the sofa. It annoyed me, but I pretended not to notice.

She started playing. She was only doing it for the attention, I realised that, but she wasn't going to get any from me. I concentrated on trying to read, and a few moments later she was as if erased from my mind.

'Do you think it's a good house I've built?' she said.

'Yes,' I said.

'But you haven't even seen it!'

I cast a glance.

'Very good, like I said.'

Again, there was a silence.

She put her hand on my crotch.

'What have you got there?' she said.

I sat bolt upright.

'What are you doing? You mustn't do that, not ever!'

She looked up at me and smiled suggestively.

'Why not? Why can't I touch you there?'

'Because you can't. It's not acceptable. It's not done.'

'Why not?' she said, and again put her hand between my legs. I gripped her hard by the wrist, pulling her hand aside as I jumped to my feet.

She laughed.

I went towards the kitchen, where Helene was still occupied.

'Are you going to tell Mum now?' she called after me.

'Tell Mum what?' Helene wanted to know as I came in. 'What's she done?'

As soon as I looked at her I realised I couldn't possibly tell her. What was I going to say? Your daughter touched my dick, I just wanted you to know? Instead, I stepped past and poured myself a coffee from the vacuum jug.

'Nothing. She emptied her Lego out onto the floor next to where I was sleeping, that's all.'

'Sleeping?'

'Well, dozing — with a book.'

But if I didn't say anything, maybe *she* would. I touched Uncle Kristian between his legs, she might say. Out of context, they could interpret it in the worst way imaginable.

For all I knew she could be one of those kids who made things up just to be the centre of attention.

Helene opened the oven door and took out a tray of Christmas gingerbreads, put it down on the worktop and slotted in another.

'Do you want one?'

'No, thanks. Well, all right. Just the one, then.'

'Not them, silly. The ones on the rack over there.'

I took one that was shaped like a heart. It was still warm, and soft inside.

'Did Mum take the car?' I said.

She nodded.

'When will she be back, do you know?'

'No, but she went to the supermarket, so it shouldn't be that long. Why, are you going somewhere?'

'I was thinking about it.'

'Can you give us a lift?'

Fortunately, Ane sat quietly in the back the whole way there. I could see her in the rear-view mirror, staring out the window, immersed in her own world. Hopefully, what she'd done was insignificant to her and already forgotten. And even if she did bring it up, it wouldn't be that much of a catastrophe. *I* had done nothing.

The wind had died down. In our wake, the car threw up a plume of snow, until we reached the main road, which having been cleared and salted now glistened black with moisture in the greys of the dwindling daylight.

'When's Liv coming, anyway?' I said.

Helene shrugged.

'She should have been here by now.'

'How is she?'

She shrugged again.

'I haven't spoken to her in a while.'

'I thought you were close.'

'We were, a long time ago.'

'Nothing unusual in that. You're different, that's all.'

'Yes, we are.'

We crossed the bridge onto the flatland on the other side, where their house was. Why anyone would want to live on a new housing estate in the middle of nowhere, next to a busy main artery, was beyond me. But there was a lot I didn't understand about Helene.

The houses were all the same, the estate lifeless, not a kid to be seen anywhere.

I turned up their driveway and came to a halt in front of the house. The sky above the trees at the end of the plain had taken on a bluish tinge in all the grey. A pair of kids' skis stood leaned up against the outside wall, a Christmas wreath with red berries hung from the front door.

'Are you popping in?' Helene said.

'No, it's all right. I need to be getting into town.'

'Ah, I'd forgotten. Your Christmas present for Ane!'

'Ha ha.'

'Thanks for the lift. See you tomorrow.'

She shut the door and went towards the house, where Ane was already standing waiting. I reversed, swung round and drove back the same way we'd come.

The thought that I actually lived in London and not here suddenly sparkled in me. Piccadilly Circus, its neon shining into the night, visible even from incoming planes as they passed low over the city. The grubby, seedy streets of Soho, their teeming crowds that seemingly contained every variation on a human being, as if they had emerged from subterranean burrows. The taxicabs that weaved their way through the city like sharks, the markets and the immigrant shops of the outer districts, the poverty there, and the wealth in the well-to-do boroughs, in some areas it was even side by side. And the faces. All the faces in a city with six millon inhabitants. Face after face after face, an endless flow, a river of faces. Who would live here, in a hinterland such as this, with nothing but fields on every side, where there were as many tractors as people, and where nothing ever happened, when at the same time there was a whole wide world out there?

Poor Helene.

But not everyone could be an artist. Not everyone could move away. What would the world look like if they did? No, those who had to stay, stayed; those who had to go, went.

What was it that decided? Why didn't Helene feel the way I did? We had the same parents, the same upbringing.

Mum and Dad liked to travel. But Helene?

Not a shred of curiosity. Not the slightest wanderlust.

If she'd been the anxious type and for that reason needed to stick to what she knew, I'd have understood. But she wasn't anxious. This was what she *wanted*.

The shopping centre was on the other side of town and by the time I got there the sky was almost completely dark. The shops would be closing soon, so there were plenty of spaces in the enormous car park.

I pulled into one conveniently close to the entrance. The last thing I felt like doing was buying the kid a present after what she'd done, but it would only be glaringly conspicuous if I didn't, and who knew what she might say then? All I could do was suck it up and head for the toy shop on the first floor.

I stood for ages waiting for one of the two assistants to find time for me. One was dealing with the customers and taking their money, while the other was kept more than busy gift-wrapping their purchases.

'I'm looking for a gift. It's for a girl, eight years old,' I said when finally it was my turn. 'Can you help me find something?'

'How much were you thinking of spending?' said the assistant, a woman in her late fifties with a backside the size of a wardrobe.

'Fifteen, twenty, something like that.'

'We've a rack with the cheaper toys over by the door,' she said. 'Have a look there and see if you find anything.'

'But I don't know what an eight-year-old would want.'

'You're not that old that you can't remember, surely?' she replied, and with that she turned her attention to a young couple behind me, each with a huge box in their arms.

I could hardly believe what I'd heard and stood there a moment just looking at her. She ignored me completely, entering the couple's purchases into the cash register. No fucking way was I going to buy anything there, I thought, if that was how they treated their customers, so I went back out and bought myself a coffee in the cafeteria. I found a table by the window from where I looked out on dismal fields while shoppers milled about the concourse with bulging carrier bags.

The coffee was sour and bitter-tasting, and I wished I'd ordered tea instead. Not that I cared much for tea, but at least it would have been freshly made.

I could donate the money I was prepared to pay to a good cause and say that was her present. Save the Children or something. At school they were taught to be against everything bad and in favour of everything good. Until at some point they realised, or at least began to suspect, that bad things sometimes paid off, after which they could start making bad out to be good.

Maybe Young Friends of the Earth? A radical organisation, always on the front foot, that never pulled its punches. Helene and Rickard probably wouldn't approve. But it was *my* present we were talking about.

Something bright I hadn't noticed before shone in the sky. It was bigger than a star. A planet, perhaps? But then I'd have seen it before, surely?

I stared at it for some time before realising that it was moving. It was a plane. Because of the angle it had looked like it was standing still.

Of course, it could be a UFO. Aliens from another planet, fascinated by life here by the river. The same way we were fascinated by the lives of lions or anteaters. Maybe they were making a documentary about us and that was the reason their spaceship was hovering like that.

'Kristian,' a girl's voice said.

I looked up and it was Stina. She was standing with a carrier bag in each hand, her eyes fixed on me, wearing a white down jacket and a white bobble hat.

'Hi,' I said. 'Christmas shopping, is it?'

'Do you mind if I sit down?'

'No, go ahead.'

She dumped her bags and sat down without even bothering to take off her hat and coat. Her ardour was all gone.

'How do you feel?' she said, and looked me straight in the eye.

'I feel fine,' I said.

'You would,' she said, 'because you've no heart. Where your heart should be, there's just a black hole.'

I felt my cheeks go red.

'How do you mean?'

'I made myself vulnerable to you. And you humiliated me terribly.'

'I wouldn't call it *humiliated*, exactly.'

She glared at me.

'I thought you were a really nice guy. But you're not, you're cold and callous. A creep, in fact.'

She stood up and picked up her shopping.

'I hope your life turns out really badly.'

And with that she turned round and strode away.

I shook my head and forced a smile, in case anyone had overheard our exchange and was looking.

It wasn't my fault she couldn't handle rejection. But it was easy to blame me. To gather up all her disappointments and toss them in my face.

No heart, as if.

Her flat had been soulless, completely lacking in any kind of human warmth. She was bringing up a kid in that cold, soulless flat. How much worse was that than turning down a girl you didn't even know?

I waited a bit to make sure I wasn't going to run into her again before making straight for the exit and leaving the whole bloody consumer trap behind.

Mum had put the goose in the oven, I realised as soon as I got in — the cooking smells assailed me as I came through the door. We'd had goose for dinner the night before Christmas Eve for as long as I could remember. Christmas Eve itself was roast pork. It should have filled me with joy and excitement, for my whole childhood was somehow contained in those smells, but instead I felt nausea. I went upstairs to my room, sat down at the desk, and stared at the sick yellow light that fell through the darkness and pooled on the snow next to the barn.

It would be too expensive to change my plane ticket and go home early. At the same time, being here was unbearable.

Mum and Dad were all right. Helene too, for that matter. So it wasn't that.

What was it, then?

I couldn't move here. I just couldn't bloody move. It didn't help to try and detach myself from it all. To tell myself that I should think of the house as just a house like any other, and go about in it as if I was a stranger who just happened to be staying a few days, with Mum and Dad as my kindly hosts.

Was there anything good here?

I switched on the desk lamp and opened my boxes of photographs and began looking through them, but then quickly sensed that at that moment it was the stupidest thing I could do, for everything was bathed in the light of emptiness and futility, and so I put them back. My records, then. They were neutral in that respect. I did as I'd been thinking the night before, created a little Cure-inspired section, the

Cure first, of course, with Bauhaus, the Birthday Party and Hüsker Dü following on. Unsurprisingly, though, a new problem transpired, because Ultravox couldn't come after Hüsker Dü. Anyway, I'd lost the momentum of the night before, so I left it all for later. Instead, I went downstairs and switched the TV on, an optimistic venture to say the least — there was never anything even remotely interesting on around this time. A puppet theatre piece from Iceland with a twist on the Christmas story had just started. It was called *The Angel Who Never Came Home*, and not even Ane would have wanted to watch it, though she, presumably, was dead centre of its target group. I switched it off and picked up one of Dad's *Science Illustrated* magazines from the pile under the coffee table. One article was about some apes in America that a scientist and her team of assistants had taught to communicate at a comparatively advanced level — they understood and could use more than a hundred different signs.

I could hear Mum occasionally attending to something in the kitchen, but apart from that all was quiet, and I imagined she was sitting at the table reading her book as she so often did. Dad would be in his office, I assumed. They never did anything unexpected, those two, were always true to type, with never a waver.

I was enjoying the article about the apes. It said when some orangutans had been taken from the jungles of Borneo to the cities of Europe in the eighteenth century, people there had believed them to be humans. The three gorillas the scientists were working with were too beast-like to fool anyone. But they could communicate quite complex notions, so apparently they had an inner life, which made them someone rather than something. Persons of a sort.

There couldn't be that much difference between them and Ane, not essentially. What was going on in her mind when she sat quietly gazing out the car window, for instance, was something I could only guess at. Presumably she was thinking child-thoughts, but what were they? She didn't know they were child-thoughts and that a grown-up could think of them as such. To her they were everything, not something that one day would be fully developed. I supposed the same applied to the apes. They thought their ape-thoughts and felt their ape-emotions without knowing that was what they were.

It was almost easier to imagine what it was like being an ape than a child.

I could make a project of it. I could go to London Zoo and take pictures there.

Mum emerged to set the table.

'Nice having you home,' she said, and smiled at me before spreading a billowing tablecloth.

'Nice being here.'

'What's that you're reading?'

'An article about apes.'

'You've always had an inquisitive nature.'

'Have I?'

She opened the sideboard and took out three plates she then arranged on the table.

'You were forever asking questions when you were little, it didn't matter what the subject. You could drive us round the bend sometimes.'

'But that came to an end.'

'Yes, it came to an end,' she said. Now she put the glasses out. 'But photography is a form of enquiry too, isn't it?'

'You could say.'

She sat down beside me with her hands in her lap.

'It's nice to have you home.'

'So you said.'

She made to run a hand through my hair, but I shrank away.

'I'm not five any more, Mum.'

'No, you're a young man,' she said, and got to her feet. 'Dinner's ready in a minute. Will you go and tell your dad?'

I went up the stairs and knocked on his door, but not wanting to know what he was doing in there I didn't open it when he answered, just told him dinner was ready and then went back down before he came out.

She'd put a bottle of wine by his plate, the corkscrew next to it. That was a way of communicating too. Standing at the table in front of the steaming goose and all the trimmings, he removed the foil from the neck of the bottle with a practised hand having first made an incision with the knife, then pressed the point of the corkscrew into the cork.

He twisted the handle a few times and then pulled hard, though with no particular effort, until the cork was extracted with a pop of suction. He poured the wine into each of our three glasses before sitting down and rubbing his hands together.

'At last,' I said ironically. 'You've been waiting for this a whole year, haven't you?'

'I certainly have,' he said, and his fleshy face was a red glow as he stood up again, this time to carve the goose.

'You're not averse to a bit of goose yourself, I know that,' he said.

'Fact.'

The carving knife, sharpened to perfection, slid through the meat.

'Cut some thinner slices too,' Mum said. He did as he was told, and soon we each had a little heap of golden-skinned grey-white meat on our plate, moments later smothered in thick, light brown gravy and trimmed with red onion, carrot, leek, prunes and apple, not to mention the roast potatoes.

We ate in silence.

Mum's movements, quick and fluttering, weightless, birdlike. Dad, her opposite in almost every respect, appeared almost unmoving by contrast, his slow, solid, level-headed progressions. If she was a leaf, he was a tree trunk.

'Cheers, then,' Mum said, and raised her glass.

'Cheers,' Dad said.

'Cheers,' I said.

'When will Liv be here?' I said as I put my glass down.

'She was meant to be coming this morning,' Mum said.

'Haven't you heard from her?'

'No. She'll be here tomorrow, you'll see.'

Liv had been the kind of teenager they'd had to go out in the middle of the night searching for at weekends. She would drink herself senseless at the first opportunity and was completely incapable of setting limits for herself; several times, she'd stolen money from home. There was nothing in her to keep her grounded.

What was it that kept me grounded?

I had my art, and channelled my transgressive tendencies into that.

So it was never a problem for me, as it was for her; I didn't need to be wild in the way I lived my life.

But I'd never really understood what it was inside her that propelled her into such insane behaviour. She wanted fun in her life, I could see that, but didn't everyone? She never saw the point in staying in and being bored. But again, she was hardly the only one. She went out. But somehow she'd never been able to see that when it came to having fun there was a cut-off point. Once you crossed that line, it was fun no more. But still that was exactly what she did, time and again. And didn't that send you back to the start? It wasn't fun to stay in, but then neither was puking in a gutter or being paralysed on ketamine – or going home with someone you didn't even like, out of your head, and letting them fuck you.

She'd never understood that it was best to stick to the middle ground. To stop before fun turned to horror.

'Delicious this year, as ever,' Dad said.

Mum beamed.

'You've got it down to a fine art,' I said.

And it was true. The meat was tender and succulent, the vegetables were sublime, their crisp freshness softened to perfection, with the particular, concentrated taste they acquired when part-boiled, part-roasted in the juices from the meat. The potatoes were crusty on the outside, soft inside. The gravy rich without being too salty, thick and full of flavour.

'Why do you think Liv's always been so wild?' I said.

They both looked at me at once in sheer fright.

'Is that what you think? That she's wild?' Dad said.

'It's not how I see it,' Mum said. 'I'd say she had a desire to taste life and try things out. There's nothing wrong with that.'

'Relax,' I said. 'I wasn't criticising. I just wondered, that's all. I thought it might be something you'd thought about too, seeing as you're the ones who brought her up.'

They carried on eating without reply.

'Maybe she's empty inside and feels she needs to compensate in some way,' I said.

'Kristian,' Dad said, 'that's not the way we talk about each other here.'

'Besides, it's not true,' Mum said.

'Who knows?' I said.

'Not you, at any rate,' Mum said.

'What's that supposed to mean?'

'It means what I said,' she said, and got to her feet, taking her plate with her into the kitchen.

Dad was still eating. He picked up a drumstick with his fingers and lifted it to his mouth. The skin was so crisp it gave a little crunch as he bit through it.

He took a mouthful of wine.

'Mum's mother to you all,' he said when he put his glass back down. His lips and part of his chin were a greasy glisten in the soft light. 'She'd never side with one against another. You understand that, I'm sure.'

'Of course I do. But she didn't have to side with anyone. All I said was that Liv was a bit wild. There's nothing controversial about that, is there? We all know she is.'

From the kitchen came the electric whirr of the hand mixer.

'You said rather more than that, Kristian.'

'Like what?'

'You said she was empty. You can't say a thing like that about your sister. At least not to your mother.'

'But to you I can, apparently?'

'You can say what you want to me. But it doesn't mean I care for it.'

He wiped his mouth at last with his napkin, before he too got up and took his plate into the kitchen. I did likewise with mine, scraped the leftovers into the bin, rinsed the plate and put it in the dishwasher along with my knife and fork. Mum stood with her back to us whipping cream, slow circular movements of mixer in bowl. On the worktop next to her, a big glass bowl contained some large reddish-brown lumps in a cloudy, viscous-looking liquid with bits floating around in it. Her home-made preserved plums.

When she came back in with the dessert, a bowl in each hand, it was with a breezy, unruffled air, as if she'd never said, only a few minutes earlier, that I knew nothing about other people.

'Christmas Eve tomorrow,' she said as she sat down. 'Isn't it lovely?'

The plums were mushy and bitter, they tasted of earth and darkness, whereas the syrup was sweet, the cream fresh and luxurious. It was a matchless combination.

'We'll have cloudberry cream for dessert then,' she added, and turned to me: 'You wouldn't believe how many cloudberries there were this year, you should have seen!'

'Do we have to talk about tomorrow's dessert while we're eating today's?' I said.

'You're right,' she said. 'I see what you mean.'

She and Dad exchanged glances. Barely a couple of seconds, but I noticed all the same.

What was in it? It looked like neither was in doubt, as if many, many hours of talk had preceded it and established a fundamental concurrence between them which required only a look in order to be cemented.

They'd been talking about me.

Cold and callous, Stina had called me.

But she didn't know me. Mum and Dad did.

'If everything's fine with Liv, how come she didn't turn up when she was supposed to?' I said. 'Has she even phoned?'

Mum shook her head.

'We haven't heard a word yet.'

'If there was something wrong, we'd have been informed,' said Dad. 'You've no need to be worried about her. If that's what you are.'

'I just hope she's coming,' I said. 'I haven't seen her in ages. And it'd be nice for us all to be together for once.'

'It will be, yes,' said Mum.

I woke in the middle of the night, hearing a car pull up outside. It lingered a while with the engine turning over. I lifted the curtain and looked out. Liv was standing beside it, clutching a down jacket to her chest, while some guy opened the boot and took out a rucksack. The headlights lit up the yard and shone out into the field, making the snow there glitter and sparkle. Fumes puffed from the exhaust in waves tinted red by the rear lights.

The guy handed Liv the rucksack. She leaned in to him, whoever he was, and they hugged. Demin jacket with a fur collar, his hair in a ponytail.

Mum and Dad's bedroom door opened as the guy got in the car and Liv, still clutching her jacket, but now also with the rucksack in her hand, went towards the front door.

So she had a driver, I thought, and went back to bed. She was fairly good-looking, so it wasn't exactly strange. But still. They'd only hugged, so they weren't going out with each other. Nevertheless, he'd driven her all the way from Oslo in the middle of the night.

It was nearly four o'clock. Another two hours and Dad would be getting up.

The next time I woke there was music coming from downstairs. I got up and found Mum sitting in her chair with a book in her hands and Bach on the stereo. Dad and Liv were nowhere to be seen. In the kitchen, rice porridge bubbled in a pan. The sky above the fields was dark, the road deserted. Slices of ham lay on a chopping board on the table. She'd put sugar, cinnamon and butter out too. A fat red candle burned with a steady flame.

'Put some more milk in, if it needs it,' she said from the living room.

I added a splash and stirred it in.

The doorbell rang. Mum turned the volume down and went to answer it. It was Andreas and his family. Dad was out there too, I could hear — he must have seen the car from wherever he'd been when it came up the drive, and gone over to greet them.

I poured myself some coffee, sat down at the table and gazed out the window. This was always the longest of days. When I was a boy, of course, it was because I looked forward to the presents in the evening. Now I didn't. Nevertheless, the day dragged on interminably. Perhaps it was because everything had been made ready in anticipation, the house tidied and cleaned, the tree decorated, everything just waiting.

Across the road, the neighbour's windows were a warm glow in the dusky mid-morning murk and fairy lights twinkled from a tree out front.

Darkness didn't care what it descended on, it struck me. It just descended.

Next Christmas I'd stay in London. Go down the pub in the evening and have a few pints. Go for a walk by the river in the morning, take pictures of everything I saw. Capture the mood. Savour the freedom.

What was mood anyway? There was nothing at all different about the fields, the road or the sky today, but still it felt like there was — as if even out there it was Christmas Eve.

Dad appeared in the doorway.

'Aren't you going to come and say hello to Andreas and the others?' he said.

'Yes, of course. Just finishing my coffee.'

I let another couple of minutes pass before going in. Andreas was hunched forward on the edge of sofa, his wife Vilde was sitting at the end of it with her legs tucked underneath her, while the baby was lying still on a sheepskin on the floor, gazing up at the ceiling.

'Kristian!' Andreas said, and got to his feet.

'Long time, no see,' I said. I shook his hand and gave Vilde a hug.

'So this is the little miracle,' I said. 'How old is he now?'

'She,' said Andreas. 'Kari. She's five months.'

'Doing well?'

'Yes, she's amazing, of course.'

I nodded and smiled.

'Nice,' I said.

'I'll make some more coffee,' Mum said. 'Or would you rather have tea?'

'Coffee for me, please,' said Andreas, and turned to Vilde. 'But you'd prefer tea, I think?'

'Please, yes. With a tiny bit of milk, if that's all right?'

'I think we can manage that!' Mum said with a smile, and went out into the kitchen.

'So, how's London?' Andreas said.

'Big,' I said. 'And bad.'

He laughed.

'But you're doing all right over there?'

'I am, yes. Never been better.'

'Aren't you going to sit down?' Dad said.

'I was thinking of going out and doing a bit of work, actually. The light's fantastic just at the moment. It won't last, though. How long are you staying?'

'Oh, just a short visit.'

'I won't be long, then. See you before you go.'

I fetched my camera, put my coat on and went out. The photography had been an excuse, but now I was outside I could just as well take a few pictures — the light really *was* fantastic, as if streaked with darkness, making it seem like the sky in some way wished ill on us.

I went down to the road. I wanted to capture the light in the windows against the near black of the forest and the sky's monumental grey.

The neighbours had a Norwegian Buhund that came bounding as soon as it saw me, only to be brought to an abrupt halt, barking madly, as it reached the end of its long tether. I took some photos of it, and of the house too, but when a figure appeared in the window and peered out I carried on walking, the same way we'd gone the day before. The air was a lot milder now. The snow had become soggier, and the dark trunks of the spruce trees showed faint shimmers of moisture.

Andreas and I had basically grown up together. He was my cousin, the son of my dad's brother, Aslak. He was three years older than me, though, solid and level-headed, always one to be trusted, even as a young boy. I understood at an early age that it was he who should have been my dad's son, not me. They had a lot more in common and understood each other.

Once, when I was about thirteen, I'd described a girl we both knew as a *dog*. It was the sort of thing we said, the jargon we used. What was it he said? 'And what do you think you are — fucking irresistible?'

I'd got nothing against him, but he'd actually driven me out of the house. I couldn't stand to be in the living room with him, and I couldn't just stay in my room either as long as they were there, it'd be taken as a protest and frowned upon by my parents. So I had no choice but to trudge about among the trees with my camera bobbing in front of my chest, like some poor birdwatcher.

The sky looked like someone had drawn a sponge across it that had been steeped in dark grey watercolours. The trees stood motionless around me, they also dark, striving upwards from the floor of white snow.

No movement, no sound.

The mood of the forest was not hostile exactly, but then not welcoming either.

It was inside me, wasn't it?

The mood.

The pictures I took couldn't possibly contain what was inside me. But since clearly they *did* possess mood, was it just something I attributed to them when looking at them? Would the photographs simply reawaken the mood I felt there among the trees?

It had to be the case.

The Dutchman believed this had to be eliminated — wasn't that what he meant? That the photographer was in the way of the photograph, or perhaps even *was* the photograph?

There was no reason to listen to anything he said. He'd failed and had given up.

But I had to find my way. I couldn't just take pictures. I had to find my own style. So that whenever someone looked at my photographs, they'd know at once that this, this was Kristian Hadeland's work.

The food wasn't far off, I realised, for the table was set with everything bar the rice porridge itself. Red tablecoth, white candles, the Christmas Oratorio on the stereo.

'Did you get anything done?' Mum said from the kitchen. She glanced up at me with a smile when I came and stood in the doorway as she was stirring the porridge.

'Yes, a bit,' I said.

'Where did you go?' she said, and began to pour the porridge from the saucepan. It coiled slowly into a big serving bowl.

'The woods.'

'Aha,' she said, and tore off a piece of kitchen paper to wipe the lip of the bowl before carrying it past me and putting it down on the table in the living room.

'Do you want me to call the others?'

'If you would.'

'Is Dad in his office?'

She nodded.

'Liv's upstairs too, in her old room.'

Dad came down the stairs as I was going up.

'Ready, is it?' he said.

'Yes. Just going to tell Liv.'

She was sitting on the bed smoking, the window next to her pushed ajar. She was thinner than I remembered, her skin tight across the bones of her face. Her grey eyes opened ironically as soon as she saw me, and she stubbed out her cigarette.

'So, the family's little artist's come home,' she said.

'And the family's little drug addict.'

'Is that what you think?'

I gave a shrug.

'It doesn't matter to me what you do. There's food downstairs.'

'Same old kid brother,' she said, and got to her feet as I turned and went back out.

The energy around the table was different with Liv there. Mum and Dad's silence, otherwise such a comfortable part of them, became at once awkward, as if now, instead of being just the way things were, it was a deficiency. Why aren't we saying anything? they seemed to be thinking all of a sudden. That it was Liv, sitting there picking at her food, who gave rise to this tension, was obvious, there'd been nothing like it the previous evening.

'Andreas told me he's bought a plot of land up the hill,' Dad said.

'Are they going to build a house there?' Mum said.

'That's what they're intending, yes,' Dad said. 'He's going to do most of the work himself, he says.'

No one spoke for a while.

'We'll be seven at the table tonight,' Mum said. 'It's been a long time since we've been so many.'

'We were seven last Christmas as well,' I said.

'Well, it's still a long time ago, a whole year. I'm looking forward to us all being together!'

Again, a silence.

I wondered what it took to set the mood like that, without saying or doing anything. I didn't have the capability myself. At least not here. Presumably, it was because I was the youngest. No one cared what I said or did.

But I felt different as well now that Liv was there.

It was easy to think it had to do with strength, that she was strong. But that wasn't the case. She was weak, someone who gave in to things.

After leaving school, she'd first gone off to attend a *folkehøyskole* for a year, then did a stint working in a clothes shop here in town, followed by six months jaunting around South America. When she came back, she took the university preparatory courses with the intention of reading psychology, but didn't get in and chose to do sociology instead, dropping out after a year and taking on casual jobs here and there, mostly in bars and cafes. After that came a half-hearted attempt to start again at uni, this time it was social anthropology, but that too went belly-up. Now she was twenty-eight, with no qualifications, no real place of her own, no kids. She lived like a teenager, or like an artist. But with no talents at all in that direction, there was nothing to justify her living as if she did. Besides, being an artist was actually hard work, much harder than people realised.

I took another portion, mainly just to highlight her own pickiness. Mum and Dad both appreciated it when people tucked in and enjoyed the food they served.

A knob of butter in the middle, then a sprinkling of sugar and cinnamon before the first tentative nibbles, from the edges to begin with, that weren't so piping hot, gradually proceeding inwards, towards the centre, the porridge thereby cooling incrementally as these new extremities were excavated, the temperature of my spoonfuls thus remaining reasonably constant throughout.

I liked the way the cinnamon seemed to remain so dry, even in its combination with the soft and creamy porridge, the melting butter and the dissolving, translucent glaze of sugar.

I poured myself a glass of squash and noticed Liv looking at me as I drank.

'Do you like it in London?' she said.

'Yes, I do. It's a good place.'

'I was over there during the autumn as it happens.'

'Were you in London?' Mum said. 'We didn't know that.'

'I thought about looking you up, but I was there such a short time, it would have been too much hassle.'

'What were you doing there?' Mum wanted to know, still astonished that one of her offspring could have embarked on such an expedition without her prior knowledge.

'I was there with Nicolai. A weekend getaway, that's all.'

'Nicolai . . .' said Dad.

'Nicolai, yes,' said Liv. 'You don't know him.'

'Was he the one who brought you here?'

'No.'

'Who was that, then?'

'That was Are.'

Mum and Dad's eyes met very briefly, and their questioning ceased.

I was looking at my photos when Liv came in.

'You might have knocked,' I said when she sat down on the edge of the bed. 'I could have been having a wank.'

'Do you want a ciggie?' she said.

'You know I don't smoke.'

'You could have started over there.'

She lit up and I opened the window. Cold air poured in.

'Can I have a look?' she said with a nod at the photos I was still holding in one hand.

'Not these ones, you can't. They're just snaps. But you can look at this series here, if you want.'

I took the photos out of the box and handed them to her.

She looked through them, pausing here and there to study an image closer for a moment, occasionally holding one out at arm's length, the cigarette dangling from her lip the whole time. When eventually the drooping ash threatened to drop from the tip, she leaned forward and released it through the window.

'What do you make of them?' I said.

'It's all been done before,' she said, and handed them back. 'You can improve, though. That's why you're at art school, isn't it?'

'And since when were you an expert?'

'You asked for an opinion. I gave you one.'

'Exactly, it's just an opinion.'

She gave a laugh, a cold report, then tossed her cigarette end out the window.

'What put it into your head that I was a drug addict?'

'It was just something I said. I know you've tried pretty much everything going.'

'You do, do you?'

'I reckon so. It seems fairly obvious to me.'

She held my gaze, as if realising only now that I existed. It felt uncomfortable, and I turned back to my pictures.

'When I was a kid, there was one thing I wanted more than anything else in the world,' she said. 'Do you know what it was?'

'No.'

'A little brother. I kept pestering Mum and Dad about it.'

'You don't say.'

'I was ecstatic when they said it was going to come true. Even more so when you finally arrived. But then I lost interest. It wasn't your fault. It was more like I didn't know what to do with you. It's a bit like that now as well.'

'You don't know what to do with me?'

'No. And it's still not your fault. But when I come in here to talk to you, part of me doesn't know why. You probably feel the same way about me.'

'I don't.'

'Oh, come on. When do you ever give me a thought? When do you ever care?'

'Quite often, actually.'

She gave another joyless laugh.

'Do you know what your problem is?' she said, and lit another cigarette. 'You're always trying to be bigger than you are. It's fatiguing. You'd feel a lot better about yourself if you stopped doing that.'

'I feel fine about myself.'

'Your photographs are ordinary. You try and make out they're art. What if you end up living your whole life like that? Pretending you're something you're not, and never will be. That's going to be pretty strenuous.'

'You're the failure out of us two, not me.'

She stood up and tossed her half-smoked cigarette the same way as the first.

'I meant well by what I said, even if it might not have sounded like it.'

She left the room.

I tried to put my mind to my work again and ignore what she'd said. She hadn't the power over me for it to be hurtful, it would have been idiotic to take her words seriously, but still I couldn't concentrate, her comments kept trickling in like water through the planks of a leaky boat.

I was trapped here. I was a prisoner.

Who had imprisoned me, and for what crime? What had I done?

I was only me, and yet I had to field so much crap.

The trick was to treat them as strangers, random generic persons, hosts of a boarding house I just happened to be staying at. I could eat well there, retire to my bed on a satisfied stomach without a care as to what they might think or say about me, for their opinions didn't matter. I could appreciate the snow as darkness fell upon it, the cosy lights from nearby houses.

There was a knock on the door.

Mum poked her head inside.

'Kristian?'

'What now?'

'Helene phoned. She said Ane suspects Father Christmas is just her dad. Would you do the honours this year?'

I looked at her in disbelief.

'The costume's too small for your dad now,' she added. 'And it should be a man.'

'Mum, seriously! Ane's eight years old. Of course she doesn't believe in Father Christmas.'

'But she wants to, that's the main thing. It might be the last time, which makes it a bit special this year. Would you?'

'No, I can't.'

She stared at me.

'Why not?'

'All right, let me put it this way: I won't.'

She nodded, biting her bottom lip as she did when something didn't suit her.

A bit later, Helene, Rickard and Ane arrived. I watched them from the window, the two grown-ups as they lugged their bulging IKEA bags from the car to the front door, strides made stiff and awkward by best shoes, their daughter dressed up, flitting about between them.

There was still a while until the boys' choir, that fixture of Christmas television, came on, so I lay down on the bed with my Shakespeare to pass some time before I'd have to go down and join them.

Shortly afterwards, I heard someone come up the stairs. This time it was Helene who opened the door.

She tossed me a carrier bag with the Father Christmas costume in it.

'You put this on later,' she said. 'And spare me your protests. You're her uncle. Now pull yourself together and start bloody acting like it.'

She shut the door again without waiting for a response.

I sat up, more resigned than angry. If I refused, which of course I was perfectly entitled to, it would sour the evening, the air would vibrate with scorn and reproaches. I couldn't be bothered with that all evening. Better then to swallow my pride. A few minutes in a stupid costume wasn't going to hurt. But next year I was staying in London. Every year from now on, in fact. They could plead and beg all they liked, wild horses wouldn't drag me back. They'd just have to sit here and wish they hadn't treated me like an idiot.

Revenge is best cold.

Tonight I'd play along and pretend everything was hunky-dory, that I was having a lovely time of it.

I went over to the wardrobe and got my white shirt out, then changed my mind as I stood with it in my hand, and hung it back. I wasn't a Christian, I didn't believe in family values, so why make an effort and dress up?

On the other hand, I couldn't go down in what I had on, that wouldn't do either. I studied my options and decided on a plain, dark blue sweatshirt and a pair of matching chinos. I stood in front of the mirror and put some gel in my hair, which without it tended to fluff.

Downstairs, I said hello to Rickard, who'd put on weight, his eyes even smaller than before in his chubby face. He didn't like me, I'd sensed that as soon as he became part of the family and would take me fishing with him just to show Helene how kind and thoughtful he was. His friendly mask cracked more than once — he'd get annoyed with the way I kept fumbling, helped me only with irritation when my spinner got caught in a tree behind us, and the interested questions he asked in the car on the way there were supplanted by silence on the way back.

'Well, look who's here,' he said, putting his hand out for me to shake.

'The one and only,' I said.

He didn't even smile. Ane was on the sofa watching the telly with her mother, Mum and Dad were busy in the kitchen. I sat down in the armchair by the window.

Rickard was wearing the same cheap suit he'd worn on every festive occasion I could remember. His thighs looked like black sausages in it now. Funny how bricklayers were often so corpulent when their work was so physical. But maybe these days his job was mostly paperwork. Probably, since he had his own little firm now. My suggestion he call it *Murmur* had only left him bemused, or else he thought I was taking the piss. But I wasn't — I actually found the pun, doubling up on the Norwegian for *wall*, to be rather funny.

He was biding his time until Dad decided to retire, then he and Helene would take on the farm. He probably fantasised about him getting wiped out by a falling tree in the forest in winter so they could get their grubby hands on the place prematurely.

Ane looked across at me now and then. Apart from that, my presence didn't seem to bother her one way or the other.

What was it with that girl?

Her unfortunate appearance made her look constantly bewildered, regardless of what was going on in her mind.

Maybe I should write a note saying her present was a subscription, rather than just telling her. Put it in an envelope with her name on it.

Rickard had a glass of wine in his hand, I noticed. So they were looking after *him* all right.

I got up and went to the kitchen, where Mum and Dad were in full swing. Mum cut the top off a silvery bag of pickled red cabbage, a bowl of steaming potatoes on the counter next to her. Dad stood with a big fork stuck into the roast as he carved. The radio was on, choral music.

'Rickard's got a glass of wine,' I said. 'Where's the bottle?'

'It's here on the side,' Mum said. 'Take it in, will you? Dinner's ready now.'

'You can open another as well,' said Dad.

I did, and took them both to the table with me. I poured myself a glass and tasted it. Odd, that something wet could taste dry, I thought to myself as Mum appeared carrying two serving bowls, one containing sauerkraut, the other pickled red cabbage.

'Do you need a hand, Mum?' said Helene.

'No, everything's done. Sit yourselves down!'

She turned to me.

'Will you go and give Liv a shout, tell her the dinner's on the table?'

I put my glass down with a measure of annoyance, went up the stairs and knocked on the door of her room. She didn't answer, so I opened it.

She was asleep on the bed.

'Liv?' I said. 'Dinner's ready.'

No response.

'Come on, for fuck's sake. It's Christmas Eve!'

When she still didn't react, I went in and put a hand on her shoulder to rouse her.

'Liv?'

She was well away.

I switched the light on and off a few times. When that didn't wake her, I went downstairs again. She could sleep through for all I cared.

They'd all taken their seats at the table. The TV had been turned off and the Christmas Oratorio put on radio in the background.

'Dig in, everyone,' Mum said.

'Don't hold back!' said Dad.

Helene started with the potatoes, putting a couple on Ane's plate before helping herself and handing the bowl on to Rickard. I skewered a juicy slice of pork with the serving fork, spooned some sprouts onto my plate next to it, then a little heap of the sauerkraut, just in time to receive the potatoes as Rickard passed them on. They were soft, and crumbly at the edges.

I swallowed a good mouthful of wine and caught my Mum's gaze as she sat with her knife and fork pointing at each other in her hands.

'Was Liv getting ready?'

'She was asleep.'

'But she's coming now?'

'No, I don't think she is. I couldn't wake her.'

'What?' She looked at Dad.

Dad got to his feet.

'I'll go and fetch her,' he said calmly.

She turned her head to glance at him several times in the few seconds it took him to reach the door. A smile was stuck to her face, and yet she looked terrified.

What was she thinking?

That Liv was dead?

I went cold.

But she'd been breathing — hadn't she?

'What's the matter, Mummy?' Ane said. 'Why did Grandad leave the table?'

'It's all right, nothing's wrong,' Rickard said.

'He's just going upstairs to wake Liv,' Helene said.

'Is she ill?'

No one answered.

Mum dabbed her mouth hastily with her napkin, put it down on the table, stood up and with a smile aimed at Ane went towards the door. In the silence that followed, we heard her hurry up the stairs.

'Why did Granny go?' Ane said.

'Not so many questions,' Rickard said.

Now it was Helene whose head turned nervously, repeatedly, in the direction of the staircase. Rickard carried on eating. I sipped my wine.

And so we sat, for a couple of minutes. Then, Dad came down again. Measured and collected as always, but there was alarm in his eyes.

'Can I have a word with you?' he said to Helene and Rickard, gesturing with a nod towards the kitchen.

Ane looked at me after they left the table.

'Why aren't we allowed to know?'

I shrugged.

Banished to the kids' table. It wasn't on. No matter what was happening with Liv. It wasn't fucking on.

Helene and Rickard returned. Dad went back upstairs. Helene crouched in front of Ane.

'We're going to have to go now,' she said. 'Your auntie Liv's been taken ill. We'll take all the presents with us and open them later at home. OK?'

'But I want to stay here,' Ane said.

'We can't, darling. Come on, let's get the presents. There's even more now, since we came.'

'Chop chop,' Rickard said. He'd fetched their IKEA bags from the hall and now began filling them with the presents that earlier had been put out under the tree.

'I don't want to go home,' Ane said. 'I want to stay here.'

She started crying.

'What's going on?' I said.

Helene flashed her eyes at me before turning her attention back to her daughter.

I got to my feet and went up the stairs. Liv was on the bed, in the same position as before. Mum was sat next to her, crying. Dad was standing at the window staring out.

'What's happened?' I said. 'What's wrong with Liv?'

Dad turned towards me.

'We think she's taken an overdose. The ambulance is on its way. You go down and help Helene. We don't want Ane to be here when they arrive.'

But there was nothing for me to do. When I went down, they were already in the hall putting their coats on. Tears were streaming down Ane's cheeks, but she was good and did as she was told. Rickard, however, looked angry. Totally unsympathetic. Furious at having his Christmas ruined.

Helene saw me standing there, and came up and hugged me.

'It'll be all right, I'm sure,' she whispered.

Then they left. The car started up, accelerated away towards the main road. Minutes later, the blue lights of the ambulance flashed into view on the plain. Dad must have seen them too, for he came down the stairs almost right away. I followed him out. Silent, we stood and watched as it turned off the road and came up the rise.

Dad went over as they pulled up. Two medics in red overalls climbed out. A man and a woman. Dad spoke to them. They each grabbed a large case and between them a stretcher and hurried into the house. Their boots, thudding against the floor, up the stairs. Dad went after them, I followed. Mum was standing against the wall on the landing, hunched over like an old woman.

'What's she taken?' the ambulanceman shouted from inside the room. 'Any idea?'

'No,' said Dad.

I stepped into the room. She was on her back now and looked completely lifeless. The woman was bent over her. The man searched the drawer of the bedside table, the rucksack. Dad pulled me back.

'I'm not in the way,' I said.

He would never normally order me about, but now he jerked his head firmly towards the stairs. It wasn't the time to argue, so I did as he wished, went downstairs and sat in the chair by the window. Shortly afterwards their boots thudded again on the stairs. The two medics came down with her on the stretcher into the hall. I got up and went to the door. She was lying there unmoving. Completely unmoving. They went past the Christmas tree, the dinner table with our Christmas meal on it, the flickering candles. Mum and Dad came after them. I followed. The medics opened the back of the ambulance and rolled the stretcher inside. Mum and Dad got their coats on.

'We're going with them,' Dad said. 'You stay here and hold the fort. I'll telephone as soon as there's any news.'

'OK,' I replied. 'What have they said? Is she going to be all right?'

'Everything's going to be fine,' he said.

Mum sniffled as he spoke. Her whole body trembled.

The ambulance went off down the drive, its blue lights flashing into the darkness above the fields. Dad scurried to the car, holding the door for Mum on the passenger side then starting the engine. The siren blared suddenly as the ambulance turned onto the main road. I waited until Mum and Dad reached the bottom of the drive before going back inside. It was the strangest feeling, the house now empty, everything abandoned. The fire crackled, Christmas lights twinkled.

She'd overdosed. The question was whether it was intentional.

Had she wanted to kill herself?

Was it that bad?

No, it had to be an accident.

Who would kill themselves on Christmas Eve, in a house full of family, with a kid there too?

I was hungry, only it didn't feel right to sit down and eat. On the other hand, there was nobody here to see me.

I picked up a slice of meat with my fingers and went upstairs. I could still see the depression in the duvet where she'd been lying. Her clothes had been pulled halfway out of her rucksack. Odd, that there'd been no trace of what she'd taken. Or maybe it had come to light after I'd gone downstairs.

It struck me suddenly that it was all still intact. Everything was the same as when they'd left. It could be documented. It *should* be documented.

I swallowed the last bit of the meat, wiped my hands on my trousers and went to get my camera. I photographed her room from the doorway, then stepped inside and photographed just the bed, just her rucksack, just the bedside table with its open drawer. I took some of the ballerina poster on her wall, from the time when she'd danced herself. After that, the living room, in its entirety at first, and from various angles, then just the dinner table, then the individual plates of half-eaten food. One of a greasy fork. The half-carved roast. The Christmas tree, still with some presents underneath it. The kitchen, in the kind of disarray that suggested only that normally it was clean and tidy. Dad's office? Yes, it was an important room in the house. I opened the door and switched the light on, and looked around as I stood there. Dad was a man without secrets. What you saw was what you got. But I wasn't looking for secrets, what I wanted was the house the way it actually was, with all the traces of the human beings who lived in it.

The desk, big and deep, like a sea in all its light-coloured wood, nothing on it but the telephone, a typewriter he hardly ever used, a hole punch and a stapler. Recent correspondance in one drawer, stationery in the other, older documents in ring binders chronologically arranged on the bookshelf, along with a complete encyclopedia in eighteen volumes. Family photos on the opposite wall — my great-grandparents,

grandparents, aunts and uncles. Underneath them, school photographs of me and my sisters.

Could I imagine a duller life?

No, I couldn't. If there was one, it would have to be Helene's.

Mum at least wanted to go places, meet people. She liked things going on around her. Life. Liv was like that too.

They were the flighty, neurotic ones, Mum and Liv. If anyone needed the security of home life, it was them.

The phone rang. It was Helene.

'What's the situation? Is she going to live?'

'Dad seemed to think so, when they left for the hospital. But that's all I know. I've not heard from them yet.'

'So Mum and Dad are with her?'

'Yes.'

'I'll get down there too, once Ane's gone to sleep. What a terrible mess.'

She started crying.

'It'll all be all right, Helene. It'll be all right.'

'Oh God.'

'I'll give you a ring as soon as I hear anything,' I said, though chances were they'd phone her before they phoned me.

'Thanks,' she said in a tiny voice.

It was as if she'd filled the whole house, I thought after I put the phone down and everything was quiet again. But it was only my mind she'd filled.

She and Helene had grown up together. Liv was Helene's little sister. It was no wonder she was distraught.

I switched the light off and went back out onto the landing. For some reason, speaking to Helene just then had made it clear to me. It was a suicide attempt, of course it was. The fact that she hadn't died meant that she didn't want to, she wanted only to be noticed.

Cocky and supercilious one minute. Utterly helpless the next. Laying her life in Mum and Dad's hands so they could see how bad it was.

The phone rang again. This time I answered it downstairs.

'Yes, hello?' I said.

'It's your dad. She's going to be all right.'

'Oh, thank goodness.'

'They pumped her stomach. She's in a sort of coma now, but they say she's out of danger.'

'I'm really happy to hear it, Dad.'

'I know you are. Anyway, we're going to stop the night here. We want to be with her when she wakes up.'

'Of course, I understand.'

'It wasn't the Christmas Eve we'd been hoping for.'

'No. But some things are more important than Christmas.'

'Exactly. I'll give you a ring again in the morning. We should be home sometime tomorrow, I think. All three of us, hopefully. You hold the fort until then.'

'I will. Give my love to Mum.'

I felt absolutely starving now, so I went and sat down at the table and ate what was still on my plate. The food was good cold, too. After I'd eaten, I went around the house with a glass of wine in my hand, thinking about what else I could do. Photographing the rooms wasn't enough. Maybe one of the house, too, from outside?

I went out, not bothering to put on a coat, and walked into the field, from where the house stood with all its windows lit up and empty, in the snow, beneath an ink-black sky. I photographed it from various angles, then fetched my old tripod and used that, shivering with cold, before going back inside, placing the camera on the dining table, activating the self-timer and going over to stand by the kitchen door. Hopefully, I'd be little more than a blurry, shadow-like figure. I took some more in the same vein, and then, reluctantly, cleared the table — they'd be outraged if everything was left out waiting for them when they got back. They'd think it was the very least I could have done, so I scraped all the leftovers into the bin and loaded the dishwasher.

They couldn't complain then.

The house was still quiet when I woke up the next morning. I liked being on my own there, it gave me a sense of freedom, of being my own master. In the best of all worlds, it would have stayed empty another couple of months, allowing me to continue taking photographs, documenting how the rooms lived on without their people inside them. The food would rot on the table, the needles fall from the tree, the plants wither in their pots, dust would settle on every surface. And onwards, through the years, the decades, the wallpaper would rot, fungi would spread, mice and rats would invade, vegetation would thrust its way through holes and cracks, walls would collapse, until the house was but a ruin, slowly consumed by grass and flowers, bushes and trees, a small mound in the flat landscape of the plain.

When Mum did her tidying and cleaning, and when Dad repaired a tile on the roof, this was what they were perpetually staving off: the slow abyss, ever present, ever close.

But what *was* it? I knew it had a name, entropy, but what *was* it? What force in the universe ensured that entropy never ceased, but untiringly pursued all that existed?

Outside, the weather was milder now and a mist clung to the fields, mantling them with its filmy grey. Sitting in the kitchen with some breakfast, I could hear the drip of melting snow from the roof onto the slabs of the doorstep. Apart from that, everything out there was still.

I finished reading the Shakespeare play, and remained unimpressed. I knew, of course, that it had been written early in his career and that his best works came later, but still I felt entitled to have expected more — after all, wasn't this the same man who produced the later plays? Or had he been injected with some potion, a witch's brew, that turned him into a genius all of a sudden?

Mum and Dad came back around twelve. I'd sat down at the window so I'd see the car when it turned up the driveway and had the camera to hand on the table next to me, allowing me to photograph their return. The car, at first from a distance, an insignificant fleck in the landscape, gradually approaching, pulling up outside, the doors opening, Mum and Dad getting out. I continued snapping away, even as they walked to the front door. Guessing they wouldn't like me photographing their return, I did so stealthily, from a distance, and when I went to greet them in the hall I'd already put the camera aside.

'How is she?'

Mum fluttered a smile.

'She's doing fine now,' Dad said and draped his scarf over the peg, unzipped his coat. His face was red and puffy. 'They're keeping her in until tomorrow, for the rest.'

'She's awake, then?'

'Oh, yes.'

'So what happened, exactly?' I said.

'She took something she shouldn't have,' Dad replied.

'I realise that. But what was it? Did she say? Was it accidental, or —'

'We'll not talk about it for now.'

He went straight upstairs to his office. Mum was already emptying the dishwasher. After that, she started on the hoovering. There was no rest or repose in her. I could forget all about getting her to sit down and talk about what had happened. Dad was equally unamenable. All I could do was let her flit about with her various appliances, let him sit upstairs on his own and grumble, or whatever it was he was doing up there. It was none of my business anyway.

Maybe I should take an overdose, too?

The rest of the day I spent in my room, working on my book, reading now and then, lying on the bed listening to music on my Walkman. At one point, I slept.

For dinner, Mum had made a stew from the leftover pork, which she dished up with pasta. There was no wine on the table, just a jug of water.

'It's freezing out there again,' Dad said. 'It's like a skating rink.'

'A good thing it's Christmas Day,' Mum said. 'There won't be so many on the roads.'

'There'll be a few,' Dad said. 'People visiting family.'

'I can't believe you're actually talking about the *weather*,' I said.

Mum smiled.

'Life is in the everyday, Kristian.'

There was a silence. I wondered what they would have talked about if I hadn't been there. Nothing, most likely. They were so melded together they didn't need to talk. They could read each other's thoughts.

'You haven't said much about your school since you came home,' Mum said after a while.

'There's not that much to tell,' I said.

'I'm sure there is,' Dad said. 'It's all obvious to you, but to us it's not.'

'So what do you want to know about?'

'Well, do you have lectures, for instance? How does the teaching take place?'

'We do have lectures, yes.'

They both nodded, looking at me with feigned interest, as if to encourage me to tell them more. I'd never seen anything so false in my life.

'Aren't we going to talk about Liv and what happened last night? About her being carried out of here on a stretcher less than twenty-four hours ago? Or are we meant to pretend it never occurred? Is that it?'

'No, of course not,' Mum said.

Dad said nothing, he just looked down at his plate and carried on eating.

'It's difficult for all of us,' Mum said. 'Sometimes it can be good to take a break from difficulties. Sharing a meal allows us to find comfort in being together.'

'But you've not talked about it since you got home.'

'What is it you want us to say, son?' Dad said, now fixing his gaze on me. It was a harsh gaze, hostile.

It flashed through my mind that this was what he was really like.

'Nothing specific,' I said. 'It just feels wrong that you're pretending nothing's happened.'

'You think so, do you?' Dad said.

'Lars,' Mum said.

Their eyes met. He didn't yield the way he normally would have done, he glared at her until she looked away. But he said nothing more.

Thankfully, we'd almost finished eating and I was shortly able to take my plate out into the kitchen, put it in the dishwasher and go back upstairs to my room. At first, I felt distressed, beside myself – I'd never seen Dad like that before – but then it was anger I felt. It wasn't me who'd tried to commit suicide. If he really did have to turn his aggression on someone, he could start with himself or with Mum. They were the ones who'd brought her up.

From the landing on my way to the loo, I could hear them talking downstairs. In case they registered my movements, I followed the usual routine — flushed the toilet, washed my hands, closed the bathroom door behind me, then my own — before creeping as quietly as I could down the stairs to stand by the living-room door, unseen, but within earshot.

Typically, they weren't saying anything now. The silence felt charged and I suppressed an urge to step forward and steal a look into the room, to find out if the tension was in them or me.

'We *must* get her away from there,' Dad said. 'It doesn't matter if she is nearly thirty. We have to intervene.'

'She won't want to stay here,' said Mum. 'We can't expect that.'

'What about Modum Bad?'

'Psychiatric hospital? Do you really think she'd agree to that?'

'Not unless she was talked into it, no. But there's got to be *something* we can do?'

Again, silence ensued. And I could only stand there, in anticipation of more.

Then Dad said:

'I could have done without Kristian being here. He's like a black hole. Sucks all the energy out of the place. Gives nothing back. Not even now, when Liv's in such a state. Even more so, in fact.'

I went cold.

'He's only twenty,' Mum said. 'And he means no harm by it.'

'He's always been the same. I know you've said he'll grow out of it. But it's not going to happen. It's what he is. He's a narcissist, through and through.'

'Lars.'

'Yes, I know. He's our son. But can't we be honest for once? I've been reading up on it.'

'Reading up on what?'

'Narcissism. He shows all the signs. Excessive need for attention and admiration. Grandiose sense of self. Arrogance, and a sense of entitlement. Manipulative and exploitative behaviour. Lack of empathy. It all adds up.'

'Nonsense. Everyone has elements of all those things in them. Including you. He's had a shock, that's all. As we have. People react differently when they're in shock.'

'He's not in shock. He just doesn't care.'

'That's enough, Lars.'

No more was said. I turned and went silently up the stairs. I couldn't think. I couldn't feel. I was completely vacant.

I lay down on my bed in the dark.

He hated me.

My own father hated me.

He'd hated me all these years.

And Mum hadn't supported me much either. She agreed with him, she just didn't care to say so out loud.

But I'd show them. I'd take off now and never come back. Never see them again. Never, no matter how much they pleaded and begged.

I got up, switched the desk lamp on and started packing. My photos went in first, flat at the bottom of the case, then my clothes, folded on top. After that, I stood for a moment, wondering if there was anything else I should take with me, mementos of any sort, but decided there wasn't. All I wanted was to forget.

My records. I wanted my records.

I took the clothes out again and arranged a few LPs in the case to gauge how many there'd be room for. I didn't want to make it too heavy to carry either. I reckoned fifteen, and impulsively selected which ones. If I stopped to think about it, I'd be here forever.

I closed the suitcase again and picked it up to test its weight, before leaving it ready by the door and lying down on the bed again.

All I had to do now was wait.

Mum came up and knocked around nine, poked her head round the door and asked if I wanted any supper.

'No,' I said.

'Aren't you hungry?'

'No.'

She smiled at me before withdrawing and closing the door behind her. The thought of it being the last time I'd see her face sent a ripple of joy through me.

I'd never come back here again.

From now on, the world was mine to discover. Never again would my thoughts have to pass through this place before I could make a decision. I would expel both house and family from my mind, erase them completely.

These thoughts shimmered in the darkness.

Dad got up at six o'clock all year round, so I set my alarm for five and put it under my pillow so they wouldn't hear it when it went off. Minutes later I was asleep, though my body had felt almost electric.

I slept in my clothes, so when the alarm rang all I had to do was get out of bed, pick up my suitcase, sneak down the stairs, put my shoes and coat on, my scarf and hat, and step out into the lightless early morning.

No note, no nothing. Just an empty bed.

I hoped they'd think I'd gone off into the woods and hanged myself or something, organised a search party, racked with guilt, fear and anxiety.

By half past five I was already standing in the railway station waiting room. The next train wasn't for another forty minutes. I bought a ticket from the machine, went for a piss, then sat down on a bench on the platform outside, feeling good in myself there in the cold, illuminated darkness.

Dad would probably ring the police and report me missing after a few hours. I hoped he was going to make the connection to what he'd said about me. If he didn't, it would be all the more baffling to them. Of course, they'd be concerned then as well, but they wouldn't feel the guilt.

This was exactly the sort of thing I couldn't allow myself to think! If what they felt mattered, it meant they still had a grip on me. I had to be indifferent. It was of no consequence what they felt or believed. The important thing was that I wasn't ever going to see them again. That I was free. Totally free.

The train came into view, a short ribbon of lights hugging the bend of the river, and rolled moments later into the station with a screeching and clattering of metal. The carriages were old and heavy, ice clung to their undersides in lumps, but inside was good and warm, and besides me there was hardly another passenger. After a short while I dozed off and slept the whole way to Oslo, where I went into a cafe for a coffee and a bread roll before taking a taxi to Fornebu. At the airport I was in luck, my ticket could be exchanged and there was a flight around one — the woman at the counter said it wasn't even half full. I told her that would do fine, checked my suitcase in, went through passport control, bought myself a beer at one of the bars, and went and sat down at a table by the window.

The landscape outside was drably monochrome. The runways black, edged with white snow, beneath a grey sky. The aircraft, though, gleamed at their gates. SAS with its bright blue logo. Braathens SAFE with its red and blue.

Wasn't it cats that couldn't see in colour?

It was easy to think they'd wish they could. But they didn't know colours existed, so they couldn't.

There had to be something similar that applied to us. Something obvious and wonderful in the world that we didn't know existed.

What could it be?

That was exactly the problem! We could only imagine that which existed. Any ruminations on something that *didn't* exist necessarily had to base themselves on what *did*.

I went over to buy myself another pint. When the bartender turned to take my order, something stopped me, not a thought exactly, but something like it. Drinking in the daytime isn't OK, it said.

Really? Why not? OK to whom? If I want another pint, and if I think it's OK to have one, then why shouldn't it actually *be* OK? Who are you to impose on me anyway? I'm alone here in the world, you see, and I can do exactly as I want. And now I want to buy myself another pint.

All such restrictions, every such rule that reared its head, came from my parents. And now I had nothing more to do with them. But when you open the birdcage, the bird will always need time to realise it's free to fly.

Slightly under the influence, though still in complete control of myself, I boarded the flight with at most thirty-odd other passengers. Among them were several Anglo-Norwegian couples, one of which occupied the row behind mine. A kid maybe four years old who kept kicking the back of my seat, a baby, too, that started crying when the aircraft hurtled along the runway, and didn't stop for another twenty minutes. I swivelled round a couple of times to make the parents aware that their boy was bothering me, but they didn't seem to take the hint and let him carry on as he pleased. Fortunately, he tired after a while and settled down. In fact, he was so quiet I turned round again to see what had happened. All four were fast asleep. The mother, flabby and pale, asleep with the little one in her lap, the father, lean, with goatish features, glasses and a few days' worth of stubble, asleep open-mouthed, the boy beside him with his head and arms resting on the tray-table in front of him.

The pictures I'd taken of the empty house could be my best work so far. They'd be an enigma. Something had happened, but what? The house was abandoned, apart from the person taking the photos, the shadow over by the wall. What was he doing there? What was it about the bed? The table with all the food?

I could hardly wait to develop them. The new term didn't start until well into January, but maybe I could get hold of a key from someone so I could use the darkroom. They were bound to appreciate the students wanting to work through the holidays.

After a couple of hours crossing the sea, land appeared below. Passing over it, I picked out a large estuary. Was it the mouth of the Thames? There was a small town, and I found myself thinking how good it would be to live just there, but by then it was already gone from view and we flew on, over patchworks of fields, dull greens and browns, with villages dotted about, meandering roads and railway lines, woodland.

It was clear just how much our cities swallowed up their inhabitants, for although they were big and grim they occupied a surprisingly small area of the landscape. Yet once you were in them, they were endless, the only thing there was.

No sooner had the thought come to me than London opened out beneath us. I looked for the house I lived in, but couldn't even locate Deptford, and then we were already descending into Heathrow, where the terminal building glinted in the light of the low-hanging sun as we approached the runway to land.

The phone started ringing that same evening. I didn't answer, of course, and when it kept on I disconnected it from the socket. In my little bedsit, surrounded by all that was mine, the events of the last couple of days appeared unreal. In particular the image of Liv being stretchered away by the ambulance crew in the midst of all the Christmas decorations, but also what Dad, invisible to me, had said. Had he really said those things?

Yes, he had, and it had changed everything. For that reason, it was not entirely without a sense of triumph that I disconnected the phone. They would just have to live on in uncertainty. The only mildly frustrating part was that I now couldn't tell them *why* they no longer had a son.

The weather the next day was bright and sunny. So much light imparted a sense of spring. I packed the camera and a couple of rolls of film into my bag before carrying my bike down the staircase, where I bumped into Collin, one of the other tenants. He was a couple of years older than me and came from one of the islands in the West Indies, I'd forgotten which one. With a Sainsbury's carrier bag of shopping in one hand, he stood back against the wall to let me past.

'Hello, Collin. You all right?' I said.

'Yeah,' he said. 'You?'

'Can't complain.'

He smiled and carried on up the stairs. I had no idea what he did, but he seemed to be at home a lot, and the smell that came from his flat was totally different from whatever came from mine. Mine didn't smell of anything in particular, his always had something exotic about it. What was it? Curry? Chilli? Food, anyway.

The air was cold in the shadows of the buildings, much warmer where the sun shone through. I'd decided to go a bit further afield than usual, and cycled all the way out to Barnes, where I had lunch at a traditional pub. The place was packed and the atmosphere lively, laughter rippling through buzzing chat. The customers seemed to be of all ages and had with them a conspicuous number of dogs. Outside, the local area verged on the rural, Barnes itself reminiscent of a village. If you ignored the modern cars, it all looked pretty much as I expected it had done back in the 1950s, or why not the 1920s, an age when Britannia still ruled over half the world. Ruddy-cheeked and fat-necked, flabby and unattractive, it was a mystery how the British, of all people, believed themselves entitled to govern others. Certainly, they possessed both wit and eloquence, at least some of them did, but also perverted minds and a warped sense of their own importance.

After a generous serving of roast lamb and potatoes, I cycled on, along the narrow roads, past meadows and copses, in search of something to photograph. When I noticed a lonely oak tree in the middle of a field, I stopped. In spring and summer it would be like a big green bauble, but as yet it was bare, its branches spiky and inhospitable.

It looked like a framework. It *was* a framework.

I took some pictures of it, from a distance to begin with, then at closer quarters. I was excited, the way I always was when an idea came to me and raced ahead of what I was doing, so that what I was doing was no longer enough. I cycled on and looked for more trees that were likewise solitary. The idea I'd got was to do a series — *Frameworks of Life* would make a good title — to show how everything that existed was in fact a construction. Even a cat was, with its inner framework of bones. Not to mention bats, their leathery skin drawn taut over a wiry skeleton.

I was never short on ideas. The problem was that the results, the pictures themselves, were always so less than I'd imagined.

It had nothing to do with talent, as Liv had believed, it was more a lack of experience.

Which was why trudging along riverbanks to take photos wasn't something I did for fun. I did it because it was necessary and important. A matter even of life and death.

Finding skeletons wouldn't be easy, though. Of course, I could go to a natural history museum and photograph the exhibits there. But that would be introducing a filter — the museum itself. My pictures would then be of the *filter* rather than the reality behind.

I would buy some fish and boil the flesh away.

Could I do the same with a cat?

It was probably against the law. Boiling a dead cat wouldn't be, but killing a live one was. Or was it? Vets did it every day.

Maybe I could find a veterinary clinic and ask if they'd got any dead animals I could have. I could say I was a biology student or something.

The sun was already low in the sky, the air swelled cold. Having photographed four solitary trees, I made for home, regretting that I hadn't brought my gloves with me, my fingers, curled around the handlebars, were red and numb. Soon my thighs too felt stiff. It was a long ride, at least an hour in the saddle, I reckoned. The prospect felt almost unbearable. So when I caught sight of a local train rocking its way through the landscape, and saw that it stopped at a station close by, I made in the same direction and took the next one that came, first to Waterloo, then to Lewisham, and biked the rest of the way from there.

Back home, I went downstairs into the basement where the bathroom was, clutching a set of clean clothes and a towel. Thankfully, no one was using it and so I undressed and stepped into the shower cubicle, turning as much hot water on as I could withstand, and stood there soaking for what felt like a quarter of an hour. There were brown stains around the drain and crinkly black pubes here and there along the edges where the water didn't reach or where they'd got caught on something that stopped them getting washed away. Two slivers of soap, thin as leaves, lay there too. I'd kept my own soap and shampoo there the first few weeks, until noticing how quickly they seemed to be dwindling and then realising that someone else was using them too. Worse, though, was that the toilet roll in my toilet on the landing kept disappearing too. I could get my head around people just *happening* to use someone else's shampoo in a shared bathroom — I could even have done so myself — but the toilet on my landing was mine alone, which meant someone was wilfully stealing. But no one was so skint that they couldn't afford to buy toilet roll, surely? Nevertheless, the upshot was that I now kept soap, shampoo and toilet paper in my room, and took them with me every time I went for a shower or needed to go to the loo.

Who could the thief be? It was a bit of a mystery. There were six tenants in the house. Next door to me lived an elderly woman, directly below me a girl whose name was Liz, a student in her mid-twenties, not bad-looking, with cropped hair and full cheeks, who often had a guy round to see her who I supposed was her boyfriend — long hair, beard and glasses, he looked like someone who was never going to finish his degree, skinny and shabbily dressed to boot. I didn't get what she saw in him, but that was her lookout, not mine. Next door to her lived Collin. On the ground floor was a flat twice the size of all the others, where an elderly couple lived. They had grown-up kids, so I gathered. A family with a pair of noisy preschoolers would often come and see them, and after a while I realised it wasn't just now and again, but every other Sunday, regular as clockwork, on which basis it wasn't hard to work out that the relationship between parents and son or daughter wasn't that close — they only came because they were expected to.

That any one of these people could steal my toiletries was by no means unthinkable, but I really couldn't see any of them sneaking into my private loo with the sole intention of stealing the toilet paper.

The bathroom with its cold stone walls was full of steam as I dressed again. Upstairs, I made myself a cup of tea, sat down on the settee and stared into the street below, almost deserted apart from a guy sitting up against the wall in his sleeping bag outside the bicycle shop, his dog stretched out on the pavement next to him, and a gang of lads who ambled boisterously past and then disappeared round a corner.

I plugged the telephone into the wall again. Not because I was going to answer if it rang, but because I was curious to know if they were still trying to get hold of me.

If they'd reported me missing, the police would have checked the passenger lists and found out by now that I was back in London. But that wouldn't stop them from ringing.

A day or two without them knowing if I was alive or dead, that was the first part of their punishment. The second was a lifetime of no contact.

What sort of person calls their son a narcissist?

Grandiose sense of self, as if.

I was better than him, that was for sure. What had he ever achieved? What would he be remembered for? What was the point of him having a life at all?

I put my mug down in the sink, took ten quid from my stash in the kitchen cupboard, and one of my unread paperbacks from the bookshelf, put my coat on and went out. No sooner had I shut the door behind me than I heard the telephone ring. I let it. There was a peculiar satisfaction in picturing my mother standing with the receiver to her ear in the living room at home, unable to get in touch with me. Its ringing filling my empty room again and again, all through the evening, while I was out drinking and enjoying myself. I could feel empathy all right, just not for them. They could go to hell.

I walked to what by now I thought of as my local, the Dog & Bell. It wasn't far from the river, oddly situated in what was almost a *terrain vague*. It was a popular place, nevertheless, with lots of regulars, and it was busy again tonight.

I was hungry, I realised. A Guinness was almost a meal in itself, so I ordered a pint. The book I'd brought with me was Ian McEwan's *The Comfort of Strangers*. A few pages in and it seemed promising.

'What are you reading tonight, then?' a voice in front of me then said.

It was Hans. I'd forgotten how tall he was. Nearly two metres, probably. What would that be in feet and inches? His hair was all over the place. His eyes sunken and dull, as if he'd only just got out of bed.

I held the book up so he could see the cover.

'Ah! Ian Macabre!'

He sat down at the other side of the table.

'Have you had a good Christmas?' he said.

'You could say.'

'In Norway?'

I nodded.

'How about you?'

'I wasn't in Norway, no. What would I be doing there?'

'The Netherlands, then?'

'I live here. Therefore I was here.'

'On your own?'

'Yes. But didn't you say you weren't coming back until the new year?'

'Did I?'

'Yes, you did. But you were rather drunk at the time. So it's no wonder, if you can't remember.'

Had I been *that* drunk?

'My vodka isn't for the novice,' he said with a wink.

'I'll drink you under the table any day.'

He laughed.

'You're offended easily, I've noticed. Relax. Not everything's a competition.'

'I don't compete with anyone. Only myself.'

'In which case you've a job on your hands,' he said, and laughed again. 'Do you want another?'

'Better not. I'm off home in a minute.'

He got up and went to the bar. I returned to my book, but not knowing if he was coming back I found myself unable to concentrate.

He put a pint and a small glass of what looked to be vodka on the table in front of me, then went back to the bar, returning again with another pint and another vodka chaser.

'I said I didn't want anything.'

'Christmas present. You can't turn that down, now, can you? Cheers!'

He'd got me there. Of course, I could have declined and left the drinks untouched. But then I'd have been an ungrateful sod. It wasn't worth it, not for something as trivial as that.

'Cheers, then,' I said.

'You can drink me under the table now.'

'Some other day. Like I said, I'm off in a minute.'

'How come you came back early from Norway?'

He was talking to me as if we were friends and confidants. But we'd only met three times. Maybe he was the sort who had difficulty setting boundaries between themselves and other people.

That was probably it.

'Family problems?'

'No, not at all. No, I came back to get some work done. Haven't got a darkroom over there.'

'What are you working on now?'

'A project.'

'Ah, a project!' he said with sarcasm, but let it drop. He looked around the room, drained his vodka glass, then looked at me. The contrast between the intelligent look in his eyes and the stupid way his lower jaw protruded lent him an ambivalent appearance, a brainy guy trapped in the body of an idiot.

'Did you know the Royal Navy used to build its ships here?' he said.

'No, I didn't know that. Must have been a long time ago, though?'

'Between the sixteenth and nineteenth centuries. Deptford was quite an important place in colonial times. You'd never think so to look at it now, but it was. The dockyard here was enormous. It was practically where we're sitting now.'

'Really?'

'And of course Christopher Marlowe was stabbed to death here. You'd know that, though?'

'I've heard about it, yes.'

'At an alehouse nearby. Unfortunately, no one knows exactly where it was any more, but the place was run by a widow called Eleanor Bull. He was with three other men. They spent the whole day there. Wednesday, 30 May 1593. In the evening, after they'd eaten, one of the other men stabbed him in the eye, killed him dead.'

'Sounds brutal.'

'It was a brutal age. On the other hand, Lennon was shot and killed in our time. Not a lot's changed.'

'What is it with Marlowe, then? Seeing as you clearly know so much about him?'

'Marlowe? He was *the* great English dramatist. Completely renewed the genre. Possibly the greatest talent ever.'

'Wouldn't that be Shakespeare?' I said, realising at once, and to my annoyance, that it was exactly what he'd been wanting me to say.

'Shakespeare and Marlowe were born the same year. Shakespeare hadn't done a *thing* of note before Marlowe died. Whereas Marlowe himself already had three masterpieces to his name. He was only twenty-nine. We'll never know what he might have written had he lived.'

'But he died. And then Shakespeare was the greatest.'

'Indeed. But there are those who believe that Marlowe *didn't* die then. At the time, he was in a bit of a tight spot, you see. It's possible he staged his own death. The three other men who were with him that night were all friends of his. They were the only witnesses, too, so it's by no means beyond the bounds of possibility. If that's what did happen, the suggestion is that he fled to Scotland — we know he was planning to do so — and lived on there under a different identity, eventually dying in 1611.'

'How come 1611, exactly? If he'd been living in secret, surely no one would know when he died?'

'That was the year Shakespeare stopped writing. He retired to his home town to live the life of a pensioner, if you like. Yet he was only forty-seven years old, and insanely successful. Why would he stop writing? Well, the theory is that Shakespeare hadn't been writing his own works. He'd lent out his name, that's all.'

'To Marlowe?'

'Exactly! They knew each other, and had even worked on a play together. Playwrights in those days were a bit like film and television scriptwriters in our day. It was the plays that were known, not so much who wrote them. They weren't that bothered about originality either — they stole like ravens, the lot of them, and from each other too. But they collaborated as well — Marlowe, for example, wasn't that good on comedy, so his comic passages were written with the help of another writer. And as for being a *writer*, well, they could be all sorts of other things too, at the same time — Marlowe was a spy and was once arrested for counterfeiting, while a couple of his friends were downright con artists, besides writing fairly decent plays. So being a writer wasn't really a profession as such. What may have happened, then, is that Marlowe, aided by his dodgy mates, faked his own death, disappeared off to Scotland and carried on writing his dramas, which he would send to his friend Shakespeare on completion — *Hamlet*, *Othello*, *King Lear*, *Macbeth* . . . Shakespeare made his name, but when Marlowe died, properly this time, the game was up, and Shakespeare went home to his family in Stratford, where five years later he died.'

'Do you believe it?'

'Of course not! Not for a second. No, no, no. The Shakespeare scholars have analysed his style and his word choices and all that, and every indication is that the works are his own. That said, I do like the idea. It messes things up a bit. And as I mentioned, it's quite plausible too. It actually *could* be the case that was what happened. Sadly, though, it seems not!'

I racked my brains for a similar story to match his own, but all I could come up with were supposed sightings of Elvis after his death, and then there was the Count of Monte Cristo, didn't he fake his own death? But that was a novel.

'Fancy another?' he said, picking up his empty pint and giving me an enquiring look.

'Go on, then. But just the one.'

He got to his feet.

'Wait, it's my round,' I said.

He smiled and winked.

'On me. I've come into some money.'

Although he was the pontificating type who clearly took it for granted that he was way above me, I stayed there with him until closing time. I hadn't that much else to do, and besides, it wasn't every day that someone was buying me drinks. He was interesting, too, I had to concede. Or knowledgeable, at least. He seldom talked about himself, and unlike many social extroverts seemed to have no pet subject to which he would invariably return. No, subjects would occur to him during conversation, and he would pursue them as far as he could, often to places completely different from where he'd started, sometimes to other ages, without me ever getting the feeling he'd lost the thread along the way. I guessed him to be a single-minded reader, one who would absorb everything there was to know on a subject, preferably for months at a time, before eventually letting it go — and that he was the sort of person whose interest could be captured by just about anything at all. What's more, and significantly, he remembered what he read.

It wasn't hard to believe that this, his monomaniacal approach to reading, coupled with a seemingly insatiable need to lecture, was a protective mechanism, a substitute even, designed to disguise the fact that he *did* nothing of note. Anyone can talk. But *doing* something important is reserved for the few. He'd been a photographer, but wasn't any longer. Now he constructed electric rats and turtles, and told himself it was art. Had he ever had an exhibition? Were there any articles anywhere about his work? Any interviews with him?

I'd certainly never heard of any Dutch rat-artist of significance. Presumably his parents were wealthy and looked after him financially while he tinkered about in his disused garage.

Thinking about it again, it wasn't entirely true that he had no pet subject. The first time I met him, in the same pub, in the late summer, he bored me stiff going on about the history and technology of the camera. And when I'd gone to see him in his studio just before

Christmas, he talked about the same thing. Now, well into our fifth pint, he returned to the subject again, albeit by way of a different artefact altogether, whose history he believed it was high time someone wrote — the mirror. A few minutes previously he'd gone out to the toilets and had obviously been inspired by the experience.

'I saw my reflection in the mirror out there,' he began. 'I was washing my hands, and then, when I looked up, there was my reflection. It gives me the shivers every time. There's something so unsettling about mirrors, don't you agree?'

'Unsettling? No, not really,' I said. 'Not that I've noticed.'

He wanted me to ask him why he found them unsettling, so I didn't. He carried on regardless, working up his own head of steam.

'What is it we see in a mirror?'

'Ourselves.'

'No. *We* are inside ourselves. We can't get out. What we see is our image.'

'A picture.'

'Indeed. When we look into our own eyes, who do we see? We know it's an image, which is to say light collecting in a certain way on a surface. And yet it's as if we're actually looking into someone's eyes. True?'

'Yes, obviously. We're looking at our own image. Seeing ourselves the way we look from the outside.'

'But the eyes are alive. There's someone there.'

'It's just a very precise image. Nobody's actually *in* the mirror!'

I laughed. He smiled.

'Let's say you're right. It's still a strange phenomenon.'

'Not really. It's easily explained.'

'The implications aren't, though. What does it mean, to see ourselves?'

I shrugged.

'I don't see that it means anything in particular.'

'Your gaze goes from you, to the image of you, then back to you again, and since that's the same thing, it's static. It becomes a loop. A closed circuit. The earliest story I know about with a mirror in it is the myth of Narcissus. There, the mirror is the very symbol of infertility, and a punishment. You know the story, don't you?'

'The outline, at least,' I said, and gulped a mouthful of beer, as if it could wash away the prickling discomfort I immediately felt at the name of Narcissus.

'The story begins with Echo. She was a nymph. We can assume she was very beautiful. Anyway, she was renowned for being talkative and for her nice singing voice. She did something she wasn't supposed to, and her punishment was to be deprived of her speech — from then on she could only repeat what others said to her. Then one day she sees this incredibly beautiful young man in the forest. That's Narcissus. Immediately, she's infatuated, and must follow him. He hears her, and calls out: Is anyone there? And of course Echo, the poor girl, can only repeat his words: Is anyone there? To make a long and very edifying story short, she eventually runs up and throws her arms around him. He rejects her out of hand. She feels humiliated and shameful, but she's still in love, and now withdraws into solitude. Some other nymphs talk Nemesis into punishing Narcissus by making him too fall fruitlessly in love with his own reflection. The moment he sees the image of himself, his life basically ends, he grinds to a standstill. Echo too dwindles away, and eventually only her echo remains. An echo, of course, is reflected sound, the mirror being the visual equivalent. Narcissus is isolated, totally cut off from life. The same goes for Echo, she can't communicate, only repeat, so she too dies. Interesting, wouldn't you say?'

'Very, even if it is a bit over the top. I mean, looking at yourself in the mirror every now and then isn't exactly harmful, is it? It doesn't mean a thing.'

He went on, as if I hadn't spoken.

'Mirrors have always been associated with magic. But also with technology. The Renaissance was mad on optical instruments. They constructed the most intricate of instruments using mirrors. Many of the most realistic paintings of the seventeenth and eighteenth centuries were produced with the aid of mirrors. An image would be mirrored from one surface to another, onto a table or a wall, where it would be traced by the artist.'

'I've never heard about that. Is it true?'

'Absolutely, and the culmination was the camera obscura, an

instrument that could literally *project* an image. From there, it was a relatively short step to *capturing* the image. A photograph is simply a mirror image that's been captured. Do you see the relevance now?'

'No.'

'We live in a world of mirrors now. Like Narcissus and Echo, we've been cut off from real life. Haven't you noticed how everything's becoming more and more the same? More and more indistinguishable? It's not just the logic of monopoly capitalism that's at work. It's the logic of the mirror, too. The repeated image of ourselves. We're living in a loop. Yes, roll your eyes, if you must.'

'I didn't roll my eyes.'

'Yes, you did. But I understand. You want to be a photographer.'

'I *am* a photographer.'

'All right. Thankfully, I'm not.'

'Was this why you packed it in?'

'Partly, yes.'

'So you could become a hobby philosopher instead?'

He didn't answer that.

'I'll get another round in,' I said, and before he could stop me I was already at the bar. The alcohol was demolishing the very walls of my soul, my thoughts and feelings flowed more freely with every drink, things no longer *mattered* as before — in fact, the whole idea that everything had to be so rigorously well defined now appeared ridiculous.

'One more thing,' he said when I returned to the table and put another pint, another vodka chaser down in front of him. 'Have you ever seen the first photograph that was taken? I know there's a couple of very blurry ones of a rooftop and some walls, but those aren't the ones I mean. I'm talking about the first clear photograph of a recognisable subject. Taken by Daguerre.'

'Maybe. I'm not sure.'

'It's from 1838. It shows a street in Paris. The Boulevard du Temple. Judging by the light, it's early morning. The street is a wide avenue, with a row of shops along one side, many of them with their awnings extended. You'd expect the street to be busy with people. But it's completely deserted. There's not a soul to be seen, only the trees and the buildings. It's actually quite spooky.'

'That'd be because of the exposure time, wouldn't it?'

'Exactly, yes. The exposure time was ten minutes, so nothing moving could be captured, only what was permanent. And yet, if you examine it closely, there's actually a figure in the picture. A solitary figure on the pavement. A silhouette. You've never seen it?'

'No. We've looked at some of Daguerre's work at school, but I can't remember that one.'

'It appears to be a man. Tall and slim, with his hands behind his back and one leg raised. A dark shadow, that's all he is. Who could it be?'

'Something tells me you know the answer to that.'

'It's the Devil.'

I stared at him with eyebrows raised. He met my gaze without batting an eyelid.

'OK . . .' I said.

'Look at the picture and you'll see what I mean.'

'I will,' I said, half expecting him to laugh, or at least flash me a grin. But he didn't. He took a sip of his beer and ran a hand through his thick hair. He was surely drunker than he looked. Or maybe he just enjoyed a good conspiracy theory. Probably, it was a combination of both. First the mirrors, now the Devil. Couldn't he see how far out he was?

'It's one of the strangest things about those early photographs,' he went on, 'that only the most permanent fixtures show up, and that everything human beings do, and are, is too fleeting to be captured. Don't you agree?'

'I've never thought about it, but I suppose you're right.'

'If you imagine a being for which time passes slowly, it would show up like that.'

'What sort of being?'

'One that's beyond time? That would have to be a divine being, wouldn't you say?'

'The Devil?'

'Exactly. The fallen angel. You can smile, but people have believed in the Divine for as long as people have existed. There have been sightings, too.'

'Of what?'

'Angels. The Devil.'

'And now even a photo?'

'It's no coincidence that the Devil is present when the first photograph is taken. That's all I'm going to say. You don't believe me, so I'd be wasting my energy.'

'Who *would* believe you?'

He held up his hands and smiled.

'That's up to them.'

'Do you know what I think?'

'No.'

'I think you spend too much time on your own in that garage of yours. Even the maddest of notions can start to resemble truths.'

He winked and took another sip of his beer.

'After all the drinks I've bought, you could at least humour me.'

I still hadn't eaten, not since lunch, so the first thing I did when I got home was open the fridge. I took out a box of eggs, boiled three and ate them while standing, somewhat unsteadily, in front of the window, my mind teeming with thoughts of mirrors and devils, staged murders, Mum and Dad and Liv. The street outside was empty and windswept. It was hard to believe it was Christmas.

Still hungry, I boiled some noodles, sprinkled the sachet of beef flavouring over them and stirred it in with a fork before wolfing them down. After that, I sat down with my photographs for a while. I didn't want to be altering the sequence in a series while I was drunk, but it was important for me to stay in touch with them so that my subconscious would carry on working on its own.

What was it I'd come up with back home? The monumental versus the levelled-off, the evened-out, the sameness of the everyday.

Maybe the two things could be combined? Maybe I could focus on the contrasts?

Some of the images of converging lines were actually very good.

They satisfied me.

I could hardly wait to get the photos I'd taken at home developed. *The Suicide*. Was that a feasible title? No, I couldn't use that. *Absence*, maybe? That was all right.

What a nutter Hans was.

Or was he taking the piss?

I couldn't rule it out. He'd winked and stuff.

Maybe the point was to get me to believe something stupid. Maybe he was acting, playing a role. If others had been there, it might have been a plausible explanation. But how funny would it be to pull the wool over my eyes with no one else to witness it?

I put the photographs back in their boxes, then made up my bed and lay down to sleep. Only then I remembered that the telephone was plugged in. I got up again, disconnected it and got back under the covers, directing my thoughts towards my work, trying to remember each and every photograph in each series I'd produced, the sequences in which they occurred, it was a good way of keeping them fresh in my mind, as well as a good way of falling asleep. Usually, only a few minutes went by before my thoughts would be infiltrated by other images, and though I would force them back on track, still more would intrude, and eventually, though not long afterwards, my will would become so weakened, so wearied, that the invasive images would come flooding and usurp my conscious thoughts entirely, I would dissolve into them, without being aware of what was happening.

I was woken by the doorbell ringing. Where was I? In my flat, yes. The sun was coming in through the window above the settee. The alarm clock on the sill said twenty-five past ten. I pulled on my T-shirt and pants, wriggled my bare feet into my shoes and went down the stairs.

A woman in her early thirties was standing on the step. She was wearing a long dark coat, her hair page-cut and brown, eyes dark and uninviting.

'Kristian Hadeland?' she said.

'Who wants to know?'

'I'm Anne Nymo, from the embassy,' she said in Norwegian. 'You've been reported missing. Were you aware of that? You are Kristian Hadeland?'

'I'm not missing. I'm here. Where I *live*.'

'I understand,' she said. 'However, your parents reported you missing. You disappeared without telling anyone where you were going.'

'It's not like I'm lost in the mountains.'

'No.'

'I take it your job's done, then?'

'I'd say so, yes.'

I closed the door in her face and went back upstairs. I was seething. They were treating me as if I'd done something wrong. As if I was a criminal. I'd gone back to see my parents, and then I'd come home to my own flat again. And they had to go and involve the bloody embassy on that account? Did they even have the *right* to do that? To send people round to check up on you? It smacked of surveillance.

I felt like phoning them and telling them to leave me alone. But then I'd be breaking the promise I'd made to myself. That I was never going to speak to them or see them again.

For fuck's sake.

I had to start doing things that were good for *me*. Start thinking of myself for a change. If only the new term wasn't such a long way off. The days between Christmas and New Year were such a limbo. Always had been, even when I was a kid. Nothing ever happened, everyone stayed in, and in our house no one ever did anything.

None of the other students from my course had stuck around as far as I knew.

I decided to cycle into the city. See if I could find a book of Daguerre's photographs in the second-hand bookshops on Charing Cross Road. It didn't matter if I couldn't, the main thing was to have a purpose, not necessarily to achieve it.

Had someone said that before? Or had I just thought of it?

It was quite snappy, so I jotted it down in my notebook:

'The main thing is to have a purpose, not necessarily to achieve it.'
Kristian Hadeland, 1985

I chained my bike to a post and walked up to where the bookshops were. A cold wind blew through the streets. Not many people were out, and a number of the shops were closed. But the bookshop I knew to have the widest selection of art books was open, and in the photography section I found several editions containing examples of Daguerre's work. I ended up buying one called *The Origins of Photography*, by Helmut Gernsheim, which I thought would be useful in various respects — as a photographer, I of course needed to be clued up on the medium's beginnings, and Gernsheim's volume looked to contain most of what I was likely to require.

I sat down in one of the cafes in Soho and began looking through it. I recognised the picture Hans had been talking about as soon as I came to it. The dark figure was small, but since there were no other people anywhere to be seen on the wide boulevard, I picked him out immediately. It was spooky, him standing there all on his own, Hans had been right about that. But the Devil didn't exist, so vaguely unsettling as the photograph was, there had to be some other explanation. Even so, all the other people — dozens, presumably — had disappeared. They had not been captured on the photographic plate. So what was it about him, this shadowy silhouette? His leg was raised in a way that suggested his foot was resting on something, a contraption of some sort? His leg was outstretched — why? Why would he be standing like that? When did a person stand like that? His hands in his pockets, his foot outstretched?

He was having his boots polished! That would explain why he was standing still long enough for his image to be captured. The bootblacker himself was busy with his work, a blur of movement, blacking and polishing, this way and that, so he couldn't be captured.

The Devil? Yeah, right.

I turned the pages, almost relieved to have come upon the explanation, as if I'd actually believed him.

But there was still something unsettling about those first photographs. They were so grainy and obscure that the world they depicted looked somehow different, at the same time as it remained familiar. It was easy to believe it was the beholder's gaze that was different. That the pictures showed the world as it appeared to another being. A being that was not human.

I stared for some time at a picture of a table. It was set with a white tablecloth, a heavy-looking wine glass, cutlery and a bowl. There was a bottle, too, as black as night, and a strange, tall, rectangular object — a canister, perhaps? Everything that was light, and everything that was outside the surface of the table, appeared coarse and rough. The air didn't look like air, but like something material — sand or grit. In the top left corner was something resembling a wing, human in size. Just an interplay of light and darkness, and the rudimentary instrument by which it had been captured. But still, a wing.

I looked up and found someone was staring at me, a thin, dark-haired man sitting on his own at a table further inside the room. Immediately, he turned away and gazed absently out the window. I took him to be around thirty. Wearing a dark brown suit. Something about him suggested to me that he could be Egyptian.

I wasn't unused to people staring at me — I looked good, and my face had something inscrutable about it that probably could arouse curiosity as well as desire. But something in the way he'd looked at me was different. Wasn't it as if he'd recognised me, perhaps even knew me?

I returned to my book, though my attention was now also directed towards him. The instant I sensed him turn to look at me again, I looked straight back at him. He averted his gaze as before, and shortly afterwards stood up and left. I wouldn't have thought any more about it, had it not been for the fact that I saw him again a few weeks later on the Tube one early morning when I was on my way to the school. The carriage was packed and I stood facing the door, holding on to the pole as we rattled through the tunnels. As soon as we drew into the next station, I turned round to see if there were any seats being vacated, and immediately there he was looking at me. This time, it wasn't just his head he turned away, but his whole body, and quickly too, as if he'd been caught in the midst of something illicit.

It gave me a strong sense of unease. For the rest of the journey I stood demonstratively looking the other way. I had no idea if he was staring at me again, or if he was even still on the train. All I knew was that I didn't want to encourage him. He'd almost certainly recognised me from the cafe, that was why he was looking at me like that, and it was also the reason he appeared to feel guilty — I'd made my annoyance abundantly clear to him the last time. Twice could be coincidence, and almost certainly was, but not three times. If he turned up again, I'd confront him. I'd punch his face, too, if I had to.

No reason to be paranoid, though.

Emerging from the Underground, I went and sat down at a cafe to look again at the photos I was going to be presenting in class. For the first three weeks of term we had a guest lecturer, his name was Rafael Figueroa. When I'd first seen his name in the course plan, I'd imagined a portly, middle-aged man with glasses and a beard, a spluttering laugh and an outgoing personality. That picture changed radically when we were introduced to his work and provided with some biography. I'd never heard of him before, but apparently he was something of a name. When still in his early twenties, he gained full membership of Magnum. In the first years of his career he'd been an out-and-out war photographer, but since then he'd broadened his repertoire to include fashion photography and celebrity portraiture as well as exhibiting more arty stuff. The photos we were shown were hard and brutal, yet aesthetic, that was his style. The only one I recognised was an Afghan mujahideen fighter with the cartridge belt and the rifle over his shoulder — he looked like a soldier from the Spanish Civil War, maybe that was why the image was so well known. Another, more powerful image was of a burnt-out Russian tank with a dead soldier in it, only the upper body visible, head snapped back, empty eyes staring into the sky. It was a photo that looked old, even though the tank was modern and everything had happened in our own time. His photos from Lebanon also had something archaic about them. Or maybe not that, exactly. More that everything seemed grand: full of gravity in a way. Having seen his work, my conceptions of him changed completely: Figueroa was no longer a jovial, cigarette-smoking Spaniard, but a strapping, keenly intelligent younger man, high-powered and dynamic, a man with an acutely international outlook, eager to share his experiences. I was looking forward to meeting him. So when he came shuffling into the room, I wouldn't say I was disappointed exactly, more surprised. Figueroa was hollow-cheeked and pale, a silent, serious man somewhere in his mid-thirties. There was no energy about him at all, in fact he hardly spoke. He wore a black shirt and black jeans, which together with his black hair and sallow skin made him look like a member of one of those bands whose name everybody knows, but nobody actually likes or listens to. It would have been hard to spot that he was Spanish, and completely impossible to guess that he was considered a star photographer.

Our first week with him was devoted to us going through our work, two students per day. In the second week, we were going to be producing new work on the basis of assignments he was going to hand out to us. The third and final week was for reviewing what we'd come up with.

Today it was my turn. He hadn't seen anything I'd done before and wanted an unbiased look at it. I'd brought my *Vertigo* series. I could have brought work that had got me into the school in the first place, but there'd have been no point, we'd already been through it at the beginning of the first term and everything that could possibly be said about it had surely already been said. *Vertigo* had been seen by no one but my mum. A lot had happened since then, I'd worked hard between Christmas and New Year, and in the first week of January, in the darkroom and all that, and had been buzzing with inspiration. And now the whole weekend I'd spent taking pictures in and out of the series, changing them around until they were as if cast in cement.

Looking through them in the cafe, I fortunately found they still were. This was it.

The school itself was situated in venerable and imposing buildings in Mayfair, whereas the photography programme, comprising no more than some twenty students, was located in a former factory premises south of the river. There were ten of us in all on the first year of the course. I'd made friends with two: Gavin, who was from Newcastle, and Håkan, a Swede from Gothenburg, or more exactly one of the islands in the archipelago — Tjörn, I think the place was called. Five were girls, though I didn't like any of them much, and I basically hardly spoke to the other two boys.

But we weren't there to be liked. We were there because we were the new generation of photographers. We were talented, all of us. Some more than others, naturally. But I respected them all, and even the dullest of the girls could suddenly sparkle and say something insightful or thought-provoking.

I didn't want to be the first to arrive and come across too eager about my work, so I left it until the last minute before walking the short distance to the school.

Gav was standing outside smoking, shivering in just a T-shirt and jeans.

'Has everyone arrived?' I said.

He nodded.

'Are you nervous?'

'Course not. Better get in, though, or else we'll be late.'

He nodded again.

'I'll be along in a minute. See you there.'

I hung my coat up on one of the hooks in the corridor and went inside. So far, people were just hanging around, some stood talking, others were sitting down reading. Neither George, our tutor, nor the gloomy Spaniard appeared to have arrived. I sat down and took my work out of my bag. The procedure was to lay our photographs out on the big table in the middle of the room, but I wanted to maintain the element of surprise, so I remained seated with the photographs in my hands, waiting for the teachers to come in and get the session started. I felt good and my body tingled with anticipation. At school, I'd always enjoyed doing presentations, be it a novel in a Norwegian lesson or a summary of some societal topic in Social Studies. It was to do with having attention *bestowed* on me, like a gift. I could talk about what *I* found interesting, without interruption.

They came in together, George talking, Figueroa listening. George Hindley was a reasonably well-known photographer in his fifties. Whenever I saw him, I couldn't help thinking he was likely to have a heart attack before long. It wasn't that he was fat as such — he carried a few extra kilos, but they were fairly evenly distributed — it was more the general look of him that made me think he could drop to the floor at any minute. His face was pudgy and bloated, as was so often the case with men in their fifties, his hair wispy and yellow as grain. A pair of black, chunky-framed glasses offered a measure of resistance to the facial fleshiness and in a way held his features together. His lips were thick and forever moist, his gaze was weak and evasive.

Figueroa sat down on a stool while George, standing in the middle of the room, made some administrative announcements, before turning to me.

'I'll now give the stage, as it were, to Kristian. It's all yours, Kristian.

Perhaps you could start with just a few short words about what you're going to share with us. Over to you.'

He smiled and gave a friendly nod.

I smiled back. I wasn't nervous, but my heart beat harder as I stepped out onto the floor with all eyes on me.

'I'd like the photographs to speak for themselves, so I won't say anything about them. But it's a series I've entitled *Vertigo*.'

I placed the photographs one by one on the table in exactly the same sequence as on the floor of my flat.

Everyone gathered around. Some scribbled down notes, others just looked. My eyes were on Figueroa, but it was impossible to gauge his thoughts, he studied the photos with the same impenetrable expression he always wore, no matter what he was looking at — uncommitted, indifferent almost. I could only assume the important stuff was going on inside him. How else could he take the pictures he took, if he looked upon the world with such a lack of interest? George too scrutinised the photographs, before going to the back of the room to survey the proceedings from there.

People went back to their seats and Figueroa then turned to the floor for comments. Usually, he left his own thoughts until last, using the students' appraisals as a kind of wall against which he occasionally would bounce a comment, a question, an impression.

'I find it interesting the way the converging lines tie together things that otherwise wouldn't have anything to do with each other,' Håkan said. 'You get the feeling of some bigger system. Even if, on their own, the pictures themselves are pretty unspectacular.'

'I agree with that,' said Sarah, an inquisitive, gossipy girl with saggy cheeks. 'But you've got to look at a lot of them together. Individually, I think they're lacking. The focus is on the vanishing point, but they're all very flat, I find. There's no internal tension. No contrasts.'

There were a lot of nods.

'The clouds above the trees, though, in that one of the track in the forest, there's a bit of something there. A little bit of life.'

'A little bit?' I said.

She turned her head towards me and smiled.

'There's some life there, yes. More of that, I think.'

Another of the girls pursued the same line of criticism. I looked across at Gav — why wasn't he saying anything? He was just sitting there tipping back on his chair as if he couldn't care less.

Martin, a fiery political type who nevertheless couldn't be taken seriously because he looked like a child — eager blue eyes, a mop of curls, and small, glistening zits arrayed on his cheeks — was looking for more punch, he found them all a bit bland. He didn't look at me as he spoke, but at the Spaniard, who sat with his arms folded across his chest as he listened. No one offered a word of disagreement, or had anything to add.

There was a long silence before George spoke.

'Thanks for sharing this work with us, Kristian. Let me just say that it's important to bear in mind that you're here to learn. If you'd all been fully fledged photographers or artists, you wouldn't be here. Isn't that so, Rafael?'

Figueroa nodded.

'Would you care to add a few words about Kristian's pictures, by way of conclusion?'

'Yes. I'm not quite sure how to say this, but yes. We talked about fascination earlier, about how incredibly important it is in order for a picture to be able to convey meaning. It can be in the subject, as in a lot of war photography. But if it was only in the subject, nearly all photography, all art, in fact, would be without meaning. And when I look at these photographs, that is what they are lacking. Why should I look at them? What's important in them? Well, they investigate a phenomenon, that of perspective. They succeed in telling me something about that, we see how the lines converge on a vanishing point. But it is not enough, Kristian. Your pictures are basically a bit dull. Without temperament.'

'They're not meant to have temperament,' I said. 'That's why.'

He nodded.

'You can think that. And you can do that, by all means. But it is as if you are singing only one note. And you're not going to get a song like that. You must penetrate the world with the camera, this is what you must strive to do. And when you work on the pictures afterwards, you must find a way to lift them. The photographs must levitate. A fence cannot simply be a fence, it must be *this* fence.'

'But the whole point is that things are the same,' I said. 'That there are no differences anywhere. If I start trying to add a dynamic in there, then there's no longer a point.'

'You can say that. But I don't think that's the way to go. You can take pictures of something mundane, but you can't take mundane pictures.'

'They're not exactly mundane, though, are they?' I said. 'You could say a lot of things about them, and I accept that, they're not to everyone's liking — but *mundane*?'

Figueroa tightened his lips, as if disguising some pain he felt by pretending to smile.

'Affirmation will never help us grow,' said George. 'Rigorous opposition, however, will.'

Fuck. It couldn't have been worse. The end of it all was now they felt they had to console me.

'Well, thanks, everybody,' I said, and got to my feet. I gathered my work together and put it back in my bag. A murmur arose as people began to make their way out.

'You OK?' said Gav.

'Yes, why shouldn't I be?'

He gave a shrug.

'Your pictures took a bit of a bashing.'

He waited for me as I put my coat on in the corridor. I slung my bag over my shoulder and we went outside, where he stopped to pick a cigarette out of his packet and then light it.

'See you, then,' I said.

'Are you off somewhere?'

'Dental appointment.'

'All right, see you,' he said, and ambled towards a little group that had congregated, while I crossed the open space and made for the Tube station.

Although I knew the others would think it was because of the critique I'd received, I stayed away from the school the rest of that week. We learned nothing in those crit sessions, everyone saw the same things, said the same things — even after a couple days, they'd already started employing the same terms and concepts as the teachers. My work maybe wasn't as good as the Spaniard's, but he was a teacher and I was a student, and I was pretty damn certain that his own work hadn't been world class when he was twenty. He wanted our photos to look like his, was trying to force his own aesthetics on us, and if that was the yardstick, then of course my pictures were going to fall short. The photos I took were of a different nature — we weren't exploring the same things. I wasn't looking for the striking, iconic image, because those kinds of pictures were just that and nothing more. What I was looking for were connections, the networks that tied things together. He, the war iconist, couldn't see that. And the other students weren't independent enough to realise when they were being herded like sheep.

Was there only one way to take photographs?

I wouldn't accept that. So I stayed at home. Took no pictures — the spark had gone. But there were other ways in which to work. I wrote down all the ideas I had, noting what they required in the way of research, equipment and time, and scheduling when I was going to do the work. Then, I drew up a plan of what I would achieve in the next five years. It was a bit timid, perhaps, but it was important to be realistic — I was a nobody, starting from scratch. So my first goal was to put on an exhibition of my work in a cafe or a shop. There were several hip clothes shops in London where they had a keen eye for what was going on in the art world. Record shops, too, were a possibility — not the big chains, but the established indie stores. The main thing was to get myself a track record so I wouldn't have to just stand there, a blank page, head bowed and portfolio in hand, but instead be able to say I'd held my own exhibition in Brixton, Shoreditch or Islington. Then there was Norway. Being a student at a London art school would be recommendation in itself over there. Maybe I could get one of the smaller Oslo galleries interested. If I could approach them with two exhibitions under my belt, they wouldn't be so inclined to slam the door in my face. That was one track I'd follow. Another was magazines. The same principle applied there. If I could get something in print in one publication, others would see it as a stamp of approval. The music papers and mags would be the easiest, so that was where I'd go first, and London was of course the right place to be in that respect. But the money was in the fashion business. It would be harder to get a foot in the door there, but not impossible, it happened all the time.

What to others would look like a culmination, having my work published by Thames & Hudson after five years, was for me simply the first step. The foundation upon which all that followed would be based.

Viewed from that perspective, Figueroa's critique paled into insignificance. No one seriously believed you could get anywhere without encountering difficulties, hurdles along the way.

I read a lot, too, in the days that followed. Partly, in the case of the novels I'd bought, for my own enjoyment, partly, in the case of the Shakespeare, for the sake of discipline — but also in order to benefit my work, and here it was the book about the origins of photography that absorbed me. I seriously liked studying the photos from the late 1820s to the 1850s, they were so very different from all other photographs I'd seen. It was as if every image, no matter what it depicted, was significant. If I photographed the coffee table, for instance — on which there were three coffee mugs, two empty glasses, a couple of crusts of bread on a plate, a half-eaten slice with cheese next to them, the cheese dried-up and lifeless at one end, otherwise soft-looking, almost incorporated into the squishy bread; a fat, unopened Sunday newspaper, several magazines, and a concave heap of orange peel, on the outside rich in colour, and presumably hard, inside paper-white with desiccated, yellowing bits of the fruit stuck to it — it would be nothing more than what it showed, an untidy coffee table, with no depth or shade to it at all. But a table photographed in 1829 somehow or other possessed something else. The same was true of the picture of a shed with gardening tools hung in place on its wall, or the one of a basket full of apples, left on the ground in front of the doorstep of a house. Such photographs were indeed *significant*, it was obvious the moment you looked at them. Perhaps because so few photographs were taken in those days. If only, let's say, sixty-three photographs exist in the world, then each one will be a rare thing indeed, a curiosity, and whatever they depict, even a basket of fruit, will for that reason alone be invested with significance. In those days, a photograph was magical. An impossibility suddenly made possible. A door no one even knew was there had opened. The world became recreated in the photograph.

The photographer was not an artist, and certainly not a technician, but a medium. A medium for miracles.

But however few photographs existed in the world, this couldn't be apparent in the individual image, for the photograph itself, I thought as I studied the fruit basket on the white gravel, had no way of knowing what a marvel it was. Besides, if that was what made those early photographs so compelling at the time, it certainly wasn't the case any longer. The world was now full of pictures — there were millions, billions of them. Photography was no longer magic. Wouldn't that influence the way I perceived those early examples?

This was something Hans no doubt would relish talking about. As it seemed to me, he had a ready-made theory about everything. And photography in particular.

In the evenings, after long days of reading and taking notes, with quite a bit of sleep in between, I got into the habit of going to the pub for a few pints, but not once did I run into Hans. Instead, I'd exchange the odd word with those who tried to strike up a conversation — it came naturally to them over here, dangling a few phrases in front of a stranger to see if they could get a bite. But mostly I'd just sit and read until I was too half-cut, then go home. I didn't knock on Liz's door, didn't even stop in front of it, but went straight past. But since the thought occurred to me every time I was a bit tipsy, I knew it meant that I'd actually do it one night when I was really pissed. The next morning, the thought would appear totally ridiculous, I hadn't the slightest inclination to see her, not even from a distance, through the window, certainly not to go to bed with her. Why would I do that? Still, being a bit drunk was always a good barometer, feelings are released then which are otherwise so inconsequential as not to be accorded a voice, whereupon you're able to consider them and make a choice: either kill them so they'll never come back, or else leave them be, well knowing that they'll accumulate into a storm as soon as you're drunk enough.

At the same time, though, it wasn't as easy as that. When I was sober I wanted nothing to do with her — it wasn't the case that I *actually* did, but suppressed it, no, I really didn't, there wasn't a shred of doubt in my mind. So what was it that stirred in me, however faintly, when I went up the stairs not long gone eleven at night? Was it me, or was it not-me? Was it a bit like how it was with matter, that also comprised antimatter? If so, and I was made up of an I and an anti-I, which part then was *me*? That clearly would be my I. In which case I ought to have crushed those tiny impulses from my anti-I, it would have been as easy as anything, only I didn't. Never said to myself: Remember this — no matter how pissed you are, don't knock on that door.

So was I going to?

No, it was exactly what I *didn't* want.

But as long as I stuck to no more than three or four or five pints down the pub, there was no real problem. What *was* a problem was school. By the time the weekend came round again, I'd decided to start back the following Monday and take in the final week of Figueroa's course. But it wasn't for my sake, I thought as I stood under the shower that morning, it was because of what the *others* would think if I didn't. A few days off didn't matter, I could have been ill, but staying away from most of an important guest lecturer's residency was bound to set people's tongues wagging. Did *I* want to sit there and have an opinion about their work, listen to what Figueroa had to say? No, thanks, I decided, the water splashing down my naked body, my thinking as if freer in a way than when I was clothed. No. Actually, I didn't. I had to be true to myself. It was more important than always being considerate to what everyone else thought and believed.

So I stayed away that week too. It didn't feel as good as it had done the week before. It was probably easy to think that I despised Figueroa, but I didn't. His work was of a very high standard, no doubt about that. The fact that he was so short on personality didn't really come into it. He knew his field. And one of the ideas behind having a guest lecturer at all was presumably that they could facilitate the transition from being a student to becoming a professional practitioner. A guest lecturer had contacts, knew where to go, who to talk to, where to be seen. Looking at it like that, boycotting his sessions perhaps hadn't been the smartest move.

It was too late now, anyway.

Although I felt a strong disinclination towards taking pictures — indeed even the sight of the camera on the table in front of me, not to mention the boxes in which I kept my work, filled me with reluctance — I forced myself to go out and find something to photograph, if only to demonstrate to myself that I possessed determination. I couldn't allow myself to be broken by a little thing like that. Reluctance was in fact a good word for it, for there were no conscious thoughts involved as I picked up the camera and put it in my bag, only a vague discomfort, a haze of negativity. A will against will. Will and anti-will.

The thing to do was to force myself, and it would be overcome.

It was cold and foggy outside. I cycled towards the river, thinking I'd follow it as far as Greenwich, and came through a relatively large area of waste ground between disused buildings and wire-mesh fencing. A JCB stood abandoned-looking, the bucket resting on the oily gravel, and facing it an empty loader. Some site huts were lined up in a row not far away. I leaned my bike up against one and walked over to the river with my camera. This was good. Clearly I was standing at the edge of a small tributary running into the main river from the right; the spit of land on the other side was occupied by a factory — a scattering of buildings, of various heights, connected by shafts and chutes, some of which ran down to the quayside where two big cranes stood. The outer walls were criss-crossed by pipes, and from beside a number of barrel-shaped structures two tall chimneys rose, smoke pouring from both. I had no idea what it all was, it could have been anything, but it made a bloody good subject! I clicked away. Everything was brilliant here: a heap of bricks and planks, probably left over from a demolition job, lay a few metres from where the JCB had been left, while behind the loader, in front of a free-standing wall, were long, rusting rafters of steel. Overturned drums. And the wall itself, blackened here and there by soot, as if shadows had been cast on it by an invisible sun.

I used up a roll of film, then followed the quayside, wheeling the bike, one hand on the handlebar, the other on my camera. More rubble, sudden areas of scrub and sandy grit, a few parked vehicles. Then the road came to an end at a barrack-like structure, behind which another building had been demolished into a towering heap of bricks and debris. With no obvious way around, I went back the same way I'd come, mounting the bike and pedalling towards more open terrain — a street, semi-industrial, garage-type businesses, the signage advertising gearboxes, batteries, skip hire, glazing. I'd never noticed the narrower body of water before, but I realised now that the road to Greenwich in fact went over a bridge. Something else I hadn't previously been aware of was the name of the street leading away to the left on the other side — Norway Street! I took a few pictures there too — of cranes reaching into the sky above a brick wall; but also of small details, like the grass poking up between paving stones; the dark, thick-looking mud that seemed to have oozed out from underneath a shuttered entrance; a cigarette advert neatly framed on its hoarding, in contrast to the surrounding disorder — a gift of an image.

Reaching Greenwich, I chained my bike to a fence and began walking along the river. Although there was no industry here, the mood was quite as disheartening. The river ahead dissolved into the mist. Barges drifted by like shadows, the occasional foghorn a mournful, resonant groan amid dreamlike silence. The wall that followed the line of the river, dank and dismal, must have been there since the Industrial Revolution. In places, stone steps led down to the water. It would've been amazing in the Med, people bathing in ancient, blue waters, but here the sight was just depressing, a descent into the river's cold and filthy, fishless element, its grey-brown jaundiced depths so utterly impenetrable.

Some disused buildings loomed up ahead. Broken windows, rubbish strewn about. Pigeons in the roof spaces, grey, as if it were they who had once been manufactured here.

I took a few photos, albeit half-heartedly, my enthusiasm drained away — and what would I do with them anyway? The Thames in fog, anyone could do that, and abandoned factory buildings were a photographic cliché.

The energy I'd felt before only irritated me now, it was a sign of immaturity. The riverside was derelict — so what? It had been the heart of the Empire in times gone by, but all hearts eventually will stop, and this one had been no exception.

What was it I wanted to *say*?

It wasn't enough just to *show*. Everyone had eyes, everyone could see for themselves.

There had to be something more. Something deeper.

I turned back. I needed to divert my thoughts towards something else, because the space they were in now was occupied too by the Spaniard's critique, and what could happen next was that my thoughts deferred to his.

If the photos I'd taken now were a cliché, it didn't mean I was a cliché. I had to distinguish between who I was and what I did.

Unlocking the bike, I decided to take a different way home. I walked up through the park, past the observatory and on to the plain above, where trees stood like giants stretching their arms into the murk. They were enormous and surely very old. Some, no doubt, went back to Shakespeare's time. I remembered the project I'd started, *Frameworks of Life*, in the days between Christmas and New Year, and shuddered.

But shortcomings were always easy to find. If all you ever thought about were the negative aspects, you'd never see what was good about a thing.

I biked across the wide-open expanse called Blackheath, a name presumably that stemmed from the Black Death when they must have buried people here. Hundreds, perhaps thousands of human bodies putrifying in the soil through spring and summer, and spring and summer again. Within the boundaries of the heath a small village lay, grey and sunken, though well kept — it made me think of a wealthy old lady — no larger than to encompass two streets of shops, from where the road sloped gently upwards to the top of a low-slung ridge before sweeping away on the other side between trees and nestling, brick-built villas, until once again more urban features began to prevail — pubs, garages, a post office, an estate agent's, a petrol station, office buildings, grimy and more or less run-down — residential properties then lining the next hill. One of these houses, I noted from the sign in the driveway, contained the premises of a veterinary hospital, and immediately I stopped. They'd have dead animals in there. I supposed they incinerated them, but the place, seemingly a converted private home, looked too small for that sort of thing to be done there. They sent them somewhere else for that. Until then, they'd be stored on the premises, though surely not indoors? No, they'd be left somewhere round the back until someone came and collected them.

Maybe I could go in and ask?

Sorry to bother you, I'm a photographer and I need to photograph a dead cat. You couldn't give me one of yours, could you? Or lend me one?

They'd look at me as if I was a madman.

No, we most certainly can't.

But they're dead, aren't they? They're only going to be incinerated. It can hardly make a difference, now, can it? And it's for a good cause.

I turned and cycled back towards home. Left at the junction, along the main road into Lewisham, past the square with the funny little clocktower, onwards from the centre, up the hill, down the road to the right, always dense with traffic, an inferno of lorries and cars, rumbling and rattling, a spew of exhaust fumes, people sat behind the wheels like automatons. Welcome to 1986.

There was a letter on the floor inside the door when I got home. Mum's handwriting. I tossed it in the bin and made myself something to eat — a few leftover potatoes fried in the pan, some spaghetti and ketchup to go with them, and a dollop of mustard for the potatoes, on the side of the plate. If I'd had a girlfriend, she'd have thought I was only eating it because it was cheap, but the truth was it tasted quite good. She wouldn't believe me, of course, she'd think I was a poor starving student, and then, if I served it again when I'd got money, she'd think I was a penny-pincher too. But I liked it. I liked pot noodles as well, and fish fingers, and another potato dish, which was fried potatoes with onions and peas. But now I was actually short of funds, my grant hadn't come through yet, and of course I'd ruled out asking Dad for money — but my imaginary girlfriend wasn't to know.

Waking up a couple of hours later after a sleep, I thought better of it and fished the letter out of the bin, the envelope now damp and stained with ketchup from the remains of my dinner, the address though still perfectly legible. I put it in the window, spooned some coffee granules into a mug and filled it with boiling water. Outside, it was dark again. The sight of my reflection in the windowpane made me think of Hans and what he'd said about mirrors. It was a bit unsettling, seeing yourself like that, especially when you were on your own in the room — it was as if you were doubly alone then. Me, and me again in the mirror — which besides *him* was completely empty. It was as if *I* wasn't there, only *him*.

Only then did I realise it was snowing. I switched the lights off in the kitchen so I could see — big, sodden flakes, drifting down into the circular pools of street lighting, descending softly onto the asphalt below, where at once they melted and were gone.

It wasn't enough to stop me from cycling. But still, it was probably a good idea not to put it off too long. Soon it would begin to stick, and no way did I want to be out in London's traffic when it did.

I put my clothes back on and carried the bike down the stairs. It took me half an hour to cycle to the veterinary hospital. I left the bike a bit further down the street and walked slowly past the place, noting that the lights were on, which presumably meant they were still at work. It also meant that the back door was likely to be open and that someone could step out into the yard while I was there. But what were the chances? I'd be done in less than a couple of minutes. They probably only went out there no more than two or three times a day, so I'd have to be unusually unlucky to be discovered. In any such situation, self-confidence and resoluteness were of the essence.

I took another recce. It was a detached house, and there was a passage between the side wall and the hedge. It wasn't as if I was taking anything of value. The animals were going to be burned. It wouldn't matter in the slightest if one of them ended up with me instead.

The snow had settled on the tarmacked entrance area in front of the clinic. No one had been here since it started to stick, I could see, as I strode purposefully forward and then veered away to slip between the side of the house and the hedge. The rear yard was small, enclosed by a wall the height of a man, yellow in the filtering light. Against the wall of the house stood three large rubbish bins. Two windows faced out from the house, partially blanked by venetian blinds. I paused in case anyone was coming, but then it struck me how idiotic that was — if anyone was going to come, they could come at any time, so I stepped out and went straight to the bins. The first two were just full of general rubbish. I opened the lid of the third. It contained maybe eight or ten bundles in dark, vacuum-sealed plastic bags. One, about the size of a baby, was probably a small dog. Two or three were hardly bigger than snowballs and could only be hamsters or something similar. The rest all seemed to be cat-sized. I leaned in and pulled one out. A cat, yes. Both the weight of it and the sleek, limp body I could feel through the plastic confirmed it. I clamped it against my chest with one arm and closed the lid of the container with my free hand.

And then the back door opened. A middle-aged woman in a white apron looked at me in astonishment.

'What are you up to?' she said.

'Just collecting this,' I said, and immediately walked past her.

'Hey!' she shouted. 'You there!'

I heard her call for someone to come as I started running. Five seconds was all it took and I was back at the front of the house. Before anyone appeared at the front door I was already on my way along the pavement. Even if they had their wits about them and were quick to give chase, I'd be on my bike and away. And, a dead cat surely wasn't worth them jumping in a car and coming after me.

Not that it would make any difference, I told myself as I skidded to a halt at my bike, put the bag down on the ground and fumbled for the key in my pocket.

Glancing back, I saw a figure emerge from the clinic driveway. A short, thickset man.

Where was that bloody key?

I kept it in the right front pocket of my trousers, always. Where was it?

The stubby man ran towards me.

Had I put it in the other pocket instead?

Yes!

He was closing in on me, and for a second I thought about leaving the bike and legging it. But for all I knew he could have been an English middle-distance champion. And the seconds I lost unlocking the bike would be gained as soon as I pedalled off.

'Stop thief!' he shouted. 'Stop thief!'

As quick as I could, I got the lock open, gripped both it and the handlebar in one hand, snatched up the bag with the other, jumped onto the bike and pressed my foot down hard on the pedal. He was bearing down on me now.

Oh no. Too high a gear.

Slowly, as if in a dream, I picked up speed before shifting into a more manageable cog, and only then was I able to really pedal. I didn't look back, but could actually hear his breathing, he could only have been four or five metres behind, and then I was away.

I didn't dare stop until I reached the busy junction, where I stuffed the plastic bag into my rucksack and fastened the chain lock around the seat post.

It had been a good little adventure, I thought to myself as I set off again, just a little shaken after the mad vet's pursuit. It could only have been some inexplicable code of honour that had compelled him to strain himself like that for the sake of a dead cat. And anyway, it shouldn't be forgotten, I told myself, that he'd killed it in the first place.

What was worse, injecting a poor animal with some lethal substance, like a Dr Mengele, or taking the dead creature home?

The asphalt, wet and black, gleamed in the street lighting, dissected by gauze-like bands of snow at its edges and down the middle. It was snowing quite a lot now, but there was too much traffic, I supposed, for it to stick properly. The rooftops on both sides of the road, usually melded into the darkness, loomed grey-white and unexpectedly defined.

I pedalled on, past Lewisham's deserted square, which at second glance wasn't entirely deserted, for a small gaggle of winos were still hanging out, drunken shouts going up in my wake.

The Beatles had played here once, Hans had told me when we'd sat drinking in his garage. At the Odeon, 1962 or 1963. He'd seen the Clash there himself five years ago.

Maybe he'd be down the pub tonight. Not that I had anything in particular to talk to him about. But I wondered if he knew anything about Figueroa. How big a name he was. I could easily have been exaggerating his importance. But if he *was* important, boycotting him wouldn't be such a good move. He might remember me then, I'd be the student who'd skipped his classes.

After lugging the bike up the stairs into the flat, I removed the plastic bag containing the cat from my rucksack and stood with it in my hands while wondering what to do. If I could get hold of a big cooking pot the next day to boil the cat in, I could just leave it for now. The plastic bag was sealed. On the other hand, I didn't know how long it had been in that container. If I was really unlucky, I'd wake up with the whole room stinking of death.

I emptied the fridge's freezer compartment and stuffed it in there. I threw the fish fingers out, but the pizzas would be all right in the fridge for a couple of days. The bin bag was full, so I tied a knot in the top and took it down to the rubbish container in the basement before going out to the pub. Hans wasn't there. I didn't know anyone else around where I lived, so I'd taken a book with me just in case, which I read while sitting beside the window. The snow eased outside, the air got colder, and by the time I got up and went home after last orders, the slush in the street had frozen into icy lumps. The five pints I'd drunk sent me spinning into almost immediate sleep.

The first thing I did the next day was buy that big pot at the ironmonger's on the main street. I couldn't really afford it — what little I'd got left was supposed to be for food, but I wasn't in London to eat, and my grant would be coming through any day now, so I chanced it.

The project I'd embarked upon no longer seemed quite such a good idea as I took the dead cat out of the freezer. It was a lot of work for a photograph, but that was exactly the kind of thought that led to nothing new ever getting done, no boundary ever being pushed back. Besides, I'd already invested so much time and energy in the venture that it would be stupid to knock it on the head now.

The bag clunked against the worktop as I put it down. I only hoped it *was* a cat. I found the scissors in the drawer and cut through the plastic.

It was. A frozen foot, a frozen belly were revealed. Then a flank, black, matted fur, the spine, and finally the head. The eyes were closed, the mouth slightly open on one side, the teeth visible.

I placed it in the pot, which I filled with water until the animal was covered, topped up for good measure, then put the lid on, turned the knob and touched the hissing burner with a match, the gas igniting with a little puff of sound.

I had no idea how long it would take to boil the flesh from the bone, only that when Mum made soup at home it would stand and simmer away for hours, and there was no reason to believe that this would be any quicker.

It was a strange thought: the cat, as black as night, still stiff and crooked in the shallow arc the spine described, languishing in a pot on the cooker. A faint discomfort pricked at me, presumably some form of guilty conscience triggered by the knowledge that this was not normal. But normal according to whom? Who said cats weren't to be boiled? People gladly dropped live crabs and lobsters into boiling water, that was fine, apparently, no one complained about that. But boil a *dead* cat and they'd have your guts.

When the water came to the boil, I turned the heat down and got my coat. Four hours was bound to be enough. I'd give it five, just to be sure.

It was twenty past eleven now. Half four, then.

Putting my arms through the straps of my rucksack before going out, my eye fell on Mum's letter. I hadn't given it a thought, but now I suddenly felt curious as to what she'd written. I slipped it into my coat pocket, locked the door behind me and went down the stairs. On the landing below, Liz's door opened and she stepped out, rummaging in her bag for a second, before looking up at me.

'Hi,' I said.

'Hi,' she said.

Bright red lipstick today. It had the opposite effect of what presumably she was intending; it wasn't until then that I saw how thin-lipped she was.

She turned and closed the door. I guessed she'd been checking to make sure her key was in her bag. Neurotic, in other words.

It was all a bit awkward after that — she followed me down the stairs and once we went through the front door and out into the street it became apparent that we were going the same way. I could have upped my tempo and left her behind, only it would have seemed a bit impolite. Keeping a few paces ahead of her would have been even odder.

I turned round.

'Are you going to the station?' I said, and lingered the two seconds it took for her to come up alongside me, before walking on.

'Aha,' she said. 'You too?'

'That's right.'

Silence.

It wasn't like I was chatting her up. She could have been a bit more encouraging, though, I thought. Anyway, what if I did try to get off with her? Her boyfriend, that skinny, long-haired wimp, was hardly going to give me any trouble.

Still, that was her business.

'Are you a student?' I said.

'Aha.'

'What course are you on?'

'English lit.'

Most people would then have expected her to ask me the same question. But she didn't. She didn't even look at me. I remembered how it felt. After I'd been going out with Hanne a few months in gymnas, I'd had to make an effort not to look at other girls when we were together. It didn't matter how innocent it felt to me — I was only looking, not touching — I gradually realised that Hanne felt differently about it, and after that it was as if I always had to put on a mental neck brace so my head wouldn't be turned. Liz's boyfriend wasn't even here, so obviously it had become ingrained in her.

We stopped at the zebra crossing. The sun shone down on the other side of the street, but we were standing in shadow. Cars and lorries thundered past.

'Who's the best English writer, then? Since you're doing English lit, I mean.'

'Shakespeare, obviously. Coleridge and Wordsworth. Virginia Woolf.'

The traffic slowed. Exhausts coughed out their fumes above the asphalt.

'How about living writers?'

She glanced at me at the same time as she tucked a strand of hair behind her ear. Nervous? Or interested?

'I don't know.'

'Who do you like?'

'Lessing. Fowles. Burgess. Murdoch.'

'Sounds like a firm of solicitors.'

The lights changed, the red man switched to green, and she strode out onto the crossing on her rather short legs. I came up beside her again.

'What about Gabriel García Márquez?'

'He's not exactly English.'

'Do you like him, though?'

'I do, yes. Salman Rushdie, too. I forgot to mention him. He's British. And Naipaul.'

'You read a lot, then?'

Her eyes were fixed on the station entrance now, and she clearly didn't think it worth responding. I gave her a bit of the same, and joined the queue at the kiosk without saying anything or even looking at her. She vanished in the direction of the platform. Not the worst outcome. No danger then of a similarly embarrassing situation on the train. We'd come this far together, so we'd probably have had to sit next to each other.

I bought myself a coffee that came in one of those thin, squashy plastic cups that got so hot it was almost impossible to drink from them. In the meantime, she could catch her train. I was in no rush and could wait for the next one.

Did she think I wasn't good enough for her? It didn't have to be her boyfriend standing in the way — she was bound to be aware that he wasn't exactly a prize specimen. And social class was still an important thing for the Brits.

Nah, that couldn't be it. Not when she was living in a grotty little bedsit in an unfashionable part of town, she was hardly going to be upper class living like that. And anyway, I didn't fit into the class system here. I was an outsider to them, impossible to categorise. My dad was a farmer — that put me at the bottom. But it was a big farm that had been in his family for generations, and it wasn't *that* long ago that such people belonged to the upper echelons in an agriculture-based society. My mum taught at gymnas. Would that be middle class? Whatever, it made no difference really, because I was an artist, and that wasn't working, middle or upper class. An artist belonged everywhere and nowhere.

When I'd presumed she read a lot and had asked her about it, she ought to have asked about me too, what I liked to read. She didn't have to like me just to ask. It was everyday politeness.

The train slowed down and came to a stop at the platform, and I dropped my barely sipped coffee into the nearest bin. You could hardly have called it coffee, anyway. England was an instant-coffee nation, the filter machine was apparently a complete unknown to them — coffee here was as thin and watery as tea, or as thick and bitter as tar.

I found myself a place to sit in the half-empty carriage. A lot of young mothers with their babies, as always at this time of day, mid-morning. The breadwinners hurried off at the crack of dawn, into cold and dark mornings, while the women took things easy and had the whole day to themselves. It was beyond me how those women's libbers could be so envious of men — couldn't they see how stressed out they were, how flustered? High blood pressure, cheap suits, low pay.

From Charing Cross I strolled over to the National Gallery. Studying the masterpieces there was more useful than trying to find something to say about the work of one's fellow students at the school. I liked the way the paintings were hung chronologically, it was interesting to see how the pictures became increasingly true to life through history, until suddenly they crashed into a wall, as it were, and after that resembled nothing. It was because photography had arrived. Even the most photo-realistic of paintings, which doubtless had astounded beholders at the time, was infinitely more removed from the real world than the poorest of photographs. They were like pictures from a fantasy world, where the grass was greener, the sky bluer, the sun yellower. The Renaissance artists were presumably aware of this, because they seemed to be hardly even trying. Perspective swung this way and that, and nature resembled nothing I'd seen before.

I lingered at a Giotto depicting a group of men gathered together beneath the ceiling of a room that had one wall missing. All were portrayed with halos — there were twelve of them, so I reasoned they were the Disciples. Above them, I suddenly noticed, was a dove, radiating light. The painting, then, depicted the moment they received the Holy Spirit. I stepped closer and studied the faces. The man in the middle was younger than the rest, long-haired, his hands, surprisingly small, held in the air in front of him. This, I assumed, was Jesus, he'd come back from the dead and had appeared to his disciples, who now numbered eleven following the suicide of Judas.

The strange thing about the faces was that nothing in them revealed any awareness of being seen — either by the other figures in the room or those who were looking at the painting.

I thought about what Hans had told me about mirrors. But it couldn't be anything to do with them living before the advent of the mirror, because there were lots of paintings from subsequent centuries in which the faces didn't show this absence of visual self-awareness.

It did something to them — each individual became interesting in his own right; something was going on in every face.

Next to this was another work by the same painter, this one showing a bleeding Jesus and a woman standing beside him who looked to be sticking her finger into his wound. The finger was unnaturally long, as it might have been if a child had painted it, for children, I knew, focused on what was important and made such elements bigger than what was less important. The funny thing, though, was the face of Christ. He didn't look at all as if he was from another age. London was full of faces just the same. He looked like a workman, a builder or, why not, a carpenter, which was what he was! Hideous, puffy eyes, a long, pointed nose, thin lips. Big ears. His gaze was distant, and not in the slightest bit benevolent. This was not a particularly good person. He couldn't have been painted like that on purpose, surely?

Turning away to move on, my eyes met a familiar gaze. A thin, dark-haired man with glasses, in a dark blue suit, was standing staring at me from the entrance into the next room. It took a second for me to realise it was the man from the cafe, and later the Tube. By the time I did, he was already making towards the exit. I wasn't as bothered as I had been the last time, accepting it could only be coincidence and feeling no desire to set off in pursuit of him, as I'd told myself I would the last time, if I ever saw him again.

Nonetheless, it was still a bit unnerving.

I dismissed him from my mind. Who would be interested in following *me*?

No one.

The cold, clear air outside, drenched with light by a low-hanging sun, took what remained of my unease. The concourse was teeming with people, who seemed as if fenced in by the steady stream of traffic around the surrounding square, and I found myself with an intense feeling that the world was wide open and filled with opportunity. It probably had to do with me just having spent an hour in solemn, dimly lit rooms, looking at paintings produced hundreds of years ago by working artists now long since dead. No wonder, then, that it felt as if the doors of the real world had been opened wide and that anything at all could happen the moment you stepped through them.

I sat down at the same cafe where I'd seen him the first time — at the same table, in fact, at which he'd been sitting. He wasn't there now, of course, and after ordering a coffee I got Mum's letter out and read it.

My dearest Kristian,

How are you? I sincerely hope you are well. It was very painful to your dad and me that you walked out the way you did, and that we have had no word from you since. It leaves us with many unanswered questions. But you are an adult now, making your own choices and living your own life. Your dad and I both respect that. Christmas proved to be a difficult time for us with Liv being so unwell. We didn't think enough about you and the problems you might have of your own. But you are so very important to both of us, as I hope you know. Perhaps one day you'll have children of your own and will discover the strength of the bonds that will develop between you. A mother loves her child unconditionally. It doesn't matter what it may do or what sort of person it becomes — a mother's love is constant. Sometimes, things may happen which cloud the feeling. One's attention may be directed elsewhere. But love remains, always. I vividly remember the day you were born, Kristian, the first time you looked at me, how wonderful it was. That feeling will never go away. Now you're a young man, finding your way in the world, and I imagine you find these words terribly sentimental. The world is yours to be conquered, isn't that how it feels? I remember it felt that way to me, too. What did I care about my tired old parents at home? I scarcely paid them a thought. My life was mine, and mine alone, to be lived to the full. So don't think I don't understand you. You've always been so very independent, always forged your own paths, as of course you must — I would never stand in the way of that. All I want is for you to know that you're in our thoughts and that you will always be welcome here.

Mum

PS: Liv is doing fine, has realised how serious things are, wants to deal with her problems, and is now in therapy. She sends you all her love, as do your dad and Helene.

So, was I supposed to be filled with warm feelings for them now? Was I supposed to dash outside and ring home in tears? She'd weighed her words meticulously, probably penned several drafts, and still it shone through that Dad had no part in it. She was barely invested in it herself. Who was this *it* she referred to? *It doesn't matter what it may do.* Was that me? It was. My own mother was calling me *it*. I'd no doubt she meant every word she said about love, but love for her was just that, a concept, a word, something she could look at and consider.

I threw the letter into a bin on the pavement outside. Not quite three hours had passed yet, but they would have by the time I'd got the train home.

Around fifty other people were stood on the platform, they all kept looking up at the display to see when the next train was due, stock-still and focused — perhaps there'd be an announcement from the afterlife if they stood there long enough.

Delays, that was all it was.

A man wearing a sheepskin coat, gloves and rectangular glasses was standing back against the wall, his eyes following me. I ignored him and went over to the newspaper stand outside the kiosk. All the papers carried the same front-page story. The *Challenger* space shuttle had exploded the day before, the crew of seven had perished, blown to bits. The image of the disaster was incredibly beautiful. A plume of smoke swelling nebula-like into the darkened sky. It could just as easily have been a picture of something being created rather than destroyed, I thought. Turning round after buying a paper, I saw that the man was gone. No need to be paranoid. Yes, he'd been looking at me, and the Egyptian had looked at me too, but it didn't mean I was being watched! Coincidence governed the world, and how many coincidences were occurring every second in this city of six million inhabitants?

The explosion had taken place about a minute after the launch, the paper said. In that time the craft had reached an altitude of some fourteen kilometres.

Fourteen kilometres in a minute!

No one knew what had happened, other than that the temperature had been lower than usual. Eight below during the night, three at the time of the launch.

I'd read everything I could lay my hands on about space exploration when I was a kid, though mostly about the Apollo missions; by the time they started sending space shuttles up I'd lost interest. I hadn't even known there was a launch happening.

Still, Cape Canaveral had been a mythical place to me. The gigantic vehicle, the largest in the world, that they used to transport the rockets to the launch pad. The enormous thrust that was required to conquer the force of gravity. The sea of flame underneath the rocket when the fuel was ignited, and how slowly it rose in those first seconds, before gathering speed and shooting into the sky, the astronauts strapped into their seats inside their little tin can, no larger than a 2CV, at the very tip. The radio signals, reaching all the way to the moon.

I looked at the picture again. It said that man was nothing. The world was pattern and emptiness. Something that was continually coming into being and breaking up again, everywhere and all the time. Slowly drifting dust, light from burning spheres.

I folded the newspaper, put it in my bag and grabbed a seat in the packed carriage of the train. In a hundred years, everyone in it would be dead and a whole new set of people would occupy their places. And still they thought themselves important and unique, as if whatever they did, thought and said was significant.

Well, it wasn't.

The thought of this made me smarter than them, but no happier.

Every building alongside the railway tracks was derelict. Graffiti, rust, broken windows. The last vestiges of snow and ice were gone. The colours were yellow-white, brown, grey, black.

Frameworks of Life was a stupid idea. It presupposed that life was something more. That the flesh that clung to the bone, the leaf that sprouted from the twig, had some value of their own, rather than being something that arose out of chance.

A fat man wearing a hooded jacket and, of all things, shorts, occupied the seat opposite and was busy telling an anecdote to his slouching mate who looked like he was falling asleep. The fat man laughed, revealing a set of yellowed teeth; his mate smiled and gave him a glance of acknowledgement before turning to gaze out the window, his face abruptly expressionless. A fumbling look of helplessness appeared fleetingly in the fat man's eye, and then his features too found repose.

I hadn't understood a word he'd said, but something told me I hadn't missed anything.

On my way home from the station I popped into the supermarket and bought one of those Vesta ready meals of rice and curry, some milk for my tea, and some oranges for the vitamin C. The woman on the checkout, with wispy white hair and patches of pink scalp showing through — I took her to be around seventy and far too old to be working — called me *love* and asked if I wanted a bag, which I did.

The day had clouded over, cloaking the rooftops grey. I couldn't get over how shallow Mum's letter had been, I was thinking about it as I crossed the road in front of the shop. Over here, they called everyone *love*, but at home I'd never heard the word uttered. Maybe I'd write back as frankly as she deserved, maybe then she'd realise what honesty meant. She could see what it felt like to have feelings then, not just act them out.

As I went up the stairs, I sensed an unfamiliar and unpleasant smell, and I knew what it was: the cat. I let myself in, and the stench almost knocked me out. The air was thick with steam, the smell so foul it made me want to vomit. Breathing through my mouth only, I darted over to the windows and threw them wide open.

Oh God.

I turned the cooker off and the extractor on. Nausea welled in me, my stomach muscles tried to push it back and I swallowed hard. Again, I darted to the windows and gulped in fresh air, my upper body hanging over the sill.

How could it smell so bad? It was only meat. Why would there be any difference compared to boiling meat and bones for a broth?

Clearly, though, there was a difference.

Oh, it was disgusting.

Maybe it was because I'd boiled it whole, fur and guts and all.

There was no way I could stay here.

I'd have to go out somewhere until the room was properly aired.

A new wave of nausea washed through me as I shut the door behind me. I'd probably remember this smell the rest of my life.

How indescribably good it then felt to be standing on the pavement outside, just breathing. Exhaust fumes, dank brick, dampness were like the most exquisite perfumes.

I went to the shop again, maybe they sold scented candles there, or those aerosols that overly anxious people used after they'd been to the toilet.

They did have the aerosols, so I bought two, one that smelled of summer meadows, the other of fresh laundry. I bought a packet of cigarettes too. I'd only ever smoked a couple of times, when I'd been at gymnas. I hadn't liked it then, but it hadn't made me feel sick either, so it didn't exactly disagree with me. Cigarette smoke and the sprays would do the trick, I was sure of it.

Collin opened his door as I went past. He must have been standing behind it, waiting for me to come back.

'What's that smell?' he said. 'Or stench I should say.'

'No idea,' I said. 'You're right, though, it is pretty horrible. Maybe the old girl up there?'

'You don't think she's . . .'

'No, no, I just saw her. She is old, though. Maybe she's been cooking some tainted meat or something, and can't smell it herself.'

He forced a smile.

'Just thought I'd check,' he said.

'No problem.'

The smell had already gone a bit. I sprayed the whole room with the meadow scent, then flopped down on the settee to regain a measure of composure. I was tempted just to dump the whole pot into the bin and get rid of it in the basement rubbish container, but having got this far I didn't really see the point in stopping now.

After a while, I'd collected myself sufficiently to get started on the final phase. Standing at the cooker, my hand resting a while on the lid of the pot, I feared I'd only be assailed by a smell even worse. I went and sat down again and lit a cigarette, coughing as the tobacco smoke etched its way down my throat and into my lungs. Another couple of drags and I seemed to have got the hang of it, feeling myself quicken, as if the brain somehow tightened and became more concentrated, and a good, satisfying feeling ran through me: I was high on nicotine. Slightly dizzy, with the flat of one hand planted firmly on the settee next to me, I sat and smoked until I'd finished the cigarette. I stubbed it out on a saucer and wobbled through blue-grey smoke to the cooker and lifted the lid.

The cat was quite as whole as before, curled in the pot, as black as night, grinning up at me.

How was it possible?

I'd been expecting a half-dissolved animal in a soup of hairs and flesh.

It must have been the skin that kept everything intact, and no doubt it was as tough as old boots.

There was only the smallest amount of water left in the bottom, I could see, and realised it was a good job I hadn't come home any later — it might have burned a hole, maybe even started a fire, or at least set an alarm off. Firemen in the full get-up, oxygen masks and everything, smashing their way into the empty flat — and what would they have said when they realised I boiled cats?

I put the lid back on.

What was I going to do?

Skin it? Get hold of a sharp knife and cut the flesh away, fur and all. It was probably tender enough by now, so maybe it wouldn't be that difficult.

But not tonight.

I took a shelf out of the fridge to make room for the pot and then put it inside. The room still smelled pretty horrible, but the air was freezing cold, so I closed the windows again. They were draughty anyway, and now at least the source of the stink was shut in.

It was getting dark outside. I was hungry, but the thought of eating in wasn't exactly appealing. There was a fried chicken place down the high street, and a chippy next door to it, a burger bar near the station. They weren't exactly sit-down places, where you'd linger over a meal, more like eating on the go, but I knew the chicken was good and spicy, succulent and crispy-skinned.

I put my coat on and went out. The high street was a ribbon of tacky signage. Boxes of fruit and veg outside little grocers' shops, buckets, long-handled brushes and stepladders in front of the ironmonger's, people popping in and out, trains with lit-up windows clattering by behind the houses and buildings. Faces in pubs, punters engaged in banter, laughing, gesticulating, drinking, smoking.

A group of noisy schoolkids in dark uniforms had invaded the chicken place. I squeezed in, ordered a peri-peri half-chicken with rice and sat down in the corner. I regretted not having taken a book with me, but the food came almost straight away, oily and glistening in the glaring light. There was no end of things I could photograph. Maybe I could shift to colour and do a series on glitzy, garish London. Or what about burger bars? The people who ate there, a month of custom. I imagined it: lonely men with ketchup on their chins, mouths filled with the mash of chewed-up bread and meat as they gazed vacantly out the windows; boisterous kids hanging out, still in their uniforms after school, ties and skirts, bound by the stiffness of civilisation, while nature, in their oozing zits, gangly limbs, the suddenness of breasts, swelled, their cries and shouts, giggles and snorts impossible to keep in check; maybe some slender, elegant woman, dark and aloof, would appear one day too.

The pictures I'd shown in class weren't good enough, I realised that now. I'd been strung along by the idea. They *were* tame. But all it meant was that I'd gauged things wrong. It said nothing about the potential I had in me.

It was just a pity it was the only chance I'd have as regards Figueroa. I'd liked him. He was sharp. Probably one of the leading photographers of his generation. If only I'd been able to show him something really good, he'd have remembered me then. It would have meant I'd be able to contact him once I'd got some more work in my portfolio. That way I could use him, his name would open doors. *Kristian is a shining talent, one of the biggest I've known. Raw and unpolished, yes, but the force of his work even now would be a draw for any gallery, if only he is given the chance.*

The spicy chicken made me aware I'd got a little sore in the corner of my mouth. I dabbed my lips with the serviette and took a mouthful of my cola.

But what if I showed him something else? A couple from the series that had got me accepted? Or maybe the ones of Liv's bed? Or the empty house, that whole batch? Plus a couple of other things, to show him I'd scope as well as depth?

I felt my heart quicken. He wouldn't still be at the school now, he'd have gone back to his hotel. It wouldn't be hard to find out where he was staying. I could ring the school and ask for him, then when they said he wasn't there, I'd ask for the name of his hotel so I could get in touch with him.

I demolished the rest of my chicken, finished off the rice, dabbed my mouth again and tried to wipe my hands, which now were orange from the spices and grease. It wouldn't come off, but it didn't matter — I'd have to go home first anyway to pick some photos out, so I'd give them a proper wash there.

I rang the school from the phone box outside the station. As I'd thought, Figueroa had gone for the day. He was staying at the Regent Palace Hotel near Piccadilly. Easy to find and straightforward getting there. Brilliant!

I hurried home, washed my hands, selected twelve pictures, put them in my bag and headed straight back to the station. The delays had been sorted now, so half an hour later I emerged at Charing Cross and walked towards Piccadilly. It had started to rain. The street lighting slid onto black asphalt. Red rear lights, the rumble and growl of traffic, horns. Pedestrians, eyes down, brollies to the wind. Wet faces, wet hair.

Now I'd be able to *talk* to him. Explain my way of thinking. I could mention my skeleton series, for one thing. Lay out the background for him. He'd realise then that I was on my way. Of course, nothing was fully fledged or perfect. That was why I attended the school. And it was why I'd come to see him at his hotel this evening. I was burning, burning, burning for this. Not everyone had that energy. Some of the other students were technically more gifted than me, but their personalities were ill-defined and ineffectual.

The hotel looked posh enough from the outside, but as soon as I came into the foyer the impression dissolved. The place had an old smell to it, the smell of lower-end London hotels, where all grandeur was a sham.

I asked for Figueroa. The receptionist, a young man with the bushy eyebrows of one much older, called up his room and informed him that a Mr Hadeland was here.

He put his hand over the receiver.

'He wants to know who you are.'

'One of his students,' I said.

He nodded and turned slightly away as he passed the information on, then hung up and turned to face me again.

'He'll be down in a while. You can wait over there, if you like.'

I went and sat down on the sofa he'd indicated with a nod, took out my folder with the photographs in it and began to arrange them on the low coffee table. Changed my mind. It was too direct — I put them back in my bag again.

Figueroa came down the stairs. I'd been expecting him to receive me in his room, but now he was on his way out, in a brown suede jacket and a black woolly hat.

I stood up with a smile.

'I'm sorry to disturb you after hours.'

'That's OK.'

'Only I was wondering if you could spare me a few minutes.'

'Sure. What's on your mind?'

'The pictures I showed you at school weren't really representative of what I'm doing. So I didn't really benefit from the critique.'

'No.'

'I've brought some other work with me that I was thinking we might look at together. You're a master, and I'm just very curious to know what you think.'

'I wouldn't say a master, not exactly. But yes, by all means.'

'Shall we sit here?'

'Let's not. I'm on my way out to see a film in Soho. Why don't we walk and see if we can find somewhere along the way?'

'OK,' I said, picked up my bag and went with him into the street. He walked with his hands in his jacket pockets and had poor posture, I noted. A listless gait. There ought to be something more vigorous about a war photographer, I thought, something vigilant, keen and acute.

'What film are you going to see?' I asked as we turned down one of the streets leading towards Chinatown.

'*Runaway Train.*'

'Jon Voight?'

'Exactly.'

The stone and red-brick buildings, old and dark, seemed to bear down on us out of the leaden sky. The rain made the light shimmer in the asphalt's millimetre-thin puddles. We passed a pub that was packed with customers, people piling in after work. Only two doors down was a quiet, unobtrusive little cafe.

'How about here?'

'Fine, yes.'

There were two other customers inside, a pair of fair-haired girls in their twenties with backpacks leaned against their chairs. I picked out a table as far from them as possible.

'Can I get you something?' I said as he took off his jacket and hung it over the back of his chair, before stuffing his hat into one of the pockets.

'Just a coffee, please.'

One of the two girls glanced away as I caught her gaze on my way up to the counter.

'Not him, he's obviously gay,' the other one said to her in Danish. 'They came in together.'

'I'll convert him, then.'

They both laughed.

Idiots.

My cheeks warm, I ordered two coffees. I'd say something to them, in Danish. That would wipe the stupid smiles off their faces. But I'd lose the upper hand then. Best to wait a bit and hear what else they might have to say.

Gay! Did I look gay?

Was it only because we'd come in together, or was there more to it? Something specifically about me?

The guy who was serving put two coffees down on the counter. I gave him some money, waved him away dismissively when he made to give me my change, and took the cups over to the table. Figueroa smiled as I put his down in front of him.

Was he gay?

No. Who'd ever heard of a gay war photographer?

'So, you wanted to show me some pictures?'

I nodded, took the folder out of my bag and carefully removed the photographs. I'd placed them in the order I'd decided on spontaneously at home. Now, I handed him the first. It showed Mum seated on a chair.

'This is part of a series,' I said, and took out the next one ready: Helene, in the same chair.

'Aha,' Figueroa said. He put the first one down and then looked at the next.

Five images — the same motif, different people. He gave each a few seconds. The next one was of the tree out at Barnes.

'This one belongs to a series as well. I'm going to call it *Frameworks of Life*. It's about the structures that keep us together. Physically, I mean. Skeletons, that sort of stuff.'

'I see.'

'These last ones are standalones.'

One was old, a perfect shot from when I was seventeen, Hanne coming up out of the river on a rainy day in summer. After that, Liv's bed, the abandoned meal, the Christmas tree.

'Actually, that's not true. The last three belong together. They're from this Christmas just gone. My sister took an overdose and was rushed to hospital.'

For the first time, he looked up from the photos.

'I'm sorry to hear that,' he said. 'Is she all right?'

'Yes, she's doing fine now. Started in therapy and stuff.'

'Aha.'

He put the final photo down, fished a packet of cigarettes from his coat pocket and lit up. I remembered my own and lit up too, making sure not to inhale at first — I didn't want to sit there coughing my guts up like an amateur.

'I'm not sure quite what to say,' he said.

'Do you like them?'

He shook his head.

'I must be honest with you, since you've placed such confidence in me. At the general level, I'd say you're photographing ideas, as opposed to reality. There is nothing wrong with that. But still there must be life. And in these pictures there is none.'

'But look at this one,' I said, going back to the one of Hanne. 'There's life here, surely?'

'Perhaps, yes. But the picture is a cliché. Clichés kill life.'

'But what do you mean by *life*? Isn't that a cliché too?'

He shrugged.

'You could say. But you see immediately when a picture is alive. It grabs you. It asks you questions.'

'My pictures ask questions too.'

'You know what you want, I'm in no doubt about that. But you don't succeed in putting it into your photographs.'

'Then how can I do that? If what you're saying is right.'

Again, he shrugged.

'I don't know. You are sure this is what you want to do?'

'Yes.'

'You could try journalism. The requirements there are different. A lot of it is about being in the right place at the right time. I know many excellent war photographers who fail when they try to do other things. But out there in the field they take very strong photographs.'

'OK.'

He gazed out through the window as I gathered my pictures together, as if he couldn't stomach that gesture of defeat. I aligned the photos with a couple of raps against the tabletop, put them back in their folder, and the folder back in my bag.

Our coffees were hardly touched.

How easy it was for him to say what he'd said. He was at the top. He could sling anything in anyone's face without it jeopardising his status.

I felt tears begin to well, turned away and got to my feet. The toilets were at the far end of the room, behind where the two Danish girls were sitting. I stared at the rear wall as I went past.

'He's dumped him now,' one of them said.

'Don't get me going,' said the other.

I dabbed my eyes with some toilet roll, flushed it away and checked myself in the mirror. The person that stared back at me didn't look like he'd been crying. And why should he have? Nothing had happened. One person's opinion was no more than that: one person's opinion.

'Are you OK?' Figueroa asked when I returned.

'Yes, of course,' I said.

'My film will be starting soon,' he said, and got to his feet. 'Thank you for coming to see me, and I wish you the best of luck in the future.'

And with that he left, seconds later passing by the window outside before he was out of sight.

I sat with my coffee for a few minutes. I didn't need to go just because he'd gone. I lit another cigarette and smoked it without even coughing. If I was as talentless as he'd suggested, then how come they'd accepted me into the school? It didn't make sense.

Just as an arse had two buttocks, there were two sides to artistic taste — and from the middle came nothing but shite.

I'd meet him again on my way up, when he was on his way down. I wouldn't spare him either. I'd be just as *honest* with him as he'd been with me.

On my way out, I went over to the table where the two girls were sitting. They looked up at me in surprise.

'Hi, mind if I say something?' I said in my best Danish. 'I'm *not* gay. But looking at your two ugly faces makes me wish I was. What a pair of absolute dogs.'

I strode out before they had a chance to say anything in reply. But one of them had been quick to get the message — her jaw dropped immediately and her eyes were as big as saucers.

Outside, I almost broke into a jog. I didn't exactly want them coming after me.

A photojournalist was the last thing I wanted to be. Dad had talked about it too. He wanted everything to stay within the bounds of normality, the way he'd always known things. Newspaper photographers belonged recognisably to the world he knew — he looked at their work every morning when he sat with his paper, so he could relate to that.

Mum was more open. Liv too. But she didn't understand things, even if she thought she did. Helene was like Dad. Her biggest challenge so far had been organising a christening. It was probably the biggest thing that had happened in her life too.

Where was I going to go now?

Not home, that was for sure. The thought of my flat depressed me. But then again, there wasn't much that was uplifting about the prospect of sitting on my own drinking in a pub in central London either.

Maybe I could give Gav or Håkan a ring?

But then I'd have to tell them why I hadn't been there. We'd end up talking school.

I could go down the pub at home, have a few pints. I'd have no trouble sleeping after that.

Not a bad idea.

Ten minutes later I was on a near-empty train rocking and rattling away from the hub. The city was occasional shimmering bands of light under a dark sky, but mostly it remained hidden behind tower blocks, tenements, embankments, the jagged silhouettes of trees. That people actually lived in those places was hard to grasp. What did they do? Why were they there? What was the point of sitting in a kitchen and staring out the window, unknown to everyone? They had to eat, of course, so they were all having their dinner, and to buy food you had to have money, meaning they spent long working days doing something absolutely meaningless — but what for? If there'd only been ten or twenty of them, or two, three hundred, it wouldn't matter — but six million?

The thought returned to me as I went through the streets of Deptford, for I recognised not a face among those I saw, and had no idea who lived in all those flats. Ants probably felt like that. Everyone around them doing what was expected of them so society didn't collapse, but with no personal relation to anyone else, they were just other ants. Replaceable, albeit useful as long as they were there. But who wanted no more than to perform a function in an anthill? Answer: everyone.

I bought a pint and found a table in the corner at the back where I could look out into the yard, teeming with customers in summer, now empty and forlorn, the cement carpeted with dank leaves, tables and chairs stacked against the brick wall at the far end, half covered by a tarpaulin. Away in the distance, red lights on top of some cranes.

Then something weird happened. Right next to me, the wall opened — that was what it looked like, but of course there was a door there that I hadn't noticed — and out stepped Hans. He didn't see me, and I said nothing, just sat there quietly without moving and watched him go through into the next room, followed by four others who likewise came out the wall. The last of these people, a black-clad woman in a pair of Dr Martens boots, closed the door behind her. She was around Hans's age, not exactly a looker, broad-chinned, with prominent, fishlike eyes, pasty skin and black hair. She was the only of them to notice me sitting there, and sent me a fleeting, apologetic smile before going the same way as the others.

So, he hangs out with goths, I thought. But the question wasn't so much why he hung out with her, than the opposite — what could she possibly see in a man who wore home-knitted jumpers and trousers that were too short in the leg?

I smiled, only then the dense black hole of Figueroa came and swallowed me up again.

Was he right?

Was I talentless?

Liv had said so too. That I was deluding myself.

But if that was the case, I'd never have got into the school in the first place. If there was one thing they were looking for, it was talent. So, I had talent. I wasn't deluding myself. I wasn't living my life on a lie. The issue now was how to manage that talent.

I had it in me.

It was just a matter of bringing it out.

My pictures so far were OK. Not brilliant, not world class, but I was twenty, I was only starting out. Anyway, art wasn't science. There was no right answer to anything. What one person understood and was enriched by, another might not get at all. This was true of artists themselves too. What's more, Figueroa wasn't an artist. He was a war photographer, which was a different thing altogether. He'd said himself how easy that was. What judge of art was he?

Shoemaker, stick to thy last.

'Sitting here moping again, are we?' It was Hans, now suddenly in front of me with a pint in his hand, smiling. 'How's it going, all right?'

'Can't complain.'

'No book today?'

'Came straight from the station, so no.'

'Listen, I'm through there with some friends, if you want to join us?'

'Nah, I'm all right. Just popped in for a quick one, then home.'

He nodded.

'Suit yourself. Catch you soon enough, no doubt.'

'What were you doing in there?' I said with a nod towards the door.

'You mean you saw us?'

'I saw you come out.'

'Why didn't you say anything?'

'I reckoned you were with them. What's in there, anyway?'

'Private rooms, upstairs. They hire them out for functions. Parties, dining, that sort of thing.'

'So what were you doing — dining?'

'No. Well, a bite to eat, yes. But no, we were having a meeting.'

'A meeting?'

'You're very inquisitive all of a sudden?'

'No I'm not. Just wondering.'

'Still a lot of questions, though! Why don't you come through and meet the others? Put your mind at rest about this mysterious meeting.'

'Nah, you go on,' I said. 'I'll see you soon enough.'

I watched as he threaded his long, gangly figure between the tables into the adjoining room. His hands were enormous — I noticed it again now. It was odd in a way that people didn't turn round and look at him, as tall as he was, with that thick bush of hair, the jutting lower jaw. He could have been intellectually impaired. He wasn't, of course, he came across smarter than most, but until he opened his mouth and spoke, you'd never have known.

I wondered who his friends were.

He'd been with a crowd the first time I met him, but not knowing him then I hadn't given a thought to what sort of people he hung out with. All the other times, he'd been on his own.

I drained my glass. I'd painted myself into a bit of a corner telling him I'd only popped in for a quick one. That wasn't what I'd been intending at all. A person was allowed to change his mind, of course, but the quick pint had been my excuse for not joining them — if I got another, it would no longer count.

Surely he'd understand if I didn't want to sit with a load of strangers?

I went up to the bar and bought myself another. When the barman put it down on the counter, I asked for a straight vodka to go with it.

I shouldn't have. Once I'd knocked that back, I'd want another. There's a tipping point in drinking, when that first tingling delight gradually intensifies and the veins begin to run with the coldest, darkest pleasure. When the sensation kicks in, it must be seized before it subsides — which requires another drink. And once seized, it must be held — another drink, and another again. By the time I got to that point it didn't matter any more what Hans thought. What was it to him if at first I'd said a quick drink, but then had a few more?

With the pint in one hand, the vodka in the other, I went through into the next room, not so drunk that I couldn't walk straight as long as I focused.

They were sitting around a table in the middle of the room. I stopped in front of them. Hans interrupted himself and looked up at me.

'Pull up a chair!' he said with a smile. 'This is Kristian who I was telling you about.'

The others nodded and smiled.

An icy hand clutched at my heart.

It was him!

The man from the cafe.

His eyes locked onto mine.

There was no doubt. It *was* him. Thin-haired, glasses. Egyptian face.

'Nice to meet you,' he said. 'I'm Victor. A friend of Hans's. Well, obviously.'

I took a chair and sat down.

'Daniella,' said the girl who was sitting beside him — fair, shoulder-length hair, lips that slipped easily about her teeth.

'Vivian,' a second girl said, the one who'd smiled at me earlier.

'And I'm Mark,' said the final member of the group. They all looked to be in their late twenties.

'I've seen you before,' I said to Victor.

'Oh?'

'At the National Gallery. Another time on the Tube. And at a cafe in Soho.'

He smiled, a bit bemused, as if he had no idea what I was talking about.

'I've never seen you before.'

'Have you got a good memory for faces?' Hans said.

'Not particularly.'

'And yet you remember me?' Victor said.

'Yes.'

'Strange. I've never seen you before. Or if I have, I don't remember. When was it you saw me at the gallery?'

'Today.'

'*Were* you there today?' Hans said.

'Yes, as a matter of fact I was. What was I wearing, then?'

'A blue suit.'

'I *was*, yes! I'm not very observant, am I?'

'Don't let him make you think you've got a forgettable face, Kristian,' the fair-haired girl said. 'Because you haven't.'

'A bit puppyish, perhaps,' said the girl in black. Her hair was cut in a goth bob. Maybe her eyes were more like a cow's, lashy like that.

'Don't listen to her.'

'Give yourself fifty years and your face'll have plenty of character. You'll look like Beckett then.'

They laughed.

I smiled and sipped my beer so as to distract from the dark countenance I sensed now clouded my face.

Who were these jerks? Who did they think they were?

'We were all students together,' Hans said, as if reading my mind. 'We've kept in touch, as you can see.'

'Don't mind me, just carry on,' I said. 'I'm off in a minute, anyway.'

'We weren't talking about anything in particular,' Hans said.

'What *were* we talking about?' said the guy named Mark.

'The School of Night.'

'That was it, yes,' Mark said, turning his gaze to me. 'A good thing you came and moved us on.'

'What's the School of Night?' I said.

'Vivian here works in theatre, she's directing a production of *Doctor Faustus* this spring,' Hans said. 'Marlowe's play.'

So that was where he'd picked it up. She'd been talking about Marlowe, and he'd just been regurgitating.

'The School of Night was a group of prominent figures in Elizabethan England who were, well, bolshie, I suppose you could call them.'

'Clandestinely oppositional,' said Vivian. 'Dissidents. A bit like in East Germany. Kept their thoughts to themselves.'

'Whatever. Marlowe's said to have given a lecture on atheism at one of their meetings.'

'He was a heretic,' said Vivian.

'But is it in any way apparent in *Doctor Faustus*? That's what we were discussing. Frances Yates, the historian, believes the play was written to *warn against* occultism, suggesting the intention was purely populist. This was the time of the witch craze, when they started burning women for sorcery. The question is how much of what we know about Marlowe can be read into it.'

Of all the people around the table, Hans now looked at me.

'How should I know?' I said.

They laughed.

I got the unpleasant feeling the joke was on me, as if they already had me sussed. Had Hans been talking? Then again, there wasn't much he could tell them.

'When *Doctor Faustus* was put on for the first time, it was rumoured the Devil himself was seen onstage,' the Egyptian said. 'People were terrified.'

'That would surely have surprised Marlowe,' Hans said. 'If it was the case he didn't believe in God, I mean. If he didn't, he couldn't have believed in the Devil either.'

'You do go on, you lot,' said Mark. 'Cheers, and let's change the bloody subject!'

'What do you want to talk about?' said Hans, not without sarcasm.

Mark gave a shrug. No one spoke.

'I went to Norway once when I was a kid,' Daniella then said, looking at me.

I was starting to wish I'd never joined them. I should have known they'd be condescending and *nice* to me.

'Oh yes?' I said.

Hans cut in and asked the question I was meant to ask:

'Whereabouts?'

'Bergen. And we drove along a big fjord there. Harding Fjord, something like that?'

'Hardangerfjorden,' I said.

'That's it, yes. Have you been there?'

I shook my head.

'It was like being in a fairy tale. I've always wanted to go back. I was only seven at the time.'

She smiled, slippery-lipped as before.

I got up and went to the bogs. The pub entrance was in the other room from where they were sitting, which would allow me to slip away without being seen. A bit of a shame to leave a pint behind, hardly touched, but at least I'd avoid the pantomime of all their goodbyes, the falseness of them saying how fantastic it had been meeting me, so from that perspective it was worth it, I told myself, swaying slightly as I pissed into the urinal. The question was, what was I going to do now? Going home definitely didn't appeal, and it couldn't be that late, they hadn't called last orders yet.

Shit, my coat!

Was I going to sacrifice that too?

No, that would be stupid of me, even if it would make a bold statement.

I went back in and sat down again. Vivian looked at me with her cowish eyes, smiled when I returned her gaze, then immediately turned her attention to the Egyptian, who was now the one talking.

Typical that she was the one who was interested, rather than the much prettier Daniella.

'Whenever there's a plane disaster, there's always a story surfaces about someone who was meant to be on board, but didn't make it or else changed their mind at the last minute,' the Egyptian was saying. 'It seems they all made it to the space shuttle, though.'

'Has anyone ever died at that altitude before?' Mark said.

Vivian's gaze caught mine again. I knocked back my vodka.

What did she want with me? She had to be ten years older than me. There couldn't be much cred in a twenty-year-old. Or maybe there was, maybe that was it?

She was almost certainly bright. Creative.

Worked in theatre. Directing a play.

'I wonder if anyone ever went that high in a balloon,' said Hans. 'Before the aeroplane, I mean. You'd think *someone* would have got it into their heads to see how high they could get.'

'Do you get the bends at altitude?' Daniella asked. 'Or is that just a depth thing?'

'Good question,' said the Egyptian. 'The answer to which we'll surely never know.'

The lights flashed a couple of times to signal last orders. I knocked another vodka back at the bar, ordered one more, and a last pint, and returned to the table with them. Not that I enjoyed sitting with these people, but nonetheless hoping they'd want to go on somewhere.

Shortly afterwards, however, they made moves to call it a night, and it was clear to me it would only be embarrassing to suggest carrying on drinking in another place. In the rain outside, Mark and Daniella disappeared off towards the trains, the Egyptian flagged down a passing cab, and Hans, it turned out, was on his bike.

When, with his hood pulled up over his head and his spine curving, he pedalled slowly away, Vivian touched my shoulder.

'Do you want to come back to mine?' she said.

'Yes,' I said.

She took a drag of the cigarette she held in her hand and blew the smoke out into the air. Black coat, black skirt, black tights, black boots.

'We'll get a cab.'

Without speaking, we walked up to the high street. A few minutes later and we were sitting in the back of one. She'd told the driver the address, but the name of the street meant nothing to me. It could have been anywhere.

The silence suited me well. The difference in our two ages was absorbed by it. What I liked less was the feeling that I was just someone she'd picked up. That she wasn't interested in who I was. My quietness then became a sign that I was overwhelmed by her.

But I wasn't. She wasn't ugly, not by any means, but she was no beauty, not with those eyes. I needed to find a way somehow to make her aware of that, to rectify the imbalance between us.

At the same time, we were on our way. There were few things I liked better. Black asphalt, dark, rain-heavy sky, night. Car headlights, shop signs, windows lit up in the flats. Figures on the pavement, some with umbrellas, others without. Everything came into existence in front of us, everything vanished behind us. Trees pricked at the darkness, an empty park opened wide. A closed-down supermarket lay like a fortress inside the expanse of its car park.

'You didn't take much persuading,' she said suddenly, still gazing out the window on her side.

'No,' I said.

'You're a good-looking boy.'

Boy?

I didn't reply.

She put her hand to my crotch. Immediately, I was rock-hard.

'Soon be there,' she whispered.

We went through a big junction, and moments later down a narrow street with a brick wall running along one side. At the bottom end, a church reached into the murk. We turned left, continued up a hill and then swung onto one of those typical English streets of terraced houses.

'Just behind the car there'll be fine,' she said to the driver.

'Right you are,' he said.

I got out while she paid, and stood looking at the house, brickwork blackened by soot and age. A crack in the glass pane of the door. Tiny front garden, overgrown, a discarded door leaned against the outer wall, a stack of bricks in the corner.

She went up the front step and let us in. I followed her.

'Top floor,' she said in a low voice.

We climbed the stairs and she turned her key in the door. There was a dark red velvet settee, an untidy desk. The black-painted walls of the room inside were taken up by two bookshelf units and two big film posters.

Blow-Up and *A Clockwork Orange*.

She took her coat off and dropped it over a chair. She had rather short legs, I noticed, and a long back. But I was up for it now, and put my arms around her.

'Wait,' she said, extricating herself and turning to the stereo, where she put a record on. A little pop of sound, then surface noise came from the speakers by the opposite wall, before the room filled with intense piano music and she went through into the next room, a small kitchen. She reached onto her toes and took something from a cupboard, returning with a little packet of silver foil in her hand, and sat down on the settee.

'Aren't you going to take your coat off?' she said as she unwrapped a small lump of hash.

I did as she said and dropped my coat on top of hers. She turned the lump a few times in the flame of a lighter. The piano kept repeating the same theme. I went over and looked at the cover. Philip Glass.

'I thought photographers always carried a camera with them,' she said.

'That's a cliché.'

'Is it?'

She teased some strands of tobacco into a cigarette paper and crumbled in some hash.

'There's as many different ways of being a photographer as there are photographs.'

'Come and sit down,' she said, and lit the spliff. She held in the smoke before exhaling with a little splutter, then handed it to me where I was standing.

I took a toke and handed it back to her. The sweet, rather cloying smell began to fill the room.

'What do you want with me, anyway?' I said.

'I want to have sex with you, of course,' she replied, and returned my gaze. 'That's why you're here too, isn't it?'

'What are you sitting there for, then?'

'My, aren't we impatient!'

She smiled, put the spliff down in the ashtray and stepped up to me. Again, she moved her hand over my crotch.

'You *are* a big boy,' she said. 'Come on, you can do anything you want with me.'

I disliked her intensely, but I wanted her too, and so I followed her into the bedroom. A narrow bed was pushed up against one wall, a small table piled up with books next to it, a chair with a heap of clothes on top. It was a small room. Clothes on the floor, too.

She took her jumper off and then stood in a black bra, white skin luminescent in the dim light, and shimmied out of her skirt. When at last she was naked, she lay down on the bed, facing upwards, and spread her legs. I pulled off my underpants and got on top of her, opening my mouth to hers, thrusting my hips as I struggled to penetrate her.

'Relax, there's no hurry,' she said. 'Lick me.'

I went down on her. She was smooth, and quickly soaking wet, moaning. I felt like a dog, accepting the role only because I was so turned on and knew I'd soon be inside her.

'Take me now,' she breathed.

Again, I got on top of her. Her cowish eyes stared at me. She took my hand and curled it around her throat.

'Squeeze,' she said. 'Hard.'

'Seriously?'

She closed her eyes and tossed her head to one side.

'Just do it.'

I gripped her throat and eased my cock into her. She gasped. I relaxed my grip.

'Harder,' she whispered.

I squeezed again, tighter now, at the same time as I was thrusting. Her breathing became wheezy, then a throaty rattle, and when she beat her fist into my back a couple of times I let go. She gasped for breath, and I came.

Panting, I flopped onto my back beside her. Then she began kissing me all over. Cheeks, mouth, throat, chest.

What sort of a madhouse was this?

'That was fantastic,' she said softly.

I sat up and plucked my underpants from among the scattered garments on the floor.

'You will stay, won't you?'

I shook my head.

'I've got to get home.'

She said nothing. I felt her eyes on me. Then she got up, and dressed.

'I'll see you home.'

'No,' I said.

'You don't know the way.'

'Yes, I do.'

In the other room, the stylus clicked in the run-out grooves as the record turned and turned. She saw me to the door. Put her arms around me. I wasn't going to see her again, so I did as she wanted, and we kissed. She smiled and did not close the door after I stepped out, but stood with both hands clutched around it, watching me until I was out of sight. Not before I reached the landing below did I hear it click shut.

The flat was freezing. As I was too: the air outside was raw, my coat too flimsy. After closing the windows I tucked myself under the duvet on the bed settee with all my clothes on, and fell asleep in an instant.

The first thing in my head when I woke up was that I had to get away. My creativity was chained here, and without it I had nothing.

I could tell from the light that it was already well into the day. I got up, realising that I didn't have to get dressed, which at least was something. I put the kettle on for some tea, made some toast, and boiled an egg, stared out into the street below, which lay in a grimy grey light, bounded by rows of faintly glowing windows.

Maybe I could go off to some war or other like he'd suggested. It would probably be a more beneficial learning experience than the one I was getting at that stupid art school.

I opened the fridge to get the milk, immediately seeing the pot with the cat in it, which for some incomprehensible reason I hadn't noticed when I'd got the breakfast things out just before.

Leaving would be giving up, wouldn't it?

I wasn't the sort to give up. I was the sort who stayed and stuck it out.

I poured some milk into my tea, placed a slice of cured ham on each of the two pieces of toast, added a smear of mustard and sat down at the table. I was going to see this project through. I was going to boil the flesh away from that bloody cat and photograph the skeleton. I was going to take pictures of scaffolding, antlers, crabs, leafless trees and fleshless fish, exactly as I'd visualised. I was going to finish *Vertigo* as well, and put together the Christmas Eve series. I wasn't going to give a toss about what other people said, I was going to do what *I* wanted.

Go back to the school as if nothing had happened, as soon as Figueroa had left. I could tell George I'd been a bit depressed. It was the kind of language they understood and accepted.

Yes, it was a good plan. Continue school, continue my work.

Continue fucking Vivian.

Did I want that?

If it was going to be like it was last night, then yes. There was something there that I'd liked. Not the end, but the rest of it.

I rinsed the crumbs off the plate and put it in the rack next to the sink. The thought of her on the bed there in the half-light actually got me going again. I didn't want to go out with her and be seen with her, and the way she'd started kissing me wasn't a good sign, but it wouldn't be impossible to just go on having her in her room as we'd already done.

I put the things back in the fridge and then took out the pot. I'd bought a set of kitchen knives when I first moved in, they'd barely been used since, if at all, so they should be sharp enough, I reckoned, and removed the lid. I lifted out the cat and laid it out on the chopping board on the worktop. The fur was matted and soggy, the teeth visible, white and hard against what was soft and black.

Gloves would be a good idea?

I opened the cupboard under the sink and found the packet of rubber gloves, likewise purchased on moving in, likewise unused.

It felt good to grip the knife with such a gloved hand. Exact, in a way. Efficient. No doubt it was the same feeling a surgeon had. My other hand positioned the cat. The best way of going about it, perhaps, would be to slit open the belly first, as with a fish. Starting at the behind, then.

I lifted the tail, parted the legs and inserted the point of the knife into the anus. It slid in with ease, so the long boil had obviously had some effect. I proceeded to slit, small incisions along the length of the belly. A pungent, repulsive smell leaked slowly into the air, though in contrast to the boiling phase it was only local and it helped to breathe through my mouth.

I'd been thinking it would be possible to simply peel the skin away from the line of incision, that the flesh would come away with it, but that wasn't the case. Everything was stuck fast. I inserted the knife to try and slice the skin and meat apart, but soon realised that it was no use, it would take hours to expose the skeleton like that, and I'd still have to boil it some more anyway, so I decided I might as well put it back in the pot. If four hours wasn't enough, I'd give it twenty-four instead — surely the skeleton would then at last be revealed, white and hard and gleaming, in its mush of flesh, fur and innards?

I filled the pot to the brim, covering the carcass, and put it on the hob. Opening the windows, I then waited until it came to the boil, turned down the heat, put my coat on, and my camera into my rucksack, and carried the bike down the stairs.

I had no idea where to go or what to do, but got on the bike and set off. A light drizzle, barely more than moisture, filled the air. The river ran grey and lifeless past the docks. The grass growing up between the buildings was flat and bleached, the scrub a greyish variation on green, the leafless trees black as tar from a distance, at closer quarters a stony brown. There wasn't much point in taking colour photographs in this city, I thought. Or actually, maybe there was! Greens verged on greys, yellows verged on white, bricks, mortar and concrete always tinged with red and yellow, regardless of wear and grime.

Reaching Greenwich, I wheeled the bike through the park, up the hill, past the observatory, where I paused and gazed for a moment, for this was the very zero point of the Empire itself, the hub from which everything radiated — or perhaps rather on which everything converged? Converged, yes! The threads of time were reeled in here, and the threads too of the earth, and of the arching firmament above. All held in a single hand.

At the top, I got on the bike again, pedalling among dog-walkers and day-trippers, emerging onto the great heath where schoolchildren were playing football and some nerds were flying kites, then onwards through the village to swing right at the next summit and fly down the hills towards Lewisham. Instead of taking the shortest way home from there, I followed the route that went through Peckham, where twenty minutes later I sat down with a coffee at a small cafe. Inspired by an old guy in his fifties with a rugged, nicotine-furrowed face who sat smoking, I dug out my own cigarettes and lit one up, and the thought that I could become a smoker caused my soul to flare and glow. I could be whatever I wanted, do whatever I wished.

I hadn't planned to, but the thought occurred to me that since I was in the area I could pop round to Hans's garage. I had no idea how he felt about people turning up unannounced, I'd just have to see. Weren't we friends of a kind now?

I leaned the bike against the outer wall and knocked on the green metal door we'd used the last time I'd been here. No one came. I knocked again, and my eyes wandered as I waited. The idea I'd had about photographing in colour wasn't bad at all. Everything around me was damp and as if drained of colour, leaving behind only suggestions that bordered on greys, faint embers in a soft and rainy light.

If he was out in the back room, he might not hear if anyone was knocking.

I wheeled the bike round and peered through a window.

There he was, munching an apple while staring at something I couldn't see.

I tapped on the pane and he gave a start, then came up and looked out. Discovering it was me, he pointed me back towards the door on which I'd knocked. But he didn't smile. Probably didn't want to be bothered.

He was already standing in the open doorway waiting when I came back round.

'I'm not disturbing, I hope?' I said.

'No, not at all. Come in.'

It sounded a bit half-hearted, and I decided to make it as short a visit as possible. I could hardly leave straight away.

I took the bike inside as before. Loud music filtered from the back room.

'Do you want a drink?' he said. 'Coffee?'

'Only if you're having.'

He nodded, ambled away into his studio and emerged with a Thermos and two mugs, the latter he then took with him into the toilet, presumably to rinse them at the sink.

'Milk?' he said when he came back, putting them down on the table and then filling them with coffee.

'Not for me, thanks.'

'A good thing too, because I haven't got any. Have a seat.'

He dropped down onto the sofa as he spoke, then sat with his mug held in front of him.

'Vivian rang me this morning. You met her last night. The dark-haired one who's putting on the Faust production.'

'Oh?'

'She wanted to know if you'd agree to take the photos for the programme, if she asked.'

'How come she asked you and not me?'

'Because she hasn't got your number and doesn't know where you live, I assume. I don't either, as it happens, so I was wondering how I was going to get in touch with you about it. And the next minute here you are! Which means you're going to say yes, obviously? A twist of fate like that would be meaningless otherwise.'

'Can I think about it?'

'If you give me your phone number, you can.'

Normally, I'd have agreed without hesitation. It was an assignment, and art-related at that. Collaborating with a London theatre company would look good on my CV. But her reasons for asking weren't artistically motivated. She was clearly interested in me and wanted to cement our association. I envisaged myself having to go out with her, to dinners and parties, thereby becoming inextricably bound up with her in the eyes of others.

'What sort of theatre is it?' I asked. 'Are they established?'

'The company itself has been going for ten years. But they're very production-based, so it's almost like they're starting from scratch every time. A lot of young people involved, often straight out of drama school. They don't have a theatre space of their own, but hire a venue for each production. They do have a permanent rehearsal space, though, in Greenwich. Maybe you should go over there? Get a better idea of what's going on.'

'Maybe I should.'

'They did the *Oresteia* last year. One of the best things I've ever seen, to be honest. For what it's worth, if it was me who'd just been given the chance to work with them, I'd jump at it.'

'How long has Vivian been involved?'

'The *Oresteia* was the first thing she did. As in, ever. It was impressive. *She* is impressive.'

'What about that other woman?'

'Which one?'

'From last night.'

'Oh, you mean Daniella! No, she's not quite as impressive. She's very good, though. Why, did you like her?'

He smiled.

'I didn't get much of an impression of anyone really.'

'If you say so,' he said, and smiled again, then got to his feet. 'Do you want to see what I'm doing at the moment?'

'Yes, all right.'

I went with him into the back room. Everything that had cluttered the floor the last time I'd been there was now gone. Instead, the space was almost entirely taken up by a low cement platform that was dissected by a meandering, water-filled gutter. Hundreds of little building blocks were assembled in rows on either side, as if to form channels or compartments. Here and there, a kind of pennant stuck up, with two letters of the alphabet on each.

'Nice, don't you think?' he said. 'It's nowhere near finished, though.'

'What is it?'

'Well, if I say the water there is the Thames, you can probably guess the rest.'

'A model of London?'

'A representation, yes.'

'And the letters?'

'Have a guess.'

'Places?'

'No.'

'People?'

'Correct. So KM, for example, is Karl Marx. CD is Charles Darwin. SF is Sigmund Freud, of course. All placed in locations the figure in question is known to be associated with.'

'WS would be William Shakespeare, then?'

'Right. And CM is Marlowe.'

'What about CA?'

'Cornelius Agrippa.'

'Who?'

'The man who the Faust legends were based on. Author of a three-volume work entitled *De Occulta Philosophia*. He came to London on several occasions. GB is Giordano Bruno, who was burned at the stake for heresy. He was here too. ES is Emanuel Swedenborg. IN is Isaac Newton, but you probably guessed that already.'

'VW, that would be Volkswagen, right?'

'Ha ha. Virginia Woolf, the suicide. She needs to be here as well.'

'And that one over there?' I said, pointing a finger. 'AC?'

'Aleister Crowley. He hated London, but lived here most of his life.'

'The Devil worshipper?'

'No less.'

We stood surveying the model for a long moment or two. It was all a bit pathetic, little wooden building blocks on a bare cement base. It looked nothing like London.

'What's the idea, then?' I said eventually.

'Ah, the idea!' he almost barked. 'There are so many it makes me dizzy! Do you remember I said that ideas have got to have some form of physical expression? If they don't, they don't exist, or else have been lost. Yes? This applies to communism, evolutionary theory, your photographs, unicorns — anything we can think of. They have to be somewhere, and they have to possess some physical form.'

'I remember you saying, yes.'

'But they have to *come* from somewhere, too. So that's what I'm doing. I'm looking for the interface, the point at which the interaction between the two vital forms, the abstract and the concrete, becomes visible.'

'And you see that in these building blocks?'

'You're not exactly a dream audience, are you? Like I said, it's not finished yet. The river's got to be running, for a start. There'll be bridges, too. The familiar landmark buildings need to be marked — St Paul's Cathedral, Westminster Abbey, the Tower and what have you. I'm going to use moss for the parks, and straw for the riverbanks, I reckon. And I'll need more names.'

'Then what?'

'How do you mean?'

'What are you going to do with it? Exhibit it somewhere?'

'I doubt it. You never know, though.'

I only suggested it to keep him happy. No one was ever going to exhibit something like that.

'Another thing I've been thinking about that could be interesting here is that the spaces between the landmarks form particular patterns. And likewise, that the dimensions — the distance between the Tower and St Paul's, for instance — carry certain numeric values. It might be overdoing things. But it's relevant nonetheless. The city itself is a network of abstract symbols.'

'What sort of symbols?'

'Seek and ye shall find. But it's a fact that one of the City's primary architects following the Great Fire in 1666 was unusually interested in Kabbalah. Or at least a Christian variant of it. So the dimensions of Solomon's Temple as given in the Bible were transposed into the City's new layout. That's a fact. In passing, I mention here that Newton himself employed the same figures in calculating the return of Christ, which he concluded would occur in 1948.'

'He was wrong, then.'

'Yes. If he'd been right, Jesus would be thirty-eight today and would surely have made himself known by now. But I've been thinking maybe Newton got his figures wrong and meant 1984 instead. In which case there's still a chance he was right.'

'That Jesus came back and is now two years old?'

'That's right, yes.'

'Well, anything's possible, I suppose. If you believe in God.'

He threw up his arms.

'What other explanation would there be?'

'Evolution. The laws of nature.'

'You don't believe that, do you?'

'What is this, Upsidedownland?'

'How old are you, Kristian?'

'Twenty. But age has nothing to do with it. If it did, I ought to be asking you.'

'I'll give you another ten years living the mystery — maybe then you'll open your eyes.'

'What mystery?'

'Life, of course.'

He gave me a wink, and smiled.

'But now I want you to go. It's two o'clock and I've hardly done a thing all day.'

Now I want you to go — what sort of a person said that to their visitors? He was patronising, he was. I supposed it was the ten extra years that made him think it was all right. I might have accepted it if he'd actually ever achieved anything, if he'd made any kind of name for himself, but when the only thing he had to show was a crap model of London with some names stuck on, there was no way he could rank higher than me. If anything, *he* should have been learning from *me*.

I lugged the bike up the stairs again, leaned it up against the wall and went over to the cooker to inspect the pot. The cat looked the same as before, except that the meat under the fur had now turned grey and thready along the incision I'd made. I put some more water in, waited until it came to the boil, then turned the heat down and went back out — it was simply too cold to stay in with the windows open. I bought the *NME* from the newsagent's at the station and flicked through it on the train into central London. The photography was unimaginative: band members in back alleys, at the beach or in the park, or else live on-stage. It was even worse when they actually tried something different and had them lying in a heap on the floor or larking about climbing trees — the limitations of the genre only became more obvious then, it was as if all the pictures said was that the framework for what they were doing was too restrictive.

It was an interesting problem. How was music to be photographed? Or how was the *experience* of music to be photographed? Looking at someone dancing wasn't the same as dancing itself.

Oh! It always came down to that. Photographing a phenomenon wasn't enough — the picture had to be a phenomenon in itself.

I read on through the Tube on the way to Notting Hill. The plan was to walk up to Rough Trade from there and buy myself two LPs. I hadn't enough money to waste it on something ill-considered that turned out to be rubbish, but then I couldn't trust the *NME* unconditionally either. How often did they hype a band who could hardly play and at best had one decent song in them? They feathered their own nest, banged their own drum. Once in a while, though, they got it right. Like with the Smiths, when their first couple of singles came out. I bought the debut album then, from Platehjørnet. Now *there* was an album that wasn't just hype.

One of the ear-splitting screeches that every so often somehow developed in the tunnels, as the Tube trains rattled along through the underground, built now into a crescendo and for a few seconds became almost unbearable. A little boy of maybe six pressed his hands to his ears a few seats away. And although it then died away, silence did not replace it — I became even more aware of the train's everyday rattle and clatter, the rushes of noise that filled the carriage. No one spoke, no one looked at each other, everyone sat or stood in their own little worlds.

I stared at my reflection in the window across the carriage. *He* stared back from his own dimension, surrounded by strangers.

Another screech resounded through the tunnel. A moment later, the train slowed down and emerged into the station. I folded my paper and stepped out onto the platform, following the mass of people, the moving wall of flesh, to the stairs, through the walkways, up the long, plunging escalators. The daylight outside was bewildering — I always expected darkness when coming up out of the ground, as if darkness was the world's natural state.

What if I stood there by the staircase and photographed every person who emerged from below? Each with their own inner darkness, vast to them, yet instantly dwindling, emptying itself into the light to become little more than a thimble of water in the sea.

Inner Darkness, Outer Light, the series could be called.

I couldn't remember exactly where the record shop was, but I was fairly sure of the direction and now made my way with the music paper under my arm and an increasing craving for a cigarette. Or was it a beer I wanted?

I'd made up my mind to buy the Cure's latest, and one more I hadn't decided on yet. I actually thought I'd given up on the Cure, they'd become so commercial, and with their latest offering, *The Head on the Door*, they'd basically turned into a normal pop band. But if I balanced it out with something more hardcore, I'd just about get away with it.

I stopped and lit a cigarette.

The smartest thing would be to accept Vivian's offer. It was a proper assignment. Which meant it was business. She'd have no right to expect us to be going out with each other just because she'd given me a job.

Was it all that kissing that had got me going again?

It was weird, though. First cool and aloof, then bloody strangulation — and *then*, a thousand kisses.

I started walking again, glancing sideways as I went, at the shop windows that now poured out their light into the beginning dusk to resemble display cabinets, or compartments on a train.

It made me remember something about Dad. We were on holiday in the car and had stopped off in Flensburg on the way south, we'd booked a hotel for the night, but Dad couldn't find it. We went looking on foot and came upon a street where half-naked women sat in all the windows. Dad became strange, I sensed it immediately, the way he stared straight ahead and briskly walked on. What is it, Dad? I said. Nothing, he replied. Why are all those ladies sitting in the windows? They live there, I suppose. Why haven't they got any clothes on? Perhaps it's too hot inside. Not until some years later did it occur to me what sort of street it had been.

Now, I saw the record shop a bit further on. There were so many LP covers on display in the window that you could hardly see in. I dropped my fag end onto the ground and pushed open the door. It was exactly the sort of place for me. The walls were papered with posters and record covers, LPs and singles were piled up everywhere, as if they were growing them. A song I knew was blasting out from the speakers, but although it was familiar I couldn't for the life of me remember what it was. All I knew was that it was something I *really* liked. I avoided checking the cover I knew would be prominently placed in front of the turntable — that would be cheating. Began flipping through the racks while humming along in my mind, straining to recall the title. Then, a familiar vocal came in, not song, but expelled sounds, a singular modulation I knew only too well, and there it was: the voice was Mark E. Smith's, the band of course was the Fall, the song 'L.A.'!

Having perused from A to Z, I stood with six LPs in my hands. The Cure, as intended, the latest by Hüsker Dü and Sonic Youth, an early Wire album, the Jesus and Mary Chain's *Psychocandy*, which I hadn't yet heard, only read about, but apparently it was brilliant, the next big thing, and the second album by the Chameleons.

I couldn't buy all six, even though I wanted to. With Mum and Dad now out of the picture, all I had was my grant, which wasn't nearly generous enough to fund such extravagance.

It was in America things were happening at the moment, a shift that had started a couple of years back, but the slew of bands everyone was liking now were all embracing elements of country, and while neither Sonic Youth nor Hüsker Dü could be accused of that, I nevertheless put them back in the rack. And since I was after something new, Wire and the Chameleons went the same way.

The assistant, standing at first with his back turned, faced me as I put the two LPs down on the counter. He looked to be around my age, spotty and bespectacled, wearing a black woolly hat and black long-sleeved T-shirt, jeans and braces. There was something vaguely unsettling about him. Then, when he opened his mouth to say how immense *Psychocandy* was, it fell into place: *he* was a *she*. The lightness of voice was enough for the round cheeks and soft gaze to suddenly make sense.

It felt provoking, like when someone lies to your face. At the same time, I felt sorry for her. The confusion she presumably felt couldn't have been good.

'I hope you're right,' I said.

'I am, trust me,' she said, entering the amount into the till.

'Can I have two sleeves as well?'

'Sure. Do you want me to pop the records in them?'

'No, it's all right, I'll do it myself.'

I pulled my wallet out of my back pocket and paid the twelve quid I'd now spent. She dropped the records into a carrier bag. Smiled as she handed them over the counter, stopped smiling the second I took the bag from her hand, then turned away and went back to whatever it was she'd been doing. I felt put out by it — it seemed to me she ought to be grateful I hadn't expressed disgust.

Outside, I decided to walk to the railway station rather than take the Tube. The longer it took to get home, the better.

The people in the streets up here looked different from where I lived. It wasn't just the clothes — furs, suits and nice overcoats — it was the faces too, they were softer, not as marked, as if those who lived around here were softer inside too, because they had money. But in order to get money you had to be hard, not soft. Hardness within was in other words obscured; only hardness from without left marks.

That was a good idea too. I could photograph poor people and rich people in the same clothes. In a studio. Everything as neutral as possible, the story would be in the faces.

Not bad. Not bad at all.

Figueroa could go to hell. What did he know about what I was capable of?

Anyone could take good pictures in war. He'd said so himself.

What if life was a war? With victors and vanquished? Beseiged and beseigers?

The thought wouldn't have occurred to him. But it did to me. Reality had to be held up to view in order for people to see it.

He'd be forgotten in twenty years. Not that he was that well known now. When I passed him on my way up, he'd already be on the floor — and I was going to kick him.

Arrogant twat.

Instead of going towards Marylebone, then on through Soho to Charing Cross, I cut down through Hyde Park to Chelsea. From there I could follow the river. I liked the melancholy in the lights reflecting from the water's darkness, but also that the river was so inconceivably dirty, the way it ran, grey as death, through the city.

I came across a bookshop and went inside. I was assuming what Vivian was offering would be paid work, meaning I could perhaps afford to spend a bit anyway. I found a copy of *Doctor Faustus* and a biography of Marlowe, and bought them both. I scanned the shelves for some of the names Hans had mentioned too. Agrippa wasn't there, and neither was Swedenborg, but they did have some Aleister Crowley. I skimmed a title called *The Book of the Law*. It looked like numerology. *I am Nuit, and my word is six and fifty*, I read. *Divide, add, multiply, and understand.* Elsewhere, *My number is 11.* What was it supposed to mean? Other statements were more transparent: *I am alone; there is no God where I am,* I noted. It brought to mind a sentence I remembered from philosophy lessons at gymnas. Was it the Epicureans or the Stoics? Whoever it was, they'd been trying to cast death in a more innocuous light. Where I am, death is not, and where death is, I am not.

Same thing in a way.

But I couldn't actually *buy* a book like that! How would it make me look? Have you seen Kristian lately? No, he's sat in his bedsit reading Aleister Crowley night and day. Instead, I picked out a biography of the man, which I thought might complement *Faustus*. I'd never probed into Crowley before, had never even contemplated it — all I knew about him was what now and then cropped up in the music papers. A teacher at school had once warned us about what he called *devil music*. If we played certain records backwards, he told us, we'd hear satanic messages. What's more, these messages would work even if we played the records normally and didn't actually hear what they said. He used the word *brainwashing*, I remembered. AC/DC were on his list, not just because they sang about a 'Highway to Hell', but also because the band name itself was slang for bisexual, as he told us, practically frothing at the mouth.

It had left an impression, what he'd told us back then. It took on much the same aura as heroin, which too seemed to us to be something deeply mysterious, removed from our lives and yet life-threatening.

Pettersen, his name was. I wished he could have seen me now, in a London bookshop with a biography of Aleister Crowley in my hand. The thought brought a smirk to my face.

It was still only half six when I got back to Deptford. I stopped by the flat to drop off the records and the books and top the pot up with water before going down the pub to while away the time until bed.

The barman put a pint of Red Stripe down on the counter in front of me as soon as I approached the bar. He was buttering me up, giving me the usual.

'Pint of Guinness, please,' I said.

He raised his eyebrows. Without a word, he poured the lager out into the sink, put the dirty glass aside and pulled me a Guinness. That'd teach him not to treat me like we were old friends, I reckoned, and took my pint over to the table where I'd sat on my own the night before.

The bitter taste of the stout on my tongue immediately gave me the urge to get hammered. I swallowed a couple of mouthfuls, savouring the sensation — my whole organism seemed almost to unfold, as if all day it had been denied its true potential. It was always the same after I'd been drinking the night before: the high somehow sat deeper and took on a golden tinge.

That was another thing we'd been warned about: drinking alone, and drinking the next day, too. No one actually said so, as far as I remembered, but still it was as if chiselled in stone inside me: The first commandment, Thou shalt not become an alcoholic. The second, Thou shalt not become a heroin addict. The third, Thou shalt not become a satanist. Apart from that, you can do as you like.

Or rather, it wasn't becoming a satanist as such that Pettersen and his ilk had been worried about. No, I supposed it was more the notion of the Devil exerting his influence on our impressionable young minds. In case, no doubt, we all of a sudden stopped listening to what they were telling us and started doing what we wanted instead.

What did they think we were going to do? Start telling lies? Stealing? Killing each other?

Two elderly women together with two elderly men, all four seedy-looking and worse the wear for alcohol, if their loud voices were anything to go by, now occupied the table next to mine. The women smoked rollies and their laughter was hoarse and joyless. Both were wearing jeans — I couldn't abide it, old women in jeans. It was no use wasting your energy on things you couldn't change, wasn't that what the Stoics had said? Still, it filled me with loathing to see them sitting there in their youthful denim, wheezing like a pair of sick birds, drinking like fish.

I got up and went to the bar for another pint. This time, I went back onto the Red Stripe just to keep him on his toes. He didn't bat an eyelid, but pulled the pint, took the money and then served the next customer.

I was nicely aglow by the time I'd finished that one, and went up for another. Just as I sat down again, Hans came in through the door. And after Hans, Vivian.

They saw me straight away and came over.

'I thought we'd find you here,' Hans said. 'I tried phoning, but you weren't in, so it was a giveaway. You drink too much, don't you?'

He laughed. I glanced at Vivian, who hadn't acknowledged me yet, but wasn't demonstratively looking the other way either. All in black, same as yesterday.

'That was what the Lord said to Swedenborg, by the way, the first time He appeared before him. Well, not exactly. You eat too much, was what He said. It was Swedenborg's first vision of Christ. The best, too, if you ask me. Mind if we join you?'

'No, course not.'

He turned to Vivian.

'What do you fancy? Beer?'

'Maybe a glass of red.'

He ambled off to the bar. She looked at me without speaking. Something told me the next few minutes would be decisive. That what happened now would determine what happened later.

I had no idea what she was thinking, where she was at, what the night before meant to her.

My mind had made her more attractive than she was, that much was obvious. So from that perspective, her being so stand-offish was neither here nor there. Nevertheless, it riled me.

'I'd be happy to take those pictures for you,' I said. 'If you'd like me to.'

'That was Hans's idea. I'm not sure if it's a very good one.'

'Why not?'

'I haven't seen your work.'

'Oh, OK.'

I picked up my beer, leaned back and drank a mouthful.

Not mentioning what had happened made it seem like it hadn't. It provoked me, but at the same time it was OK given that I didn't want to start seeing her. All the same, I'd have felt better about it if the decision had come from me.

On the other hand, it was just as much me who wasn't talking about it.

Hans returned and put a glass of red wine down in front of Vivian, then pulled out a chair and sat down still clutching his pint.

'Cheers, my friends,' he said. 'And may good fortune accompany us on all life's paths.'

We chinked our glasses together.

'Now, have you come to an agreement yet?' he said, putting his beer down with a little clunk as his eyes queried first me, then Vivian. I looked away, straight into the gaze of one of the elderly women at the next table. She'd been sitting staring at me, and now smiled.

'Vivian's not sure I'm good enough,' I said.

'How about making it provisory?' Hans said. 'If you like the way he starts out, you let him go ahead. If not, you don't.'

'I won't do it if there's going to be a trial period,' I said.

'I didn't say you weren't good enough,' Vivian said. 'All I said was I haven't seen your work yet.'

'Well, we can soon sort that out,' said Hans.

'So you want me to audition? I'm not sure I can agree to that.'

'Come on, mate. You're a blank page. It's perfectly reasonable if she'd like to see what you do first. After that, you take the photos. It's no big deal.'

I held my hands up in a shrug.

'It's not like I asked for the work. It's not my doing.'

I stood up, drained what was left in my glass and put it back down on the table.

'I can't be bothered with this,' I said. 'See you around.'

As soon as I got outside I started wondering if I hadn't overreacted. I lingered a few seconds in case one of them decided to come after me, but when it didn't happen I headed home. It was only right to maintain a measure of professional pride, even if as yet I'd only photographed for the local paper back home. Hans was just trying to be nice, I realised that, whereas Vivian's motives were harder to work out. Why had she come to the pub, if she didn't want me to take the pictures?

Sod it. I hadn't liked sitting there with them anyway.

It was as cold inside the flat as it was out. I switched the cooker off, shut the windows and got under the duvet with my clothes still on. When the phone began to ring shortly afterwards, I let it. It would be Hans, wanting to smooth things over. It rang ten times, then stopped. Then it rang again, and again I let it. If it rings again after this, I'll answer it, I told myself. The tenacity he'd be demonstrating would be hard to ignore. And surely he'd be offering an apology? Or maybe it was Vivian, not Hans. Maybe she'd thought better of it and decided not to play games with me any more.

For a few minutes it was quiet, but when it rang again I got up, went over and picked up the receiver.

'Hello?' I said.

'Hello, Kristian. It's Mum.'

I hung up.

I thought the letter would be the last I heard from them. Clearly though, she wasn't finished yet. What was it she hadn't understood? Did she think I hadn't a shred of willpower in me?

Crossing the floor to go back to bed, I stopped and spun round, and pulled the little plug out of the wall.

I was a bit down when I woke again. Without school, it felt like there wasn't a lot to get up for. It didn't help much that almost the first thing I clapped eyes on almost was the big pot on top of the cooker. Why did *that* have to be my project? Next week I'd go back and everything would be like it was before. The school would lead me on to something big, the cat's skeleton to something small, or maybe nothing at all — it was a little step along the way, but not insignificant. The main thing was to give it all I'd got — what lay ahead, bigger and better or not, depended on here and now.

And yet the thought didn't exactly fill me with delight and enthusiasm.

How long did it have to boil before the flesh and the skin came away? A week? A month?

Whatever, I wasn't going to give up until it happened.

I supposed I ought to have a shower. I hadn't had a good wash in days, and in the interim I'd had sex, so I probably wasn't smelling that good down below.

A shower, yes.

I found some clean clothes and went downstairs into the basement, which, mid-morning, was deserted. Afterwards, I found I was in better mood — maybe that was all it took. Back upstairs, I put the new Cure album on and sat looking through the books I'd bought. The first track was good. The drum intro promised something epic, while the instrumental part that followed was almost frivolous, certainly for the Cure, but then the vocals came in and the epic quality turned into something intimate and close, and frivolity became darkness.

I slotted the books onto the shelf and went over to the kitchen area, where I put on the yellow rubber gloves, lifted the cat from the pot and laid it out on the chopping board. It was more amenable now, the knife went more easily through the meat and I was able to remove large chunks at a time. But the photograph I was after, I soon realised, of the clean, blanched skeleton, was still a long way off — sinews and tendons and lumps of fur clung as yet to the bones, and then there were the innards to contend with. Cleaning the skull was going to be a terrible faff. The whole endeavour was really getting me down. I dropped the soft clods I'd cut away into the bin and wondered if I should just give up, when suddenly it occurred to me that I didn't *need* a clean skeleton. Why hadn't I thought of it before? It was nature I wanted to photograph, not something purified and sterile! Frameworks. What did it matter if the picture took in meat and guts, blood and fur? It didn't matter at all! In fact, it would only be the more authentic for it, so much closer to reality. I could take the photos *now* — photograph the carcass as it was lying there in front of me, on the chopping board!

The light was even good!

I pulled off the gloves and tossed them in the bin, fetched the camera, put in a new roll of film, metered the light, adjusted the aperture, and began snapping away. Some I took from above, standing on a chair, framing the composition in a variety of ways, now simply the cat on the chopping board, now including the worktop; some I took from the side, with and without zoom; some widened the perspective to take in the window and the sink. I'd decided I was getting rid of the carcass today, as soon as I was finished; it meant this was my only chance, and so I used up the whole roll, put in another, and used that one up too.

Before clearing everything away, I documented the carnage: the boiled animal in the bin; the knotted bin bag, viewed both in isolation and as an element of the room; the staircase; the bins outside, where the carcass was laid to rest. At last, at last I was rid of it.

So much work, and all for just a photograph!

They couldn't fault me for effort, that was for certain.

The only darkroom to which I had access was the one at the school. I rang George and told him I'd been down with depression and hadn't been able to attend teaching, hadn't been able even to get out of my bed. I told him too — reckoning it would be the first thing that came into his mind — that it had nothing to do with Figueroa's critique of my work. Critique was a vital part of our training, I underlined, and I hadn't the slightest objection to it. He understood what I was saying and told me he was glad I was feeling better and looked forward to seeing me back on Monday.

Afterwards, I wondered if it had been such a good idea to mention the crit session — I couldn't help thinking how insisting on something not being the case would often have the opposite effect and make people think it *was* the case. But it didn't really matter what he decided to believe — I had no influence on it one way or the other. The important thing was to get back to school.

I heard from neither Vivian nor Hans that week, so I assumed I'd offended them by getting up and leaving so abruptly like that. I didn't care about Vivian, she didn't matter, but it disappointed me that Hans could be so touchy. Still, I reckoned he'd come round soon enough.

Our first year at the school was focused very much on technique, with courses in street photography, studio work and portraiture. Scattered in between were various workshops, excursions and lectures by guesting professionals. During the second year, we were expected to work more independently on our own projects with a view to a final exhibition. The practicalities of working as a professional photographer would also be drawn in — we'd be networking with gallerists, curators, picture editors from some of the major fashion magazines. We would also be going on a field trip to New York for a week. What we did there would be up to us, and together we would edit the pictures we took into a book.

But now the next eight weeks were all about the portrait. It wasn't really my cup of tea — portraiture was so restrictive, it allowed so little leeway: basically, you just stood in front of someone and took their picture. Of course, you could play around with it a bit, as many did, ask the subject to put their hand over their eye, for instance, or hold out a strand of hair. You could get them to dress up, or, more adventurously, even bodypaint them. Another tried-and-tested trick was to plonk the person in an unfamiliar setting: dinner-jacketed in Brick Lane, evening-gowned in the woods.

When I returned on the Monday, it was to a two-day lecture on the history of the portrait, given by an art historian. He was particularly interested in a series of sarcophagus paintings found at Faiyum in Egypt, which in his opinion remained unmatched in every respect, even in a modern context; unprecedentedly individual and brimming with the personalities of those whose portraits they featured, he held, but when he showed us a series on the overhead, I immediately saw that the eyes were all painted in the same way and that on the contrary they all resembled each other without exception. Nonetheless, it was interesting, because the people who'd been painted were of course long since dead, and their portraits had been attached in each case to the mummy, so that body and face would live on — at least that was what I assumed was the point.

Would it be feasible to photograph dead people as if they were living? A photograph would only be showing a body, and it would be intact, even if dead.

It would make a brilliant series.

But how would you get hold of the bodies?

No one was going to lend their dead mother to a twenty-year-old photography student, not even for five minutes.

There was something hypocritical about it, wasn't there? Everyone wanted their photo taken, and yet it was deemed unacceptable to photograph the dead, who were no longer people but something else, more comparable to lumps of meat.

The lecturer — somewhere in his thirties, smooth-cheeked and balding, with the beginnings of a paunch, sporting a tweed jacket and exuding all the self-confidence of the Englishman, however awkward or unattractive — turned then to a self-portrait by someone called Dürer, who apparently in his time had broken completely new ground.

'A portrait — *any* portrait — comprises three aspects,' he said. 'The first is the inner aspect, the subject's character or personality — his or her soul, if you like. The second is the outer aspect, the body itself — through which the inner aspect reveals itself. But the third, what would that be?'

He scanned the room for a few seconds. The question was cringingly rhetorical, and since we weren't eight-year-olds, none of us responded.

'The third aspect is the social aspect. The period, the culture to which the subject belongs. You'll see it in the clothes, the hairstyle, the jewellery, but also in the style of painting. And of course, in classical painting at least, in the pose, and the gesture. No one, I venture to claim, has combined these three aspects as compellingly and as credibly as Albrecht Dürer in this self-portrait painted in the year 1500.'

He pressed the remote he'd been holding in his hand and turned towards the slide that appeared on the screen behind him.

Aha.

A guy with long hair and intense eyes staring straight out at the beholder. Clad in a brown coat, there was a hippieish, 1970s aura about him. He could have been the bass player in Jethro Tull. Or rather, not the bass player, no, there was something overbearing and self-satisfied about him — a typical frontman.

'So, here we have it,' the lecturer said. 'The perfect portrait. You sense his presence, yes? Even today, five hundred years on, we get a feeling of this person straight away. There's a smouldering kind of fervour in him, which he's holding back — do we agree? His gaze — outwardly directed and yet reserved at the same time. But what's most interesting about the picture, regardless of how powerfully it conveys the character, the personality, is the social aspect. Dürer has painted himself in fully frontal pose. For a secular portrait, this was unheard of. The frontal pose was for Christ, and no other. Now, look at the positioning of the hand. Here, too, he's quoting, as it were, the iconography of the Christ figure. So if you're thinking this is an honest self-portrait, that he was simply painting what he saw, you need to think again. Dürer had reddish-blond hair. This man has dark brown hair, exactly as Jesus has always been depicted. The artist, then, is identifying himself with Christ and with Christianity — to whom, and to which, in so doing, he paradoxically severs all ties. But he's not presenting himself in the likeness of Christ, he's presenting Christ in his, Dürer's, likeness, thereby making Christ a secular figure. He's elevating the ordinary human and ordinary human life to a higher level. Now, this heralds a new age in the history of our Western civilisation — we could almost refer to it as a new world: the secular epoch we inhabit to this day. For that reason, my friends, this is the first picture of *us*. Not bad going, I'd say, for a single painting. But of course, there's a lot more to Dürer's portrait than that. He's looking at us, yes — but when he was painting the picture he was looking into a mirror, so what we're seeing is his mirror image. We're looking into Dürer's mirror and what we're seeing is another person. What feelings come towards us from that mirror? Are they his? We don't know, and never shall. He painted himself in his own image, yet it is we who give his portrait life, by virtue of our own experiences as individual human beings. And I say *life* meaning quite literally that — even though Dürer himself has been dead nearly five hundred years. The picture is about that, too. Look at the background — it's completely black, and why is that? Because the background is eternity, the timeless void — there's nothing there to connect the image to his own time. The clothing too is rather neutral, wouldn't you say? That's appropriate to mention, I think, in the present company, because photography, of course, is the art form most attached to the moment. Photography is about here and now, is it not? I'd say that applies especially to the photographic portrait. The image halts time. Yet the fun truly starts when time floods — as it does in Dürer's self-portrait.'

He glanced at George, who was seated at the rear of the room with his back against the wall, arms across his chest.

'But perhaps now would be a good time to break for lunch?'

George gave a nod and got to his feet. I went up to him.

'Do you know if the darkroom's free this afternoon, by any chance?'

He shook his head.

'But if you pop by my office after the lecture, we'll book you in.'

I nodded and made my way outside, where Gav, sparrow-like as ever, stood smoking.

'Fascinating stuff,' he said.

'He's obviously never heard of punk,' I said, taking out my own unopened packet, bought from the newsagent's that morning. 'It makes me want to tear something down just listening to him. Smash a window or something.'

Gav looked at me, elbows tucked tightly into his sides.

'Have you started smoking?'

'What does it look like?'

'But why? I mean, why *now*?'

'When are you supposed to start?'

He smiled.

'Sixteen, maybe?'

'The brain's not fully developed then. When you're twenty everything's fallen into place. The decision's properly reasoned then.'

Håkan appeared through the door.

'Have you started smoking?' he said too. 'The more the merrier.'

A riverboat with a long tow of barges drifted slowly past, smoke coiling from its chimney into the still, sun-drenched air.

'Where have you been, anyway? Have you been ill?'

'No, just doing some work on my own, that's all. School gets a bit much for me sometimes.'

It seemed to exhaust what we had to say to each other.

'Simple Minds are playing Wembley on the second,' Håkan said, breaking the silence after a while. 'Anyone fancy going?'

'Not sure I can afford it,' said Gav.

'If it had been five years ago, maybe,' I said. 'I'd rather die than go to a Simple Minds concert now.'

'You're joking, aren't you? The new album's brilliant.'

'If you like prog, I suppose it is.'

'Kristian's a punk at heart – he's given himself away now,' Gav said.

'Ha ha,' I said.

'Some friends of mine are coming over from Sweden just to see them,' Håkan said, as if that vouched for the quality.

'It doesn't surprise me,' I said. 'They're from the land of Abba, so of course they'd like Simple Minds.'

'And what brilliant bands has Norway fostered, if you don't mind me asking?'

'There's a lot of good Norwegian stuff, as it happens.'

'Such as?'

'Garden of Delight. Holy Toy. De Press. Circus Modern. Babij Jar. The Cut. White Lord Jesus. To name but a few.'

'Never heard of them.'

'That's because they're not Abba. They don't come to you, you have to go to them.'

'You're not a punk, Kristian. You're a snob.'

'That's as may be. But at least I'm not Swedish.'

'I think this might be getting a bit internal for me,' said Gav. 'Why don't we get some lunch?'

I spent every evening that week developing the new photographs. I was nervous about the cat on the chopping board — the subject was gone forever now, so if I'd got it wrong that would be it. I stood motionless and watched as blotches of darkness emerged onto the white paper in the tray. How they shaped into a catlike form, which for a few seconds looked as if it had been photographed in the nineteenth century, until light and shade too seeped into place and the picture consolidated itself, as it were, and became — well, pretty damn good.

Oh, it was good. It was very good.

I pegged it onto the drying line, sat down and stared at it.

It was a powerful photograph. Compelling.

Now was a new beginning, I felt, with all my being.

I developed three more copies. Watched with relish the image appear as if out of nowhere. The way the abstract pattern seemed almost to stutter before becoming recognisable, as if it didn't really know where to go, and then realised, made it hard to grasp that there was no will or thought involved. The shadows behaved as if they were alive. It was chemistry, yes, and it was quantum mechanics, yes, atoms and molecules, attraction and repulsion, according to very particular formulas — but how did the atoms know *that* was where they were meant to go? How did the darkness know it was a cat they were fetching up this time?

Somewhere, there was an explanation, and someone too who knew all about it — that was enough for me. I didn't need to know things, as long as everything worked.

It applied generally, that.

I didn't need to know what Vivian was thinking. Or Mum and Dad. It was enough to look at what they did.

How many problems would cease to exist if everyone thought that way? How simple life would be! *Face value*, as they said over here. What you see is what you get.

I reached into the inside pocket of my coat and took out my notebook.

What you see is what you get.

A motto for my first book.

A photographer's mantra, credo, maxim.

Something in me countered:

The earth isn't flat, the sun doesn't rise, colours and sounds don't exist on their own!

But why do we need to know that? To us, the earth is flat. To us, the sun rises in the east and sets in the west. To us, blood is red and the sky is black.

What does it matter if none of these things is *actually* the case?

I resolved to give the matter some more thought at a later date, and returned my attention to the images that were now strung out on the line, studying them one last time before taking them down, placing them in their respective boxes, packing my bag and heading for the Tube.

Although the rush hour had long since passed, the carriages were still filled with people on their way home from work. Office slaves, instantly recognisable in their cheap suits. Narrow-eyed, heads nodding. Another day dead.

Two girls who could only be twins, about sixteen years old, were sitting next to each other a bit further down, in identical pale pink tracksuits, their blonde hair put up like a pair of palm trees. One of them noticed me staring — her eyes met mine for a second before she looked away, and then, just as she did, the other one noticed as well, her eyes likewise latching on to mine before she too averted her gaze. They seemed to be used to people's stares. To being objects of the first thought that entered any man's head — what it would be like to have them both at the same time.

Was there a pair of twins anywhere in world history that had achieved anything momentous? Statistically, at least, there ought to be a few. But no. Churchill had no Churchillian lookalike at his shoulder. The same applied to Napoleon, to van Gogh, Mozart, Plato.

Elvis would be the one who came closest with his stillborn twin brother.

Why was that?

Maybe having each other sufficed, maybe it eliminated the need to go out and make a splash in the world, because they were fine as they were, having someone else just like them.

What would that be like?

Waking up to see your own face beside you. Having breakfast together, slinging your school bags over your shoulders and setting off in the mornings, chatting along the way, or else saying nothing, always together, never alone — but never really being two either.

I looked up and into the gaze of my reflected image in the window.

Keeping the eye contact, I turned my head slightly, as he too turned his.

Yes, it was a bit unsettling. It was me, and yet it *wasn't* me.

An illusion, that too.

The train rattled and rolled through the darkness. I felt an urge to take the photographs from my bag and look at them again, but I couldn't. While no one much cared what others around them were doing — we were all in our own worlds here — and although one day I'd be exhibiting the same photographs, meaning that any one of these people would be able to see them anyway, if they wanted, getting them out here was unthinkable.

Why?

Weren't they finished?

Was *I* not finished?

The train began to brake. I got up and went and stood by the door. Before stepping out, I glanced to see if the twins were looking at me. But they too had risen — I picked out their pale pink tracksuits among the commuters at the next door down.

The train to Deptford was as good as empty, at least the carriage I'd sat in was. Not long before, though, it had probably been packed. There was rubbish all over the floor. Newspapers, plastic cups, chocolate wrappers. A man was slumped in his seat with his feet extending into the aisle, unkempt and grubby-looking, though in a hat and suit. A woman in her thirties, moon-faced and as big as a hippo, occupied the seat opposite him, where she sat with a small handbag on her lap while staring anxiously out of the window — that was what it looked like to me, anyway, perhaps because of the way she kept twitching her head.

A quick look at the photos here wouldn't matter.

I couldn't think anything else but that the cat on the chopping board was a masterpiece. Raw, enigmatic, perfectly poised between life and death. What more could anyone ask of a photograph?

Three hundred years from now, the photographs of our time would have the same aura, the same clout as Rembrandt's paintings had to us today. The lightweight, insignificant ones would have fallen by the wayside, of course, and only the masterpieces would remain. A hundred in all, perhaps. I wasn't deluded enough to think that this one of mine would be among them. But I did think it possible that hindsight one day would mark it out as a door that had suddenly opened for me. Those hundred pictures had to come from somewhere, so why couldn't one of them come from me?

I ambled towards the station exit among a scattering of other passengers, and the train pulled slowly away again. Turning for some reason to watch it go, I noticed a fox further down the platform. It was staring at us, a mangy, skinny specimen. The eyes in its triangular head faintly reflected the lights that glared above it. They seemed full of sorrow, those eyes. Not until it turned and slunk away did I realise it had only three legs. It must have been run over, I thought, as with its hopalong gait it scuttled off along the side of the tracks and then disappeared from sight.

I popped into the supermarket on the way home. Bought a loaf, a packet of sliced salami and a jar of mayonnaise I suddenly fancied, some oranges and a carton of juice. The hell of boiling the cat was over, the flat wouldn't be freezing, the stink was gone, and I looked forward to closing my door and putting a record on, a bite to eat, lying down with a book.

A piece of paper, ragged along one edge, torn from a notebook, lay on the floor inside the door when I stepped in. I picked it up. In biro on the other side was written:

Kristian,
I want to see you again.
Vivian

I bet you fucking do, I said out loud, and crumpled the note in my hand. The arrogance of her. Did she think I was a dog? That all she had to do was call and I'd come running? *I want to see you again.* Oh, you do, do you? Well, thanks for the information. Do I want to see you? No. Maybe you should have asked me that. *Kristian, do you want to see me?* There might just have been a possibility then, you see. A tiny, tiny possibility.

Or rather, no, there wouldn't. Hadn't she, this very same *Vivian*, backtracked on the photo assignment she'd been offering, for the single reason that she wasn't sure I was good enough?

I put the kettle on and buttered three slices of bread while I waited for it to boil. Salami, cucumber and generous dollops of mayo on top. The mayonnaise over here was different from the Mills I was used to from at home, thinner in its consistency, paler in colour, and ever so slightly tangier on the tongue. It was like that with nearly all food here — it looked to be the same, but always lacked that little *something*.

The exception was tea. Although the brand, Twinings Earl Grey, was the same as at home, it was better over here. It could only mean they reserved the Grade A leaves for the domestic market, while Grade B was for export.

They hadn't a clue about coffee.

I put my mug of tea down on the little table by the armchair and kneeled in front of my records, took out *Block to Block* by De Press, still the best album ever by a Norwegian band, placed it on the turntable and lowered the stylus into the myriad black grooves, sat down in the chair, took a sip of my tea, and closed my eyes.

Imperiet were a Mickey Mouse band by comparison.

No, it wasn't a dog she made me feel like. It was a stud. A bull used for breeding purposes, led to the heifer to do its job.

She could have been here just before I got home. If I was her, I'd have gone down the pub, had a drink or two, then come back after closing time to see if I'd returned. Seeing as she'd come all this way in the first place.

In which case, she'd be here any time soon.

I got up and turned the music off, the lights too, and sat back in the chair.

Perhaps ten minutes later, footsteps sounded on the landing, and stopped outside my door. There was a knock. I sat unmoving in the darkness.

'Kristian?' she said. 'Are you there?'

She knocked again, harder this time.

Then she gave up and I heard her go back down the stairs, waited until I heard the front door shut, its bang in the silence of bated breath, before switching the light on again and returning to what I'd been doing.

The only trouble with the cat picture, I discovered the next day, was that it stuck out so much. The other photos in the series — which so far comprised only the ones I'd taken of trees — paled in comparison. The cat was simply too powerful an image. Tentatively, I tried integrating it into earlier work, but only with the same results — the others in the series became at best indistinctive or else faded away into nothingness.

This was good in that it meant I'd created something extraordinary at long last. But it gave me a problem too: I'd raised the bar, and from now on this was the standard against which all my pictures would be measured.

Still, I was glad I hadn't let Vivian come inside the night before. It would have been the same as letting her inside *me*. I needed there to be something in between. A barrier of some sort, whether in time or space, that had to be surmounted first.

But it was interesting to know she wanted me. I wasn't *completely* unwilling myself. The problem was that one thing would lead to another, and then I'd be stuck with her on my lap. I had to find a way to keep it all in check.

I rang directory enquiries and noted down the address they gave me for the theatre group. I found it on the map, memorised the route and was on my bike.

The building they used, down by the riverside, was big and rundown, presumably a warehouse or something like that in former days. I chained the bike to a railing and went down some steps to the entrance. There was nothing to indicate who rented the premises. I banged on the door, green-painted metal. When no one came, I went over to the nearest grimy window and peered in. The space inside was empty save for a lot of stuff that had been pushed back against the walls. It didn't look like anyone had been here for years.

I banged again.

If they *did* hang out in this place, they certainly weren't here today. I pulled the handle down anyway and found to my surprise that the door was open.

Inside, it was dead quiet, no one around. At the far end was a steep wooden staircase. I crossed through the room and went up it. I could hear voices now, and when I got to the top I immediately saw a group sitting in a circle on the floor, while Vivian stood a bit further away together with two other people with whom she was engaged in conversation.

Everyone turned towards me.

'Thanks for your message last night, Vivian,' I said. 'Here I am. But don't let me disturb you.'

'Sit over there,' she said, indicating the floor by the wall.

Her voice and body language conveyed only irritation. So why the note?

I sat down.

'So, this is the relationship we need to focus on,' she said. 'Throughout, of course, but especially in this scene. What does Mephistophilis *mean* to Faustus? *For love of thee, I cut mine arm*, Faustus says. It may well be that this is him giving himself up to darkness or evil or transgression, but we can *see* nothing of that. The soul is invisible. All we *can* see is Mephistophilis and Faustus. *For love of thee, I cut mine arm*. This is where we need to focus.'

'So Mephisto and Faustus love each other, is that what you're saying?' one of the actors said.

'What do I know? *Love* is just a word. It says everything and nothing. Our job is to explore. To probe into the relationships and see what happens. Perhaps we'll find love, perhaps something else.'

'Love on the edge of the abyss?'

'For example, yes! Self-destruction holds a key position in all Marlowe's plays — it was something he knew himself, so the abyss is never going to be far away. Here, he's literally standing on the brink of Hell. So symbolically this is crucial. Even so, it's not enough to make good theatre. We have to get inside what it feels like to *him*. He cuts open his arm — and says he's doing it for love.'

'What about Mephistophilis? Is he consumed with love too? And what about the Devil?'

The question from the floor sounded sarcastic, but Vivian declined to take up the gauntlet.

'Only you can find that out, all of you together,' she said. 'Does Mephistophilis wish Faustus *well*? Bear in mind what he says, *I'll fetch him somewhat to delight his mind*, whereupon he re-enters with devils bearing gifts for him and dancing for his entertainment.'

'Wouldn't that be because he wants to take his soul and take him to Hell?'

'Yes — but maybe that's what Faustus himself wants too? And so Mephistophilis helps him. And what *is* love, anyway? It's not all good, surely? Destructive love exists too, as you know. But all this is going to reveal itself. It's what we're hoping to find. Right, how about we break for lunch now, and we'll run through the scene when we get back?'

The actors dispersed, and Vivian came up to me.

I got to my feet, uncomfortable with the idea of sitting while she stood.

'Have you had lunch?' she said.

'I'm from Norway. We don't do lunch.'

'Oh?'

'A slice of buttered bread with something on it, maybe.'

'I'm sure we can find a place that does sandwiches. If you want?'

'OK.'

She took me to a pub down by the river. I didn't want to eat with her, so I just bought myself a pint, while she ordered a hamburger and chips.

'Have you read *Doctor Faustus*?' she said once we'd sat down and she'd got her cigarettes out. The river ran grey outside. Grey, with a faint touch of sand.

'I've got a copy at home,' I said.

'You've got a copy at home. But have you read it?'

'I've skimmed it.'

She raised her eyebrows, studying me from behind her glasses. She was more and more like a teacher every minute.

'I know the story,' I said.

'It's a terribly difficult piece to stage. It's all over the place. Part horror, part comedy, part medieval morality play, part *Hamlet*. There's very little cohesion.'

'I can see that.'

'You can take the photos, if you still want. I may as well trust you.'

'Because you feel sorry for me?'

'Don't be so sensitive. Just say yes or no.'

'I'm not sensitive.'

She smiled, her smouldering cigarette held high, elbow propped in the cup of her free hand.

'You seem to think you know me.'

'Oh?'

'You don't, though. Sensitive is the last thing you could call me.'

'If you say so, fine.'

She was annoying the fuck out of me, and then her food came to the table. She attacked it straight away, the hamburger gripped in both her hands. There followed an extended moment of mastication until she swallowed and wiped away a crumb from the corner of her mouth.

'I'll do it,' I heard myself say.

'OK. Good.'

'How do you envisage it?'

She bit again into her hamburger and didn't immediately answer. Another riverboat, another tow of barges, glided by outside, black on grey. Tears for Fears came on the jukebox.

'I was actually thinking of using this for the play,' she said.

'What?' I said. I'd heard well enough, I just didn't know what she meant.

'I said, I was thinking of using this for the play. The song. "Everybody

Wants to Rule the World". We need music for when the devils do their dance. It'd be all wrong, though. Too contemporary. Too poppy.'

'It's absolute crap. I can't understand how you could even consider it.'

'What would you suggest, then?'

I gave a shrug.

'Einstürzende Neubauten. Something like that. Noise.'

'The Devil's got to be menacing. You don't think Tears for Fears would be a good fit?'

Before I could even answer, she carried on:

'As far as the photography goes, you can do what you like. We do need some photos from rehearsals, though. Can you manage that?'

'Of course I can. I can do some now, if you want.'

'No, it's too early yet. We've only just got onto the floor, so it's still too nervous and tentative at the moment. I'll let you know when they're ready.'

'OK.'

I didn't know what to do with all the humiliation I got from her. It wasn't on a scale that would warrant telling her to go to hell. But it was enough for me not to be able to ignore it. It was as if she was playing a game with me. She may have been really intelligent and confident with words. But at the end of the day, when she was lying there naked on the bed, wanting me to strangle her, or smothering me with kisses afterwards, all that went out the window. It didn't count for anything then. And that was where the truth was.

The easiest thing would have been never to see her again. If not exactly repulsive, she wasn't much to look at, had an ungainly way of walking and no idea about clothes. Besides, she was ten years older than me, which to a certain extent gave her the upper hand. But no, I'd push back. I'd show her, teach her, make her understand what was truth and what wasn't. The assignment wasn't unimportant either.

'I'd best be getting back,' she said, and got to her feet. I finished off my pint and went with her outside. She waited while I unlocked the bike.

'We've got a deal, then?' I said, mainly to break the silence.

'The pictures, you mean? Yes, the job's yours.'

'Right. I'm off this way.'

'Come round to mine tonight.'
She held my gaze in earnest.
'OK,' I said, and set off on my bike along the embankment.

When I got home there was a postcard on the floor. I immediately recognised Mum's pedantic handwriting. On the front were three views of Jerusalem, reminding me they'd been due to go there.

Dear Kristian,

Jerusalem is a beautiful city amid all its great tensions. The hotel has its own pool, and we wake in the mornings to prayer being called from the minarets. So many layers of history, from Jesus to Lagerlöf. We miss you and hope you're well. Will we be seeing you for Easter?

I wondered if she'd ever give up, and binned the card straight away. It didn't bother me in itself, her sending a postcard. It was the bit about Easter that annoyed me. She thought I was weak. It could only be because she'd known me as a child. She hadn't adjusted the picture she had of the needy little boy wanting to sit on her lap. Why would I want to *see* them now? I had nothing in common with them. It was a torment. But to her, conventions were a bond in themselves. It mattered less whether family get-togethers were pleasant or disagreeable, interesting or dull, fun or misery — the important thing was that they took place at the established intervals.

I held off as long as I could on cycling out to Vivian's place. The less time I spent there, the better. It was just gone ten when I set off. The stars were out for a change, though it wasn't cold. It gave me a sense of spring being just around the corner. But in London the seasons were much of a muchness, they ran together and succeeded each other more or less seamlessly.

I paused by the church I'd last seen melding into misty gloom — now its contours were sharply drawn against the night sky, illuminated by floodlighting from below, reaching above the buildings by which it was so closely surrounded. One of these was a bank, old-fashioned, with columns flanking the entrance, a relief above the doors. Money and God alongside each other, I thought with a smile.

It was a moment worthy of memory. I was living in one of the world's greatest cities. I was a budding young photographic artist. I had a lover I was on my way to meet. She was sophisticated and intelligent. She saw something in me.

I leaned the bike up against the low stone wall and lit a cigarette. The stars winked down. Traffic backed up at the nearby junction.

'Can you spare one of them?' a voice said. I looked round to see where it came from. In the small enclosed space in front of the church, a shabby-looking man with long, matted hair was sat up against the exterior, his legs stuck into a sleeping bag, a shopping trolley next to him with all his stuff in it. That he'd been able to see me the whole time, while I'd thought myself alone, was unsettling.

'A smoke, you mean?'

'Yes.'

'Sorry, I've only got two left,' I said, flicking the one I was smoking onto the pavement as I got back on the bike. Halfway up the hill, I thought better of it and turned back. There weren't two in the packet, there were eighteen. I pulled up in the same place as before and dismounted.

'Seems I had more than I thought,' I said, and tossed him two.

'Thanks,' he said impassively, as if he'd been expecting just this. He leaned forward to pick them up where they lay, faint-white, on the ground in front of him.

'Have you got a light?'

He knew I had, because he'd seen me light one up just before — it'd be odd to say I hadn't. But giving him a light meant I'd have to step up close to him.

That was the thing about being good, it got so easily out of hand. All of a sudden you found yourself involved in something you didn't want to be involved in.

But he'd sussed me, so I went in through the open gate to where he was sitting. He didn't bother getting up, just lifted his head towards me with the cigarette in his mouth.

I wasn't going to light it for him.

'Here,' I said, and handed him the lighter.

He was actually wearing a suit, underneath a shaggy oversized coat that was covered in grime.

In the light of the flame, I saw there was a weeping sore in his forehead the size of a ten-pence coin. It looked to be infected.

He put the lighter in his coat pocket. His hands were covered in sores as well.

'Could I have that back, do you think?' I said.

He stared up at me.

'What do you mean?'

'The lighter you borrowed. Can I have it back, please?'

'What lighter? I never saw any lighter.'

'The one you put in your pocket. Can I have it back?'

'Are you calling me a liar?'

'No.'

'Well, then.'

He leaned his head back against the wall, his eyes still fixed on me.

I stood for a moment, not knowing what to do.

He'd taken my lighter. I couldn't let him get away with that. But I wasn't exactly going to fight him for it either.

Should I just let it go and leave him to gloat?

I'd look stupid, I'd look like an idiot.

'All right, you've had your fun,' I said. 'I lent you my lighter. I saw you put it in your pocket. Now I want it back.'

'I don't know what you're talking about.'

I leaned forward to stick my hand in his coat and get the bloody thing myself. He gripped my wrist. He was stronger than he looked. His eyes, glaring into mine, were full of aggression. Before even thinking about it, I got my hand under his chin and banged his head back as hard as I could. He didn't cry out, didn't so much as whimper, he just went completely still. The hand that had gripped my wrist was now limp. He must have gone out like a light. I drew myself upright. His head had flopped to one side, his open eyes were vacant.

I glanced around in case anyone had seen what had happened. It was his own fault, but a passing witness wouldn't necessarily know that. For all I knew, it could have looked like I'd jumped him for no reason, an unmotivated attack. You could go to prison for that. Assault and battery.

But there was no one around.

I retrieved the lighter from his coat and went casually back to the bike as if nothing had occurred. My heart was thumping, all I wanted was to get away, but still I put my foot on the pedal and pushed away as calmly as you like, swinging my other leg over the saddle quite as deliberately before pedalling slowly up the long, shallow slope of the hill. I could have done with a few minutes to myself to go through what had happened, but it was late, Vivian had probably been waiting several hours already.

My bike safely chained to a lamp post on the pavement outside, I pushed open the gate and went up the steps to the front door. It was locked. Next to the three doorbells were only surnames. Was the top one for the top floor or the ground floor? The bottom one presented the same dilemma. So, was Vivian's surname Jarman or Moore?

Vivian Moore had a better ring to it than Vivian Jarman. If her parents had the same good taste, then it was the doorbell at the bottom I needed to press.

I did.

It hadn't taken much. A knock on the head and he was out.

Someone came down the stairs and the door opened, just a fraction at first.

'What time do you call this?' said Vivian.

There was something different about her. Her face was bare somehow. It took a few seconds for me to realise she wasn't wearing her glasses.

'We didn't agree on any time,' I said. 'Had you gone to bed?'

She shook her head.

'Come in.'

I followed her up the stairs. The place was tidier than last time. Three scented candles stood flickering on the coffee table. The wax still looked hard. She must have just lit them before answering the door. So it meant something to her that I was coming. She'd tidied up, and waited.

I felt a strong urge to wash my hands. I'd touched him, and with those sores of his he could have had AIDS.

'Mind if I use the bathroom?'

'Through there,' she said, indicating the door next to the kitchen.

I washed my hands thoroughly. While I was at it, my face too. I leaned forward, hands propped against the sink, and saw my reflection do likewise. The face was like a mask. Nothing about it revealed what I was thinking or felt.

'Do you want a drink?' said Vivian as I came back into the living room.

'What have you got?'

'Red wine. White wine. Lager. Gin.'

'No brandy? Calvados?'

'Nope.'

'Just a beer, then.'

She fetched me one from the fridge. Poured herself a glass of red from a bottle that was already open, a bit more than half full, I noticed. She put the glass down and went over to the stereo.

'What do you want to listen to?'

'Not bothered.'

'As long as it's not Tears for Fears, I take it?' she said, and looked across at me with a smile.

'That's about it, yes,' I said.

I wondered how she'd react if I told her about what had happened. She'd be horrified. You mean, you just left him there? I could hear her say. And then perhaps she'd drag me back down there to see how he was. Maybe call an ambulance. It'd be impossible to explain what had led up to it. A lighter wasn't something to fight about. But it wasn't the lighter in itself. It was the fact that he thought himself entitled to steal from me. The cheek of it. He only had himself to blame. There was no need to go and check on him, not when he had his sleeping bag and that warm overcoat.

She straightened up having picked out an LP, tilted the inner sleeve out of the cover, then allowed the record to slide into her hand. She put it on the turntable, lifted the tone arm and lowered the stylus into the lead-in groove. When the first crackles came through the speakers she turned towards me.

'I'm guessing you like this,' she said as the drums pounded into 'Lust for Life'. 'Am I right?'

'I like Iggy, yes.'

She made a couple of dance moves, arms flailing above her shoulders.

'Want to dance?'

'Certainly not.'

She laughed and smoothed a hand over my arm.

'I should have known. You take yourself far too seriously to dance.'

I returned her gaze, gave a little shake of my head, and went and sat down in the armchair. She followed suit, plonking herself on the sofa.

'Just teasing,' she said. 'You can take a bit of teasing, can't you?'

I didn't reply.

'I like you, you know that. A lot, actually. Do you like me?'

'Would I be sitting here if I didn't?'

'That's not an answer. That's a question.'

I took a long swig from the can, then remembered my cigarettes, not yet an integrated part of who I was, but they'd have been a perfect distraction here.

'But the question contains the answer,' I said, and was about to get up and fetch the packet from my coat when the full force of what had happened assailed me, rooting me to the chair. I'd have to get rid of the cigarette packet, obviously, it was tainted now, and would remind me of the incident every time I reached for a smoke.

'Are you restless? Don't you want to be here? You can go, if you want.'

I looked at her. I'd have to do something she'd like, put her mind at rest.

I stood up and went and kneeled in front of her. She gave a look of puzzlement, and sat up a bit straighter. I placed a hand on each of her knees and parted her legs.

'What are you up to?' she said with a grin, still holding her wine. I put my cheek against her thigh and moved my head slowly up and down, caressing her.

'Let me get rid of this,' she said. I nuzzled my face into her crotch, then undid the button and drew down the zip. White knickers on. I hoped she'd washed herself, I heard myself think as she twisted to one side to put her glass down on the armrest and I started pulling off her jeans.

Moments later, she was well away, lying there as if entranced, breathing heavily as my tongue explored her wet folds. She wouldn't think about anything else for a good while now. When after a bit I stood up, she crossed hands and gripped the hem of her jumper to take it off. I stopped her. It turned me on to see her naked from the waist down. I entered her and gripped her throat, only for her to pull my hand away.

'No. Not that,' she said.

So it was only something she did when she was drunk or stoned, I reasoned. I pressed my cheek against hers so as not to be distracted by her face, then turned away and looked at the room as I came.

'Aaah! Aaah! Aaah!' she said.

I pulled out and sat up. Put my underpants and T-shirt back on. She lay there looking at me without covering herself.

'Can I cadge a smoke off you? I've forgotten mine.'

'On the side in the kitchen.'

When I came back in, she'd already got dressed. I sat in the armchair and smoked. The cigarette brought the incident back, but I managed to shove it away.

'Will you give me one?' she said, perched on the edge of the sofa with her knees together.

I tossed her the packet.

'And the lighter, if you don't mind.'

Oh Christ.

The lighter did it. I couldn't think of anything else now. It was all I could see in my mind. His head knocking back against the wall, dropping to one side. I was sorry now, though, wasn't I? I was, I was sorry. It wasn't my fault. He provoked me. He gripped my wrist really hard, when I was only trying to take what was mine. Still, I was sorry. Was that not enough for you?

'What are you thinking about?' she said, having lit her cigarette.

'Nothing,' I said. 'What about you?'

'I'm wondering who you are, to be honest.'

'I see.'

'Wondering what goes on behind that beautiful exterior. I basically know nothing about you.'

'What do you want to know?'

'Your favourite book?'

'Haven't got one.'

'Favourite record?'

'*In the Flat Field.*'

'Film?'

'*Apocalypse Now.*'

'What about political views?'

'Haven't got any. Are you satisfied now?'

'Everything you're saying fits. It's what I'd expect from someone who dresses the way you do. But you can't *really* tell who a person is until you see what *doesn't* fit. The bits that stick out. Don't you think?'

'No idea. I've never thought about it.'

'Perhaps you need to read a few more books. But tell me something about yourself that I'd never have guessed.'

'How about you go first?'

'All right. I absolutely love Tears for Fears.'

She laughed, pleased with herself.

What if he *did* have AIDS? It was transmitted by blood, wasn't it?

I looked at my hands to see if there were any scratches or sores I hadn't noticed before. Turned them over. One of the cuticles was a bit ragged. But was that enough? I hadn't actually *touched* his sores.

'What's the matter?'

'Nothing. I'd best be off home. It's a bit late.'

I thought she was going to beg me to stay, as she'd done the last time, but she didn't.

'OK,' she said.

She'd already got what she wanted.

It couldn't go on. Treating me like a stud. I wasn't.

I stood up and put my coat on. She got to her feet.

'Have you given those photos any thought?' she said.

'What do you mean?'

'The ones for the programme. Have you thought about what you're going to do?'

'No, not yet.'

I went to the door.

'Only I had an idea. How about photographing Marlowe's London places as they are today?'

'I thought it was up to me.'

'It is. But it's a good idea, don't you think?'

I opened the door without answering. She came towards me.

'Thanks for coming round,' she said, and smiled.

'Thanks for asking.'

'We'll need to talk some more about those photos. But don't turn up at rehearsals again unless we've agreed on it. OK?'

It wasn't hard to work out why she found it necessary to reproach me, I thought as I went down the stairs. She'd been desperate and had turned to a twenty-year-old to get what she wanted. The whole set-up put a bad taste in my mouth. It couldn't go on, not like this. I'd have to find a way of managing the assignment without too much involvement from her.

Outside, the sky was still scattered with stars. Dipping into my pocket for the key to unlock my bike, I felt the lighter against my hand. The front garden was so overgrown and cluttered with stuff that I could simply toss it there. But I'd be acting as if I was guilty of something then. Getting rid of the evidence. Or what made me think about what had happened.

But why shouldn't I think about it? Wasn't that too an admittance I'd done something wrong? I hadn't. He'd stolen my lighter, I'd taken it back. The skirmish had been his doing, not mine. He could have just given me the lighter back, he knew full well it wasn't his to take. But he wouldn't, and so it had ended in a scuffle. He'd banged his head on the wall and knocked himself out.

There was nothing to run away from.

I'd keep the lighter. In fact, I'd even look after it. It would remind me of the truth.

With these thoughts, I got on the bike and sailed off down the hill through the still, nocturnal street. Here and there, a window flickered television-blue. In two, the light changed in unison.

Nearing the bottom end, where the church rose up around the corner, I touched the brakes. The chances he was still there were slim. If he was, I'd check and see if he'd moved. If he hadn't, I'd have to find a phone box and call an ambulance. Tell them there was an injured homeless person near such-and-such a place.

I didn't think he'd still be there, but my heart thumped in my chest as I approached.

What was that bluish glow?

I turned the corner to see three police vehicles pulled into the side with their lights flashing.

Oh Christ.

But why were they there?

I cycled towards them as slowly as I could without appearing suspicious. I had to see what was going on without drawing attention to myself.

A policeman was cordoning off the area with tape. Three others were standing in a huddle, meaning I couldn't get a view of where the incident had taken place. Walkie-talkies crackled. From the other direction an ambulance appeared and pulled up quietly.

Was he lying there?

Yes, he was. Exactly as before. A camera flashed as a fifth policeman took photographs, momentarily illuminating the scene.

Was he dead?

This had to mean he was dead, surely?

But how?

One of the policemen turned towards me. His eyes caught mine for a second, before I looked away. But I was just a cyclist on his way home. I had nothing to do with it. I was only going slowly because I was curious to know what was going on.

He was dead!

Oh no, oh no.

He must have had a heart attack.

That little knock on the head couldn't possibly have been enough to kill him.

He was probably weak with AIDS. Half dead already.

Had anyone seen me?

No.

I was certain of it. No one had seen me. No one knew anything. I was safe. As long as I didn't tell anyone, I was safe. They didn't know who I was, so how would they ever find me?

Fingerprints.

On his chin? Don't make me laugh.

And the lighter lay snug in my pocket.

I was safe. Safe, safe, safe.

At the end of the street, I turned my head again. The ambulance had pulled up. Two paramedics, or whatever, were wheeling a stretcher through the gate.

It was a terrible night. Although I knew it was completely irrational, I kept waiting for the police to ring the doorbell and take me away. The slightest sound inside the house became footsteps on the stairs. Likewise any car that pulled up outside — surely the police, and my heart stopped in fear. I'd put the lighter on the bookshelf, in plain sight, mostly so as to reassure myself that I had nothing to be afraid of. I'd done nothing wrong. More importantly, no one had seen what had happened. There was no way the police could find me.

But still I was not at ease. It felt like the boundary between me and the world was gone. Now, anyone at all could get to me. My locked door was no help. The certainty I'd done nothing wrong was no help.

I went over to the bookshelf and flicked the wheel of the lighter. Its flame burned yellow and clear, like the flame of any other. The lighter, too, was indeed wholly unremarkable.

Returning it to the shelf, the metal casing at the top still burning hot, the thought of him having AIDS came back to me, and with it the thought that the lighter had been in his hands. The chances of it infecting me were tiny, but quite apart from that his fingerprints would be on it, and so I took it over to the sink and washed it thoroughly, before scrubbing my hands. I dropped the towel I used to dry them with in the laundry bin, put the lighter back on the shelf, switched the lights off and returned to bed. For some time, I felt a calmness. Lying there in the dark, my head resting on the pillow, my body underneath the duvet, was like being removed from time, as close to being eleven years old and lying with the window open on a hot August night as it was to lying here in London with the events of the previous night playing in my mind. Nothing of what had occurred outside my bed existed any longer, other than in my mind, where it lay tucked, a tiny bump of memory. Most of what had happened was not even there. It was gone. What's more, it would never come back. Nearly everything that had ever happened was gone without a trace. Why would this be any different?

The sound of distant sirens jolted me with anxiety.

Oh, why had I done it? How completely unnecessary it had been. If only I'd cycled on, instead of trying to be kind, everything would have been the same as before. I wouldn't have been tormented, not by anything.

Regardless that it had been his own fault entirely, that he was the one who'd become aggressive, and had actually stolen from me, that he'd gripped my wrist when I'd only been trying to take back what was mine — regardless of all this, I was the only person who knew. The police might believe something else. I could have avoided it all, if only I'd cycled on. That which now, in spite of everything, was something, would not have been anything at all.

How many times had an occurrence lain in wait for me, only to remain unrealised, because instead of turning left I carried on my way?

The crux of the matter was that no one had seen me. No one knew anything. What had happened existed now only in me. And I could do anything I wanted with it.

Erase it completely?

Yes, I could do that.

It didn't exist in the world outside, only in me. So what was I afraid of?

It was a huge relief.

The next morning, I walked up to the newsagent's at the station and bought all the newspapers. I felt extremely visible, like in wide-open terrain, surrounded by the enemy, so instead of reading them in a cafe, the way I'd envisaged when I first woke up, I took them home with me and went through them there. There wasn't a word about what had happened. I checked and double-checked. Not even a little notice. Either it was because it had happened too late to be included in the early editions, or else no one considered it important enough. A homeless destitute who'd hit his head and died wasn't much of a story. They probably died all the time, people like that. Overdoses, falls. Drownings too, no doubt. Some would likely freeze to death in the coldest snaps of winter. Whatever, their lives were surely misery, worthless to anyone but themselves, perhaps even also to themselves. Unable to maintain any kind of dignity, constantly in search of food, drink, dope, wandering about looking for somewhere to sleep at night. Begging, fighting, stealing.

I was giving it too much space again.

It was nothing.

I hadn't done anything. I'd given him two cigarettes and a lighter. He'd been extremely ungrateful and stolen from me, a scuffle had occurred.

Too much space. Don't think about it. It'll go away then. It existed only in me.

But it didn't matter what I did, in my mind I kept returning to the night before. I couldn't read, or listen to music. I had to get out. See someone. Talk about something else.

I took the newspapers downstairs and dropped them in the rubbish, then went back up to get the bike. What had happened, I suddenly discovered, had attached to it too — now it was the death bike, but I knew there was only one thing I could do about that, which was to carry on using it, over and over again, until the unfortunate event had been worn away and it became once more a normal, trusty bicycle.

Outside on the pavement it occurred to me that I could take the cat photo with me and show it to Hans. It was a good excuse to go round there, otherwise he'd wonder why I'd come, so soon after we'd seen each other last. I chained my bike to the lamp post, went back up and gathered the whole series I'd taken, and, as an afterthought, those of the empty house at Christmas. There was a risk he wouldn't like them, but it was a risk I didn't mind taking — already, as I sorted through the pictures and packed them into my rucksack, I found all my thoughts were staying away from what had happened, as I knew they would do too when I showed him the photos.

A police car came towards me up by New Cross. I spotted it from some distance and consciously avoided looking at it when it passed. I didn't look away, which could have made me look guilty, but kept my eyes on the road ahead, fully concentrated on the traffic around me. I knew, of course, that they weren't looking for me, but I still had to be careful not to attract unnecessary attention.

A few minutes later, when I looked over my shoulder to get into the right lane, I saw it was coming back. At once, all energy drained from my body, my legs suddenly weak and trembling. They were looking for me, of course they were. They'd have patrol cars everywhere. Now they'd seen someone matching the description and had come back for him.

There was a park on my left-hand side. I pulled up, got off the bike and wheeled it in through the big, open gate. They couldn't get through in a car, and on foot they wouldn't be able to catch up with me on the bike.

I glanced over my shoulder in time to see the police car glide slowly by in the flow of traffic.

Out of sorts, I sat down on a bench to get back on top of the situation. What was I thinking? No one had seen me. The police had no idea I even existed.

I was letting myself be chased by my own ghosts.

Oh, please, when was it going to stop?

London was full of police cars. I couldn't allow the world to come apart every time I saw one. For a start, I'd done nothing wrong. And besides, no one had seen anything. I was totally safe.

I got on the death bike again, feeling sick in my body.

I'd frightened myself. It was as simple as that.

The last part of the way to Hans's place, I walked. I needed to get myself together before seeing him. Apart from Vivian, I hadn't spoken to anyone since the incident, hadn't seen a familiar face, and it felt like I had to prepare myself mentally for it. I toyed with the idea of telling him everything. Since it was me, he'd understand what had happened, as well as why. He wasn't stupid. But then my ingenious device of the incident existing only in me would no longer hold. It would be out in the world again then. Telling him would serve no other purpose than to give me the small comfort of confession, which doubtless would evaporate after only a few minutes.

He might not even be in.

But he was, appearing in the doorway seconds after I'd knocked.

'Kristian,' he said. 'What a nice surprise!'

Did he have a slight lisp? I'd never noticed before.

'Just passing by.'

'Come in. Coffee?'

No s's in that.

'Thanks, I wouldn't mind.'

I leaned the bike against the wall while he disappeared into the studio. He returned with two mugs, rinsed as last time at the sink in the toilet.

He had on a black T-shirt, with a band logo in silver lettering. I noticed it as he handed me my coffee. At least, I assumed that was what it was. Hellhammer, it said.

'Who are they?' I said with a nod.

'Hellhammer? A Swiss band. A lot of people would say they're sick in the head. Sick music.'

It was a very faint lisp, almost inaudible. But it was there, definitely.

'Not you, though?' I said with a smile.

'I love them. Crap musicianship, crap production. But immense power. Like punk, only wilder. Darker, too. Blacker than night.'

We sat down.

'What's the rucksack for?' he said. 'Off on your holidays?'

Why hadn't I thought of it before? Getting out of London. Going up to the Lake District. Away from it all.

'I brought some photos with me I thought you might like to see. You didn't much like the last lot. These are better.'

'I never said I didn't like them. What I said was they're not bad.'

'*Not bad*,' I said in air quotes.

'OK, I'm curious. Let's have a look. Or do you want to finish your coffee first?'

'No, you can look at them now, of course you can.'

I unzipped the rucksack and took out the box. I'd put the photo of the cat on top, and now, as I removed it, I kept it hidden with the lid so that he wouldn't form an impression before seeing it properly.

'It was basically just this one I wanted to show you,' I said, handing it to him over the table.

He held it out in front of him and studied it for some time. Then, lowering it a fraction, he stared at me.

'Kristian, this is bloody *good*.'

'No need to sound surprised.'

He smiled.

'Maybe I am, a bit. This is on a different level altogether compared to the other stuff you showed me. This is . . . well, superb. Are there any more? Is it a series?'

'Sort of. I've got a couple more belonging to the same sequence, at least.'

I handed him the others.

He skimmed them quickly, then shook his head.

'No. The first one's the one. The others here actually detract from it. It's discovering the context that does it. The magic has to do with the mystery. Our not knowing the context. There *is* a context, of course, and we sense that as we look at the picture. But we don't know what it is. That uncertainty makes the image extremely compelling. At the same time, there's something universal about it. It's life and death. Flesh and blood. Matter and spirit. Destruction.'

He fixed his eyes on me.

'I'm pleased for you, Kristian. But you need more. One's not enough.'

'I do have some more, as it happens. Only it's a different series. Do you want to have a look?'

'Hit me.'

He spent a while scrutinising, even spreading them out on the table in front of him and standing up to get an overview.

'These aren't half bad either. But what's the story here?'

'You remember I told you about my sister who tried to kill herself on Christmas Eve? These are the pictures from that night. Immediately after the ambulance had come and taken her away.'

'You never told me that?'

'Didn't I? I'm sure I did. Maybe it was someone else.'

'It must have been. Was it this Christmas just gone?'

I nodded.

'Is she all right?'

'Yes, much better, thanks. It looks like she's come through whatever it was that was troubling her.'

'What's her name?'

'Liv.'

'Hm. Well, I like them. They're perhaps a bit short on context, though. You're telling a story, but because we're not quite getting the background, the pictures lose some of their value. The trick is to get them to give out a little bit more information, without turning them into notices.'

'Do you think I could put them together with the cat?'

He shook his head.

'No, you mustn't do that. The cat needs its own universe, and you need to create that.'

'I've thought about it, actually. The idea I've been toying with is for the cat to be part of a series called *Frameworks of Life*. Skeletons, that sort of thing. Scaffolding. The structures that hold life together, in physical terms.'

'Why not? The risk, though, is that it becomes too cerebral.'

I gathered the photos together and put them back in their box.

'Thanks for having a look,' I said.

'Thanks for showing me. I'm glad you did — and really pleased to see you're getting it together.'

He stood up again.

'Do you remember my turtles?'

'Of course I do.'

'I want you to see one more thing in that respect. Hang on here a minute.'

He went off into the back room and then emerged with one of the turtles in his hands. He put it down on the floor, taking care to position it correctly. It began to move slowly across the floor. Hans himself disappeared for a moment again, returning with a large mirror he then leaned up against the wall.

'Is that a real turtle shell?' I said, stepping closer.

'It is, yes.'

'Where did you get hold of them? I had a hell of a job getting my hands on a cat, and they're a lot more common than turtles.'

'It wasn't a problem,' he said. 'But now look.'

The turtle had turned round over by the wall and was on its way back. Passing the mirror, it changed direction again. It looked like it had discovered the mirror and went over to investigate. It got up close to it, drew back slightly, then moved towards it again, angling itself first one way, then another as if looking at itself from different perspectives.

Hans laughed.

'Amazing, don't you think?'

'You mean it can *see*?'

'That would depend on how you define the word. It's certainly registering, at least.'

'Why did it go towards the mirror? It can't possibly be aware of itself, surely?'

He laughed again.

'No. I've mounted a little light on it. And programmed it to do two things: avoid obstacles and follow light. When it sees a light in the mirror, two conflicting impulses occur: it wants to go towards the light, but also to avoid the obstacle, which is to say its mirror image. And so it performs its little dance!'

His laughter bounced off the concrete walls.

He switched off his turtle, returned to the sofa and sat down. 'More coffee?'

'Don't mind if I do.'

Being there was good, completely apart from the world outside.

He took my mug and filled it up.

'But what are you doing it for?'

'Doing what?'

'Playing around with turtles.'

'I could ask the same question about you and your cat.'

'That's different.'

'I'm not sure it is. I can tell you my thoughts behind it, though.'

'But the rat and the turtles are just old inventions, aren't they? Someone was telling me about it. So there can't be much of an artistic project there?'

'Maybe not. It's exploration, that's all. I'm exploring something.'

'Which is?'

'OK. You photographed a cat. What were you doing?'

'Photographing a cat.'

'But what's it all about? You're so used to it that you don't give a thought to the medium. The technology. What does the camera do? It captures light. In other words, it stores something. It doesn't change anything in the world, all it does is keep hold of something. But it does change *us*. Come on, let me show you something.'

He led me to the back room where I stood in the open doorway and watched as he took an antique gramophone from one of the shelves and put it down on the metal bench.

'A record player,' I said.

He didn't respond, but stooped to wind the little handle while looking up at me, his face beaming gleefully — like a child's, I thought — before lowering the needle. An old voice, full of feeling, crackled from the horn of the speaker, accompanied by a tinny-sounding orchestra.

'Isn't this amazing?' he said, straightening up. 'Giovanni Martinelli, 1915.'

He smiled.

'You're not impressed, I sense.'

'A record player,' I said again. 'Music.'

'It's the same as with your photography. The photograph stores light. The gramophone stores sound. Neither interacts with the world, only with us. Do you see what I'm getting at?'

'No. But I sense you want to give me a lecture.'

He stepped past me, and I followed him back to the sofa. The ensuing seconds of silence brought the horror crashing back inside me.

'What I like about it is that it's so simple: a needle, a groove, a funnel are all it takes and you've captured sound. The same goes for the photograph: a light-sensitive plate, a few chemicals, and you capture light. Paracelsus could have done it — all he needed existed even then. Pythagorus, for that matter, too.'

'Everyone whose name starts with P, you mean?'

'It's not that different when it comes to the computer. But of course you're not interested in computers.'

'No.'

'The principle is simple indeed,' he went on regardless. 'You feed in information, it's manipulated according to certain parameters, and a result comes out the other end. The first computer was Greek and dates back to two centuries before Christ. They found it on a sunken ship. A mechanical construction that allowed you to plot in the position of a celestial body in order to discover the positions of others relative to it.'

'I'm still not very interested,' I said, and it was true. The more he went on about it, the more thoughts of the world outside encroached — they didn't get all the way in, but they were coming close enough for my emotions, slightly ahead of them always, to prick me with discomfort.

'I just wanted to put those turtles into a context for you. The computer can only store information, it doesn't interact with the world directly, it contains its own world within itself. It can only interact through us telling it what to do. So, what we have is a closed system.'

'A loop?'

'Yes!'

'Your term for it, not mine.'

'But you remembered! Anyway, the turtles are a computer too. But *they* do interact with the world — they react to what they encounter. Imagine a body of water that's never replenished. It stagnates, and the life that's in it dies. But it's still water. The turtles here are constantly given new things to encounter. Random things — that's important.'

'But they don't do anything. They just trundle about in here.'

He sighed.

'It's the principle, Kristian. The principle.'

No sooner had I said goodbye and got on the bike than the events of the previous night milled in my mind. Inside the studio, they'd seemed like signals from the beyond, unable to penetrate these bunker walls. Here, in the outside world, they were free to assail me, and yet, somehow, they seemed fainter now. Yes, in fact it was almost as if they couldn't harm me, as if the visit to see Hans had been a hot bath that for a while rendered the body impervious to the cold outside. All right, so I'd been involved in an incident the previous night, but it had been local, there had been no witnesses, so the area through which I now cycled, with its rows of identical brick houses, its pitiful little shopping precinct, its waste grounds and industrial sites, its exhaust-smothered road junctions, was removed from what had occurred. Mainly, I was just glad that he'd been so enthusiastic about my pictures. All the negative responses I'd been receiving had probably affected me more than

I'd been willing to acknowledge, and cycling home it felt like I'd been relieved of a rucksack filled with bricks.

I *was* talented. My work *was* up to scratch — and far better. I *did* have a future in photography.

Or maybe even the future of photography was me?

A couple of hundred metres from the house, I saw a familiar figure walking along the pavement. It was Liz. I swung in and pulled up alongside her.

'How's the English lit?' I said.

She looked at me with surprise, but seemingly without aversion.

'Fine,' she said, and carried on walking. I walked alongside her with the bike.

'What are you reading at the moment, then?'

A few seconds passed without her answering.

Why was she hesitating? I hadn't exactly asked her anything personal. Or maybe she felt that her reading was in some way intimately bound up with the person she was on the inside.

'Why do you ask?' she said eventually.

A cautious, wary little creature she appeared to be. Alert to any danger.

'Just wondering. Curious to know what English lit students read.'

'*The Time of the Angels*,' she said. 'Iris Murdoch.'

'Aha.'

'Perhaps you've read it?'

'No. Should I have done?'

'I wouldn't know.'

We passed the ironmonger's with its jumble of brooms, buckets and tubs on the pavement outside, then the old barber's shop. She clearly wasn't prepared to say anything off her own bat, but walked sullenly beside me with her arm resting on the large, bulging bag that hung from her shoulder.

'Do you know anything about Christopher Marlowe?' I said.

'Of course,' she said.

'Have you read him?'

'Yes.'

I let a few seconds go by to allow her to ask why I was asking, but she didn't.

'It's just that I'm going to be taking some photographs for a production of *Doctor Faustus*. For the printed programme. I may not have mentioned it, only I'm a photographer, you see.'

'You don't say.'

'Well, anyway. When I saw you just now, I remembered you were doing English lit and realised you probably know everything about him. Maybe we could get together and talk about it? If you like?'

The front doorsteps loomed.

'I don't think so.'

'OK,' I said. 'You've probably got plenty of other things to be getting on with. Finding room in your diary to help a neighbour with something relating to your field of expertise was always going to be difficult, I can see that.'

'Exactly. Good luck with it, all the same.'

She unlocked the door with the key she must have been holding in her hand, perhaps all the way from the station.

'If you change your mind, just come up and knock,' I said. 'We'll have a drink and talk about Marlowe.'

She turned round and her mouth curled fleetingly into a dismissive smile before she started up the stairs. I picked the bike up and followed her. By the time I got to her landing, she'd already let herself in.

I could have found it really annoying that such a grey little mouse as she thought herself too good to talk to someone like me, but right now I couldn't have cared less. What she thought or didn't was totally uninteresting to me.

The first thing my eyes saw after I leaned the bike against the wall was the lighter on the bookshelf — it drew my gaze towards it as if it was in possession of some mysterious force.

I'd killed a man.

Only I hadn't. Not really. There'd been a minor altercation. It wasn't my fault at all — he'd started it, not me. I hadn't done anything.

But it could easily look as if I *had*. Easily.

Oh, what a terrible fucking mess.

I went over to the window and looked down into the street below.

Everything was the same as it had always been. A cloudy sky, drizzle, a hundred variations on grey, brown, black. The occasional car shimmering blue or red.

It would do me good to get back to school the next day. Get myself into a routine, structure my time.

I put on Tuxedomoon's *Holy Wars*. It had to be the best album of the year so far, I thought as the apocalyptic bass opened 'The Waltz' ahead of the majestic solitary trumpet. They were Americans, of course, but so deeply immersed in the European tradition that I forgave them that. And both Blaine Reininger's and Winston Tong's solo works were really good, too.

Music was mood, period. Music was atmosphere. Music was something other and more than reality. So who could understand Americans and their 'genuine', 'authentic', 'roots' music? Springsteen and all that crowd.

It was naive, it was stupid, and beyond credible.

But music wasn't directly comparable to photography. Music was art from the word go, it was sounds, whereas a photograph reproduced a visible world. What would photographs look like if they were like the music of Tuxedomoon? European. Rain-wet streets of Prague at dusk. Tree-lined Parisian boulevards. Auschwitz. Swiss sanatoriums. The Berlin Wall. Spandau Prison. Cabaret Voltaire. Castles and palaces scattered along the Rhine. The battlefields of Flanders. Lisbon trams. Vienna, Budapest, Baden-Baden. The Po Valley. Lake Como. Milan. Genoa.

In other words, everything Springsteen and Åge Aleksandersen weren't.

My eyes found the lighter again. It *did* possess a force. But only to me.

What if I took pictures of objects that were laden with meaning, things that had a history and meant something special, but only to me? If there were enough pictures, everyone would understand that each object carried a certain meaning in its own right, it just wouldn't be accessible.

Would that be an idea?

How would it work?

I went and got the camera and took a few pictures of the lighter, first upright on the bookshelf, then on its side on the table.

There was no harm in trying.

No one would know it had been in a dead man's pocket. But it had — and the photograph would show it. Or rather, only the lighter would be shown, while the history would be within it, shrouded from view.

I took off Tuxedomoon and put Cabaret Voltaire on instead, their last good album, *Red Mecca*, turned up the volume and spread out on the floor the two series I'd shown to Hans. He was right, I saw it immediately: the cat photo was in a class all on its own.

A sense of despair gripped me: I'd never do anything as good as this again. And who had ever heard of a great artist with only one picture to his name?

I gathered up the photographs and sat down in the armchair with the boxes in my lap.

A rancid smell rose to my nostrils. I bent towards my crotch and sniffed.

Ugh. I hadn't washed down there since I'd been with Vivian. It wasn't exactly my fault — I'd a lot on my mind. Besides, the smell wasn't so foul as to reach beyond my own personal space, so Hans surely wouldn't have noticed.

I found some clean clothes and went down into the basement to have a shower. But someone else, it turned out, had the same idea — the door was locked and from inside came the sounds of cascading water.

I knocked.

'Yes?' Liz's voice said.

'Just checking if the shower's free.'

'It isn't.'

'You won't be long, will you?'

She didn't reply, but knowing I was standing waiting would surely prompt her to be as quick as she could. Unless she decided to take her time in protest. I hadn't got her marked down as the vindictive type, though.

Sure enough, barely a minute later the shower was turned off, shortly after which she emerged, wrapped in a bath robe, with a towel around her head. Without her glasses, and her hair hidden from sight, she looked very different — almost like a child, I thought, as without a word, though with a surly look, she stepped past me. Her problem, not mine. I hadn't done anything.

The rest of the day and evening I spent reading the Marlowe biography, at the same time as listening my way through my small record collection. I didn't much fancy going out to get something to eat, so I fried some potatoes and boiled some spaghetti, eating while perusing a map of London I spread out on the table in front of me along with a list of places Marlowe was known to have frequented. There weren't many. The biography contained barely any facts about his London life — as good as every trace of him was gone. He was born in Canterbury and attended the King's School there before commencing university studies at Cambridge. For two weeks he was held in a London prison for his involvement in a violent episode. I found the place, Newgate, close to the Old Bailey and St Paul's, and put a ring around it. Shortly before his death he was staying at the Chislehurst estate of his patron, Thomas Walsingham, when a warrant was issued for his arrest on charges of blasphemy, and I drew another ring. London had only a small number of theatres in the sixteenth century, I discovered, and of course these were all long since gone. I ringed a location in the Shoreditch area, where Marlowe had also lived for a short time, and another, south of the river in Southwark, the Rose, where most of his plays had first been performed. Then there was Deptford, where he died. No one knew exactly where or why. His final resting place was unknown.

The Old Bailey, Shoreditch, Southwark, Chislehurst, Deptford. These were Marlowe's London places. I could cover them all in a week. And then there were the rehearsals to photograph.

The urge to get started made me restless. Hans being so positive had seemingly triggered something in me. It felt as if I was on the crest of a wave. All difficulty had been put behind me. Ahead lay only opportunity.

Was I so easy to manipulate? Was I not my own person? Was I really so dependent on the appraisals of others? It wasn't meant to be like that, and I wasn't going to allow it to be either. I had to forge my own path, do what I needed to do, and stick to my guns no matter the circumstances.

It was dark outside by the time I rinsed the ketchup and mustard from my plate before leaving it in the sink with the cutlery and the glass. The sight of my reflection, alone in the room, outside the window, gave me an idea. One of the assignments we were bound to be given as part of the portraiture course was to photograph ourselves. Some would doubtless do this before a mirror, either with the camera in front of their face, thereby to include, albeit in the banalest of ways, the meta-perspective — as the painter painting himself painting, so the photographer photographing himself photographing — or else held more discreetly at chest height, which would be quite as hackneyed. Those with a bit more nous would use a self-timer to capture themselves either in some everyday situation — I imagined them darting for the Hoover or diving into a casual posture on the sofa in front of the telly as the camera counted down — or neutral full face, in the manner of the passport photo. What I would do would be to combine the two approaches, photographing my reflection using the self-timer, so that the camera wouldn't be visible, and at the same time capturing the reflection in the window rather than the mirror, meaning the whole room would be included.

Brilliant.

I set up the tripod, adjusted the camera settings, switched on the ceiling light to heighten the effect, activated the self-timer and went and stood in the middle of the room, motionless so as not to make the figure in the window more blurred than it was already. I repeated the procedure a few times using various aperture settings. It was hard to say whether it would turn out well or not, but I sensed it was going to be good. The idea, at least, bordered on the ingenious.

The equipment packed away again, I felt inexplicably tired all of a sudden — I hadn't done anything the entire day, and had slept well into the morning — so although it was only just gone half nine, I went straight to bed and out like a light, as if shot in the back of the head.

I was woken by the alarm clock and was hurled directly into myriad thoughts and emotions, which for a few seconds were vague and unclear before settling meaningfully into place. Something very good had happened. Hans had declared my photograph of the cat to be a masterpiece. There would be order in my day, because I was going back to school. But from somewhere deep within me, something else stirred, likewise vague and unclear to begin with, a faint, trembling unease. Then, almost instantaneously, it too fell into place: the incident with the lighter.

Oh no, no. I swung my legs out of bed and put my feet to the floor, scratched my scalp a moment, my crotch, the scrotum loose and floppy, a slight, pulsating ache in my balls. But nothing had happened. Not really. If anyone had witnessed what had happened, they might plausibly have made something out of it, but no one *had*. Any concern was in my head, and only there.

Good was in any case stronger, and it was good that tugged at me, not stupid fear, which could only keep sending out its signals into the darkness like some lighthouse of anxiety.

I got dressed, ate some muesli and milk, and packed my bag. The lighter and the bike were still tainted by the incident — it was impossible to look at either without it being brought to mind. But in a few days that too would recede. Our days are open and transparent, but enveloped too by the faintest membrane of time, almost imperceptible when our gaze passes through it to consider a single day on its own. But come another day, and another after that, the membrane will thicken, that which before was as *clear as day* will then be blurred and faintly obscured; come yet more and only the outlines will be perceptible, until they too recede and dissolve, and what happened inside them will then be hidden from us, sealed away by time.

Outside the window it was grey and rainy. I put my rain jacket on, slipped my arms through the straps of my rucksack and went down into the street. No police cars pulled up outside. No one stared at me on my way to the station. People were turned inwards, behind dour faces. They shook their umbrellas in front of entrances before folding them up. They pulled back anorak hoods. Some scurried, others strode businesslike and determined, still more came ambling along. Yellow waterproofs, black and red brollies, grey and navy suits. Olive-green wellingtons, light brown brogues, white trainers. Moments opened and closed like sea anemones, colours swam by like fish.

I plucked the day's papers from the stand and joined the two-man queue at the kiosk. The umbrella of the man in front of me dripped onto the flagstones. He wanted throat lozenges and *The Times*. I glanced around and immediately recognised a face. It was the Egyptian. He smiled as he saw me. But his eyes did not.

'Nice to meet you the other night,' he said. 'Kristian, isn't it?'

'Yes, it was a good night,' I said.

'Are you off to the National Gallery, by any chance?' He laughed.

'Not today.'

'Why all the newspapers? Searching them for something?'

'No. No, I like to keep up, that's all. It's a good way of passing time, too.'

'What, murder and devilish deeds?'

He touched my arm and winked as he smiled.

'Be seeing you soon, I shouldn't wonder,' he said. 'You do live around here, don't you? I do.'

The guy was a creep, I thought as I smiled back and said goodbye before turning to the newsagent inside the kiosk and paying for the newspapers. In order not to end up on the same train, I decided to get a coffee at the caff over the road and skim the papers there.

I draped my jacket over the back of a chair, bought a coffee at the counter and wiped the table with a serviette before sitting down and opening the first of the newspapers.

Oh no.

Oh no, no, no.

There was a picture of me.

A picture of me going through the gate.

Where the hell did they get that?

Who'd taken it?

It was blurred.

But it was me.

I could see it was me. If I could see it, then others could too.

I was wearing the same jacket.

I glanced around. No one was looking at me.

Turn the page, for goodness' sake. Don't sit and stare at that damned picture. Drink your coffee. Pull a face, as if it's too bitter. Now, fold the paper. Put your coat on, nice and calm. Pick up the pile and go out the door. Go slowly, but not too slowly.

I'd have to get rid of the bloody coat. Cut my hair. Stay indoors.

A girl went past all in black, kohl-lined eyes like a panda, a big, unruly pile of hair, closely followed by a man in grubby work overalls. Neither of them noticed me.

Even if people had read the paper that morning and seen the photo of me, it didn't mean they were going to recognise me. The papers were full of pictures, and the streets were full of people. But if my behaviour attracted attention and their eyes were drawn to me, the penny might drop. Same coat, same hair.

I went to the crossing looking firmly at the ground. Traffic rumbled past. One, two, three people were stood waiting for the green man. I scanned them quickly: an elderly woman with a shopping trolley, a grey-blue hat balanced on peeping white curls; a middle-aged man with a beer gut, arms held ape-like at his side, a briefcase in one hand — he could have been a train driver or some other railway employee; a postman in a red coat.

I stopped beside them, half turned away. As the light changed from red to green, I stepped out, the first of us onto the crossing. Reaching the other side, I slowed down, reminding myself not to look like I was running from something.

The air was raw and cold. The end of the street, where it twisted away behind a building perhaps a hundred metres away, was almost completed erased by the fog.

It hadn't said I was suspected of murder, only that the police would like me to come forward. If anyone recognised me, they were asked to contact their local police. I was a witness, nothing more. Probably the last person to see him alive. It was only natural they'd want to talk to me. Had I seen anything, noticed anything unusual? Was he perhaps already dead, was that why I'd gone up to him?

I needed to get my story straight.

Go through the whole thing.

Anyone I knew who saw that photo would be bound to realise it was me.

Oh God. Of course. Vivian. She knew I'd been in the area that night. And she'd remember my coat.

Approaching the house, I looked up as the front door opened and someone stepped out. It was Liz. The same bulging bag, the same grey-black mottled coat. She glanced in my direction before coming up the road towards me. She must have seen me. Nevertheless, she pretended she hadn't as she came towards me. Like she was absorbed in her own thoughts.

Had she seen the paper?

No, she wouldn't be ignoring me if she had.

Or maybe that was exactly what she'd be doing?

'Hi, Liz,' I said.

She looked up as if she hadn't seen me until then.

'Oh, hi,' she said.

Not a smile, not a sign to indicate even the slightest interest. Her lips were tight, and the haste with which she'd been walking suggested she was late for something.

'Listen,' I said, needing to find out if she knew or not.

She stopped.

'What?'

'Have you given it any more thought? Filling me in about Marlowe, I mean. You know I said I was going to be taking some photographs for a production of *Doctor Faustus* . . .'

'I don't think I'd be the right person,' she said. 'And actually I'm in a bit of a hurry.'

She flashed an apologetic smile before hurrying on up the road, and I knew she didn't know.

That was something, at least.

But Vivian. She would know. If she read the papers, that is. Maybe she didn't.

If they wanted me to come forward, it could only be as a witness. If they thought I'd done it, wouldn't they come straight out and say I was a suspect?

They couldn't possibly have evidence of anything. Evidence of what? Nothing had happened. There'd been a slight scuffle, but it was unclear what had actually taken place. I'd just wanted my lighter back, he resisted and somehow our forces just fused and flared.

Could I tell them that?

I let myself in and went up the stairs.

No, I couldn't. I couldn't mention anything about any form of physical contact.

Anyway, someone would have to turn me in first. Who would that be? How many people did I know in London who read the newspapers? And even if they did, how many took enough notice of what was in them? How many would be so interested that they began to study the picture and wonder if there weren't certain resemblances to me?

I locked the door behind me as soon as I stepped inside the flat. I couldn't think straight. My head was full of noise. But I needed a plan. I needed to cover every eventuality and know what I had to do.

I filled a glass with cold water from the tap and drank it standing while looking out into the street.

Perhaps it would be easier with a pen and paper.

I put the glass down in the sink and wondered where my notebook might be. In my bag, surely? But no, it wasn't there.

Where could it be?

I checked the bookshelf. It wasn't there either. Nor had I left it on the table in the living room.

What the fuck. It was only a room, how could things disappear?

I got down on my knees and looked under the settee. I even went out to the toilet on the landing to see if it was there, though I knew it wasn't.

Exasperated, I emptied the contents of my bag onto the floor. I didn't care if my camera did take a knock. I wanted that notebook, and I wanted it now.

Could someone have been here and taken it?

Don't be stupid, Kristian. You've left it somewhere. At the school, perhaps. Some cafe or other.

There was nothing secret in it, so it didn't matter, not like that.

Rage and frustration nevertheless seethed in me. I could write on any piece of paper, the back of an envelope or a blank page in a book,

I knew that, but it was the notebook I wanted, nothing else would do, and if I couldn't find it, then I didn't care what happened, the shit could just as well hit the bloody fan.

I checked the pockets of my two coats.

Stood in the middle of the room and looked around me, surveyed the floor inch by inch, then the bookshelf and the table, the settee, the worktop in the kitchen.

It was gone.

Then, footsteps sounded on the staircase. I froze, held my breath and stood motionless as whoever it was reached the landing. Outside my door they stopped. The flap of the letter box opened, and a thin parcel slid through with a swish followed by a gentle flop.

Oh, thank God for that.

Still, I waited until the coast was clear before I went to the door and picked it up off the floor. It was almost completely flat, and so tightly packaged I had to fetch a pair of scissors from the kitchen before I could open it.

Inside was a photograph mounted on white card. I recognised it immediately.

It was Daguerre's Parisian street scene.

Was it from Hans? Why would he do that?

Most likely he just wanted me to see what he'd been talking about.

It was thoughtful of him, but unnecessary. The picture was in the book I'd bought.

I turned it over. On the back, in pencil, it said:

He who is dead is dead, and cannot be saved.
Choose life, Kristian, and you shall do well.

What?
Who had written this?
And what did it mean?
Dead? Why dead?
Reeling inside, I sat down in the chair.
Did someone know?
Who could it be?

Hans? Yes, it had to be Hans. He was the one who'd spoken about the photograph. But what did he mean? Why had he written such a thing?

And how could he possibly know what had happened?

Stay calm.

Breathe.

Vivian.

She knew. She must have told Hans. And then he'd sent the photograph.

Choose life.

It was advice. Don't turn yourself in, carry on with your life as if nothing had happened.

I would do well — this was obviously a reference to the photo of the cat I'd shown him, which had made him believe in me.

It was as simple as that.

And of course he was a bit weird himself. Something like this wouldn't exactly be out of character for him.

But Vivian knew.

No, *no one* knew.

No one had seen me, and nothing had happened.

I went and got my death-tainted cigarettes, which now all of a sudden ceased to fill me with terror. Instead, I felt a positive urge to taunt fate, as it were, and lit one with the deadly lighter itself, sitting down again to study the photograph as I smoked. I liked the way the tobacco crackled at the glowing tip as I inhaled, and the slowly eddying smoke that subsequently curled about my mouth. The man standing with his leg outstretched and his hands behind his back was clearly having his boots polished. There was no mystery about it. But there, to the right of him on the wide pavement, wasn't that another figure, this one seated? I hadn't noticed before, probably because of the small format of the reproduction I'd been looking at previously. Yes, it was. He was holding something white in his hands, what looked to be a newspaper.

One man having his boots polished, therefore standing still long enough for his image to be captured on the plate one morning in 1838, another sitting quietly with his newspaper, he too thereby immortalised. Everyone else, every busy pedestrian, every horse and cart, an entire bustling boulevard in all its restless movement, evades the plate and dissolves in the light that on this particular morning floods from the heavens.

But still there was something unsettling about the picture. It was their alienation. That they were so unnaturally alone there on that big, broad, normally so busy pavement.

Two beings of a different order from the human. They were among us, so like us that we did not see them for what they were, beings of another order, until this morning in 1838, when everyone else fell away, when all that was human evaporated, and only the two remained. One having his boots blackened and polished, another immersed in his newspaper.

The explanation was different. But the mood was exactly that.

I got up, the cigarette dangling from the corner of my mouth, found the packet of Blu-tack in the drawer and stuck the photograph to the wall between the windows above the bed settee. No sooner had I done so than my eye fell on my rucksack and all the stuff that was scattered around it, and at once I knew where my notebook was — in the bag's small outside pocket.

Everything resolved itself. All was good.

I put *Caught in Flux* by Eyeless in Gaza on the turntable and began to write:

First eventuality: The police receive a tip and take me in for questioning. A photo connects me to the scene of the crime, so I can't deny having been there. What happened was that I stopped to light a cigarette. A homeless person inside the gate asked if he could cadge one. At first I said no, and cycled on, but then I changed my mind and cycled back, went up to him and gave him two. He looked a bit worse for wear, I noticed some injuries to his face, but apart from that he seemed to be all right. I cycled on to my girlfriend's. If they ask why I didn't come forward, it was because I didn't know anything had happened. He was alive when I left him, and I don't read the papers, so I had no idea about all this until you people knocked on my door.

Second eventuality: Vivian has seen the picture in the newspaper and recognised me. She confronts me with it. If I admit to having been there, but tell her nothing happened, she'll almost definitely say I should go to the police. I want to avoid that, so the best thing is to deny all knowledge: I've no idea what you're talking about. A picture of me in the paper? Let me see! That's not me. I cycled straight up to yours that night, I swear. This should work, because the picture is blurred, and apart from the coat it could be just about anyone my age. But then the fact that it happened just down the road from hers, and just before I came round that night, might mean she won't believe me. What'll she do then? Turn me in herself? That's the thing. Much safer to say it's me in the photo, but nothing happened. But then I'll have to go to the police myself, and God knows what sort of information they've got. Maybe something I haven't thought about, that proves there was an altercation. At the moment, they've no idea who I am. Best then to deny everything to Vivian. She'd never turn me in. But if she does, the first eventuality kicks in.

<u>Third eventuality</u>: George or somebody else at the school jokingly mentions there's a picture in the paper of someone who looks a lot like me. Just go with the joke and laugh along with them, maybe elaborate on it and say I've got multiple lookalikes, some apparently shadier than others.

It was no worse than that.

With every eventuality accounted for, my behaviour that morning appeared hysterical and overwrought. I was as good as unrecognisable in that photo, no one was ever going to pull me up in the street and tell me it was me, not even the police. I should have gone into school, it wasn't good with all my absences, even if it was an art school. The structure it gave was beneficial to me as well, otherwise I'd be slobbing around the flat all day, which in the long run could only distort every sense of proportion — the smallest, most inconsequential of matters could grow in the mind and be made to seem more important than it was, until eventually it cast a shadow so big that no other thought could thrive beneath it.

But it was too late now, half the day would be gone by the time I got there.

Vivian *must* have said something to Hans. Why else would he have written those words?

I removed the photograph from the wall and read again what was written on the back:

He who is dead is dead, and cannot be saved.
Choose life, Kristian, and you shall do well.

It couldn't be understood any differently, surely? Let's say he knew nothing about the incident. What could then have prompted him to write such a thing? As far as I remembered, we'd never talked about death. The only thing I could think of was the photograph of the cat. In that case it was the cat that was dead, I carried on living, and the photo suggested I was going to do well. Was that it?

It didn't fit.

Maybe it was more philosophical than that. A photograph shows only what is dead, removed from time, but there's a way around it that can bring it to life — was that what he was saying?

I needed to talk to him. It was the only way I'd find out.

But I'd been to see him only yesterday. I couldn't exactly inundate him there at his studio.

There was no point in thinking about any of this. It was speculation, nothing more. I had to stick to fact. And the fact was that no one could possibly know what had happened.

The synth bass on 'Skeletal Framework' suddenly shattered my thoughts. I'd always loved it. Then, breaking in on top of its relentless progression, the lift of guitar, a jangling, near-aggressive riff.

It reminded me of something. Another song, different band.

Diggeliggeliggeliggeliii

Diggeliggeliggeliggeliii

What was it?

Diggeliggeliggeliggeliii

Echo and the Bunnymen, that was it. But the riff there was a lot slower, more majestic. Loaded with mood.

Was it from *Heaven Up Here*?

I kneeled down in front of my records and flipped through them, picked out the Bunnymen and put it on. The songs on it melted together in my mind, so I put the needle down at the beginning. It was sheer joy.

I'd listened to that album so many times, thousands surely, that it was like coming home. My *proper* home.

It was funny, too, that it was 'Skeletal Framework' that had wrenched me away from my futile worries. For there was the series I was planning. *Frameworks of Life*. It was a good sign. Hans's enthusiasm, too: a good sign. The daguerreotype: a good sign.

I swayed about the room, immersed in the wonderful music, which was dark, but not bottomless black; desperate, but not helpless; atmospheric, but not sentimental.

The riff was from 'Over the Wall'. Lazier, bigger, richer, and yet the same. It too spread from a single, hypnotic bassline. Still, it wouldn't be unfair to say it was a better song, that the Bunnymen were the better band. At the same time, though, they were more polished than Eyeless in Gaza, and there lay the trap, the bog they'd stepped right into with their latest album — it was the U2 syndrome, the illness of becoming great.

It was a shame. They'd had everything.

A bit like all the poor Europeans who went to America at the end of the nineteenth century to seek their fortunes. Some, indeed, found them, or at least became wealthier than they'd been before, but the price they paid was high, for it turned them into Americans.

On the other hand, it meant they'd opened up space for those they left behind, and those who succeeded them.

I stuck the Daguerre photo up on the wall again and stood for a moment considering it. There was something about those two people, the man with his hands behind his back — or were they in his pockets? — one leg extended, long and thin, his foot on the boot-blacker's box, and the other man, seated on a cafe chair ten metres away, his newspaper spread out in his lap. Since all the other people who'd been present had dissolved in the light, it was as if the two of them somehow belonged together. As if they were connected. Two parts of the same whole.

When they were there, at eight o'clock that morning, the Boulevard du Temple had almost certainly been a hive of activity, and the connection between the two men would have been completely unnoticeable. No one would have thought they had anything to do with each other. Most likely, they hadn't. It was the photograph that stirred the feeling.

Vivian was the only threat. She was the only way they could get to me.

I'd be able to tell how much she knew as soon as I saw her again. I'd be able to control it then.

I supposed they'd be rehearsing today. I couldn't use my bike, that was for certain. For all I knew, the police could have a lot more photos than the one they'd made public. And if they knew I'd been on a bike, that was what they'd be looking for. Young man, fair hair, long at the neck, wearing a dark-coloured rain jacket, riding a bicycle.

I put my black overcoat on. It wouldn't take long to get a haircut, the barber's wouldn't be particularly busy at this time of day — but it would arouse Vivian's suspicions. The same went for the jacket — even though the urge to get rid of it now burned in my chest, I knew I couldn't, I'd be a person destroying evidence then, and why would I do that, if I hadn't done anything? It made no sense to even say I was innocent, because that implied someone thinking I could be guilty.

Although the weather was too mild for it, I pulled on a black woolly hat, tucked my hair inside it, and hey presto, the young man on the bike with the long hair at his neck and a dark rain jacket on was gone. I dropped a couple of rolls of film into my bag, locked the door behind me and went down the stairs in a fairly cheerful mood, all things considered.

The door of the former warehouse was open the same as last time. And just as before, I heard voices from the floor above as I approached the staircase. I paused a moment to get myself together before going up. If she knew anything, I'd be able to tell right away from the look on her face. If she confronted me, I'd deny everything. If she knew nothing — well, everything would be all right.

These were reassuring thoughts. And yet my legs felt weak and wobbly as I climbed the stairs.

Two men in their thirties were standing facing each other in the middle of the floor with Vivian, their only audience, slightly removed.

Both men were shaven-headed and were dressed in white T-shirts and baggy black bottoms.

On seeing me, a look of astonishment passed across her face, but nothing like the fear or trepidation that would have signalled to me that she knew.

On the other hand she'd expressly said that I wasn't to come here. Shouldn't she have been angry?

'Hi, Vivian,' I said. 'I thought I might find you here.'

'This is Kristian,' she said to the two actors. 'He'll be taking pictures for us. Are you OK with him being here?'

'Yes, I'm OK with that,' said one. The other nodded.

I sat down on the floor over by the wall. All three ignored me and carried on where they'd left off. If she'd known anything, she'd have been glancing in my direction. No one could have that much control over themselves.

On a table a bit further away, a newspaper stuck out of what I assumed was her bag.

She could have bought it and not had time to read it yet. Or she could have read it and not noticed the picture.

'We'll take it from where you come back in,' I heard her say.

One of the actors went over to the far wall.

'OK,' Vivian said.

Now he came ambling towards the other one.

'Now, Faustus, what wouldst thou have me do?' he said, halting in front of him.

They were oddly alike, not only because of their clothes and their bald heads, it was something about their type.

Faustus didn't reply, but simply stared back at him. After a moment, Mephistophilis looked down.

'I charge thee wait upon me whilst I live,' said Faustus.

Vivian raised her hand.

'Hold it there,' she said. 'This is a key moment. Their first encounter. Can you hold each other's gaze a bit longer? Until it gets uncomfortable?'

The actors nodded.

Not even in the few seconds it took Mephistophilis to return to his starting point did Vivian look in my direction. It felt almost contrary to nature. Wouldn't she want to check my reactions to seeing her in the director's role? Was she so determined not to look at me, because she knew?

Mephistophilis halted in front of Faustus again.

'Now, Faustus, what wouldst thou have me do?'

They stared at each other.

'Rory, step closer,' Vivian said.

Faustus stepped closer. Mephistophilis held his gaze another moment, then looked down.

'I charge thee wait upon me whilst I live,' said Faustus. 'To do whatever Faustus shall command.'

Mephistophilis smiled, his eyes still lowered.

'Be it to make the moon drop from her sphere, or the ocean to overwhelm the world.'

'I am a servant to great Lucifer,' Mephistophilis replied, 'and may not follow thee without his leave. No more than he commands must we perform.'

'Did not he charge thee to appear to me?'

Mephistophilis now lifted his gaze.

'No, I came hither of mine own accord.'

'Did not my conjuring speeches raise thee? Speak!'

'That was the cause, but yet *per accidens*. For, when we hear one rack the name of God, abjure the Scriptures and his Saviour Christ, we fly, in hope to get his glorious soul. Nor will we come unless he use such means whereby he is in danger to be damn'd. Therefore the shortest cut for conjuring is stoutly to abjure all godliness, and pray devoutly to the prince of hell.'

'So Faustus hath already done, and holds this principle, there is no chief but only Belzebub, to whom Faustus doth dedicate himself. This word "damnation" terrifies not me, for I confound hell in Elysium: my ghost be with the old philosophers! But, leaving these vain trifles of men's souls, tell me what is that Lucifer, thy Lord?'

'Arch-regent and commander of all spirits.'

'Was not that Lucifer an angel once?'

'Yes, Faustus, and most dearly lov'd of God.'

'How comes it, then, that he is prince of devils?'

'O, by aspiring pride and insolence, for which God threw him from the face of heaven.'

'And what are you that live with Lucifer?'

'Unhappy spirits that fell with Lucifer, conspir'd against our God with Lucifer, and are forever damn'd with Lucifer.'

'Where are you damn'd?'

'In hell.'

'How comes it, then, that thou art out of hell?'

'Why, this is hell, nor am I out of it.' Faustus stared at him blankly. 'Think'st thou that I, that saw the face of God and tasted the eternal joys of heaven, am not tormented with ten thousand hells in being depriv'd of everlasting bliss? O, Faustus, leave these frivolous demands, which strike a terror to my fainting soul!'

Mephistophilis now fixed Faustus in his gaze. Tears were in his eyes.

'What, is great Mephistophilis so passionate for being deprived of the joys of heaven? Learn thou of Faustus manly fortitude, and scorn those joys thou never shalt possess.'

'Thank you,' said Vivian. 'That was good. Really, really good. Did you sense how the balance of power between you kept tipping? It's almost as if they swap parts as they go along. I think we can close in even more on that dynamic. It's partly in the lines, of course, but I think we can seek to bring it out a little bit more in the acting in between. What do you reckon?'

'Yes,' said the one who was playing Mephistophilis, 'it still feels a little static. I mean, we're just standing there saying the lines really. There must be some way we can inject something more physical into it.'

'Like what? Any suggestions?'

'Not immediately, no.'

'Let's take some time out to consider it. I don't think it needs that much doing to it, to be honest. There's a lot of tension in there as it stands, and it may be the case that they come across stronger if that tension isn't transmitted into physical action. One thing you're playing up against is expectation, yes? Mephistophilis is the Devil's envoy, so why is he so submissive? He seems to allow himself to be dominated by Faustus. Another thing is the play's whole narrative arc: Faustus starts out full of bravado, there's nothing he can't do, nothing he doesn't know — here's a man who's not going to let himself be pushed around. By the time the play ends, all that's gone. All that's left are terror and remorse. Maybe the point there is: Who does Faustus become in Hell? He becomes the Devil's servant. He becomes Mephistophilis. So, in this scene I think it's reasonable to imagine that this is Faustus encountering his doomed self. He's standing in front of the man he's to become, who in turn is trying to warn him. Don't go down that path. Yes? So, I think you have to trust that everything's there already, every bit of tension, every slice of meaning. It's there, in the writing, Faustus challenging and gloating, Mephistophilis humbler. But yes, let's take a break now, and then we'll go through the whole thing again, OK?'

The actors nodded.

There was no way she knew anything, I told myself as she went over to the table and took a packet of cigarettes from her bag.

'I thought you didn't want me just turning up like this,' I said.

'You thought right,' she said, lighting one. 'But you're here now. Was there anything in particular you wanted?'

I was longing for you, I should have said. But I couldn't make myself. I shrugged.

'Just wanted to see you. I thought you'd be here, so . . .'

'I'm meeting Hans shortly.'

She looked at her watch.

'In half an hour. That pub we went to the last time you were here. You can meet us there, if you want.'

'You don't want me here, then?'

She shook her head.

'No. They're not comfortable with it, even if they did say it was OK. They need the intimacy of the three of us together. You sitting there watching is an intrusion.'

'So you want me to go now?'

'That's right.'

Normally I'd have been annoyed by her arrogance. But as I now got to my feet, I felt only relief. She knew nothing. No one knew anything. I was completely safe. The only element of uncertainty was that newspaper of hers.

'Mind if I take that with me?' I said with a nod.

'Take what with you?'

'Your paper. It'll give me something to do while I'm waiting.'

'No, not at all. Take it.'

With the rolled-up newspaper stuffed into the pocket of my overcoat, I headed over to the pub at the riverside. The mist had lifted, the sky was an unbroken grey-white with a bulge of light, so it seemed, where the sun was. The pub, which inside had a maritime feel, with old-looking wooden beams, was half empty. I bought a pint and went to sit down in the lounge. Immediately, I saw Hans seated by the window, hunched over a small sketchpad.

I spun round before he noticed me, went back and found a seat at the bar. I had to prepare myself mentally. Hans, it occurred to me the moment I set eyes on him there, was just as much a threat to me as Vivian was. Had he not sent me that photograph? Until I knew why, and what he'd meant by the words he'd written on the back of it, he was indeed a threat. Or rather he wasn't, but *I* was. I had to make sure I reacted in the right way. Vivian could have mentioned to him that I'd been to see her that night; he could have seen the picture in the paper and then put two and two together.

Could I tell him?

Listen, Hans, there's something I need to tell you. Two days ago, a tramp dragged me into a fight with him. He banged his head. I think he might have died. Now the police want to talk to me. What do you think I should do?

Ha ha.

No way.

I took a long pull on my pint. As I put it back down, I sensed out of the corner of my eye a figure come towards me, and looked round.

'You're not hiding from me, I hope?' Hans said.

'Are you here?'

'Don't pretend you didn't see me.'

'I'm not. You were occupied.'

'So why are you asking if I'm here?'

'I don't know, I didn't realise you knew I'd seen you. And maybe it was a bit strange of me not to come over. That's why.'

'You know, don't you, that if you stick to telling the truth, you'll never get yourself all tangled up like that?'

'What do you mean? I'm not lying. I just didn't want to disturb you.'

'It's OK, Kristian. Everyone tells lies. Lies are the oil that lubricates the social machine.'

I disliked intensely that smart-arsed tone of his. The stupid face on him didn't help either.

At the same time, I realised he didn't know anything.

So why the photo he'd sent?

Why hadn't he mentioned it? Asked me if I'd seen it?

'Vivian'll be along shortly,' he said. 'Do you want some lunch with us?'

'I know,' I said, and slid down from my stool. 'I just talked to her, at the rehearsal space. I've got to do those photos, haven't I?'

'Is that today's?' he said, swiping the newspaper from my coat pocket before I could answer.

'Hey, you can't just take things, you know!'

He fixed his eyes on me and lifted his brow exaggeratedly.

'You mean I can't borrow your paper, is that what you're saying?'

'You can ask first.'

'Can I borrow your paper?'

'Yes.'

We went and sat down at a table, where he opened the newspaper. I had to distract him, I realised, and drained what was left of my pint.

'What were you doing just before, anyway?'

'Sketching,' he said without looking up.

'What for?'

'*Doctor Faustus.*'

'You mean *you're* doing the set design?'

Now he did look up.

'No need to sound so surprised.'

'I just didn't think . . .'

'Think what?'

'I didn't know you worked for the theatre company as well.'

'I don't,' he said, and turned the page.

If he did so again, the article would be there staring him in the face.

'I'm doing it for Vivian's sake.'

'Is that why you're meeting up now?'

'Mm-hmm.'

'Thanks for the photograph, by the way.'

'What photograph?'

He looked up again.

'The one by Daguerre you were telling me about. It came through the letter box today.'

'What are you talking about?'

'You sent me that photograph by Daguerre, didn't you?'

He shook his head.

'Who else could it be? You were talking about Daguerre, and that photograph in particular. It couldn't be from anyone else I know.'

'Well, it wasn't me.'

He turned the page.

'Are you sure about that?'

'What do you mean, am I *sure*?'

'I mean you're sure you didn't send me the photograph?'

'What's the matter with you today? Of course I'm sure I didn't send you a photograph by Daguerre. It's not the sort of thing I'd be likely to forget, is it?'

'Maybe not. It's just so weird that someone would send me the exact photograph that no one else has been talking about, only you.'

He was no longer listening. He was reading about the incident. He lowered his face demonstratively to the page to study the picture closer, then looked at me.

'This looks like you! Have you seen it?'

'Seen what?'

'This picture here. It looks like you.'

'Let me see that.'

He turned the paper towards me.

'I suppose it does a bit,' I said. 'Do you want another pint?'

'It's *not* you though, is it? Or *is* it?'

'Of course it's not me.'

I felt his eyes on my back as I went up to the bar, and cursed myself. I should have stayed put, remained seated until we'd exhausted the matter. Now he'd think it *was* me, that it was the reason I got up. That I was guilty.

Oh, for crying out loud.

I could still make light of it, joke about it until it was no longer an issue. He didn't *know* anything.

But he'd be wondering.

I bought a pint of lager, a Guinness for him. Even as I turned round to go back to the table, I could see he still had the paper open at the same page.

'Here you go,' I said, putting his pint down in front of him. 'I assumed it was Guinness you wanted?'

'It *is* you,' he said. 'Isn't it?'

'What are you talking about?

He turned the paper towards me again.

'This. It's you.'

'No, it's not. It's someone who looks like me, that's all. Now, give it a rest.'

'Why haven't you asked what it's about?'

'Why should I?'

'Because it'd be the natural thing to do, seeing your doppelgänger in the newspaper, anyone would be curious to know what the man had done.'

'So what's he done?'

He closed the paper and gave me a look that was half exasperation, half disappointment, which then dissolved into a smile at the same time as his gaze shifted slightly to one side.

I turned and saw Vivian come towards us.

'Hi,' she said, dumping her bag on a chair, unwinding her scarf, noticeably flushed, as if she'd been running . 'Just need to go to the loo.'

Hans smiled again as she made for the ladies.

'You've gone quiet, Kristian.'

If he mentioned it to Vivian, it'd be pointless to keep on denying it. I'd have to sacrifice my queen.

'Listen, Hans,' I said.

'Yes?'

'You don't need to mention that picture to Vivian, OK?'

'Why not? It's only someone who looks like you, isn't it?'

'Can I trust you?'

'Of course.'

'OK. Then I'll tell you everything. But you've got to promise me you won't tell Vivian.'

He nodded, the same smile on his face. I picked up the newspaper, folded it, and tucked it away by the window beside me. The chances of Vivian remembering it were surely small.

'Feel better now?' Hans said.

'I feel fine, thanks. As I have done all along. Did you say something about lunch?'

'Well, it's a meeting, primarily, but I'm sure there'll be some food on the agenda. Are you hungry?'

'No.'

He bent down and took a big sketchpad from his bag on the floor.

'You can trust me, Kristian,' he said. 'No need to worry.'

I believed him. But I wanted to make the incident go away, not disseminate it.

Vivian returned and sat down beside Hans. She didn't even look at me.

'So, what have you got for me?' she said.

'Why don't we order something to eat first?' he said.

'I haven't really got time for lunch. Do you mind?'

Hans shook his head.

'Two proposals. The first following on from what we've already talked about. Very simple. *Very* simple. A black box. Black walls, black floor. No props. But glittering stars projected onto the rear wall. Everything stays the same throughout the performance — until the end, when the clock starts ticking, and then suddenly there's a sun, and the whole stage is flooded with light.'

'Explain. Run me through your thinking.'

He gave a shrug.

'It's the basic idea that Hell is here, I suppose. As Mephistophilis says at the beginning. But also, it's trying to show us the dispossession he feels when everything is lost. Or make us understand.'

'I like it. What about costumes?'

'If we go with this, then they'll almost have to be neutral. Timeless. Everyone in white or black or grey, something like that.'

'How about everyone in red?'

'Wouldn't that be overdoing it a bit?'

'How do you mean?'

'The colours become codes then. Red for blood, life. Black for night, death, demise. I think it'd be too obvious, we'd be giving too much away.'

'I'm not sure I agree. But OK. What's the second proposal?'

'Right, let me show you,' he said, flipping open his big sketchpad. 'This is pretty much the direct opposite. Stuff going on everywhere.'

Vivian leaned in for a closer look.

'It's a blend of Faustus's study and a *wunderkammer*. Science, in other words.'

The sketch looked a bit like his own studio. Shelves with books in the middle, from where spread a miscellany of animal heads, skulls and skeletons, glass jars and myriad more items as yet undefined.

'Now, all this clutter here can be ordered, if we want — for example, we could have the *wunderkammer* and all the alchemy together in the middle, the more modern scientific stuff advancing as it were from the sides —'

'No, no.'

'Or we can tie it uniquely to the age — that particular seventeenth-century hotchpotch of science and magic.'

'What's this over here?' Vivian said, pointing a finger.

'That's a staircase. So the study is inside and the staircase is outside. I was thinking Wittenberg and the church steps. For the outdoor scenes.'

'I'm not so sure about this one. The difficult element in this play is precisely the connection between the Elizabethan age in which it takes place — the late 1500s — and the more universal resonance of it, the fact that it still speaks to us now. All that will be a lot easier to get across, I think, if the design holds back on explicitly flagging time. But I'll think about it. You're doing a great job.'

Then, she looked at me.

'What do you think, Kristian?'

I didn't want to say the same as her, they'd think I couldn't form an opinion of my own. But I did agree with her. The first proposal was the best.

'Can I have a look?' I said.

Hans turned the sketch towards me and I gave it my most scrutinising gaze.

'I think this one's probably a tad too heavy on detail,' I said. 'I'm more for the first one.'

It was a bit too simply formulated, I realised straight away.

'It's more timeless,' I added. 'And good and evil are beyond time, if you see what I mean.'

They exchanged glances. Hans's lips tightened a moment, a fraction of a second, but long enough for me to notice and comprehend. They were laughing at me. They talked about me behind my back, and when they did they laughed at me too.

My cheeks burned with indignation and contempt.

Or was it something else? Did Vivian *know*?

It wasn't implausible. Good and evil, I'd said. They knew why, and had exchanged glances.

They confided in each other.

Maybe they were fucking each other.

Did she fuck everyone?

No, she knew nothing. No one could be that good an actor.

'I have a third proposal actually,' Hans said, closing his sketchpad. 'An idea I got from the opening of Thomas Mann's *Doctor Faustus*, if you remember it?'

He looked at her, not at me.

Did he think I wouldn't have read it?

She nodded.

'Adrian's father is initiating the two boys in some of the secrets of nature. One of these concerns the boundary between the living and the dead. He shows them how inorganic, chemical growths at the bottom of a crystallisation vessel move towards the light. But they're dead, they're just dead matter. How about if I film that process and run the film during the entire performance? Projected onto the rear or side walls.'

'Wouldn't it distract from the acting?'

'No. It wouldn't be intrusive. At least, no more than the stars would be. I imagine it fading in and out, dissolving. But it would be there nonetheless. I'm thinking a permanent, but discreet, unsettling presence could be pretty cool.'

'I understand the thought. And it's a good idea. Could you do us a test version or something, so we can see how it might look?'

'Sure, no problem.'

'Great. Thanks a lot. I really appreciate your work here.'

'It's only ideas at this stage. Nothing I've spent loads of time on or anything.'

'Maybe we could talk about my photos a bit,' I said. 'While we're at it, I mean.'

'OK, tell me,' Vivian said.

'I've given it some consideration, and I think it would be a good idea to photograph Marlowe's London. I've done some initial research. He lived in Shoreditch for a time, so that's one place to start. He was in prison there. Then there's where his plays were performed. And Deptford, of course.'

'Sounds good,' Vivian said, and stood up.

I looked at her with astonishment. Was that all?

'Now, I really must be getting back to my actors.'

She put on her coat, twirled her scarf around her neck and picked up her bag. At the same time, I had a powerful urge to look towards the newspaper in the window beside me, probably because it was the one thing I knew I shouldn't do. Fortunately, I resisted.

'See you soon,' she said with a fleeting nod before turning and leaving.

'Toodle-oo,' said Hans.

'She didn't exactly seem interested in my photos,' I said as she disappeared through the door.

'That's because they belong to the final phase. She's still at the beginning. I doubt she's got the time to give them a thought yet.'

'She found the time for your sketches.'

'Yes, but the set's thought out long before photos. She's an incredible talent, you know. She's going to go a long way.'

He tucked the sketchpad into his bag and then sipped his Guinness, until then untouched, before wiping the froth from his mouth with the back of his hand.

'Anyway, you were going to tell me something.'

'Not here.'

'OK, I get you.'

He smiled.

'Maybe we should walk afterwards. I assume we'll be going in the same direction.'

The cover of cloud was white and stretched out like a sheet over the city. The river water, lapping high against the wall of the embankment, was the colour of tea with a good splash of milk in it. The concrete and brick glistened, a tarry near-black at the bottom, verging towards grey further up, and drier too, but still as dark.

Hans hadn't spoken since we'd left the pub. I supposed he was waiting for me to confess. I for my part baulked at even beginning. Telling someone was going to change everything. But I had no choice. He knew it was me in that picture. I couldn't control him, who he talked to, or what he said. But if I came clean with him, he'd be personally embroiled. The question then would be how deep his loyalty ran. I'd be telling only him. He alone would be privy. It would be a bit like presenting him with a gift. A gift of friendship. The ultimate confidence: I'm telling you something now that I've never told anyone, and never will again.

The only thing was, the same would apply the other way round: he'd have something on me, and always would.

I glanced sideways at him as we walked. No one could ever accuse him of looking cool, that was for sure. The same old trousers flapping above his ankles, the woolly jumper, the quilted waistcoat that had to be at least ten years old; the jutting lower jaw, the big mess of hair. I could only guess what people thought when they saw us together: what's he doing with such a deadbeat?

But he was brainy. Vivian was too. And they were creatives.

We emerged onto the paved open expanse where the *Cutty Sark* was, tourists and school classes swarming as ever.

'I'll catch the bus from just up here,' he said.

'OK,' I said.

It was now or never.

My eye caught his.

No. I couldn't do it.

It was nothing really.

But it wouldn't be nothing once I started talking about it.

'So, you're wanted by the police,' he said.

'No, I'm not,' I said.

'That's what it says in the paper. Assuming of course it *is* you in that picture. Which it is.'

'It bears a resemblance, yes.'

'Well, the police want to speak to the person in that photo. So you're who they want to speak to.'

'They don't know who I am.'

'Tell me what happened.'

'Nothing.'

'Nothing?'

'No, nothing. That's what's killing me about it. The picture makes it look like I had something to do with it.'

'With what, exactly?'

'Well, with what happened there.'

'A tramp getting murdered, you mean?'

'No one got murdered.'

'That's not what the papers are saying. They're calling it murder. According to them, there's a killer on the loose.'

'For God's sake, keep your voice down.'

'Relax, Kristian. No one knows what we're talking about.'

We went through the entrance to the market. He'd made me lose control of my narrative. My hands were clammy, I couldn't get my head straight.

'So what happened?' he went on. 'What were you doing there?'

A double-decker came teetering up the shallow hill towards us, passing only a hand's breadth from Hans, whose face for a second seemed faintly to take on a blush of London Transport red.

'Nothing happened, I've told you,' I said. 'I stopped to light a fag and this homeless guy on the other side of the wall where I was standing asked if I had any to spare. I went in to where he was sat and gave him a couple and came straight back out again. Then later, when I went past on my way home, there were police everywhere.

'If that's all that happened, why don't you step forward and tell them? They're looking for you in connection with a murder investigation. It's serious, you understand that, surely?'

'I just don't want to be —'

But Hans cut me off.

'If it *isn't* what happened, and you actually *did* kill him, the last thing you should do is go to the police. They'll see right through you then and have a confession out of you in no time.'

'I didn't kill him.'

'But you did cause his death?'

'What makes you think that? Why would I?'

He tightened his lips in obvious exasperation.

'Listen, Kristian. There's my bus. Let's talk about this another time.'

I went home in a fog of despair and anger. It felt like he'd deceived me, drawn me out into the open, and then left me high and dry. Hurrying for the bus like that — as if he couldn't have caught the next one instead! But most of all it was the words he'd used, they tormented me, ricocheting about like bullets in my mind: Murder. Killer. Police

I didn't feel safe, not even after I'd locked my door. It felt like the whole world knew who I was and where I lived, as if anyone at all could come barging in at any minute. I thought of wedging a chair under the door handle, but I'd be giving in then to irrational emotions, according them power and influence, it'd be a bit like appointing Hitler chancellor of the Reich to bring peace and order to the country. Instead, I cut a pair of spare bedsheets to size and hung them up in front of the windows with drawing pins. That wasn't irrational — I didn't have any curtains and it wasn't normal allowing people to stare in through your windows, not even when you lived on the second floor.

They dampened the light significantly. I lay down on the bed settee and closed my eyes. A hour or two's sleep would surely sweep away the pile of aberrant thoughts that right now cluttered my mind. The board would be cleared, as it were, white and pristine, and other patterns would form.

It was dark outside by the time I woke up, nearly night in fact, almost ten o'clock. I'd slept soundly and without dreaming, and opening my eyes it felt like I was emerging from under the soil. But sleep had worked its wonders. All despondency and despair were gone. The police didn't know who I was and the photo in the paper was inconclusive. No one I knew was going to turn me in, to think they would was beyond credible. And even if anyone did, there was no evidence against me. I hadn't done anything, at least nothing criminal. I was in the clear.

I took the sheets down from the windows, scrubbed five potatoes and dropped them into a saucepan of water, then searched the cupboard for something to go with them. I hadn't eaten all day and hunger gnawed at the walls of my stomach like some nightmarish goblin. I'd run out of spaghetti, but there was plenty of rice, as well as a couple of tins of baked beans.

The sky above the rooftops was clear. Not many stars were visible, but the ones I could see shimmered as if in eagerness. I put Ultravox's *Vienna* on and stood for a moment in front of the stereo, taking in the ticking intro of 'Astradyne'. It was so definitive: stillness, and then the first tick. But the instrumentation that followed, so faint at first as to be almost inaudible, sounded like the piece had been playing since time began, as if the ticking somehow pulled the music from out of the darkness, and then, when the rhythm section came in with its old-fashioned drums and bass, it felt like the world itself had now been invoked into being. The overlay of synths and that fabulous little violin were so full of longing, a yearning for a *different* world, but what the music couldn't understand was that it *was* that world. None of this was in any sense real, of course, there was nothing about it of a material nature, apart perhaps from the drummer's beating of his kit — it was all conjured forth out of nothing.

New Europeans. Young Europeans.

Vienna.

I had to go there. Vienna. Düsseldorf. Berlin. Zürich. Frankfurt. Machines and rain. Asphalt and concrete. The past consigned to rubble, longing the only thing left of it. The future not bleak, not nineteenth-century dark, but pale and hopeless.

I took the album off the turntable — it had done its job — and replaced it with NEU!, the first album, which I hadn't played for ages.

It was fantastic! The only downside was that it was old. From the early seventies. But there was nothing hippieish about it, nothing organic.

Those two diabolical figures would have understood none of it, I thought, as again I studied the daguerreotype with the two nineteenth-century gentlemen in it, one having his boots polished, the other engrossed in his newspaper, eerily alone in that vast and empty city. What's the idea? they would have asked, and shaken their heads. Where is the matter? Where is the sap? Where is the darkness? The thousand-year gloom? Well, gentlemen, I shall tell you. The past is a storage room, dark and dusty, in which nothing happens besides things being added to the pile, things which likewise in time become dark and dusty too. You can hear the creak of boredom. You can see your mother and father shuffle about, doing what they've always done, thinking what they've always thought, the same as their parents and grandparents. Matter, yes, but dead meat. Sap, yes, but the purge fluids of the corpse. Imagine if you saw all that come crashing down and being destroyed. Everything after it is new. The music is new. Gone are the hand-crafted, hand-played instruments of old, for their sound is now but mould and rot. Let now the machines play. Let the machines long, that we may dance.

I turned the record over and stuck a knife into a potato. The blade went through it easily, detaching a small piece which the bubbling water immediately began tossing this way and that. I decided I could do without the rice, and opened a tin of beans after straining the potatoes and leaving them steaming at the bottom of the saucepan.

It was impossible to carry out, of course, and perhaps not that desirable in itself, but the thought was certainly worth entertaining: What if everyone over the age of twenty-five was exterminated? And every book, every record, every music score, every painting burned?

It's our world — we can, and must, do with it as we please.

I picked up a potato between my fingers, its heat immediately searing my skin, but when, no more than a second or two later, I put it down on the plate, all that remained of the sensation was a slight prickle. Three was enough to begin with. I cut a cross in each, pulling the flesh slightly apart to accommodate a small knob of butter. I tipped the baked beans, cold as they were, onto the plate beside them.

Food would be a problem. It came from nature and had always been the same. Grain and milk, meat and vegetables. Even Stone Age man had the same diet.

It might not have to matter. Food could be prepared by machines and made available, full of additives, from vending machines. It wasn't being human that had to go, it was the past.

The butter melted into the potatoes, soft enough now to absorb the salty yellow liquid. I savoured a couple of mouthfuls of the first potato on its own, enjoying both taste and consistency, then forked up some beans, the sweetness of which went well with the butter.

Some would surely think it pathetic to be sitting alone in a second-floor London bedsit eating only potatoes and cold baked beans. But they didn't know me. For one thing, I liked it. For another, I had my own admission ticket to the big wide world: my pictures.

To pass the time before I could sleep again, I settled down with the Marlowe biography. It was rather boring, basically because so little was known about his life. They knew where he'd grown up, so the book was rich on local fact-finding — how a hatter with sixteen children had eventually gone out of business, that sort of thing, with Marlowe himself nowhere in any of it. Sentences began with 'He may have . . .', 'It is not inconceivable that . . .', or 'One can imagine . . .' What little was actually known stemmed from public documents, and the author strove to augment these arid pieces of information with equally mind-numbing facts culled from elsewhere. There was, though, one particularly substantial exception to this. Towards the end of Marlowe's life, a certain Richard Baines, a dubious character with whom Marlowe had once apparently shared lodgings during a stay in the Netherlands, delivered a note to the authorities about him. It concerned Marlowe's 'monstrous opinions' — that Christ had been gay and John the Baptist his bedfellow; that Christ had been illegitimate, a bastard, his mother a dishonourable liar; that if the Jews, his own people, crucified him, it was only because they best knew him, and whence he came; that Christ deserved to die more than Barabas, and the Jews thereby made a good choice, even though Barabas was both a thief and a murderer. Moreover: that the Sacrament might be better administered in a tobacco pipe; that the New Testament was 'filthily' written; and that Moses was but a 'juggler' who abused and tricked the Jews.

In the sixteenth century this was obviously explosive stuff — in fact it felt like it probably still was. He must have been an outrageous figure, and reckless too, for these were not simply thoughts given in confidence, but were delivered in 'table talk or otherwise', as the book said, not private, innermost musings, but opinions specifically worded for an audience he wished to shock. Vile and heretical. He got into a few brawls, so he was fiery and violence-prone too. In short, he didn't give a fuck.

If he believed what he'd written in *Doctor Faustus*, that devils would come and seize the soul of anyone who forsook the Scriptures and his Saviour Christ, he must surely have felt those same devils to be coming for his own.

But the point about his atheism was not that he didn't believe in God, but that to him God did not exist. Accordingly, the Devil did not exist either.

So why did he write *Doctor Faustus*?

Not long after he did, he was killed when a dagger went through his eye.

By his careless and unshackled behaviour, and perhaps too an increasing sense of invulnerableness, he had sown the seeds of his downfall himself.

Unless, that is, he had sold his soul to the Devil and redeemed himself that night in Deptford.

Or taken a boat to Scotland and begun writing Shakespeare's plays.

I slept a while in the hours before morning, got up early, showered in the basement, and then had some breakfast and a mug of coffee, enjoying this brief lull before packing my bag and getting off to school. The terror of the last couple of days was ungraspable, it was as if I'd suffered a psychotic episode. The faces of my fellow students showed no unusual reaction on seeing me, everything was the way it normally was. The only thing different was that George took me aside to tell me I was walking a fine line as regards my absences and that it was now required of me that I attend all our remaining sessions through until the end of term. I didn't mention the depressions I'd already told him I suffered from, down periods when I literally couldn't get out of bed, for although such a serious health issue ought to have been taken into account, there was also something feeble about it that I couldn't believe I'd allowed myself to be taken in by. So, I'd attend every session, take part in every activity. I'd work hard, give it my all, and at the end of the day I'd be the star of the school.

The week passed quickly. Mainly, I spent the days in the darkroom, developing the self-portraits as well as most of the other rolls I'd shot of late. I could tell from just scanning the contact sheets that almost without exception the photographs were going to be good. It was as if something pivotal had occurred, all of a sudden my work was on a higher level, not simply the odd photo that could be put down to chance, but across the board. Even the photograph of the lighter had something special about it. The book I'd bought on creativity devoted a chapter to the phenomenon, how creativity could be an uphill struggle, year after year with no apparent progress, wheels spinning without ever gaining traction, until suddenly everything came together and you shot upwards to the top, onto a plateau, your new level. Ahead of you then would be a new hill, to be negotiated in the same way at some later point.

The first print of the self-portrait was good enough, but I wouldn't let it suffice, repeating the process again and again until it was perfect. The humiliation I'd suffered at the hands of Figueroa still smarted, and I wanted to be certain there'd be no repetition the week after, when we'd be sharing our work again in a new crit session.

Not that I had any real doubts. No one else's work would come close. I'd already sneaked a look at what Håkan had been doing, and it was disappointingly ordinary.

The only thing that worried me was Vivian and where I stood with her. I was half expecting her to appear at my door one night, but so far she'd stayed away. I assumed she was thinking I'd go round to hers. Or maybe I wasn't important to her. But why wouldn't I be? I was ten years younger than her, yes, but that was about the only legitimate reason she could have. Did she think I was too immature? What I'd said about the set design hadn't impressed her. But seeing as I'd never worked in theatre the way they had, it was surely only to be expected.

It hurt, the thought of her not wanting me. If she'd been beautiful and had lots of admirers, it might have been easier to deal with. The ten years between us would have been like an abyss then. But she wasn't beautiful, no one would ever say so. She was intelligent, maybe even gifted. Intellectual. But not much to look at.

She'd be sitting around at home, waiting for me to come, surely? She wanted me, but wanted me to take the initiative. Of course. She was unsure of herself. Afraid I wasn't interested enough.

So when the doorbell rang one night, my first thought was that it was her. I hesitated. It rang again. Something tingly and delightful, the tiniest little shower, like when you blow on a dandelion, filled my chest. She wanted me.

I wriggled my feet into my trainers and went downstairs to answer it.

But it wasn't Vivian, it was Hans.

Of course it was Hans.

'Mind if I come in?' he said, his face stretching into a wide smile.

'No, of course not. How did you know where I live?' I said.

'You told me.'

'Did I?'

'Maybe you were too drunk to remember,' he said and smiled again.

'Maybe,' I said.

He followed me back up the stairs, paused inside the door and took in the room. It was the first time anyone else had seen the place, though the thought that someone might one day come round had been at the back of my mind when I first moved in and arranged my stuff— the furniture, my records, the posters on the walls, the books on the shelves.

'Do you want something to drink? Coffee? Or maybe something stronger?'

'Coffee's fine. Thanks.'

He went over to the Daguerre photograph.

'You mentioned this,' he said. 'Someone sent it you, right?'

'That's right.'

'Hm.'

'Are you *sure* it wasn't you?' I said as I put the kettle on and sprinkled some instant coffee into two mugs.

'It wasn't me.'

'Could it have been someone you know? That Egyptian guy, for instance?'

'What Egyptian guy?'

'The one down the pub that night when you were there with your friends. I'd seen him before, if you remember. He'd been wearing a suit.'

'Victor!'

'That's him, yes.'

'Why do you say he's Egyptian? He's from Norwich!'

'He looks Egyptian.'

'Why would he have sent it to you?'

'No idea. He does keep turning up everywhere, though. At the station, the last time I saw him. I thought maybe you might have mentioned it to him, what we'd been talking about. That it was a joke of some sort. With the two devil figures.'

'No, no, no, you're barking up the wrong tree there, Kristian. I'm sure he's never given you a thought.'

'I didn't mean like that.'

'How did you mean, then?'

He stepped over to the bookshelf and stood for a moment with his back to me. I poured the boiling water into the mugs and saw the dissolving brown granules froth against the white insides of the mugs.

'Aleister Crowley?' he said. 'I didn't know you were interested in Crowley?'

'I wanted to check him out.'

He turned towards me with the book open in his hands.

'He was a poser and a fraud. What used to be called a charlatan.'

'Are there any mystics who aren't?'

'Oh yes, certainly,' he said, slotting the book back between the others. I went over and handed him his coffee. I was about to ask him for some names as an example, when he asked if I'd got any milk.

I went back to the fridge. He came after me and held out his mug as I pressed open the top of the carton to shape the little spout.

'I was at the funeral today,' he suddenly said.

'What funeral?'

'Ian Moore's.'

'Who's Ian Moore?'

'Ian Moore, Kristian, was that tramp who got killed.'

'You went to his *funeral*? What for? What are you up to? What is this?'

He took his coffee and sat down on the settee, crossed one leg over the other and sipped from his mug.

'You still haven't told me what happened,' he said.

'*Nothing* happened.'

'You realise you must have been the last person to see him alive?'

I didn't reply.

'He had two kids, you know. A son and a daughter. Around the same age as you. They must have given up on him. They came to his funeral, though. They cried.'

'What are you telling me for? What do you want?'

He gave a shrug.

'I don't *want* anything.'

'You had nothing to do with him. What reason would you have to go to his funeral?'

'A lot of other people did, in fact it was quite well attended. You wouldn't have thought so, would you? You'd think a homeless person would be someone who'd cut all ties. It may have had something to do with him being killed, though.'

He turned the mug between his hands, jiggling slightly his suspended foot.

'They live and die in the shadows, people like him, don't they? No one sees them when they're alive, no one sees them when they're dead. Unless they're killed. A killing is like a light. They're seen then. Even from a distance. And people come to their funerals. I suppose that's how it works.'

I couldn't tell him to leave. I couldn't exactly change the subject either. But listening to him was excruciating.

'It must be a weight to carry around.'

Again, I said nothing.

'I can tell you're beside yourself, Kristian. Who wouldn't be? But I think it would help if you stopped pretending. It won't get you anywhere. It'll only get worse, and then worse after that.'

'I'm not pretending.'

'Come on, you're wanted by the police in connection with a killing. You're not reporting to them, even though you're fully aware they want you to come forward. Any fool would realise you were implicated. Even more so if they'd seen how you're behaving. Suspiciously, by any measure.'

'What's it got to do with *you*, anyway? Going to his *funeral* — what kind of behaviour is *that*? It's obsessive.'

'I just want to help you.'

'I don't need any help.'

'This conversation, Kristian, is a *cry* for help. But OK, I'll leave you alone, if that's what you want.'

He stood up and went towards the door.

'You know you can trust me. If you want to talk about it, or if you need help of any kind, you know where I am. OK?'

He winked at me before closing the door behind him.

I took his mug, still warm, and poured his coffee out into the sink, washed the mug meticulously, dried it and put it back in the cupboard. There were no other signs of him ever having been there, but still I got the Hoover out of the little cubbyhole and vacuumed the room. After I'd finished I stood for a moment and looked around. It was only nine o'clock and too early to go to bed. The prospect of sitting in on my own with only my thoughts for company was unbearable. Half an hour earlier and it wouldn't have been a problem. It was *his* thoughts that bothered me. It was as if he'd left them behind there in my flat. And without their proper owner, they wormed their way into mine.

If what made him suspicious was that I hadn't gone to the police, even though I knew they wanted to talk to me, then I supposed I'd just have to go to the police.

There was nothing to be apprehensive about. And once I'd spoken to them, it would be gone from the world. No one could point a finger at me then, not if I'd turned myself in and explained what happened.

'Hello, my name's Kristian Hadeland. I'm here in connection with a death . . .'

'Hello, my name's Kristian Hadeland and I have some information which I believe may be of help to you regarding a death . . .'

A counter, behind it a police sergeant. He asks me what death I'm talking about. I explain it was a tramp, a homeless person, that someone had made me aware there was a picture of me in the newspaper and said the police would like me to come forward and help them with their inquiries.

'And so here I am,' I say with a smile. I'm asked to wait a moment, and shortly after he returns with a detective. The detective ushers me down a corridor, into a room. An interview room? Or more informally, perhaps, his office?

No, an interview room. I'm a witness they've been looking for.

A glare of strip lighting. A tape recorder on the table.

'Well, a friend of mine told me there was a picture of someone in the paper and it looked like me. It *was* me, so here I am.'

'And here you are.'

'Yes. Shall I tell you what happened?'

'We'll come to that. Name, date of birth, address?'

I give him my details, understanding fully that procedure must be followed and everything correctly noted down.

'So what happened was that I stopped on my bike to light a cigarette. There was a man behind the wall, I realised, because he asked if he could have one. I tossed him a couple, but then he wanted a light, so I went over to him with my lighter. We didn't speak apart from that, so I've no idea who he was or anything. He was alive when I left him, I can tell you that. I suppose it was a CCTV camera somewhere that caught me? The picture in the paper, I mean. Anyway, that's basically all that happened. I don't know any more than that.'

The detective would then ask me what this man had looked like, what sort of state he appeared to be in, and so on, details that were relevant to their inquiries.

I had nothing to lose by it. If I went through it enough times in my head, my statement would be watertight. They might try to trip me up, they had to, it was their job, but as long as I stuck to my story, everything would be all right.

Maybe I should even take the lighter with me? 'This was the lighter he borrowed from me.' It wouldn't harm, surely? In fact, it would only enhance the credibility of what I was telling them.

Hans wouldn't be able to say anything more then. 'Listen, I stopped by the police station yesterday and gave them my statement.' His insinuations would at once be groundless and make him look like the smug, suspicious twerp he was.

But it was too late to do it today. The detectives would all have knocked off by now and they'd all be uniform on the night shift. I could do it after school tomorrow.

The thought put a lid on everything that had been tormenting me. By going to the police, I'd not only be doing my duty as a citizen, but also formalising what had occurred. Any suspicions towards me that people such as Hans for whatever reason might harbour would only evaporate like mist in the morning sun.

I put *Shock of Daylight* on by the Sound, and when 'Longest Days' came through the speakers I lay in the dark listening to it with eyes closed. Not passively, in the sense of simply lying there and allowing the music to wash over me, but more as if I was following the music's trail through landscapes it kept opening up before me, the way a hunter might follow the path of an animal. Now and then, I encountered thoughts there, or thought-like feelings, and these were without exception good. It was as if I had been redeemed. I'd been in peril. Now the danger was past.

The next morning, George kicked off the first of our planned crit sessions focusing on the self-portraits we'd submitted. Mine would be looked at the day after, and my confidence was growing with every piece of work he put under scrutiny. The thought of going to the police that afternoon was a bit like having a dental appointment looming while I'd still been at gymnas — I remembered daydreaming at the back of the classroom, toying with the idea of not turning up, though not seriously considering it, for I knew the pain that awaited was comparatively small and insufficient to warrant running away from, it was just one of those things you had to face.

I went for lunch with Håkan, Gav and Martin, and withdrawing some money from the cashpoint I discovered a sizeable sum had been deposited into my account. Ten thousand kroner. It could only have come from Dad. He'd done the same thing at the beginning of the autumn term, only then it had been agreed, I was to buy a camera I'd been hankering after for some time, Nikon's new FM2n, which I'd used just about every day since. This time it was just money. It was his way of leading me back into the fold again. I'm your father, you're my son, and whatever you may think, say or do, nothing can change that.

'What would you do if you'd just broken off with your family and they went and paid a load of money into your account?' I asked them as we sat around a table scoffing fish and chips out of newspaper while buses, vans, lorries and cars rumbled by outside.

'I'd say thanks very much,' Gav said. 'There's no such thing as dirty money, not in my book.'

'It would depend on why I'd broken off with them,' Håkan said.

'What do you think?' I said, turning to Martin.

'Send it back, of course.'

'You would say that,' said Gav. 'Ever the idealist.'

'Why are you asking?' Håkan said. '*Have* you broken off with your family?'

'Yes. I don't want anything to do with them ever again.'

'In that case you can't take their money.'

'Think of all the records you can buy,' Gav said. 'Not to mention lenses. How much are we talking about, anyway?'

'Quite a bit.'

'How about giving it to me instead? That way you won't be accepting anything from them. At the same time, you'd be helping a poor impoverished student. Someone who *really* needs the cash.'

'Ha ha.'

'Why have you broken off with them?' Håkan said.

'Because they're cultural illiterates. Especially my dad. All he thinks about is material things. The house and money. I was there for Christmas and had to come back a week early, I couldn't stick it.'

'You don't see eye to eye, then?'

'You're telling me.'

'Did he hit you when you were growing up?' Gav said.

'My dad? No, nothing like that.'

I studied him a second.

'Why are you asking? Did your dad hit you?'

'Sometimes. Nothing to get worked up about, though. A clip round the ear once in a while, that's all. He did give me a good hammering once, but only because I deserved it. No, I was just wondering if there was more to it than just not seeing eye to eye. It sounds like a bit of a step to take, breaking off with them just because they look after their money.'

'That's not the way I see it,' I said.

'Anyway, it's straightforward enough,' Gav said. 'You can't take money from your parents when money's the reason you've broken off with them.'

'He's not doing it for the sake of philanthropy either,' I said. 'There's more to it than that.'

'You can donate it to a good cause,' Martin said. 'If he's as fixated about it as you say, it'll get his back up. And you'll be helping someone at the same time.'

'That's exactly what I was suggesting!' said Gav.

'The miners are bound to have a strike fund you could donate to. Or you could give it to Ethiopia.'

Ethiopia? Ten thousand kroner to Ethiopia? Was he off his head?

'He wouldn't know where it had all gone, though,' I said. 'All he'd know would be that he'd paid it into my account, not where it went after that.'

'You could send him the receipt.'

'But I've broken off with them!'

'Do you realise how little it takes to save a child from starving in Africa? What's a human life against hurt feelings?'

'Who said anything about hurt feelings?'

He expelled air through his nostrils in what was either a snort or a snigger. Whatever, it was definitely scornful, and it annoyed me.

'And what are you doing for the starving kids of Ethiopia, if you don't mind me asking? What tangible actions are you taking? Or are you just full of wind as usual?'

'All right, steady on,' he said.

'Well, if we're all finished, I'd say we'd best be getting back,' said Håkan, and stood up. 'I don't know about the rest of you, but I've got work to do.'

It wouldn't surprise me if his parents were wealthy, I thought as we went back along the street, me alongside Håkan, Martin and Gav in front of us. Only the spoiled kids of the upper classes could afford to be communists.

Before going in, he turned towards me.

'I'm sorry, Kristian,' he said. 'I didn't mean to poke my nose into your business.'

He was looking me straight in the eye, and everything. I felt embarrassed for him.

'That's all right,' I said. 'I might even heed your advice.'

His hair, fair, verging on white, shone in the grey and drizzly light.

Gav held out his cigarettes and I took one. Martin grinned gormlessly and went through the door.

'Which one of you do you think's going to go bald first?' I said. 'You or him?'

'Why not yourself?'

'I come from a long line of luxuriant hair.'

'So you did get one thing positive from your dad?'

'You could say. Does it bother you? That you're going to go bald?'

'No.'

'You sure about that?'

'Quite sure.'

'I don't believe you.'

'I've got a big dick.'

'Ah.'

'Have you?'

'Big enough.'

'A small one, then.'

'Big enough.'

'I don't believe you.'

'Touché.'

We stood and smoked for a few minutes without saying anything, then went inside. If this was all I had, I thought, photography, the school and nothing else, it would all have been perfect.

But in fact it nearly was. The only loose end, crying out to be tucked in, was Hans and his stupid suspicion. I could sort that, and I would too. I'd go to the police station and give them my statement as a witness.

The picture in the paper would no longer mean a thing. Everything would be mended. The police had appealed to the public because they wanted me to come in as a witness. Once I'd done so, the picture, the incident and me would all be one, there'd be no loose ends.

After school I went back home and carried the bike down the stairs. I could tell them it was *this* bike I'd been on when I'd stopped and given him the cigarettes. It was *this* lighter he'd used. It would show them I'd nothing to hide.

Two police cars passed by with barely a minute between them as I cycled along and my heart beat harder. I was afraid they'd stop me and take me in. There was a world of difference between coming forward voluntarily and being taken in. But neither vehicle stopped, which made me think. If they hadn't found out who I was by now, there was a good chance they never would. What's more, there was always going to be a certain risk involved in turning myself in. I didn't know if they had any more pictures for one thing, or if they would show there'd been physical contact. Perhaps there was some other evidence connecting me to the time of death? I thought it unlikely, but still, I couldn't be sure.

But then neither could they. If I just told them what happened, that I'd tossed him a couple of cigarettes but didn't want to lose my lighter and had therefore stepped up to where he was sat to give him a light, that he'd been fine when I left him, there was no way they'd be able to refute it. It stood to reason that they wanted to talk to me — they'd been looking at the CCTV footage and had seen a young man go behind a wall where a homeless tramp had later been found dead. If nothing else he was an important witness, so of course they'd had to appeal to the public in order that he could come forward.

And now that was what I was doing. I hadn't known about the CCTV image until a few hours ago. A friend had shown it to me, and I could tell it was me. I came straight here, as quickly as I could.

What friend?

Could I give them Hans's name?

What if they checked, would he go along with it?

I didn't need to be specific about the time. In fact, I didn't need to mention anything at all about when I'd seen the image. But if they asked, what would I say?

I cycled past a long brick building of several storeys, imposingly Victorian, its dark windows as if blind to the modern age. It stood edged up to the road, a park at its rear, the opposite way round to what would seem natural. Built for a different infrastructure, I imagined.

The branches of the trees were as yet bare, but spring was in the air, spring was in the light.

As I freewheeled down the hill, cars and lorries thundering by, the wind gusted from behind, sweeping me with it. It was exhilarating, and felt like a good sign. The powers were on my side.

After the railway bridge, where the tacky high street began, I dismounted and wheeled the bike the last bit of the way to the police station, a large, looming building with an open concourse in front. I felt ill at ease, unsure as to whether I was sufficiently prepared; the building was full of police, and apart from that anyone coming along the pavement could be someone who worked there, they might recognise my face and grab me by the arm. So I crossed the road and carried on along the opposite pavement in search of a cafe or somewhere else where I could sit and gather my thoughts.

When had I seen the picture in the paper? Two days ago. So why hadn't I come forward before now?

But I didn't need a friend to have shown it to me! I could have picked up the paper on the Tube, or off a bench, skimmed the pages and seen the picture then.

That was it.

I looked back across the road at the police station.

Ready?

Why was I doing this again?

Hans. He knew it was me in that picture. If he'd realised, then others could too. But Hans knowing was enough. He knew that I knew the police wanted to speak to me. The fact that I hadn't stepped forward cast a suspicion on me. That was why.

Oh Christ.

A smoke?

Yes. Lit by the deadly lighter.

I carried on down the road until I came to a newsagent's and bought myself a new packet, lit up and leaned back against the wall outside.

This was the lighter he borrowed, I said to myself, and held it up in front of me. Do you need it for fingerprints or something?

So there I was on my bike. I wanted a cigarette and stopped to light up when this tramp on the other side of the wall asks if he can cadge one off me. I toss him a couple, only then he wants a light. I don't want to throw him my lighter, so I go up to him — that'll be when I show up on the CCTV. I hand him the lighter and he lights his cigarette. I go back to my bike and carry on up to my girlfriend's flat. She can verify that. Her name's Vivian. Well, she's not actually my girlfriend as such, but a friend, anyway. The next thing I know, I see my picture in the paper today and realise I'm wanted as a witness. So here I am.

I dropped the cigarette end to the pavement and crushed it under the sole of my shoe.

Breathed deeply. My heart fluttering like a bird.

I didn't need to. I could turn round and go home. They didn't know me from Adam.

But that loose end would stay loose. Sooner or later everything would unravel.

I knew what I was going to say. There was nothing to be afraid of.

I gripped the handlebars and walked to the crossing. Before I stepped out, the green man turned to red, so I had to stand there and wait while a cluster of pedestrians gradually gathered around me. Three teetering red double-deckers came by one after another and I stepped back from the kerb. The passengers inside stared out, blank-faced, as if in a different reality altogether from the one in which I stood.

The light changed and I crossed in the midst of the throng. Reaching the opposite pavement, I was seized by an urge, wriggled from my rucksack, took out the camera and snapped a few shots of the police station. It was a bit like the case of the lighter, I thought, a subject saturated with significance to the photographer, but to anyone else simply a lighter, a police station.

And it wasted some time.

Then, as I put the camera back in the bag, I felt sick. The police station was right there, the entrance perhaps only twenty metres away.

And now was the moment I had to go in. Report to the duty desk. Explain to them who I was and why I'd come.

It was now.

I didn't want to.

But I had to.

I put my arms through the straps once more, curled my hand around the handlebar and started walking towards the entrance, wheeling the bike at my side.

The same bike.

The same lighter.

I didn't want to throw it, so I went in through the gate and handed it to him.

I only saw the picture in the paper today. And so here I am.

I halted in front of the steps, scanning for somewhere to chain the bike when someone called out my name.

I turned to look. A woman, her coat tails flapping as she half ran towards me. Fair hair, gorgeous. It was the girl from the pub that night, Hans's friend.

'Kristian!' she said again, slowing now to a halt. 'Remember me?'

'Yes,' I said. 'You're Hans's friend, right?'

'That's right, yes.'

'Daniella, wasn't it?'

'You remembered my name!'

'Of course. You remembered mine.'

'What a coincidence, seeing you here! I thought you lived in Deptford?'

'I do. But maybe you live around here?'

'Not really. But not far. What are you doing here anyway?'

It was all I could do to stop myself glancing towards the police station.

'Doing here?' I repeated, buying time.

She gave a slight nod in confirmation.

'Nothing in particular,' I said.

An awkward moment ensued, the gust of energy with which she'd appeared subsided.

Then I remembered I had the camera with me.

'Just cycling around taking a few photographs,' I added.

'That's right, you're a photographer. Interesting!'
She smiled.
'How about you? What do you do?'
'I'm trying to get a foothold in the fashion industry.'
'Oh?'
'Yes, I'm working as an assistant to a designer. It's not my final destination, if you understand what I mean.'
'No. I mean, yes. I understand.'
She laughed, and touched my arm.
'Do you fancy a coffee somewhere? There's a new Italian place just along the road.'

I wanted to tell her I had something important to do. But glancing across at the police station entrance, I realised I couldn't possibly go in there now. It was as if she'd changed me.

I nodded.

'Sounds good.'

We crossed the concourse, and such was my relief that I laughed out loud as if for no reason. Not surprisingly, she looked at me.

'Sorry, just something that occurred to me, that's all.'

She smiled again.

Not until we were inside the cafe were my suspicions aroused. How could she have remembered my name? I was a peripheral friend of a friend. She'd only seen me the once, heard my name uttered only a single time. Either she'd been interested in me from the start, or else someone had been talking about me. I was ten years younger than her and she was beautiful, not like Vivian, who was ugly, so the chances were she wasn't interested. She'd asked me out for a coffee, yes. But it was probably nothing more than curiosity.

Vivian must have told her about us.

The Italian coffee machine hissed and spluttered at the hands of the white-aproned proprietor. What a lot of fuss just to make a cup of coffee, I thought. Daniella had found us a place to sit and was looking out the window, elbows propped on the table, hands clasped.

The notion that only a few minutes ago I'd been about to turn myself in to the police now seemed completely absurd.

Her face was full of life even when she was absent in thought.

'Two coffees, please,' I said to the man when he turned to serve me.
'What sort of coffee?'
'Just plain.'
'Americano? Espresso? Macchiato?'
'Just ordinary black coffee, please.'

Even that appeared to be a major undertaking, but eventually he put two minuscule cups down on the counter in front of me. I couldn't be bothered to complain, but handed him a five-pound note, dropped the change into my pocket and went back to the table with a cup in each hand.

Her eyes were grey, I noticed. It was unusual, anyone would have expected them to be blue, with her fair hair and pale skin.

What did she want with me?

She'd touched my arm. There must have been at least something in it.

'Thanks,' she said, and threaded an index finger through the tiny handle.

'Pleasure,' I said.

She leaned forward at the same time as lifting the cup to her lips, and glanced up at me as she sipped. Oh God, she was gorgeous.

'So how do you like London?' she said, putting her cup down.

'It's great,' I said.

I had to say more than that.

'I like it.'

'It must be very different from Norway?'

'It is, yes.'

A silence followed. It didn't seem to bother her. Everything about her was so light and unencumbered. I tasted the coffee. It was as strong as tar and bitter as hell. But she'd tasted it without comment, so I said nothing either.

'Vivian says such a lot of nice things about you.'

There it was. She was here as the friend.

'Does she?'

'I hear you're going to be working together as well. On *Doctor Faustus*.'

'That's a bit of an exaggeration, I'm afraid. I'm going to be taking some photos, that's all.'

'Vivian might seem tough, you know, but she's one of the most vulnerable people I know.'

Vulnerable? Who was she kidding?

I nodded.

'I realise that.'

What about you? I felt an urge to ask. Are you vulnerable too? But I said nothing. I didn't want to jeopardise the little spark there was between us.

'Has she talked to you about *Doctor Faustus*? She will have done, I suppose. She's absolutely obsessed.'

'A bit.'

'It's amazing the way she's able to bring out the essence in every scene. So that we can see it for ourselves. Don't you think?'

'Yes, absolutely.'

'He who is dead is dead, and cannot be saved.'

My veins turned to ice.

Was it *her*?

'What did you say?'

'He who is dead is dead, and cannot be saved. Hasn't she talked to you about that?'

I shook my head, scrutinising her face, which was still open and unaffected, without a sign of anything untoward. If she was acting, she could have fooled anyone.

'It's a quote she's got into her head, by Paul Becker. Do you know him?'

'Erm . . .'

She laughed.

'It's quite all right if you don't! He was a poet, from Austria. Anyway, he wrote something about choosing death in life, which of course is what Faustus does. According to Vivian, at least.'

Her smile was disarming. It occurred to me that I was still staring at her. I looked down.

It couldn't be her.

Vivian, then?

The quote came from Vivian.

It had to. But did it mean that she knew?

Did Vivian know?

'Earth calling Kristian. Hello, are you there?'

'Something just came to mind. Daguerre, do you know who that is?'

'The photographer?'

'Yes.'

'Of course I've heard of him. Why? Trying to get me back for Becker, are you?'

She laughed again.

'No, no reason,' I said. 'Just wondering.'

She drained the rest of her coffee and looked at her watch.

'Gosh,' she said. 'I need to get going. It was really nice bumping into you, Kristian.'

'Same here.'

She placed a hand on mine.

'Be good to Vivian,' she said, then rose, shrugged into her coat and left.

I waited a few minutes before following suit. Outside, the light was fading and the rush hour had begun. In a long, impatient line at the traffic lights, cars, vans and buses snarled. I unlocked the bike, wheeled it out onto the road and cycled away, past the police station, under the railway bridge and onwards up the long, shallow hill, harder to negotiate this time on account of what was now a strong headwind. Not that it bothered me. The only thing I could think about was that Vivian knew. That the photo could only have come from her.

Had she and Hans been talking about it? Or had they arrived at the same place from different directions?

It was already dark when I got home. I carried the bike up the stairs and leaned it against the wall inside the door, put the kettle on and spooned some coffee into a mug, then stood at the window, gazing into the street as I waited for it to boil. A white carrier bag had snagged in a tree. The gusting wind made it look like it was alive and struggling to extricate itself. Something else out there rattled and stilled, rattled and stilled.

I poured the boiling water into the mug and stirred a few times with the teaspoon even though it wasn't really necessary — the granules dissolved immediately — then took the mug over and put it down on the table before removing the Daguerre photo from the wall so I could look again at what was written on the back.

He who is dead is dead, and cannot be saved.
Choose life, Kristian, and you shall do well.

It was written in capitals, ruling out the possibility of identifying the hand. Not that I knew Vivian's handwriting.

But I did! She'd left a note here.

What had I done with it?

It wasn't on the table and it wasn't on the bookshelf.

I couldn't remember throwing it out.

I dipped my hand into my back pocket where normally I archived my receipts, removed the little bundle my fingers found and saw immediately her note. I unfolded it and smoothed it out on the table next to the photograph.

Kristian,
I want to see you again.
Vivian

She'd written in cursive, but the three capital letters would be the same. Only they weren't. Her *K* was broad and rather round, the *K* on the rear of the photograph was long and slender.

But it couldn't be coincidence, surely? Vivian had quoted an obscure Austrian poet in conversation with Daniella, and then someone had sent me the exact same quote.

Who else could it be? She knew Hans — he could have mentioned to her that he'd been telling me about the Daguerre photo. And she could have quoted the poem to him that was written on the back.

It wasn't as if this Becker was someone well known who people went around quoting all the time.

I'd never heard of him.

I kneeled down in front of my records and flicked through the titles, settling eventually on *First and Last and Always* by the Sisters of Mercy, then took a pizza out of the freezer compartment and stuck it in the oven. If Vivian *had* sent the photo, it would actually be a good thing, because the choosing life bit would then presumably mean that she was telling me to simply carry on and not look back. He who is dead is dead. And Hans was on my side too, no matter how annoying he was.

Would Liz have Becker on her shelf? She was interested in literature, she studied it. But Liz was stony and awkward.

As far as I knew, Daniella wasn't going out with anyone. Nothing suggested it — there'd been no *I must be getting home to Eric* or *John says this and that*. And she'd asked me out for coffee. She'd touched me on the arm.

I could feel her hand on me again as the thought materialised. A little tingle, electric.

But she was only a designer's assistant. Nothing to brag about exactly, not at her age. She was probably shagging him as well, the fashion designer. But then again, men were all gay in that business.

I ate half the pizza and was leaving the rest on the worktop for later, when the phone rang. I let it. When it stopped, I went downstairs and had a shower, went back up and stuffed my dirty clothes into a carrier bag I dumped next to the other three that stood bulging. I'd have to go to the launderette soon. Tomorrow after school, maybe.

My hair still wet, I went down and knocked on Liz's door.

'Who is it?' her voice called from inside.

'It's me,' I said. 'From upstairs.'

There was a rattle of chains. Was she that neurotic? Who in their right mind would break into this house? No one could possibly imagine there'd be anything of value here.

She was opening the door, at least. That was something.

'You wouldn't happen to have a book by Paul Becker by any chance, would you?' I said as her sour face appeared.

She looked at me with what I took to be mild astonishment.

'Paul Becker?'

'Yes, the Austrian poet. I thought I might be in luck, with you studying literature.'

'Well, you're not.'

'Do you know anything about him?'

'Paul Becker?' she said again.

'That's right. Paul Becker.'

She shook her head.

I smiled.

'It's just that I need something for an assignment. A book of his, preferably ... Or just some biography, maybe a history of European literature, if you've got something like that I could borrow for an hour or so?'

She hesitated a moment before giving a nod and vanishing back behind the door. I stepped into the little hall, identical to mine apart from being painted a different colour and containing different things, then gently pushed open the door into her living room, much the same, only cosier. A low coffee table with a cloth over it, a flowery throw draped across the sofa, soft carpeting on the floor. Bookshelves along the length of the rear wall. A television on with the sound lowered.

She turned round with two heavy volumes in her hands, and discovered me standing there.

'Did I say you could come in?'

'You've got this place looking really nice,' I said.

She gave a reluctant smile. Stepped towards me with the books.

'Here. An hour, OK?'

'Just the one volume will do, I imagine.'

'I don't know which one will say anything about him. And I want you to go now.'

'Fair enough,' I said. 'See you later, then.'

Only after searching back and forth without finding any mention of Becker at all — I knew nothing about him, not even the period he belonged to — did it occur to me to consult the index, where of course I immediately found a page number that directed me to his entry.

Paul Becker (born 7 March 1883 in Graz, Austria, died 2 September 1914 in Lemberg [Lviv] in what is now Ukraine) was an Austrian poet and occultist.

Biography
Paul Becker grew up in Graz, the son of a schoolteacher. He attended secondary school at the city's Akademisches Gymnasium between 1893 and 1899. At the age of sixteen, Becker wrote his first poems, some of which would be included in his debut collection, *Nights of*

Anger, Days of Sorrow (1904). The title here refers to the loss of his mother, who died when Becker was five years old and whom his father henceforth forbade him to mention. The youthful Becker was socially unruly, displaying an often conflictual relationship to authority, and soon began to experiment with drugs. In 1900 he commenced philosophy studies in Vienna and quickly entered the city's intellectual circles, notably that centred around the journal *Der Brenner*, in which he published several poems. Becker abandoned his studies in 1902, from which date he earned his living as a writer. His poetry was expressionist in style, groundbreaking in its highly peculiar, feverish qualities, and combined with Becker's self-combustive lifestyle and eccentric behaviour elevated him in certain quarters to near-mythological status. The years immediately following his debut were particularly productive and saw the publication of no less than five collections of poems, culminating in 1910 with his first and only novel, *Parmenides' Secret*. This marked a turning point in Becker's writing, which from then on amounted only to prose fragments of a larger, never-completed work with clear overtones of the occult, referred to by Becker as *The Book*. When war broke out in August 1914, Becker was conscripted into the army as a medical orderly. He was killed during the Battle of Galicia only a month later when the field hospital where he was at work was hit by Russian shelling.

Writing

With its radical zooming-in on physical and spiritual detail within the frameworks of traditional poetic forms, Becker's first book of poetry, *Nights of Anger, Days of Sorrow*, has most often been referred to under the heading of 'biological modernism'. In the collections that followed, the lyrical subject, in the debut work comparatively coherent, becomes increasingly fragmented, to the extent that in the final collection, *Sacred, Sacred, Sacred*, the very notion of the I-speaker becomes contrived, insofar as here it is the world that speaks, the world whose voice is heard. In this, Becker approaches Spinoza's idea that God is neither separate from nor within the world, but rather, pantheistically, that God and the world are the same thing. Another consistent source of inspiration in Becker's poetry is the later Hölderlin. Indeed, it was his fascination for Hölderlin that led Becker to his studies of pre-Socratic philosophy and thereby to the departure so marked in his final writings. *Parmenides' Secret* appeared in the same year as Rainer Maria Rilke's *The Notebooks of Malte Laurids Brigge*, and the parallels between the two Austrians' only novels are many — though the differences too are great. In their sketch-like descriptions and use of both the diary format and the note, the two works share many of the same formal characteristics, just as their subjects, quiveringly tense and acutely observant young men, bear much resemblance to each other. But while Rilke's novel is non-epic, centred entirely around the protagonist's observations and reflections, Becker's exhibits clear characteristics of plot: his nameless main character journeys to Greece, embarking there upon a classic Grand Tour to take in Athens, Delphi and Olympia. Presently, however, he encounters a couple, adherents of a mysterious sect, is beguiled by them, and accompanies them to Sicily. At the same time, he falls ill, his diary entries then gradually disintegrating into feverish ramblings, blurring the boundary between fantasy and reality. In this enfeebled state he takes part in an ancient ceremony at the entrance to a system of caves. The last thing he notes in writing is that his body has been filled with darkness, the novel then concluding with an epilogue in the form of a letter written by an English tourist who describes the discovery of a corpse at the caves, a notebook at the unfortunate person's side. Combining elements of the Romantic and Gothic genres, *Parmenides' Secret* exhibits traits of the popular novel, while also embracing exquisitely lyrical and expressive description. At the time of its publication, critics were confused by the novel, which in recent years has however been much acclaimed. The same applies to the writings belonging to Becker's final phase — though largely ignored at the time, post-structuralist interest in the fragment as a literary form has resulted in this part of the *oeuvre* latterly being hailed. Here, Becker posits that the pre-Socratic philosophers were in fact not philosophers at all in the modern sense of the word, but mages, and that their writings would be better understood as initiations into the deepest mysteries.

There was a picture of him too, an epitome of the disturbed poet, gaunt and sallow, with staring eyes, a narrow, tightly pinched mouth.

But it made sense: Vivian was putting on *Doctor Faustus*, in which a kind of mage evokes the Devil; she'd quoted Becker, he too an occultist, and had sent me a photograph Hans had said depicted the Devil himself, inscribing it with that same quote.

Yes, it made perfect sense. And I didn't like it.

Hans had talked about Aleister Crowley too, and Agrippa, and Swedenborg.

It felt like they were in on something together, which I wasn't a part of.

Not that I wanted to be a part of it. Not that sort of stuff.

But I didn't need to have anything to do with them. I wasn't tied to them. I wasn't obliged. I could simply stop seeing them.

I went downstairs to return the two books to Liz.

More rattling of the chains, the little snap as the lock was turned.

'Did you find what you were looking for?' she said.

'Yes,' I said, and handed them back. They must have been heavier than she remembered, because her hands sank maybe twenty centimetres as she received them.

'Good,' she said, clamping the books under her arm and closing the door in my face with her free hand.

Was I a leper or something?

'Thanks a lot, then!' I said exaggeratedly, and went back upstairs. I put the Fall on, *This Nation's Saving Grace*, and turned to my boxes of photographs, laying the pictures out one by one on the floor. The new ones were so much better. But it was impossible to say what exactly it was that *made* them better. The cat, of course, was in a class of its own. The self-portrait, too. You couldn't see at first that it was a reflection, it looked just like an ordinary room, though with something faintly unnerving about it, something ghostly, there was no weight to anything, not even me, I was almost levitating. The blurred contours brought to mind the first photographs ever taken. And if you looked closely enough, you saw that there was a second figure in the room, a shadow by the wall in the background. My heart nearly stopped when I discovered it, so vivid and lifelike it was. George probably wouldn't notice, but I'd mention it during the crit.

When I woke up the next morning, the room was filled with light. The sight of a blue sky from the kitchen window was oddly uplifting. I didn't normally care about the weather and had barely given a thought to the preceding weeks of cloud and rain until now, when it was over.

The thermometer, mounted outside the window by some previous tenant, showed fourteen degrees. It looked like it could easily rise to twenty during the day.

I decided to bike it to school. For some reason, I'd never done it before, though I often cycled much longer distances. I hadn't even contemplated it until today. School meant taking the train, somehow I'd seen no alternative.

Breaking habits was another thing that creativity book went on about. Good, then.

I devoured a bowl of cornflakes, packed my rucksack, carried the bike downstairs and set off. It was still early, but I didn't know how long it would take, and I didn't want to risk being late, not today!

The city was as if transformed around me. The sunshine drew out colour everywhere. What yesterday had slumbered in shades of grey, now kaleidoscopically shone and glittered. Fruit-and-veg stalls were detonations of colour. Cars gleamed, blues, reds, greens, yellows. Windowpanes, now suddenly all around, refracted glorious rays at all angles, sending them criss-crossing, arrowing through the air. Even the people were different — I saw smiles, lightness, a turning outwards to the world in everyone I passed. It was ridiculous, of course, the notion that something so prosaic as the weather could affect the soul in such a way, as if we humans were little more than receptors of air and light. And yet I was in no way unaffected myself, I conceded as I sailed through the streets of Southwark. Life wasn't so bad after all. Certainly there was no need to bemoan that my inner being was so seedling-like, invigorated by only a little light, especially not if it was able to create art. Great art, even — perhaps not now, but at some future time.

I relished the thought of the impending crit session and could hardly wait to see the reactions of my fellow students when I revealed my photograph to them, and to listen to what George would say about it. I imagined his response as I cycled. Kristian, he would say, you've actually created a minor masterpiece here. I wouldn't have thought it possible that a student, still to complete his training, not yet a full-fledged photographer, could inject such new life into a genre. Grand words, I know, but I stand by them. And I say this not to take anything away from the other pictures we've reviewed up until now, which have been of a very high quality indeed. But this one, this one is exceptional.

As I dismounted outside the school, I still had three-quarters of an hour in hand. I went across to the station and bought myself a coffee. I'd done so before the previous crit session too, I remembered. Regardless of how much I'd disliked Figueroa, I had to concede that he was right, my earlier photographs weren't up to scratch. Well conceived, but poorly executed. Maybe even poorly *felt*.

No, feelings had nothing to do with it. Feelings couldn't be transferred from the inner folds of the brain to the external world via a camera lens — any direction of travel could only be the opposite, from the subject, through the lens, onto the negative.

I pointed my camera at a road stretching away towards a horizon, and the picture was flat. I pointed my camera at a lighter, and the picture bristled with verve and meaning.

Try explaining that.

Ten minutes before the session was due to start, I strolled over again, nodded to the others as I entered the room, exchanged a few words with Håkan, who like me would be showing his work today, then sat down and tipped back on my chair before George appeared.

This particular session would be done a bit differently than previous ones. There would be no open discussion, only George giving his critique. As he talked, the picture in question would be passed around the table, while behind him other images, ones he found relevant in some way to our own, would be projected onto the screen. Only after this minor lecture was concluded were we allowed to comment.

He lowered the blinds, slowly and meticulously as ever, and switched on the projector.

'Right, first off today then is Kristian. And I can say right away, Kristian, that you've done this rather differently than everyone else. But before I send your photograph round, I'd like to show you this painting, by one of your compatriots. Do you recognise it?'

An image of a man appeared on the screen behind him. It was Munch. I'd seen it before, it was very well known. Perhaps it was his pose, the way he was holding his cigarette, that made it so recognisable.

'Edvard Munch,' I said.

'Indeed,' said George. 'Painted in 1894, the title *Self-Portrait with Cigarette*. Now, as you can see, the subject and the darker area here at the bottom seem almost to melt together. In fact, it appears as if the figure is rising up out of darkness. A bit like the genie of the lamp, if one were to be flippant — which, I hasten to add, would be very much out of place, because there's something rather unsettling about the picture, don't you think? The figure seems almost weightless in a way, as if it were floating. Conversely, we could say that the darkness possesses a very distinct density. Now, if we turn to your photograph, Kristian, you've managed to bring about the same effect. Did you have Munch's painting in mind, can I ask?'

He held my picture up.

'No, I've never seen it before,' I said.

But my photograph was reminiscent of Munch.

He was comparing me to Munch!

'The differences are of course many, but the mood you've created is very similar indeed,' he continued, and handed the photograph to the nearest student for it to be passed around. 'The figure in the middle melts together with the interior, in a way. There's also something *unbodied* about him, can you see that? Again, it's almost as if he's levitating. At the same time, he draws all our attention towards him. We want to look at him, don't we? Which of course is the aim of any photograph. The image must draw our attention irresistibly towards it and engender in the beholder what we might refer to as a visual craving. Now, this might lead us to believe that all that's required is for the photographer to photograph something we deem to be striking in some way. But beware! Kristian here, for example, is in every respect a fine and striking young man, and yet we're not drawn to look at him, or indeed anyone else here today, with anything like visual craving. But with this photograph, Kristian, you have transcended reality, as represented by the mundane, kitchen-sink setting, and in doing so you have created something other than and more — and you've achieved this by means of method rather than subject. The subject of course remains quite as real to us, yet the image as a whole compels us on a completely different level. I could speak at length about this. Also, Munch's self-portrait embraces elements of the occult, there's a sense here of the beyond — and at the time he painted the picture, Munch was keeping frequent company with the writer August Strindberg, who was *hugely* obsessed with all things occult, as indeed many such people were at that time, it was all the rage. This of course adds an extra dimension to Munch's self-portrait. I don't know how much you've considered it — perhaps not at all — but your photograph, Kristian, has something of that same dimension about it. It looks like a room, an interior, and yet is *exterior* to the world, wouldn't you all say? Anyway, I'll leave it at that for now, but let me conclude that you've really done something extraordinary here, Kristian. Do please carry on in the same vein.'

He then moved on to the next photograph, which showed the upper part of Sarah's face, the eyes and nose, in such close-up that every pore was visible.

It wasn't a bad portrait, but it was undistinguished, I'd seen it a thousand times before. But of course it satisfied me, bringing as it did my own into even clearer relief. George was a generous teacher, spending just as much time on Sarah's portrait as he had on mine, and passing not a single negative comment. But anyone could see with their own eyes that mine was in a different league.

Gav, next after Sarah, had made a right mess of things, imagining himself as a painter at his easel, a mirror behind him allowing the beholder to see both the camera on its tripod and the picture on the easel, which of course was a photograph of Gav. It was a clever idea, but way too complicated, the composition too cluttered by half and with far too many layers to it. But George congratulated him nevertheless and showed us a painting that used mirrors to effect, and another in which the artist had depicted himself at his easel. Though photography was a relatively new medium, George said, its visual language plugged directly into two thousand years, if not more, of art history. Mirrors had been employed with frequency throughout that time, so Gavin and I had both feet planted firmly in the tradition, he said. In fact, he added, was this not true of us all? What was a camera, if not a mirror? And was a photograph not merely a fixed reflection?

We broke off for fifteen minutes after that and I went outside and smoked with Håkan and Gav. They didn't say a word about my photograph. Whatever the reason, it didn't bother me. I knew now how good it was, so whatever they thought didn't matter.

'What did you do about that money?' Håkan said. 'Did you give it back?'

'I haven't decided yet. But if I do give it back, I'll only be showing him he matters, in a way. Whereas spending it, without any contact with him, would be a stronger signal: I don't care, just send your money, if it makes you feel better.'

'Sounds like a bit of a cop-out, if you ask me.'

I gave a shrug, tossed my fag end away and went back inside. Two more critiques to go, and then done for the day. As I sat down on my chair, it struck me that I could photograph a couple of Marlowe's haunts after we were finished. Or at least check them out. I'd been imagining fog or grainy dusk, but it didn't matter, the sun would lend them other qualities. Anyway, coupling the past and the dead with murk and gloom was a cliché.

The room had filled up again by the time George reappeared and held up the next photograph.

Everyone immediately went quiet.

Jenny was lying naked on her side, her head propped on her hand as she gazed provocatively at the camera. Her breasts were plain to see, her bush only partly covered by her other hand.

'Right,' said George. 'Jenny's turn now. You'll no doubt be thinking, nudity, honesty, forthrightness, unfiltered reality. Am I right? It's a fine portrait, let me say that right away. Yet it belongs just as much to the world of art as to our own real world. Perhaps you'll be familiar with Manet's *Olympia*?'

He pressed the remote and an image, another painting, appeared on the screen.

At the same moment, there was a knock on the door.

George paused and responded — 'Come in!'

All heads turned towards the door, mine included.

Two uniformed police entered.

Everything in me went cold and drained away.

'Is there a Kristian Hadeland here?' one of them said.

Everyone looked at me.

I put up my hand.

'That's me.'

'Come with us, please.'

I wanted to ask why, but couldn't. I didn't want the others to know. I stood up.

'What's it about?' George said. 'There's teaching going on here. You can't come barging in like this.'

Neither of the two officers replied, though one seemed to raise a questioning eyebrow as if to say, 'Really?' The other ushered me from the room, a hand at my elbow.

A police car was parked in front of the entrance.

'Stand still and put your arms behind your back.'

'You're going to *handcuff* me? But I haven't done anything!'

He said nothing, but fixed his gaze on me, the cuffs dangling from his hand.

I did as he said and he snapped them around my wrists, opened the door of the vehicle and pressed my head down with the palm of his hand as I bent to get in. His colleague was already next to me on the back seat.

It was the most insulting treatment. I looked at the officer beside me. He stared coldly, insensitively out in front of him. The other one slammed the door shut and got in behind the wheel. He turned the key in the ignition and we rolled slowly across the tarmac, out into the street, and picked up speed.

'Am I under arrest?'

The one beside me turned his head.

'You're wanted to help with inquiries. We're taking you in.'

'Am I under suspicion for something?'

Neither of them answered.

Was this even lawful?

'I haven't done anything.'

Silence.

They must have got something on me. It wouldn't have come to this otherwise.

I'd given him two cigarettes. Hadn't seen the picture in the paper, didn't know they were looking for me. He'd wanted a light, so I lent him my lighter. That'd be when the camera picked me up. It was *this* lighter, here.

I stared out the window. People passing by as if in a dream. A man outside a corner shop, angling his head to attack a sandwich. Two pig-tailed girls in school uniform, arm in arm. A chubby man with a dog on a lead, forced to change hands when the dog went the wrong side of a lamp post.

If only I knew what had happened.

There'd been no altercation. Nothing. Just the cigarettes and the lighter.

We went up a ramp and then swung right, stopping in front of a roller shutter that slowly went up. Inside, police cars were parked. It was as if I was completely empty. I felt nothing, thought nothing. Got out of the car when one of the officers opened the door, and when again he gripped my arm I allowed myself to be led through the vehicle pool to a door at the far end. Inside, the handcuffs were removed and I was instructed to take off my belt and empty my pockets, the sergeant behind the counter dropping my loose change into a transparent plastic bag and then entering my name, address and nationality into a register. Procedure complete, I was taken along a corridor to a lift that carried us down to a basement level. The place was like a bunker. Another corridor followed, with heavy doors on either side.

The policeman leading us halted at one and pulled it open.

'Someone will be down to fetch you,' he said.

'How long will that be?'

'You'll find out soon enough.'

I stepped inside and the key turned in the lock behind me.

Sparsely furnished was an inadequate description. An iron cot with a thin plastic-covered mattress on top. A tiny table bolted to the wall. A two-in-one stainless-steel toilet and sink. The faint, yet pungent smell of piss.

I sat down on the cot with my back against the wall.

It couldn't be lawful. They couldn't just put me in a cell like this without telling me why, surely?

No one knew I was here.

That wasn't lawful, definitely not.

Didn't I have the right to a solicitor?

Or would that be admitting guilt?

No, it was to make sure everything went by the book.

Thrown in a cell without recourse to the law.

A prisoner of conscience.

The bastards.

I jumped to my feet and knocked on the door with my knuckles. The sound it made was small and inconsequential. I banged my fist against it a couple of times instead.

'Hello?' I called out.

It was impossible to tell if there was anyone there. I banged again, and this time I shouted.

'Hello!'

I stood for a while waiting for the door to open. No one came. I went back to the cot again.

Surely I was allowed to phone someone and let them know I was here? What was this, the Soviet Union?

They could only know something I didn't.

Maybe they'd got a picture.

Fear rippled through me.

His head hitting the wall. His head dropping limply to his shoulder.

No.

No.

I'd done nothing wrong. Nothing had happened. If they claimed anything else, I'd have to deny it. It was all I could do. Deny it.

What would the other students be thinking?

Two uniformed police. What could he have done? Something serious, obviously.

Talk would circulate, and soon everyone would know. It would pursue me. Perhaps forever.

Could I sue them for destroying my reputation? Just as my career was beginning to take off.

Fight fire with fire.

I got up again and paced the floor. I needed a strategy. It had to be foolproof.

The first thing to do was phone someone and tell them where I was. I needed someone on the outside who could help. Even if it was only to get me a solicitor.

Dad was too far away.

The other students at the school were no use.

Hans, maybe.

He knew what it was about as well.

I lay down on the cot and closed my eyes. The mattress smelled of disinfectant. They thought I was stupid enough not to realise that they'd put me in here so as to soften me up. As if being left on my own between four bare walls with only my thoughts for company would cause me to cave in. That was what they wanted, for my thoughts to pile up confusedly, making me more amenable to being led by the nose when the investigating officer started questioning me. He'd come on like a dad, no doubt, calm and affable, put me at my ease, as if he'd come to get me out of this mess. Yes, I did it. Yes, I killed him. Thank you for helping me say so. I'm relieved. I feel much better about myself now. Oh, I'm so grateful to you, Dad. You've taken a great burden from my shoulders. I feel so light and pristine.

But: nothing happened.

The cigarettes and the lighter. Stick to that.

No idea what you're talking about.

I've told you, there *was* no altercation. How many times do you need to know? He was grateful for the ciggie and for the light. I don't think he'd been expecting me to give him anything. No, my guilty conscience can't be alleviated, for the simple reason that I haven't got one. I appreciate you being so agreeable, but you're wasting your time. I've done nothing wrong.

*

I was woken by the sound of a key in the lock. The situation was at once crystal clear to me again. I sprang to my feet — I didn't want to be lying down when they came in.

A man entered, wearing a light blue shirt, a beige jacket and jeans. I took him to be in his fifties. Bald on top, bushy at the sides. Glasses. Pasty-looking. One of the policemen who'd brought me down earlier stood in the doorway.

'Kristian Hadeland?' the man said, extending his hand.

'That's right.'

'DCI Dunne,' he said. 'Thank you for coming. We've been trying to get hold of you for some days now. Did you know?'

'I had no idea.'

'In that case, you'll no doubt be wondering why we want to talk to you.'

'Yes,' I said. My voice was so feeble it nearly cracked. They only wanted to talk to me!

He smiled. His lips were an unusual deep red.

'Come with me and we'll have a little chat.'

He gestured with an open hand and I stepped out into the corridor. He came up alongside me.

'So you're a photography student, is that right?'

'Yes.'

'Not bad. A fine school too, I believe.'

I nodded.

'I dabble a bit myself. Nothing in your league, of course. I do have my own darkroom, though, in the basement at home.'

'Really?' I said.

We stepped into the lift and he pressed the button for the fourth floor.

'Yes,' he said. 'Had a picture in *Amateur Photography* once. A competition, you understand. Didn't win. Honourable mention. The best I could have hoped for, really. A picture of the wetlands along the Thames. A lot of sky. Ominous clouds.'

A typical amateur photo, in other words.

'Sounds very good,' I said.

He smiled at me and a moment later ushered me from the lift, along a corridor and into what I took to be an interview room. But for a table and some chairs, it was bare. White walls, grey lino on the floor. A tape recorder on the table. The other policeman didn't come in.

'Do have a seat,' Dunne said.

No sooner had I done so than a woman in her forties entered.

'This is DS Witt,' he said.

She was tight-lipped, with a severe gaze, a flabby, faintly freckled face. Loose, reddish-brown hair.

'Well, as you understand, we'd like to talk to you,' Dunne said. 'You've a right to legal support, if it makes you feel more comfortable. There's always a duty solicitor here in the building. Independent of us, of course. Or you can contact your own, if you have one.'

'Who has their own solicitor?' I said with a smile. 'No, I think I'm fine without. I can speak for myself.'

'Good,' he said. He pressed the record button on the tape recorder and said the time and date, then his name and who else was present, all the while doodling with a biro on a sheet of paper. He looked up at me again and smiled amiably.

'You said you didn't know why you've been brought in, is that right?'

'Yes.'

'You're taking it all very calmly, I must say. Dragged out of your lecture like that by a pair of uniformed police officers, brought here in a marked police car? And yet you haven't asked me once what this is all about.'

'No.'

'A bit odd, wouldn't you say?'

'No, I don't think so. I'm just assuming there's been some misunderstanding and that it'll all get sorted out quite soon.'

'The thing is, we're investigating a killing,' the female detective said.

'A killing?'

'On the evening of March 10, a fifty-two-year-old man by the name of Ian Moore was killed in Lewisham.'

'I've never heard of him.'

She produced a photograph and placed it on the table in front of me. It was him, sitting up against the wall in his sleeping bag.

I felt sick.

It was exactly the way I'd left him. Did they have other images, from the CCTV, showing what had happened?

'Is that him?' I said.

'That's Ian Moore, yes. Have you seen him before?'

'Was he homeless?'

Neither of them replied, but watched my reactions.

'I did encounter a homeless person recently, yes. He asked me for a cigarette. This *could* be him. You're saying he was killed?'

'Where did this encounter take place?'

'I'm not sure exactly. I was on my way to my girlfriend's. Well, we're not exactly going out with each other, but ... she lives in Lewisham as a matter of fact, yes. So it could have been there. It must have been, really.'

'And what happened?'

'Nothing happened. I stopped to light a cigarette and this man behind me asked if he could have one. I suppose it must have been him. I gave him two. And then I carried on up the road on my bike. That was it.'

'Really?'

'Yes. I haven't even thought about it again until now. Like I said, nothing happened.'

'Can you describe to us the place where this occurred?'

'Yes, he was sitting behind a wall. I didn't see him to begin with. I thought I was on my own, lighting my cigarette. I didn't know he was there until he asked if he could cadge one. I just tossed it to him then.'

'You didn't go any closer?'

'Not that I remember. It's a while ago now.'

'Is it?'

'Well, perhaps not. But if something isn't important, it's easily forgotten, isn't it? Why would I go around thinking about this? It was nothing. Can you remember what you did after reading the paper a week ago yesterday? No one would.'

I looked at her. She turned to the small pile of papers in front of her, produced another photo and placed it on the table between us.

'Is this you?'

It was the picture from the paper.

It meant they probably had no more than that.

'It looks like it,' I said. 'Yes, that's me.'

'Can you see where you are?'

'Yes, it's the same place we're talking about.'

'Can you explain to us what you're doing in this picture?'

'It looks like I'm going through a gate.'

'What gate would that be?'

'Well, it must be the gate in front of the church.'

'Where he was sitting?'

'Yes, it must be.'

'Do you remember more clearly now?'

'Not really. A bit, maybe. I think he wanted a light. I was going to toss him the lighter, too. That was it. Only then I didn't want to throw it, so I went up and handed it to him. He lit his cigarette and I went back to my bike. That was it. I remember now. I'm sorry if I didn't at first.'

'How was he?'

'The tramp?'

'Ian Moore.'

'Just normal, I suppose. The way you'd expect.'

'Did you speak to him?'

'No. Well, I may have said "here" or something when I handed him the lighter. But apart from that, no, we didn't speak. He was just a bloke cadging a fag off me, you know? There's nothing to say about it, really. And yes, I know now that he was killed soon afterwards, but that doesn't change the way I remember it. I didn't know he was dead until now, so it's not like I've been going around thinking about it. It was nothing. I can't help it if it means more now, to you. I'm sorry.'

'We'd like to show you some CCTV footage. It might jog your memory a bit.'

She stood up and went over to a TV trolley that was tucked away against the wall behind me and which until then I hadn't been aware of. She rolled it out into the room and then pressed a button on the video machine underneath the television. My nausea came rushing back, stronger now.

This was the end.

The screen flickered black and white, then some grainy footage was sort of wrung out of it. The tramp could be seen up against the wall. I saw myself go up to him, at the same time obliterating him from the camera's view, only my back visible now as I bent forward. I couldn't make out what happened. Then, the figure that was me straightened up and left, leaving the tramp behind, his head dropped slightly to one side.

The detective sergeant paused the tape. The image of me going through the gate, as Ian Moore still sat there, remained.

'Do you remember now?' Dunne said.

'Seeing it now, yes. He was playing silly with the lighter. He put it in his pocket and wouldn't give it back, so I had to take it from him.'

The sergeant sat down again.

'Would you like a solicitor now?'

'You don't seriously think I killed him, do you? That's not why I'm here, is it? Am I a suspect?'

'We'll be charging you with manslaughter, Kristian.'

'But I didn't kill him! He must have had a heart attack or something.'

'You didn't answer the question. Would you like us to appoint a solicitor?'

'Is this lawful? Questioning me on my own like this? No one even knows I'm here. I want to make a phone call. I know it's my right.'

'Of course.'

The two officers got to their feet. She tapped together her pile of papers on the table before leaving, and he then stepped aside in the doorway to allow me to go first.

'Here,' he said, handing me some change. 'There's a payphone just down the corridor.'

Who was I to call? Not Mum and Dad. They'd be able to help money-wise, pay for a good solicitor, but I didn't want to be the one to tell them what had happened. Besides, they were in a different country. They would fly over, of course, but I didn't want them to. The school, then? George? No, no, no. That left basically only Vivian and Hans. I didn't know where I stood with Vivian. Hans, in that case.

The phone was on the wall, where the corridor turned right. Dunne hovered a bit further away. I dialled the number.

Thankfully, he answered at once.

'Hello?' he said.

'Hans, this is Kristian. I'm in a spot of trouble and was wondering if you could help me out. You're the only person I can ask.'

'Of course I can. It's what friends are for, isn't it? But what's happened? How can I help?'

'It's the police. That matter, you know. They want to charge me for manslaughter. I need a solicitor.'

He was silent a moment.

'OK, I'll get one sorted for you,' he then said. 'In fact, I know just the person. He's very good indeed. A Dutchman, as it happens. Not that it matters to you. And if he can't help, he'll know someone else who can. Top drawer, I promise.'

'Thank God. I'm in the shit here.'

'So I understand. Have they actually charged you yet?'

'I don't think so. They said they were going to, that's all so far.'

'OK, good. But listen.'

'Go on.'

'Don't tell them anything. As in nothing at all. Don't answer a single question, not even the most innocuous. You're not to open your mouth until the solicitor arrives. OK?'

A bit late now, I was about to say, but I didn't want him to know how stupid I'd already been.

'OK,' I said instead.

'It'll be all right, Kristian,' he said. 'No need to worry.'

'But I am worried. Scared stiff, to be honest. Thanks for your help, though.'

I hung up and glanced at Dunne. The uniformed one from before had appeared again and was standing beside him.

'We'll want to talk to you again later,' Dunne said, stepping towards me. 'PC Johnson here will look after you in the meantime.'

Johnson motioned with his hand and nodded in the direction of the lift. I went with him, he stood close to my side on the way down and locked the door behind me without so much as a word. I lay on the cot and closed my eyes.

There was no way out of this.

My life was destroyed.

Everyone at the school would know, and everyone at home. Kristian's been convicted of murder.

But I wasn't a murderer.

There had been no murder.

If only I hadn't given him those bloody cigarettes!

I folded my hands.

Dear God in Heaven. Please, help me.

It was impossible to say what time it was, and soon I lost all sense of it. It had been mid-morning when I'd been taken in, after which I'd been left in the cell a few hours, and judging by the light I'd glimpsed outside the questioning had taken place mid-afternoon, around three, perhaps. Now, as I paced about the cramped space, it could have been anything between six and nine at night. At some point, presumably not late, they'd have to give me some food, so more likely it was closer to six than nine.

I was dying for a piss. But the toilet bowl was so tiny and so low down I surely wouldn't be able to stand up and relieve myself without it all splashing everywhere, and there was no way I was going to sit down with my pants around my ankles when they could come in at any minute.

At last a key rattled and turned in the lock. A rather squat policeman with broad hips and a fleshy face came in with a tray of food and put it down on the little table.

'Can I ask what time it is?' I said.

He shook his head and went back out, locking me in again. I stood in front of the repulsive toilet, wet some paper at the sink above it and wiped the seat before sitting down. The force of my urine stream was so great and the clearance to the bowl so shallow that it sprayed my arse.

'Ughhh!' I blurted out. 'For fuck's sake!'

I wiped myself meticulously, first with moistened, then dry toilet paper, and washed my hands thoroughly. There was something obscene about shitting in the same room in which you ate, so I'd held back on that. Pissing was bad enough.

The food looked stodgy, almost like a pudding, yellowy-white with a couple of burnt-looking peaks on top. I sat down and prodded at it with the fork. The whitish part, it seemed, was just a topping, underneath was something I took to be minced beef. Not until I put some in my mouth did I realise the white stuff was mashed potato. It tasted watery. The meat was dry and oversalted. But I hadn't eaten since breakfast, and attacked it hungrily. As always when eating something I didn't like, I tried not to breathe through my nose, thereby diminishing the taste, occasionally eliminating it completely.

I'd barely finished when the same pudgy policeman, as expressionless and silent as he'd been the first time, came back in and took away the tray. The meal sat like cement in my stomach. I lay back on the cot.

The papers would soon pick up on it. *Young Photographer Kills Homeless Man*. In Norway too: *Norwegian Convicted of London Killing*. Or perhaps even: *Kristian Hadeland (20) Guilty in UK Death Case*. None of it would be in any way representative. I hadn't *killed* anyone. But the papers wouldn't care as long as they could shift a few more copies.

Why did I have to go and give him those bloody cigarettes? Why did I have to be so nice? If only I'd ignored him and cycled off again! My life would still have been on track then. I would never even have dreamt that this could be my reality, lying here in a police cell, my future in ruins. The thought would never have existed.

Mum and Dad would have all their misconceptions about me confirmed. But not even that would make them disown me. No, they'd probably see it as an opportunity to bring me back into the fold. A bit like they'd done with Liv. Since they themselves were so decent and upstanding, they'd doubtless receive so much sympathy and support from everyone they knew that they wouldn't even feel shame.

England was dead. Norway was dead. And even if I upped sticks and went to live in France or Italy or Spain, rumour would pursue me. Perhaps not at first, in a small and insignificant town, but the moment I made a name for myself in the art world, all boundaries would dissolve, my name would resonate as strongly in the US as in the UK, in Germany as in Norway, and would be tarnished immediately. Hadeland, wasn't he involved in some hideous business with a homeless person in London once?

Unless of course it had the opposite effect and accorded me a special, enigmatic aura. Whenever I entered the room at any vernissage, there'd be hushed whispers, a collective awestruck gasp: he killed a person.

How would I have reacted if I'd been told that a guest lecturer at the school, Figueroa, say, had once killed a man?

Gav lets it slip as we stand outside smoking:

'You do know Figueroa's been to prison for killing someone, don't you?'

'Figueroa? You're joking?'

'No, it's true. He's a hard case.'

And then, the first time he comes in, of course, there's an aura about him. Something resolute and uncompromising, something dark and evil. We look for it too in his pictures. And we find it, it's everywhere in them, because it's in him.

Manslaughter. It would carry a few years, but not that many. I'd still be young when I got out. I wouldn't go home to disgrace in Norway. Paris? No, too last century. Madrid? Nothing came out of there. Rome, the same. London was the place, and there was no way I could stay there.

No, for fuck's sake: Berlin.

Berlin!

The Wall. *Christiane F.* Bowie and Iggy. Einstürzende Neubauten. Neon. Rain. Concrete.

Never mention the past. Let it seep as it will. Never confirm, never deny.

I could change my name.

Werner Zimmel. The most astonishing photographer the world has ever seen — and he has an outrageous story to tell.

Black overcoat, always. Face ravaged by life. Authoritarian gesticulations to assistants in the enormous studio. Every boundary between photography and art long since broken down and transgressed.

A wooden leg? Nah, overdoing it. The next thing would be an eye-patch and a parrot.

But a clearly defined aesthetic. A clearly defined project. Wild and against the grain.

The big city. I know no one. I go about at night taking pictures. Of people in the windows. Bars, galleries. A lonely figure in a commercial building. Night after night. Picture upon picture. The city's spirit, the city's soul. We see it, but we're not a part of it. We are on the outside.

No, no change of name. My own. Kristian Hadeland. He's never tried to hide, always stood by what he did.

I opened my eyes and it was as if what they saw was stronger than everything I contained, for every thought and fantasy at once disintegrated as the room in which I lay became manifest to me.

Concrete floor, concrete walls, heavy metal door.

I was in jail.

I was unappreciated, undesired. Removed from society. Prohibited from association. And soon I'd have to stand up in court and be humiliated as much as a person could be. It would take place in public. Everyone would know. Everyone from junior school, everyone from secondary school, everyone from gymnas. Everyone in my family. Everyone at the art school. Every conceivable lie about me would be circulated.

All because of those bastard cigarettes.

If only I hadn't stopped!

Why hadn't I just cycled on?

I could close my eyes and do so in my mind, but as soon as I opened them again I was here, chained to the moment, like a dog was chained to its master.

What a mess I was in. What a complete and utter mess.

I stood up and began again to move about the space, but then after a few minutes I got sick of it and lay down again. Sitting still at home was no problem, the same with being alone, quite the opposite in fact. So why was it so difficult here?

It was all in the mind.

And then the lights went out and I was plunged into impenetrable darkness. I couldn't see a hand in front of me. It didn't matter, I wasn't exactly going anywhere, but it was unpleasant nevertheless.

I assumed they just switched them off at a certain time every night. Eleven o'clock, maybe? Or perhaps ten?

I closed my eyes in search of sleep, but quickly sensed it was no use — that particular respite felt hours away. Normally I'd have been quite comfortable lying awake in the dark, a bit frustrated, perhaps, but now

I found myself focusing on not thinking about the man who'd died, which of course only made him appear even more vividly to me, as clear with my eyes closed as if I'd been looking at him in real life: the sores on his face, the matted tangle of greasy hair, the moist, glazed eyes.

His eyes rolled in their sockets and went as white as if he'd been blind.

He put a hand up in front of him to protect himself.

'Don't kill me. Please, I want to live.'

I blinked into the darkness, struggling to find something else to think about. For some reason, the river back home came to mind. The flat, bare rock midstream in the rapids, where we used to stretch out to dry in summer after swimming and splashing around there. Chart hits on the cassette player one of us always brought. The girls in their bikinis.

The blind eyes of the tramp stared at me.

Come on, Kristian, pull yourself together.

I stood up in the dark, stepping forward cautiously until my outstretched hand touched the wall. I groped the few steps to the end wall. The handleless door, the opposite wall.

'Life is always worth living,' said the tramp, now firmly ensconced my mind.

This was absurd.

It was only happening because I didn't want it to happen.

I found the cot again, lay face down this time, my head pillowed against my arm.

I'd been afraid of the dark once. But it was a long time ago now.

The television had been on in the living room one morning with no one there watching it. I'd come in and paused a moment to see what was on. A headless man coming up some steps. It filled me with such terror that I ran outside to find Mum or Dad. After that, I couldn't close my eyes without seeing the headless man. That, or else the picture of the man with the skull on the front of one of Dad's magazines he'd kept from when he was a boy.

Look, no tramp here.

And if there was anywhere I was safe, it was surely here, locked inside a police cell.

Only not from the dead.

They were known to pass through even the most solid walls.

Ha ha.

Then there was the man who'd hanged himself in the forest, on the rise beyond the track. He appeared every year on the day of his death, there were people who'd seen him, trudging towards his tree. I'd believed it too, and was scared stiff whenever I went past on my bike.

But none lie stiller than the dead. None to be less frightened of than them.

He who is dead is dead. Wasn't that what he'd said, that Becker character?

It was meaningless, tormenting myself with thoughts of a homeless tramp. He'd died, and nothing could alter the fact. If a thing can't be changed, better it be left alone.

I knew that. But still the vision of him kept coming back to me as I lay twisting and turning, anxious to sleep. There he was, slumped against the wall, head dropped to one side, eyes staring blindly. It was as if he'd returned to haunt me. And yet he didn't exist as anything but a figment of my untethered imagination.

What was I to do with myself when I couldn't even find peace in my own mind?

I had no idea how long it took, but at last, presumably in the early hours of morning, I finally fell asleep. And then, abruptly, woke when the lights came on. I needed a piss, desperately, but with no way of knowing when they'd bring me breakfast, I lay slumbering, tightening my sphincter or whatever it was that stopped the piss from streaming out at will, until the door soon afterwards was opened and a policeman, a different one now, came in with a tray.

This time I tried to piss gently rather than just powering it all out. I no longer felt I needed a shit, but I knew it was only a matter of time before my stomach started cramping up. Helene, in one of her more vulgar moments, had referred to giving birth as like shitting a melon. I could identify with that. Few things in this world hurt more than having a massive load to deliver.

Breakfast was porridge and an apple. After eating it I sat waiting for the policeman to return. I found myself actually looking forward to it. And I'd been here less than twenty-four hours.

Some time after he'd been and gone, perhaps an hour, perhaps two, which I spent sitting on the cot trying to think only about things that were good, the door opened once more. This time it was Dunne. Still wearing the same jacket, but now in a different pair of trousers, these ones olive-green, a tenacious look in his eyes.

'We'd like to talk to you again. Are you ready for that?'

'I won't be telling you anything,' I said.

'You'll still have to come with me.'

'Can I refuse?'

'I think not.'

'OK,' I said and got to my feet.

Upstairs in the interview room, the woman DS was already waiting. On my side of the table sat an elderly-looking man, bespectacled and dressed in a light brown tweed jacket and dark brown trousers, his bald pate flecked with liver spots. Some hairs bristled from around his Adam's apple, as if he kept missing them when he shaved.

'This is Mr Edward Hughes, Kristian. Your solicitor.'

The man stood up and I shook his outstretched hand.

'Yes, I've been appointed to represent you,' he said.

'But I've got my own solicitor.'

'If that's the case,' Dunne said, 'I'm afraid he hasn't been in touch.'

'But I phoned him yesterday. He said he was going to contact you.'

'What's his name?'

'I can't remember. It went through a friend.'

'So what's your friend's name?'

'I only know his first name,' I lied.

'His address, then?'

'I don't know offhand.'

Dunne glanced at his detective sergeant. I couldn't for the life of me remember what she was called. Webb, or some such thing. White, perhaps. Not that it mattered.

'We'd very much like to conduct an interview with you today, nonetheless,' Dunne went on. 'Therefore I suggest that Mr Hughes represent you for the time being, until such time as your own solicitor, whoever he may be, appears and can take over. How does that sound?'

'Unacceptable,' I replied. 'I've a right to my own solicitor.'

'You have, yes,' said the DS. 'But after thirty-six hours you're appointed one automatically.'

'It really makes little difference, if any,' said Dunne.

'I want my own solicitor.'

'All right. In that case, I hope to hear from him sometime today. If not, Mr Hughes here will represent you tomorrow.'

It felt good, not letting them have things all their own way, a small triumph almost, I thought, as Dunne led me back down into the basement again. But once the door was shut behind me and I was left on my own again, I started having second thoughts. Another twenty-four hours. Another sleepless night.

But I had to stick it out. I'd spent plenty of days alone in my bedsit. OK, so I could do as I wanted there, listen to music, read, smoke, eat, whenever it suited me, but none of those things were necessities, all could be done without.

It was in my mind. Knowing there was nothing I could do made me claustrophobic. Sitting on my own in my bedsit doing nothing was never claustrophobic.

Mentally I was strong. Empty time was nothing, a doddle.

I stepped over and washed my hands meticulously, then dried them quite as carefully.

Five minutes gone.

I looked around for something to occupy me. The only thing that wasn't bolted fast was the toilet roll. I could unravel it and then fold it up again. A bit trivial, though.

I could save it for a crisis.

It was OK just to sit quietly for now.

I'd spent at least two minutes scanning the room.

Would they give me a pen and some paper? I could write down the titles of all my records then. Work out the perfect sequence.

It didn't need pen and paper. I could do it in my head.

The coolest cover first. Nothing too well known, or else people would think I was going with the flow. So not *Closer*, even though the sacral image was stunning. Not *Faith* either. No, something more like Cabaret Voltaire. *Red Mecca*? Or Throbbing Gristle, perhaps? *The Second Annual*

Report could be just the job. Stripped back and straight. Only someone was bound to think it was experimental jazz or something.

No, of course. Tuxedomoon. *Holy Wars*. The burning object in the sky above the cornfield and the woods. Not that many people had heard of them in the UK, and it was a fabulous cover.

OK, that first.

Then *The Second Annual Report*?

No, it suffocates everything.

Red Mecca, then?

Yes, that next.

Bold colours both, and yet they were very different. A third now, equally vivid, then fade back into grey with *Faith* before bringing in the colours again.

How much time had gone now?

Ten minutes, at least. I hadn't given a thought to where I was.

Maybe Hans was just a bullshitter.

Maybe he didn't know any solicitor. Maybe he hadn't lifted a finger. I could just see him sitting there laughing his head off.

So it'd be the old bloke tomorrow.

At once, a surge of terror gripped me.

I was being charged with killing a man.

I'd be in prison for years.

My life was destroyed.

Completely, utterly destroyed.

'Oh, for fuck's sake, no!' I shouted.

'Quiet in there,' a voice said straight away. 'Stop shouting.'

Was there a guard outside the door?

No, surely not. Just someone passing.

I moved restlessly about the room. Lay back on the cot. It was as if my mind was racing, but when I tried to pin down what was going on in it, there was nothing there. No thoughts, only hurtling motion.

Again, I got to my feet. Again, I lay down. I punched the mattress a few times.

Oh, oh, oh!

I was done for. My life was finished. I sensed the imperative of life's speed matching the speed inside my head. If it didn't, I'd go mad. And right now it was touching zero.

Don't think about time.

Don't think about that tramp.

Don't think about not being able to go anywhere.

Just take things easy. Breathe. Relax.

What could the time be? Ten? Eleven? Twelve?

I stood up and stepped over to the door.

'What time is it?' I called out, and felt stupid, for there was bound to be no one there.

If there was, they didn't answer.

Was there any more sleep to be had, to permeate from the reservoirs of my subconscious? If there was none, and my thoughts did not mist, eventually recede and dissipate completely, I'd be left on my own with them the whole night.

Tuxedomoon, *Holy Wars*. Cabaret Voltaire, *Red Mecca*.

No.

What was the point?

I wouldn't be seeing my records again, not for many, many years to come. I'd be cut off too from all the new ones that came out.

I sat down on the cot and put my forehead on the tabletop.

And then, the key in the lock. Lunch, maybe? I sat up as the door opened.

It was Dunne.

'Kristian,' he said. 'You're free to go.'

'What?'

'You can go home now. You're no longer a suspect. I'm sorry we kept you.'

'Seriously?'

He nodded and stepped aside.

'But how come? What's happened?'

'Some new information has come to light.'

'So I can just go?'

'Yes,' he said, with a suggestion of impatience.

I glanced at him as we went along the corridor. Was it a trick? A ploy, designed to throw me off balance and confess or something?

He pushed the button for the lift, the door opening immediately, and in the few seconds it took to reach the ground floor he said nothing. My personal belongings lay waiting in a tray on the desk. The sergeant nudged it towards me.

'Straight ahead for your way out,' Dunne said. 'Look after yourself.'

He gave a brief smile before turning and walking off towards some stairs. As if in a haze, I stepped forward to the exit. Pushed open the door, looked back over my shoulder. No one came.

The area outside the building was nearly deserted, the sky big and wide and blue.

I went down the steps. A figure was sat on a bench across the way, pigeons milling darkly at his feet. More came sailing through the air towards him.

It was Hans. He had half a loaf in one hand and was tossing crumbs with the other. He hadn't seen me, and for a moment I thought I might just make off before he did. But his presence, at the same moment I was released, could hardly have been coincidence.

Abruptly, he threw back his head and stared into the sky, the orbs in his sockets rolled white. Three times in quick succession his mouth opened and closed like a fish's.

Then, he turned to look at me.

'Hello, Kristian,' he said. 'Enjoying your freedom?'

PART TWO

Several months have passed now since last I picked up a camera, and still it feels as if something important is missing, as if I'm not whole. I've taken photographs nearly every day since I was fifteen and am used to the weight of the camera around my neck, used to seeing the world in terms of potential subjects, to subconsciously gauging the light wherever I am. Without the camera I feel the sort of phantom pain of its absence; habitually my hand reaches for it, only to find that it isn't there, and at once I feel emptiness. Less so now, thankfully, than in the first few weeks. I have built my days around writing; everything I do supports it, and the key, so I've discovered, is to always do the same as the day before. I rise at the same time in the mornings, put on the same clothes — apart from on Sundays, when I both shower and change — sit with my coffee and smoke a couple of cigarettes in the chair by the window downstairs before commencing the first session of the day. It takes me to lunchtime, when I'll eat two pieces of crispbread and an orange, before the second session begins. Only then, once it's done, do opportunities arise for variation: either I'll cross over to the store with Viggo in his boat and buy some essentials there; or else I'll go out with the rod and line to fish from the rocks, if not deciding to walk around the island — not a long walk by any means, forty or fifty minutes, perhaps, to go the whole way round. Afterwards I cook myself a meal, fish usually, before sitting down in the chair beside the window to read and listen to music until I'm tired enough to go to sleep.

My father was a creature of habit — as good as a clock when I was growing up. I felt only contempt for it then: life was not to be regulated like a waterway, but allowed to flow as it will. This was not only unfair towards him, but also a misunderstanding on my part. What regulated my father's time, more than any wristwatch, was the daylight and the rhythm of the wildlife. As well, presumably, as the insight that it is in the ordinariness of the day that things get done. The opposite of habit, that which is transgressive and irregular, and which belongs to romantic infatuations, to intoxication and art, is freedom, yet freedom will also always comprise some destructive element — like a burning stove its fire must continually be fed; eventually one must give it the furniture, and finally the house itself. I don't think my father knew this, but perhaps he had an inkling. He must have seen it, first in Liv, then in me, and he must have been afraid of it. Fear, when presenting in a level-headed man, may take the form of disapproval and scepticism, but sometimes verge on revulsion. That Dad could react so differently in the cases of Liv and myself was something I for a long time failed to understand. Liv, he perhaps believed, had been stricken with something beyond her control that had pursued and eventually overpowered her, whereas I actively went looking for it. While to his mind she was a victim, I was a narcissist. And as is often the case with those who are bound to habit, that notion became a truth which nothing, not even unequivocal experience to the contrary, could shake. Liv's behaviour was to those around her a source of endless distress and anxiety, called for endless amounts of solicitude and patience, which met with neither thanks nor reward, only new situations, no less demanding. And yet she was a victim, and they gave her warmth and love. I, on the other hand, who not only looked after myself without any help, but also did well, remained less than worthy. Not that I would have it any other way. For even if now like my father I live by a clock and understand what value he found in it, I've nonetheless brought to such a way of living the kind of experience he himself never came near. His lack of appreciation for the art world was grounded in his inability to understand it. In my case it was because I understood it all too well. For twenty years I was dazzled, but then came darkness, and all meaning was sucked out of everything.

The island lies some way off the coast and the weather here is indeed changeable — hardly two hours are the same. The birdlife is abundant and in constant flux, as too the non-avian wildlife, I began to realise, especially after the first snows had fallen. Not far from the house, an otter lives, and in the evenings I'll often see him scuttle across the jetty in the glow of the artificial lighting there, to slip headlong into the water, and only a fortnight ago, when the snow still covered the ground, I discovered he'd made a slide for himself on the shallow incline of the rock. The house itself is home to a number of mice, so used to my presence here that they have no qualms about venturing into the room as I sit and read. And there are the insects too, a constant humming and buzzing about the grass — and the seals that I often see basking on the skerry. Fish come and go, and I never know quite what will wriggle on my hook when I lift the rod, only that *something* will. Jellyfish collect now and then around the jetty, like suspended suns in some alternative planetary system. The island is home to two cats, as well as a dog that often runs loose and will come into the house if I happen to leave the door open. But the greatest changemakers in this little biosphere are of course the people — in the nearest house, some fifty metres away, live three, another in the house across the way, and one occupies the loft of one of the boathouses in the harbour. The regular boat service, a small hydrofoil, puts in twice a week, and from it occasionally a passenger or two might alight. These numbers seem smaller still when held up against the seven billion or so who inhabit the globe, and yet their activity here is more than sufficient to fill the days of a life. On Sundays, the closest neighbours, an elderly couple and their grown-up son, put on their best clothes regardless that no one is likely to see them. The son, Viggo, is much the same age as me, though possesses the mental register of a child. The man across the way, the dog owner, is from the same generation as Viggo's parents. The two households have not spoken to each other in nearly thirty years. I've yet to discover the reason for this animosity, but am fascinated by its continued currency. Both parties take pains to avoid all contact, but of course now and again it can't be helped that their paths should cross during the course of a day — I've seen it happen myself a few times — and in such cases they simply turn their heads and look the other way. I know nothing at all about the man in the boathouse, having waved the odd greeting but never spoken to him. He'd be somewhere in his fifties. He keeps a light on at night, and I wonder what it is that occupies him then — none of the other inhabitants has been inclined to answer me when I've ventured to ask. A number of vacant dwellings are found here too; some are occupied in summer, by families who presumably once inherited them, as did Emil, the owner of the property I now occupy myself.

Emil is wealthy and lives in London, and mentioned the place to me some years ago. We were talking about Norway and he told me that one side of his family hailed from a group of islands out west, a line of fishermen going back goodness knows how many generations. 'I actually own a house there,' he said, 'that belonged to my grandfather.' Hearing that the place stood empty and that the former fishing community was now all but depopulated, my interest was at once awakened and I began to probe, though discreetly so as not to indicate the depth of my interest. In that way I found out the name of the island, the property's location on it, and the information that a key was kept under the front steps. All this occurred a matter of months after I met Yelena, when all was still promise and a beckoning future, so there was as yet no real reason for me to take note of any of these things, other than the fact that I have always, even at the best of times, toyed with the notion of living a life other than the one I had.

And now I'm here. Although I didn't plan it, it feels nevertheless as if it had been planned all along and I'd merely followed a path that had been tramped down for me by others. I suppose the word for that feeling is fate.

The house was neat and tidy when I arrived, though unmistakably unused for quite some time, something you immediately sense on entering such a place — you're assailed by emptiness. Worse by far was the weather — wet and windy, the rain pouring, the sea battering the land below the house — and the fact that I felt so dislodged. It had been dark when the boat sailed from the mainland, and I'd never been in these parts before and barely even knew the region. Eight degrees and rain, the boat filled with passengers, screaming kids, the smell of hot dogs from the kiosk, the drone of a television drowning in the deep, monotonous rumble that seemed to come from the very hull itself. I was in a coma of sorts, travel-induced, and sat motionless in my seat, staring out into the darkness, looking at no one, without a thought. Grief gnawed at the wall of my stomach. Nothing mattered, anything at all could have happened and I wouldn't have cared. The very fact that I was sitting there at all, in that seat, on that boat, on my way to a near-uninhabited island, was therefore in itself something of a miracle. I remember almost nothing from the journey, though it had been long and slow — the train to Dover, the ferry to Calais, the train again, first to Hamburg, then to Copenhagen, Oslo, Bergen. The boat to Florø, the bus to the quayside there.

The hydrofoil made its many calls at quays and jetties in the darkness, many got off, none got on, and eventually only myself and an old man remained. He concealed his curiosity well when we both alighted at the same place. I strode off ahead of him, locating the house at once, set back somewhat from the harbour on a small rise. A tall, white-washed dwelling built of stone, from sometime in the 1930s. And the key hung underneath the steps just as Emil had said. A good stack of dry firewood there was too, the house ice-cold inside, the sea crashing without. Duvets on all the beds in the rooms upstairs. I lit a fire in the grate and stetched out on the sofa with two duvets to cover me, and slept well into the next day. I woke up when someone knocked on the door. I guessed it would only be the neighbour. My first impulse was not to answer, but I was anxious to avoid suspicion — the last thing I wanted was for whoever it was to get on the phone to Emil and tell him there was someone in his house, and so I dragged myself from sleep and went through into the hall preparing myself to be friendly and accommodating.

It was the old fellow who stood there, beside him a man my own age. Both were in blue overalls and brown wellingtons. The rain had stopped, but the rock behind them remained darkly moist. The air was noticeably fresh and still.

'Hello,' the old man said. 'We saw someone was here. Just wanted to make ourselves known. We're from next door, so to speak.'

'Yes, we were on the boat together yesterday,' I said. 'I'm a friend of Emil's. Borrowed his place for a few months. Arild's the name. Arild Kvam.' I put out my hand.

'Einar Olsen,' he said. 'And this is Viggo.'

Viggo, wide-faced with a square jaw and high temples, had stood staring at me the whole time. Though his features were rather distinguished, I sensed there was something about him that wasn't quite right.

'Do you want to come out in my boat?' he said.

There.

I glanced at the father, who smiled faintly and lowered his gaze.

'Perhaps I will, at some point,' I said.

'Viggo goes across and stocks up for us from the store. He can do the same for you, if you like. I don't think you've your own boat here, have you?'

'No, that's right.'

'The regular boat only comes twice a week. And you'd have to wait three hours to get back.'

'Ah.'

'Didn't Emil mention it?'

'He said the infrastructure was a bit of a challenge, yes. He never got round to telling me the details, though.'

It was important not to leave them wondering who I was or what I was doing there, I didn't want them talking too much about me to others, so I'd prepared a cover story which I now laid out for them.

'I live in London normally,' I said. 'I lecture at one of the universities there and have taken a few months off to gather some research together into a book. Emil's house here seemed the perfect place to work in peace, and he was kind enough to let me use it.'

'I see,' Einar said. 'What's this book about, then?'

'Oh, nothing very interesting,' I said. 'A textbook on sociology.'

'Well, you'll have plenty of peace here — we won't disturb you! But come over and knock if you need anything from the shop, and Viggo'll fetch it for you. Or take you over, if you prefer. Won't you, Viggo?'

Viggo gave an earnest nod.

'Appreciated,' I said, and watched them arc away along the line of the inlet and across to where they lived, the father first, the son following on behind him. They wouldn't be a problem, I felt sure of it. Not unless he got in touch with Emil. But the way he'd accepted my story didn't seem to indicate there'd be any risk of it. He probably didn't even have his number.

I carried in a couple of armfuls of logs and dumped them next to the fireplace. By the time I'd got another fire going, the strength had somehow drained from me and I lay down again on the sofa, dozing as once more the light faded into darkness, until I could no longer ignore my hunger and got up to butter some bread, which I ate while standing at the worktop in the kitchen. I drank a glass of water. Outside, the sky was stunning; a full moon hung upon the blackness above the sea, its pale light a shimmer in the harbour. Everything was so still that it felt almost unreal. The hard plastic buoys, faintly red; the crates stacked on the jetty, the boats that lay at their moorings almost without moving. The boathouses with their blocks and tackle; the rock, worn smooth, rising up behind them; the silvery black sea beyond, as great and majestic as a waiting god.

I dressed and went outside. My footfall resonated in the terrain. The lights in the houses behind the quay shone only dimly, the few who lived here were asleep. I clambered up a slope and saw far in the distance a row of mountains, more solid in their darkness than the sky. I tipped my head back and gazed up at the stars. Then, I set off walking, reaching after a while the other end of the island and returning along the opposite side. There, all vegetation had been eroded away by the wind, the rock left bare but for the odd patch in sheltered dips and crannies. I sat down on an outcrop. Never had it been clearer to me than then, that death was the rule, life the exception. The moon, the sea, the rock, the sky, the stars, everything I could see was dead. And almost nothing separated me from being dead too. It wouldn't need to be dramatic. All it would take was to slip into the sea and I'd be drowned in minutes. But I couldn't. I imagined it, getting to my feet, going down to the water's edge, crouching to slide into the element — but I knew it wouldn't be possible, that physically I wouldn't be capable of making my body do what was necessary in order for it to die.

It was too soon.

But why? I really hadn't anything to live for. There was nothing left of my life.

I would have to force myself. Resolve to do it — and then do it.

The warmth of the house when I returned seemed almost indecent. Indecent and shameful compared to the forces that prevailed outside.

There were a hundred billion stars in our galaxy. The universe contained at least a hundred billion similar galaxies. And here in this little cranny we sat, clinging to human life, regardless that it amounted to no more than an inexpressibly trivial gust of wind. We built churches and dug in.

I chose a room in which to sleep. No one knew I was here, and if I could help it no one ever would. There was no hurry.

The next morning I knocked on the neighbour's door to ask if Viggo might be going across to the store at some point during the day. He was. When? Whenever I liked. Ten minutes later I climbed down into the boat, a plastic seventeen-footer powered by a 20 hp Yamaha outboard, which Viggo unmoored and launched with a familiar hand. It felt unnatural to be out on the sea in such a small craft. I'd been expecting him to give it full throttle as soon as we left the inlet where the harbour was. Perhaps it was his childlike manner that led me to think so; nonetheless, he kept a leisurely speed. The store was right by the quayside, which was bigger by far than our own small jetty. This was a hub for the outlying island communities, I understood. I bought oranges, noodles, crispbread, sliced meats and spreads, as well as coffee and cigarettes. They had all sorts of other things too — clothing, kitchen equipment, fishing tackle, even office supplies — and so I added a set of waterproofs and a pair of rubber boots, observing already that the locals considered them obligatory. Viggo didn't buy much, just milk, bread, carrots and two tins of snus. I found him looking through the DVD shelves while waiting for me.

The sky was bright blue, only a thin veil of wispy cloud draped the horizon. The sun hung low in the sky, consigning to shadow the ground beneath steeply sloping rock and buildings. Behind the store, smoke rose up out of house chimneys. A pair of fishing boats put in; on one, a man in blue overalls attended to the nets on the deck. Viggo dumped his carrier bag of shopping on the edge of the quay to clamber into the boat. I handed it down to him along with the two of my own. He had hardly spoken on the way over, and I began to wonder if I hadn't misjudged him. After all, the only thing I had to go on was a simple question he'd asked. That, and the fact that he still lived at home with his parents.

I decided to test him.

'A nice life you live out here?' I said, seating myself in the stern as he bent to release the moorings. He said nothing, but I registered a nod of his head, which was pitched forward, his face turned away from me. It wasn't a particularly intelligent way of communicating, but not necessarily revealing of anything either.

He took up position behind the small windshield and started the engine, backing carefully away from the quay while looking over his shoulder.

'What sort of work do you do, exactly? I didn't quite catch.'

'I help Dad with things.'

'What does he do, then?'

'He's a pensioner.'

He sat down and pushed the throttle lever forward, swinging the vessel into a tight arc before straightening up and making back towards the island again, perhaps a kilometre away.

There was no doubt that he was backward, even if it wasn't much. For all I knew, he could have been one of those people with autism who had an extraordinary talent of some kind.

Still, it was strange that he said so little. I would have thought he'd be bubbling over with chat, too simple to be able to see himself from the outside and gauge the reactions of others. Maybe he was only borderline and aware that people would laugh and make fun of him if he blurted out his every thought. Though perhaps without really understanding why, putting it down as just one of life's facts?

The other explanation of course was that there wasn't much going on in his head at all.

A wave of sorrow swept through me and I started to cry.

He was facing away, but if he did happen to swivel round and look at me, the tears that streamed down my cheeks could just as easily have been caused by the wind.

It had been a couple of days since the last time, and it felt good.

I wiped my eyes with the back of my hand. The waters around the island glittered with sunlight, its tiny outcrop so negligible beneath such an immensity of sky. Viggo sat unmoving in front of me, one hand on the steering wheel, the other on the throttle. To the right, which I took to be north, a white-tipped wave rose from an otherwise still and blue-black sea. Moments later we arced slowly into the inlet. The water there was clear, the bottom shimmering green beneath us as we glided up alongside the jetty.

'Bye,' was all Viggo said where the trampled path divided in two, he veering away towards his house, I in the opposite direction towards mine.

I put the bags down on the worktop in the kitchen and took out my items. The boots I placed in the hall, and hung the rainwear on the peg, while the packets of sliced meat went into the fridge. For a terrible moment, the meaninglessness of my life out here was clear to me. No future awaited. The way ahead was closed, and behind me lay nothing to which I wished to return. So this was it, these rooms, as they were now.

The feeling was compounded by the vast and empty sky, the sun that burned in it.

It was all so insufferable. Yet why should I suffer it? The crux was that there was nothing to suffer it *for*. There was nothing beyond.

But suffer I did. I had nothing to live for, so I lived for that. The days passed. Or else I passed into the days. I found a fishing rod under the stairs, a typewriter in the upstairs junk room among boxes of objects that had once belonged to the life that had been lived in the house. There were photographs too, though the albums that doubtless had been kept were gone, someone presumably had taken them away. The loose photos were perhaps duplicates, or perhaps they'd simply not been interesting enough to have warranted inclusion. I took them downstairs to the sitting room and looked at them there. Judging by the cars, the hairstyles and clothes, they were from the 1960s and 1970s. There was nothing unusual about any of them — there had to be hundreds of thousands of similar photos in homes all over Norway. A picnic in a lay-by, with a cooler box and a foldable camping table; a child holding up a fish on a jetty; the same child a few years older, stiffly dressed beneath a fluttering flag; a table set indoors around which a dozen or more people were sat in their Sunday best. That sort of thing. It was disheartening to look at them, even though I loved that special 1970s glow of Kodachrome, for the people in the photographs meant nothing to me, the events of which they were a part completely arbitrary — without context they were devoid of meaning. Which meant that context *was* meaning. It was *context* that was the loss, not the events being gone.

I put them back. But the typewriter, which rather than having been consigned to a box had been pushed into a corner along with a large, heavy iron and an antique porcelain washbowl, was something I could use. The next time I went to the store with Viggo I stocked up on office paper, and bought too some new fishing line and a box of lures. And gradually, from being something inside me, which no one knew anything about, what had happened to me changed and became something external. Word after word, day after day, page after page. It didn't give meaning to my life, but it held my terrible emptiness at bay. And, it lessened my grief. At least in the hours in which I wrote.

The present interlude isn't because the story ended there, with me stopping in my tracks on seeing Hans feeding the pigeons outside the police station that day in 1986. It's because I had to come up for air. Now that I've filled my lungs, I can go back again. I don't even need to close my eyes in order to see it in my mind. All I need to do is think of the police station, and a chain of nerve endings in the enormous network that makes up my human memory becomes activated. Before I know it, the building lights up to my inner eye, the sunlight on the facade, a pale blue sky overhead. Hans, I think to myself, and there he sits, smiling with his half a loaf of bread in one hand, surrounded by pigeons, dressed in his habitual ankle grazers and dark green anorak, with his thick pile of unruly hair, his big hands.

Wasn't there something going on across the street?

Yes, a water main had burst, water was gushing up from a grid, flooding the surrounding asphalt and paving with its gleaming grey. Cars growled in their traffic jam, coughed out their exhaust fumes in front of the garish row of tacky shops on the other side of the street.

His eyes held me as I approached.

'Weren't you supposed to get me a solicitor?' I said.

'What do want a solicitor for? You're a free man!'

He stood up and looked like he was going to hug me, but to my relief made do with a friendly slap on the back.

'We should celebrate!'

I shook my head.

'Come on,' he said. 'It's over. As far as you need to be concerned, the matter's dead and buried. You don't have to think about it ever again. You're free.'

'How do you know?'

'I've got good sources.'

'In the police?'

'Where do you fancy going? The pub? Or somewhere more lively perhaps?'

'Listen, Hans. If you know why they let me go, then tell me.'

'You're innocent, aren't you?'

He laughed.

'Someone else confessed. They could hardly charge you both, now, could they? So they had to let you go.'

I looked at him in bewilderment.

'You owe me a favour,' he said. 'Come on, let's go.'

I couldn't see it any other way than that I'd been given a new chance. Still, I wasn't exactly starting with a clean slate. Sure, I could go back to the school and laugh off the dubious, stupefied looks I met with my head held high, and explain that it had all been a misunderstanding, but on the inside I was tarred, my soul was unclean.

'I know the feeling,' Hans said when I described it to him. 'I think most people do. We each have our own self, and then there are the demands and expectations of the social sphere, which are impossible to fulfil. Every time you fail to live up to what's expected of you, every time you can't meet a demand, shame and guilt are deposited in what you refer to as the soul, or, as my mother preferred to call it, the heart — otherwise known as the self. A tainted heart is the most human thing of all! So don't you worry about it, Kristian. Your soul will become only grubbier and grubbier. But it is from earth you have come, and to earth you shall return. What's grubbier than that! Think of it as a gradual transition.'

'You're not very good at this comforting thing, are you?'

'Oh, but I am. Comfort is exactly what it is. And it's our only comfort. You're simply not mature enough to have grasped it yet. Your heart's still too pure, simple as that. It remembers its innocent state.'

But I wasn't innocent, was I?

If someone else had confessed, though, I had to be.

In other words my torment was simply down to my conscience going obsessive-compulsive on me, punishing me for no reason. Even though I did everything in my power to escape it, it remained with me throughout the spring, a bedimming shadow. Not as a thought, nor indeed a specific emotion as such, more a coating on every feeling, even the good ones. At the same time, there was a distinct development in my work, and it was hard not to see this in the light of what had happened to me, though most likely it was simply coincidence, much more to do with what my creativity handbook referred to in terms of 'breaking the plateau effect' — after slogging away on the same plane, thousands and thousands of hours, suddenly, from one day to the next, one found oneself having performed a leap to the next level, where what until then had seemed beyond one's reach was now not merely achievable, but very quickly incorporated into one's day-to-day practice. Another few thousand hours after that and the same thing would happen again — another leap, another level. Whatever the reason, I found myself taking considerably better pictures. They were more interesting and laden with meaning, regardless that I'd done nothing to make it happen. It felt like it was something inside me. My photo of the cat, so much better than the work I'd done previously, suddenly represented a new norm. And it wasn't just me who noticed this either. George, our lecturer, said he didn't think he'd ever seen such improvement in such a short space of time. I could photograph a glass of water and somehow make it compelling. This new situation quickly became intoxicating — it was everything I'd wanted and striven for, and now I was living it. My evenings would be spent in the darkroom, while at weekends I'd be cycling around taking pictures. I procrastinated about the Marlowe project, mainly because it would be difficult to do sufficiently well — the connection between Marlowe and his London localities was by the nature of things not visually apparent and I could see no way of evoking the sixteenth century in contemporary surroundings, short of hiring someone to dress up in period costume or some such cheap and corny trick — but also because the incident with the tramp in some way stuck to Vivian. I'd been on my way to see her that night. She was also Hans's friend and he'd been too involved in what had happened — in retrospect there'd been something almost unhealthy about his interest. Not to mention that I owed him 'a favour', as if my exoneration was something he'd pulled out of his hat. I didn't exactly avoid him, but I saw no reason either to look him up. I'd half expected him to turn up of his own accord, to be suddenly standing there in the pub in those ridiculous trousers, but it didn't happen. After a while, however, this state of affairs began to prey on my mind, until eventually curiosity got the better of me and I cycled over to his garage studio one afternoon after school. He was not at home, though I knocked for some time on the door and window, before leaving with matters unresolved. Instead, I tried phoning, several times, yet with no reply. With no photographs to present, I didn't want to go and see Vivian — what would my purpose be otherwise? Because I wanted to see her? It would only indicate that I wanted our relationship to continue. Since nothing could have been further from the truth, I stayed away. But I wanted to take the pictures, they were my first proper assignment, and if I could deliver to her, my work would be noticed. At the very least, it would be something to put on my CV.

So it was that one Saturday in April — the nineteenth, to be exact — I cycled out to Scadbury Park, countryside in the 1500s, now swallowed up into Greater London, surrounded by trunk roads and bypasses, warehouses and storage facilities behind heavy-duty fencing, cheap housing with junk-strewn gardens. Here was the estate of Marlowe's patron, Thomas Walsingham, where Marlowe had been staying when arrested days before his death in 1593. The manor itself was long gone, but ruins of it remained, a few detached walls, some Roman columns, consumed by grass, shrubs and bog. It was impossible to grasp that four hundred years earlier people had sumptuously dined there, populated opulent rooms, sat in front of mirrors while performing their morning ablutions, all in what now was but thin air, metres above the ground. Indeed, that Christopher Marlowe himself had once occupied the very space, within the same walls, where I stood and pondered. Only time separated us. *Only* time? Surely there was no greater divide! Even a minute was an abyss. That, I determined, was what I would photograph, and set about the work. When I was finished, I discovered a grand and ancient oak that could easily have been there in Marlowe's time too, and so I photographed that as well. When evening came I cycled back to Southwark, where I took a shot of a young man around my own age standing on a street corner drinking from a can of beer. His gaze met mine, and I knew at once that the image would be stunning – his eyes, simultaneously filled with aggression and indifference, the cropped hair, the high cheekbones, white T-shirt and dark blue cardigan; the rakishly self-confident posture. I took some more – of people in Shoreditch, the dockside cranes in Deptford, a few down at the embankment – and then I was done.

I developed them the following weekend and spent all Sunday evening putting them together into a series. It was London now, London then, and a young man wired with reckless abandon, as I imagined Marlowe himself to have been.

It was good work. I could put it out there.

On the Monday after school, as I pulled up outside the house and got off the bike, Collin came out. He was smiling as ever, but instead of hurrying off the way he usually did, he stopped in front of me.

'Have you heard?' he said.

'Heard what?'

'There's been an explosion at a nuclear power plant in the Soviet Union.'

'What?'

'Yes. On Saturday, apparently. They only found out because the readings in Sweden are going haywire. It's just a matter of time before it reaches us here. If it hasn't already.'

'You mean, radiation?'

'Yes. I'm off out to buy some masking tape now.'

'Masking tape? What for?'

'The windows. So it won't get in. You should too.'

'No need for that, surely?'

He gave me an exasperated look before heading down the street. I looked up at the grey, dismal sky a moment before taking the bike inside and up the stairs. An explosion at a nuclear power plant. It sounded serious. A lot of people would be dead over there.

As soon as I got in, I turned the radio on. It wasn't often I listened to the news, but this was something I needed to hear. However, after only a few seconds I realised they were talking about unemployment. I put the frying pan on the hob, cracked an egg into it once it was hot enough, and a few rashers of bacon. As I sat down to eat, the five o'clock news came on. It was true enough, an explosion at a nuclear plant outside Kiev. That was about all they knew. Apparently it had just been announced on Soviet TV. The first indications, though, had come from Sweden, where readings had been so high they'd at first thought it was coming from one of their own plants. Due to prevailing weather conditions, Great Britain, they said, was so far unaffected by any radio-active fallout.

So where had Collin got that idea of taping up his windows? There wasn't a speck of radiation here.

What kind of a wimp was he?

I felt like throwing the window open and breathing in a good lungful or two.

I put the dirty plate in the sink, lit a smoke and looked at the photographs again before tucking them away into my bag, lugging the bike back down the stairs and heading out into the city. My impulse said to take the long way round, thereby avoiding the place where the incident with the tramp had played out, but the thought of Collin's anxiety seemed somehow to trigger a restlessness of my own and I decided to do the opposite, cycling directly there and even stopping to smoke a cigarette exactly as I had done that fateful night. Maybe I just needed to get it out of my system once and for all.

There was no fog this time, the sky was clearer, but apart from that everything was much the same. The police cordon was of course gone. And the tramp, naturally.

I leaned the bike against the wall and lit up while glancing across to where he'd sat. Only then did I think of the CCTV, and fear immediately prodded a finger into my chest. So, back at the scene, are we? Guilty after all, is that it?

But I wasn't guilty. I'd thought our small altercation had been the cause of the man's death, but obviously that couldn't have been the case if someone else had confessed to killing him. He must have been all right when I'd left him. Then someone else must have come, another homeless person perhaps, a drug addict; they'd argued about something and this other man had killed him. They lived outside the law, these people, and were chronically aggressive, so what had happened probably wasn't that unusual. The only thing that didn't fit was the CCTV. If someone had turned up after me and done him in, wouldn't they have got that on tape too? Why had they taken me in, then?

For all I knew, the camera might have stopped working.

It didn't matter now anyway. Someone had come clean. The case was closed.

I flicked my cigarette end into the street and stepped through the gate to the spot where he'd sat. There were no traces of anything, not a bloodstain, not a tuft of hair, nothing. But then I'd never thought there would be.

What had happened there had passed. It no longer held.

The only way it could come back would be in the form of a reconstruction, a theory in other words. Something that could be discussed, but which in itself was only an abstraction.

Oh, it was a good thought.

Everything that happens will pass.

Soon, me being here for the second time would no longer hold either.

So in fact we were free. The past releases us perpetually from its grasp. It's only us who can't release the past.

I went back into the street and got on the bike again, cycled away through the bend and then stood up on the pedals to propel myself up the hill, which wasn't that steep, more a long, taxing drag. Chaining the bike to the lamp post outside and glancing towards the front door, I suddenly felt turned on — she was upstairs, in the flesh, a quick manoeuvre or two and she'd be naked, all wobbling tits and wet pussy, and I'd thrust up inside her.

It wasn't what I'd been intending, the plan had been to keep her at arm's length, just show her the pictures and keep things professional, but now I could only swallow and accept that physical arousal ruled.

I rang the bell. A few moments passed before someone came down the stairs.

'Kristian?' she said in the doorway, dressed as ever all in black, her face bare-looking without her glasses. 'I wasn't expecting you.'

'I've got some photos for you. Do you want to have a look?'

'Photos? For the programme, you mean?'

'That's right.'

'I'm afraid you're too late.'

'What do you mean? You gave me the assignment, didn't you?'

'Yes, but you didn't deliver, darling.'

'I'm delivering now.'

'The programme's already been printed.'

'But it can't be. You can't do this.'

'Sorry. Not my fault though, is it?'

'You never said. How was I to know there was such a hurry?'

She shrugged.

'You could at least let me in, so I can show you what you've missed out on.'

'I can't.'

'Why not?'

'There's someone here with me.'

'Who?'

'It's not exactly your business.'

I stared at her blankly. She smiled. It was meant to be a comforting smile, I realised. As if she thought she'd hurt me and now felt sorry for me.

'Please yourself, then,' I said, turned away and went back to the bike. I suppose I was expecting her to say something – *I didn't mean it like that*, perhaps, or, *Why don't you come round tomorrow instead?* – but she said nothing, and the only sound was of the door closing behind me.

I was really pissed off with her as I cycled away. How unprofessional she was! You couldn't just commission someone to take pictures and then without so much as a word give the job to someone else!

But the worst thing was that she thought she'd rejected me. That I wanted her, but she didn't want me. When in fact the opposite was true. But now she could go back to her lover boy and feel a bit sorry for having turned me down.

It annoyed the hell out of me.

I'd lost face suggesting she invite me in. I'd lost face even coming out here.

Instead of making a right at the junction, I carried on straight through, under the railway bridge, up the long hill through New Cross, over to Peckham. I wanted to see if Hans was in, maybe show him the new photos, then probe a bit and find out if he knew what Vivian was playing at.

Music was coming from inside and I knocked as hard as I could for him to hear me.

The door opened and a guy in a pair of paint-spattered overalls appeared. White T-shirt and clogs, pockmarked cheeks and a flash of anger in his eyes.

'Is Hans in?' I said.

'No.'

'Do you know where he is?'

'I don't know any Hans.'

'He lives here. Or at least, this is his studio.'

'I live here.'

'Are you renting the place off him?'

'I told you. I don't know anyone called Hans. Now, get lost.'

He shut the door in my face and for the second time that night I was left standing like an idiot. I thought about knocking again to ask him the name of the landlord — in that way I could maybe find out where Hans had moved to, but then I realised I wasn't that bothered. Besides, I didn't need any more aggression from this bad-tempered geezer.

I'd just got back on the bike when the door opened again.

'Do you know him well, the guy who lived here before?' he said.

'Fairly.'

'Well, he's left some stuff behind. I was going to chuck it out. Do you want it?'

'How much is there?'

'A carrier bag.'

'OK.'

As if he'd been anticipating my reply, his hand reached out immediately with the bag. No sooner had I taken it than he closed the door again without a word. Not so much as a nod of thanks.

I opened the bag. It was full of contact sheets. I picked a couple out and looked at them. They seemed to be landscapes. Not that exciting. Probably from when he first landed here and still wanted to be a photographer. I'd look at them more closely when I got home, I decided, and stuffed the bag into my rucksack before getting back on the bike. Then, as I set off, I suddenly, desperately needed a shit. Carrying on a bit down the road, I realised there was no way I could keep it in.

I was touching cloth.

I turned and cycled back. Dismounting, I sensed the first moist beginnings of evacuation.

I knocked on the door.

No one came.

I knocked again, and now it was flung open.

'What the hell do you want now? I'm trying to get some work done.'

'Can I use your toilet?'

'No, you bloody can't.'

He slammed the door in my face.

If he was going to be like that about it, I'd just have to shit on his property. I glanced around. There were a couple of shrubs out front, but nothing that could stop me being seen from the road.

Round the back, then.

There were some other buildings there, but far enough away to mean that no one would realise what I was doing — all they'd see would be a crouching figure beside a wall.

I hadn't done a dump outside since I was a kid. In no time, my trousers and underpants were down and I was on my haunches, legs spread wide, back to the wall. My shit was a bit soft and stringy, but came out in one piece. I wiped myself with some leaves and pulled my trousers up again as I wondered how best to get back at him. I ended up emptying Hans's contact sheets into my rucksack and gathering up the shit using the carrier bag, which I then turned inside out and left dangling on the doorknob.

On my way home, I found myself thinking that someone should work out a code of conduct for artists. There were too many who thought they had the right to act like a wanker just because they painted or whatever. You could draw a scale, the work of art at one end and the artist's conduct at the other. If the work was poor, the artist had to behave themselves. If the work was good, he or she was entitled to be a prick. A scale of quality could go up to a hundred, where zero was rubbish, fifty was mediocre and a hundred world class. On the behaviour side, zero quality would require exceptional decorum, fifty demanded a good measure of politeness, and a hundred would green-light total recklessness. A system like that, I reckoned, would absolutely *compel* ninety-five per cent of all artists to be nice to others the whole time. Four per cent would basically have to toe the line, though would be allowed the odd hissy fit now and again, perhaps twice a year. The final one per cent would be free to behave badly, most, however, only a bit badly, while the very, very best, a handful, perhaps, could go around screaming at people and slagging them off in public, slamming doors in their faces and being a total pain in the arse. Maybe two or three per generation.

If a system like that had been in place, the guy who'd taken over Hans's studio would have been obliged to invite me in for coffee and then made calls to find out where Hans had moved to, all with a smile and the utmost kindness. Figueroa would have had to bow deeply before me and ask my forgiveness, well aware that apologies were insufficient, and drop to his knees to kiss my feet.

With these playful thoughts in my head, I biked past the station, swung right and freewheeled the last bit of the way to the house. Once upstairs, I leaned the bike against the wall, dumped my bag, slung my coat over the chair, found myself a clean pair of underpants, a towel in the cupboard and went down into the basement to have a shower.

Maybe leaving the carrier bag there had been a bit much, I thought as I stood under the thin jets of water and rubbed a sliver of soap over my body. He only had himself to blame, though. I'd asked him nicely enough. All he had to do was say yes.

Where could Hans have gone?

I had a feeling it was definitive. That he hadn't just moved to another address in London, but had gone somewhere further away and for good. Maybe even back to the Netherlands. Which would explain why he hadn't let on — moving back home would most definitely look like he'd thrown in the towel.

Vivian would know where he was. But I was done with her. More than done.

Those photos were bloody good and she hadn't even *looked* at them. She hadn't even been curious.

Still, that was her problem.

I had to stop caring what other people thought. The pictures I'd taken were brilliant whether Vivian had seen them or not. And it was the work that was important.

So why did I feel like a failure?

I turned the shower off and dried myself, spread the towel out on the floor and stood on it while I got dressed.

It was because she'd humiliated me.

The thing was that I was actually the sort of person it was possible to humiliate. Not everyone was. A supreme human being — and they did exist — *couldn't* be humiliated.

Wasn't that the case?

I unlocked the door and stepped out into the passage, bending down to pick up the towel and wring the end of it that somehow had got soaked, then went back upstairs, draping it over the radiator before going to the fridge to see if there was anything to eat.

Invincible were those who didn't care about others.

I fried some of those disgusting little English sausages that inside were as soft as apple sauce and boiled some pasta shells to go with them. With liberal amounts of ketchup and mustard it wasn't bad. After I was finished I reached over to the windowsill to turn the radio on and felt a sudden inexplicable twinge of excitement, it was something to do with the radio, but what?

The explosion at the nuclear plant. I'd forgotten. They'd know more about it now, surely?

I switched it on and lit a cigarette while trying to work out what they were talking about. Peter Weiss, I picked out in the stream of words, and seconds later Auschwitz was mentioned. It sounded like a radio play.

I should have had a television. Hearing about a burning nuclear plant wasn't the same as watching it. Of course, there might not even be any images. After all, it was the Soviet Union, it wasn't certain there were any getting through the Iron Curtain.

Did Collin have a telly? He'd be glued to it if he did, trembling with fear, his windows taped shut.

Liz! I was forgetting Liz!

I stubbed out my cigarette, switched the radio off and went down the stairs to knock on her door.

Footfall, the rattling of the chains.

'Hi,' I said as meekly as I could when her face came into view. 'I don't suppose you've got a television, have you?'

'What if I have?'

'Do you think I could watch the news with you? This terrible nuclear accident in the Soviet Union. I feel a bit lost not knowing what's happening.'

'I suppose that would be all right.'

She turned and went back through, and as I followed her I noticed she was barefoot. The TV was already on, and on the table in front of the settee a mug steamed. She'd been sitting there all cosy, her legs tucked underneath her.

'Would you like a cup of tea?'

I was about to say that only girls and the English drink tea, but thought better of it — she was definitely the stuffy type, easily offended.

'No, thanks. Coffee would be nice, though, if you've got any.'

I sat down on the settee.

In the kitchen area she put the kettle on and straight away it began to make noises. She was wearing blue jeans and a checked shirt with a lot of different colours in it, though not splashy in any way.

'Shall we turn the sound up a bit? *Newsnight*'s just starting,' she said.

'Yes, do.'

She went up to the set and turned the volume dial. A mousy-haired woman, lipsticked and wearing a red dress, sat behind the news desk, clutching a pen in one hand, and looked up at the camera.

'But first that explosion at a nuclear plant in the Soviet Union. What caused it, and how many people did it hurt?'

She put down the pen and folded her hands.

'Scanty information has come so far from the Soviets, but here's Peter Snow to help fill out the gaps.'

'They're saying it's the worst nuclear accident ever,' Liz said, opening the fridge. 'It's an awful thing to say, but I'm glad it's so far away.'

'It's not awful,' I said. 'It's only natural we're glad. The Russians'll have to deal with their own misery.'

Clearly, they didn't have any images yet, because Peter Snow, whoever he was, kept on talking, and what he was saying sounded in the main to be guesswork. The only thing they had to go on were the readings first picked up in Sweden and a bulletin on Soviet TV in which an announcer confirmed that an incident had taken place. That was it.

Liz handed me my coffee and sat down next to me. It was a two-seater settee, but still she managed to keep a gap between us. The coffee was a cloudy off-white.

'Ah, I don't take it with milk.'

'Don't you? Sorry, I wasn't thinking. Force of habit.'

She got up again and hesitated a moment before taking the mug as I handed it back to her. Maybe she was waiting for me to say it didn't matter. But coffee with milk was a despicable practice — it tasted absolutely horrible.

On the screen, Peter Snow sat now with a telephone receiver pressed to his ear talking to someone in Moscow via a very poor connection. But whoever that person was, he didn't know anything either and was merely supposing.

Maybe it wasn't that bad?

Disasters in the communist countries suited the West down to the ground.

Liz was standing by the kettle now, looking at the TV as the water came to the boil again. I hadn't seen her boyfriend in a while. I guessed he wasn't welcome any more. They were never a good match, you could tell a mile away — he, mangy and unkempt, a wine-drinker judging by the hair, whereas she was studious, neat and petite.

I'd prefer her a thousand times over Vivian with her quasi-intellectual posturing, all that flirting with darkness. If you were that world-weary, you wouldn't be pleading with people to strangle you.

'Coffee, black,' said Liz, holding out my mug.

Was she being sarcastic?

She smiled faintly as she sat down.

Her tits looked quite big in that shirt. It seemed to be roomy, but sat tight across the chest.

'Is it Norway you're from?'

'Yes.'

'What are they saying there? The radiation levels are highest in Scandinavia.'

'No idea. I don't keep up with what's happening there.'

In the TV studio they'd now called in a Russian scientist whose name was Medvedev. He was talking about a previous nuclear accident in the Urals.

So they knew *nothing*.

The item came to an end without new information having been forthcoming.

I should have got to my feet then and gone back upstairs. But I hadn't finished my coffee yet, and anyway it was quite cosy sitting there. Perhaps it was because unlike me she'd made an effort with the place — there was a tablecloth on the table, a rug on top of the wall-to-wall carpet, potted plants, green and flourishing, on the floor and windowsills.

'It might not be anything to worry about when it all boils down,' I said. 'Probably just the usual fear of communism. They don't seem to actually *know* much, do they?'

'Soviet TV wouldn't have made an announcement, unless they had to. That would seem to indicate it's serious enough for them not to be able to keep a lid on it. Don't you think?'

I shrugged. She got up and went over to the television set.

'It was just the nuclear accident you wanted to see, wasn't it?'

'Are you throwing me out?'

She laughed.

'But that *was* why you came, wasn't it? Anyway, you don't have to go, if you don't want to.'

She switched the TV off and went over to the small stereo on a shelf unit that was fixed to the wall.

'Do you like Depeche Mode?'

'I hate Depeche Mode.'

She laughed again.

Was she taking the piss?

'How about Bronski Beat?'

'Not sure.'

'Bronski Beat, then.'

She put the record on and lowered the pickup into the lead-in grooves. A wailing male falsetto floated from the speakers, and then a disco beat kicked in. She shimmied in time. It was meant to be funny, a semi-ironic pretending-to-be-cool, and yet I sensed there was something authentic about it too, that she meant to be a bit seductive.

But it threw her into a merciless light. Physically she was so innocent in respect of her body, so awkward and ungainly, that she had absolutely no idea that what she was showing me was sheer and utter helplessness.

'Good, don't you think?' she said, and came and sat down again.

I'd heard the song before, of course. It had been impossible to avoid a couple of summers back. I could understand people dancing to it when they were out clubbing. But not that anyone would want to listen to it at home.

'I don't see how you can stand it.'

'Really? You make it sound like there's something wrong with me. But do you know what, I've got this lecturer at the moment and his favourite phrase is, "What if the opposite is true?" He says it all the time, so much so that I've started using it myself. It's actually very liberating. So what I'm thinking now is: What if it's you there's something wrong with for not liking Bronski Beat?'

'But there isn't. Quality's the key here, not popularity.'

'I've met loads of boys like you. They cling to one style and ignore everything else. Do you want me to guess what sort of music you listen to?'

'Go on.'

'Joy Division. The Cure. Suicide. Killing Joke. Velvet Underground.'

'Couldn't be more wrong.'

'Oh? So what *do* you listen to?'

'A lot of different stuff. It varies. European, mainly. German, Belgian.'

'So there's no Joy Division or Killing Joke in your record collection?'

'No, as a matter of fact. So your theory doesn't stand up.'

'Seriously?'

She fixed me in her gaze, eyebrows sarcastically raised.

'You should use that question of yours on me too,' I said. 'What if the opposite is true?'

That would give her something to think about.

She smiled.

'Maybe.'

One—nil to me.

She scratched her ear, rapidly like a cat, then tucked her legs up under her.

'How come you've got nothing on your feet?' I said. 'Is it an English thing?'

'No, not that I know of. I don't much care for socks, that's all. They make me feel trapped.'

'Trapped?'

'Yes, claustrophobic in a way. I like the feel of carpet under my bare feet. Don't you ever go barefoot when you're at home?'

'I wouldn't dream of it.'

'No, I don't suppose you would.'

She threw me a faint smile.

'That guy who used to come round. Is he out of the picture now?'

'Nick?'

'I don't know his name. The hippie type who lived here.'

'He didn't *live* here. But yes, that was Nick. We're still friends. Why do you ask?'

'Just wondered. I used to see him all the time, then suddenly he was gone.'

'He had a name for you.'

'Oh?'

'He called you Polar Bear. He thought it was funny. The polar bear upstairs.'

'Why?'

'I don't know. Perhaps because you're from way up there. The Arctic and all that. Or maybe it was because you come across as cold and solitary, but a bit cute as well. No offence.'

'None taken.'

'How did you get on with your Marlowe project, by the way?'

'It turned out well.'

'It's finished, then?'

'Yes.'

'Have you got the pictures upstairs?'

'Yes.'

'I'd find it interesting to see what you do.'

'You're suggesting I go all the way upstairs to get them, then come back down again, is that it?'

'Is that a problem?'

'I'm not sure I can be bothered.'

'Ah.'

'If you really want to see them, you can come upstairs with me.'

'I'm not sure I can be bothered,' she said, a poor attempt at mimicry.

'You should put your socks on, at least. It's cold on the stairs.'

'I've got slippers, I'll have you know.'

Not until a few minutes later when she was standing in the middle of my room looking around did I think about my record collection. If she started investigating, which I wouldn't have put past her, she'd discover straight away that it took in both Killing Joke and Joy Division. The Cure and Suicide too, for that matter.

'Have a seat,' I said, indicating the settee. But she'd already noticed the photograph on the wall and was transfixed.

'What's this?'

'The first photograph of a living being, as far as is known. Taken by Daguerre. It's called *Boulevard du Temple*. From 1838. The subject is actually just the street seen from his window, but when it was developed these two figures here were in it.'

She gave a theatrical shudder.

'It's a bit creepy, isn't it?'

Apparently, she was full of such little pantomimes.

I liked it and didn't at the same time.

'Creepy? Why's that?'

'Because it's so depopulated, I suppose,' she said, and sat down, crossing her legs and folding her hands on top of her knee.

'In reality there were lots of people there. It's just that the long exposure time meant that nothing moving could be captured.'

'That makes it even creepier. A photograph full of people we can't see!'

'Yes, it does,' I said, relieved that my records were now out of reach. 'But it was *my* work you wanted to see, wasn't it?'

She nodded.

I pulled Hans's contact sheets out of my bag and shaped them quickly together into a pile before putting them aside on the chair, then took out the cardboard box containing my own photographs. The table was a clutter of mugs and glasses, magazines and newspapers. I shoved it all over to one end.

'This is a series,' I said. 'So you mustn't look until I've laid them out in the right order. OK? Now, close your eyes.'

'Are you being serious?'

'Serious? Are you joking? Of course I'm being serious. They have to be seen as a complete set.'

She looked sceptical.

I threw up my hands and gave her a gormless look, mouth open and eyebrows raised, as if she was a complete idiot. Perhaps she was.

She closed her eyes.

I laid out the photos in two rows of four, then made sure they were neat and aligned before giving her the word. I went over to the window and gazed out while lighting a cigarette.

'Wow,' she said. 'I mean, *wow*. Did *you* take these?'

'They're good, aren't they?'

I stepped up beside her to see what she was seeing.

'It's like they're coming *towards* me. How did you do that? They're completely alive.'

'I just took them. There's no hocus-pocus.'

She looked up at me.

'I'd never have thought, to be honest.'

'Thought what?'

'That you were so good. This is *art*.'

'Why wouldn't you have thought that?'

She gave a shrug.

'I don't know. Just . . .'

'Go on.'

'No, it was nothing.'

'Come on, spit it out. You thought what . . . ?'

She shook her head.

'That the Polar Bear guy upstairs was a talentless poser. Yes?'

'Not exactly.'

'But sort of?'

She laughed that silly laugh of hers and got to her feet.

'I must be getting back. Thanks for showing me your work!'

Her movement crossing the room was aerial, as if she was placing her entire weight on the balls of her feet alone — 'walking' rather than walking.

She turned in the doorway and smiled back at me before slipping out and leaving me on my own. Only when I heard her door shutting on the landing below did it occur to me that she could probably hear rather clearly what sort of music I listened to up here.

But she could have just known those bands by name, without knowing anything about the music. Most girls were like that.

I lit another cigarette and put on 'Sex Beat' by the Gun Club, found my magnifying glass and sat down at the table with Hans's contact sheets.

I wasn't sure if I wanted him to be talented or not. Anyway, it wasn't easy to decide on the basis of what was in front of me. The first one showed a large tree growing next to a gate in a drystone wall. Beyond, a grazed meadow stretched away towards dense woodland. A few metres away from the tree, three cows were standing. The ground at their feet was churned-up mud. A track ran parallel to the wall, muddy, it too, with deep wheel ruts. The subject was quite unspectacular, but the picture itself nevertheless possessed a somewhat eerie air, there was something downright weird about it — mostly it resembled the very first photographs, the light areas were grainy, while elsewhere it was darkly toned. The tree looked more like the shadow of a tree than an actual tree.

It would have been typical Hans to have used antique equipment, a tripod, glass plates, the camera shrouded by a black cloth.

But contact sheets didn't belong to that technology.

The landscape too seemed old, ancient even. He must have spent a long time setting it all up, seeking out places where there was no trace of our own age. But that wasn't the only reason the images appeared old, I sensed as my eye scanned. Wasn't there something about the very form of the landscape too? The drystone wall, the meadow, the ruts, perhaps from a cart?

He'd photographed old photographs!

That had to be it.

The question of whether he'd first taken the pictures using old equipment and then photographed them after developing, or had simply come across some old photos somewhere, was resolved as soon as I moved on to the next sheet and leaned forward with the magnifying glass to my eye. These ones depicted a child standing beside a farmyard well. The house in the background was low-slung with a thatched roof and whitewashed exterior. The yard looked to be no more than trampled soil. It was all wretchedly impoverished. The long handles of a cart intruded into the right of the picture. But it was the child that held one's attention. It was hard to tell if it was a boy or a girl. Four years old, perhaps, barefoot, grubby-faced and yet with the most unusually bright and gleaming eyes.

These photographs could only be of the period. Late nineteenth century. Hans had somehow laid hands on them and exploited them for this project of his, whatever it was.

I pulled the third contact sheet from the pile and picked out an image. The style was the same, grainy areas of light, void-like darkness, but the setting here was urban, wooden buildings alongside a river, and on the river were three sailing ships with tall masts. Was it the Thames? Or the Seine? No, I couldn't imagine sailing ships on the Seine. And when did they become obsolete in trade? Wouldn't they have been using steam by the late 1800s?

There had to be some overlap — most likely there were still sailing ships in abundance then, before steam gradually took over.

But it was a fantastic photograph.

What had he been planning to do with it?

The shadow beneath the wall of one of the riverside structures was perhaps a human being, I thought, and moved the magnifying glass closer. It was impossible to tell for sure. But the shadow on the water below the ship in the foreground was definitely a rowing boat.

I turned my attention to the final image in the series, a small castle situated at the top of a hill and surrounded by parkland. Was it London?

This was a treasure trove. Unknown photographs of the period were surely few and far between. Or maybe they weren't unknown. All I knew was that they weren't in the book I'd bought about the origins of photography.

The topography resembled Greenwich Park, the hill leading up to the observatory. But the observatory had a dome, so it couldn't be there. It didn't have to be London at all. France was where photography was happening back then.

I gathered the contacts together again and put them on the shelf with the magnifying glass on top, took the record off the turntable, brushed my teeth at the sink, undressed and went to bed. The photos must have been part of a project he'd been working on when he first moved here. I'd have to remember to ask him about it the next time I saw him, wherever it was he'd gone.

He'd still have the negatives, perhaps the original photographs too, so the contact sheets would be worthless to him. As they were to me too.

I sat up, swung my legs out of bed and reached for my cigarettes, and smoked one while sitting there in my underpants. It wasn't a matter of simply *taking* photographs like that, but of creating a similar mood.

Another world, quite beyond reach, which nonetheless resembled our own — indeed *was* our own.

I opened the window to let some fresh air in — sleeping in a smoky room couldn't be very healthy. It occurred to me that Liz would be lying in bed directly underneath me, and it was not an unpleasant thought. There was something invigorating about her that I had to admit I liked. Apart from that, though, she was decidedly average. Average-looking, averagely intelligent, averagely interesting. An average person living an average life. She was at uni and would get her degree, a job, a house and a couple of kids; she'd get old, maybe see a few grandkids, and then die. All without having done anything of note, without even having thought anything of note. Her kids would grow up to be like her, a bit uglier, perhaps, depending on the husband she found — though it could go the other way too if the husband was handsome, the kids then that much better-looking than their mother. But the chances weren't that good, she had nothing much to offer a handsome man that he wouldn't be able to find in a beautiful woman. And what man would choose average looks when beauty was just as attainable?

And yet I felt what might best be described as a tingle in the chest every time I went past her door on my way up and down the stairs in the days that followed — brought on by the mere thought that she might be in and that I could be with her if only I knocked. She would let me inside, I was certain of it, as far inside as I wanted to go, to her very innermost self. Maybe that was what I felt? The trajectory of movement into another life, where door after door would open, more than into the person whose life it was.

The way in which she'd danced, at once self-conscious and outgoing, and her small, illustrative gestures, were perhaps what I thought about the most, though not for very long at a time, and not seriously. It was a facade, a shield against the world — it wouldn't have made any difference no matter how much she'd wriggled her body.

But this tingle I felt was small and never compelling enough for me to take the step of actually knocking on her door, and soon it melted away. At the school, another guest lecturer was introduced to us, an American this time, who seemed mainly to be obsessed with geometry. Lines and angles were certainly in focus when he presented his work to us. His name was Dan Bennett, a man in the prime of life, carrying rather too much weight and judging by his clothes not that bothered about the way he looked — jeans and shirts that sat tight around his stomach, glasses crookedly balanced on the bridge of his nose. His favoured theme was small-town America — an endless variation on Main Street with its banks, liquor stores and supermarkets; open, sun-drenched squares fractured by the intrusions of people, cars or the shadow of a building; the clutter of signage, street lighting, billboards. Occasionally there'd be a huge horizon in the background, while in other instances — interiors taken in diners, bowling alleys or some other typically American establishment — everything was somehow closed in itself and claustrophobic. And yet it was not American life he talked to us about, but lines, angles, surfaces. His pictures were a world apart from my own, his thoughts about photography as an art form likewise at odds with mine. I couldn't have cared less about coordinate systems and geometry — what concerned me was the soul of the subject. Oddly, Dan understood this immediately when I showed him my portfolio.

'This,' he said, 'is great work. It grabs the beholder.'

I'd shown him the young man in Southwark, the ruins of Scadbury Park, the lighter and the cat, the trees, and the riverside cranes.

His eyes fixed on me, a keen, intense gaze from behind the disorderly angled spectacles.

'I get the feeling you're photographing the last day. You understand what I mean? These trees, they look like they're being seen for the last time. And this guy here,' he said, picking up the print of the young man in Southwark, 'comes across as if he's the most interesting guy in the world. I know he's not, but there's so much tension in him. These are damn good photographs. Would you mind if I asked you for a copy of each of these?'

'No, not at all. No problem.'

'Terrific.'

I spent the evening and half the night in the darkroom making copies, eventually sleeping a few hours in a chair, my head tilted back against the wall. I gave him the prints when our first session started that same morning. I had no idea why he wanted them, but clearly his interest was a good sign — as far as I was aware he hadn't asked for work from the other students.

These were heady days. I was taking pictures as if in a frenzy, and they were dazzlingly good. Every photograph seemed incandescent, it was as if I was being carried forward by some momentous force. Or rather, it was like I was a *part* of that force. And all around me, spring exploded into being, trees burst manically into leaf, the days grew longer and longer, were like vessels into which someone was pouring increasing volumes of light.

Our sessions were centred around a new theme — the urban landscape. It was why Dan Bennett had been invited, and I spent several days traipsing about the city with a camera in my hand, another around my neck. The most obvious locations were the outlying boroughs, both visually and culturally these were by far the most interesting, but everything was coming so easily to me at that time that I decided to turn things around and venture into the realm of cliché — the tourist's London, Big Ben, Westminster Abbey, Soho, Oxford Street. I was playing at being Dan Bennett, seeing people as figures, buildings as geometric patterns. To make it work required distance, and the only way I could achieve that was by using elevation, and so I found my way into the staircases of office buildings and hotels to photograph from the windows there. Daguerre's boulevard came to mind, it too photographed from some height, but this did not occur to me until late in the week while standing on a landing somewhere in Soho photographing the street below from four flights up. But when it struck me it was like a lightning bolt: I would use the same equipment as in Daguerre's age. The streets would come out deserted. There would be only light and shadow, space and structural mass. It would be a unique series. The thought of it fired me with excitement and transfixed me as I stood. It wouldn't be the same as with Hans's pictures, for they were from another age, but the same pictures, infused with the same mood, only depicting the present day.

It would be impossible to get my hands on a camera like that at such short notice, so it was something I would have to put off until some later date. Anyway, what I was doing now was only an exercise, no one was expecting a masterwork. Nevertheless, the thought of waiting was unbearable — what if someone else beat me to it?

I went back down into the street, which was teeming with people and flooded with the bright, inexhaustible rays of spring. Borne along by the crowds, I kept looking up in search of suitable locations from which to photograph. It struck me that no one else lifted their gaze in such a way, but looked only straight ahead, seeing each other and what was in front of them, though nothing besides. Dogs were like that too, they saw other dogs in the street and nothing else, sniffed for dogs, looked out for dogs, listened for dogs. But I, I looked up. I looked outwards. And took in images.

'Kristian!' someone suddenly shouted.

I turned, scanning first one side of the street, then the other.

A hand shot up and waved.

It was *Vidar*.

Beaming, he hurried towards me.

'I thought I might bump into you!' he said. 'Great to see you!'

'What are you doing *here*?'

'We're on a study trip. Been here since Monday.'

He took hold of my arm. Some people became more outgoing when they were away from home, abroad.

'What about you? Do you live around here?'

I shook my head.

'Hardly anyone lives in the centre of town.'

He glanced around, taking in the buildings above shop height as if to find evidence to the contrary.

'I live south of the river. A twenty-minute train ride.'

'Let's have a beer somewhere, eh?'

'I'm working just now,' I said, a lift of my hand indicating the camera. 'But when are you going back?'

'Tomorrow afternoon.'

'Still time for a pint before you go, then. Where are you staying?'

'Kensington.'

'I don't know Kensington that well. But there's a big pub on Charing Cross Road, just after Cambridge Circus, on the left-hand side going up. You can't miss it. Do you want to meet me there tomorrow?'

'Sounds good to me.'

'What time's your flight?'

'Not until seven.'

'How about two o'clock, then?'

'Great. See you there!'

We smiled at each other, like the two childhood friends we were, before going off in our separate directions. It was more than a bit annoying that he'd seen me. Now he'd go back home thinking London was like Elverum, a place where you met people you knew on every street corner.

I pictured him sitting in the pub, his bags beside his chair, checking his watch, hesitantly sipping his pint, not wanting to get started properly before I'd joined him. But where had I got to? Sorry, couldn't make it in the end. If only I'd been able to get hold of you. Hope you worked it out, anyway.

What was the past other than a great big rubbish dump? Where everything that had ever happened, everything that had been said and done, lay piled up. Here and there, smoke curled from small fires, elsewhere rose a rotting stench, while other parts were doomed to rust. A healthy person never looked back. A healthy person lived in the present, with a gaze that was fixed on the future.

Some would perhaps say that the Daguerre pictures I was going to take were merely dredging up the past, but that was wrong, they'd be reaching out of time itself into the timeless. Or rather, into a much slower time. A time so slow that human life left no trace on it.

It was going to be fantastic!

Excited by this new idea, and by all the light, surrounded by great swathes of new green foliage and the impressionable hordes, filled with upbeat energy, that the sun had drawn out into the streets, the thought of going back to my bedsit wasn't particularly appealing. I sat for a while at a cafe in one of the parks under the shade of a chestnut tree, but with only my thoughts for company I soon became restless and after two beers headed off to catch a train home.

Arriving back at the house, I heard music coming from upstairs, and quite loud too. Collin, I knew, had had a few parties for his friends, so I was surprised when I reached the first-floor landing and realised it was coming from Liz's flat. The song that was playing ended abruptly, and before the next one started I heard the lively murmur of voices inside.

Although we hadn't spoken since our Chernobyl night — and in order not to get involved in something I didn't really feel up for with this pert little lit student, I'd signalled a certain hesitancy the few times we'd met on the stairs since then — I found myself feeling a bit put out, for surely it would have been natural to have invited me? We were neighbours, after all, and had now been in each other's flats.

Not that I didn't have anything else to do. I needed to get some shopping in and make myself something to eat, and I was also running out of clean clothes again. On top of that there was my work — I could concentrate more on my pictures at home in the evenings than I could at school during the day.

The first thing I did when I got in was open the windows. The music sounded louder and I leaned out and saw that her windows were open too. I went and got my cigarettes from my coat pocket, then returned to sit on the windowsill and smoke. The sky was deep blue and there was a chill in the air where the sun didn't reach. I decided I couldn't be bothered going to the launderette. I didn't fancy going to the shop either. I'd do my washing tomorrow and as for food a kitchen was never so bare that you couldn't find *something* to eat, even if it was just a crust of bread and some gherkins.

I stubbed my cigarette out against the brickwork and tossed it to the street below, before turning to my photographs and spreading them out on the floor. Much of the excitement I'd felt about the Daguerre idea remained and I thought perhaps I might be able to channel it in some way into the pictures I already had while waiting for an opportunity to start work on the project.

Was there any sense of slowed-down time in them?

No.

What was it Bennett had said? That they looked like they were taken on the last day.

I scrutinised them with that in mind.

The last day.

It drew them together.

It drew them together!

I took one of the lids from my photo boxes, pressed down the sides and tore them off, found a black marker pen in the kitchen drawer and wrote the title on the cardboard.

The Last Day

Photographs by Kristian Hadeland

I put it to one side and started categorising the photographs. There were more than forty in all. I gathered the ones I found exceptionally good into a pile marked AAA. Those that were very good I marked AA, while those that were simply good received an A. Those that were fairly decent were given a B, those tipping towards the mediocre were BB, leaving BBB for what I considered useless. That done, I set to work sifting through the A categories, twenty-three pictures in all, which I spent perhaps an hour arranging and rearranging in various constellations before taking a break. But even then, as I sat smoking, I stared at the images and had to resist the urge to start again. They were good, but I needed at least twice as many to work with in order to exploit it to the full.

I got up and fetched Hans's contact sheets, anxious to see if the mood I'd sensed had come from the pictures themselves or from me. It felt like there were some similiarities and I was curious as to what they might be more exactly, given that my own pictures were from before I'd even seen them.

I stared at the poor peasant kid with the bright eyes. The melancholy of the photograph lay very clearly in the boy's compelling presence, but also in that presence being so fleeting, it revealed itself and at the same time was gone — the child was long since dead. The strange thing was that the images in which humans were absent were quite as compelling and in the same way: something revealed itself and then in the same instant was gone. The castle building on top of the hill stood splendidly against the darkness of the surrounding parkland, the grass, the trees, the ponderous sky.

It did look like the park at Greenwich.

But it couldn't be — the observatory had been built in the late 1600s as far as I was aware, so if the image was from there, it must have been taken before that, which of course it couldn't have been.

I put the stack back on the shelf and lit another cigarette, put the Pale Fountains' *Pacific Street* on and returned to my own photos hoping to see them now in a new light.

There was the cat. It shuddered almost with potency. So too did the ones I'd taken in connection with it — the bin bag, the rubbish container — albeit more faintly, as if absorbing the reverb. The same was true of the images of the empty house. In those ones, Liv's bed was the nerve centre, charging the others in the series with its energy.

That could be my organisational principle. A sun with a circle of planets around it. The planets in turn circled by moons.

The title was certainly perfect. Dan had given me the key, the unifying factor that brought everything together: *The Last Day*.

My name didn't come across that well, though, too provincial, too redolent of rural parts, of stagnation, the edgelands of a country that was itself an edgeland.

I left the pictures as they were and instead began toying with names, experimenting with variations on my own at first, until *Christoper Adel* emerged onto the sheet of paper in front of me. There was something about it I liked.

> The Last Day
> *Photographs*
> *Christopher Adel*

Or maybe Adelbaum was better? Adel didn't look entirely authentic. Adam? Adams?

> The Last Day
> *Photographs*
> *Chris Adams*

That, on the other hand, was too ordinary. Besides, people might think I'd taken the name from Ansel Adams. Christian Adelheim? Too pretentious. Mum's maiden name had been Pedersen, nothing pretentious about that. Kristian Pedersen? That looked good!

The Last Day
Photographs
Kristian Pedersen

Right on the button. Down to earth, yet elegant with its K and P, and, most importantly, enigmatic. Kristian Pedersen, who was he?

No one knew, I could put into him anything I wanted. There was a whiff of the nineteenth century about it, Copenhagen 1890, but something empty too.

Kristian Pedersen was me. Kristian Pedersen was my name. And I would make it famous.

I had no idea how much time had passed when eventually I turned my attention from work. The light was dwindling outside, so at least a couple of hours.

I noticed then that the music seemed to have stopped. I leaned out again and looked down. Liz's windows were now closed and I could hear neither music nor cackling girls.

It was a relief. Partying neighbours were always going to be a pain when you were on your own like me.

I could pop down to the shop, buy a pork chop, some oven-ready chips and a couple of beers, then concentrate on my work the rest of the evening.

Yes. I put my shoes and coat on, tingling with this new resolve. Liz had left a little note taped to her door. The writing was so small I had to step close to read what it said:

Sylvia. We're at the Cutty Sark pub. See you there!

It was a free world, as we always said when I was a boy, and no one could stop me going to the Cutty Sark too if that was what I wanted. I'd sit with a pint by the river and see what Liz and her mates were up to. I could do with going somewhere anyway, and the fresh air would do me good. I went back up the stairs to get the bike, dropped the camera into my bag just in case — and then, in a sudden flash of insight, it occurred to me that with the pub being in Greenwich I could take Hans's contact sheet with me and check his photo against the park, if only to put an end to the stupid restlessness I felt.

The temperature had already dropped somewhat outside, but the chilly, knife-like air was still saturated with light. Not the bright, direct rays of the sun, which touched only the tops of the tallest buildings now, but their flaky remnants; wearied, they came to rest here and there at the bottom of the world, at the feet of buildings, among trees and shrubs, between fences and walls, detached now from their origin, the mighty star, abandoned to their unhappy fate, to be gobbled up by the hungry dusk.

Cycling past the hoardings before the railway bridge, my eye was attracted by the haphazard collage of fly posters and suddenly I noticed that among them were several advertising Vivian's theatre production. I braked immediately. *THE CLOCK WILL STRIKE*, they announced, black lettering against a blood-red background. The play's title, along with the dates and venue, were relegated to a small box in the bottom corner. I assumed the pictures the other photographer had taken hadn't been deemed good enough for the poster, and the thought gratified me.

I wouldn't be going to see it, whatever the circumstances. I didn't want anything more to do with those people. The very thought of her production put a bad taste in my mouth.

There were more posters in Greenwich. If I hadn't known anything about Vivian and the play and had just seen them with no prior knowledge of what it was about, I'd have been curious. What clock? Whose blood? Ah, Doctor Faustus. The clock would be striking for him. The Devil was coming to get his man.

He must have walked these streets, Marlowe.

Only twenty-nine when he died.

And yet he'd done enough in that brief time to be occupying the thoughts of another man four hundred years later. It was a legacy bestowed on the few.

Stabbed through the eye. That happened near here, too.

A violent life, a violent death.

The Last Day.

Kristian Pedersen.

He broke down the boundaries of photography to penetrate the very core of existence. His long career was a constant grapple with God. Which of them came out on top cannot be said. Yet it matters not, for rather than the single outcome what is significant are the wider ramifications of the struggle itself. A great man is no longer with us, but his work remains for the edification of generations to come.

The Daguerre project was a blaze inside me. I mustn't die before it was done!

I cycled into the lower streets of Greenwich, to the gate at the corner of the park, where I locked the bike to a railing before ambling off down one of its wide avenues. Approaching the observatory, I stopped and took Hans's contact sheet and the magnifying glass from my bag. I felt rather stupid, but whatever I was doing or thinking it was nobody's business.

The thumbnail image was minuscule, the landscape sweeping away in front of me enormous. But the more I peered at the details through the magnifying glass and lifted my gaze to compare them to real life before me, the more compatible the two worlds appeared. The topographical variations seemed similar indeed. The vegetation, of course, was different, yet a couple of trees appeared to occupy the same locations, low and spindly in the photograph, now looming giants — but yes, definitely in the same place.

It could only be coincidence. There had to be somewhere else in the world that looked exactly like this. If not, the photo would have had to have been taken in the mid-1600s or before, since that was when the castle that set them apart had been pulled down.

I put the contact sheet and the magnifying glass back in my bag and returned to the bike. He must have manipulated it during the developing, some kind of double exposure, subtle enough for me to be unable to trace.

It didn't matter. It wasn't worth thinking about.

But I did hope he'd soon be back so I could get to the bottom of the mystery — and no doubt he'd have a good laugh about it too.

I cycled through Greenwich's small town centre, chained the bike to the foot of a signpost and walked the last bit of the way along the riverside to the pub. The place was packed with customers, their voices a high-spirited babble, the way people get when sufficiently fuelled by alcohol as to cast aside all pretensions towards self-observation and simply indulge in the palaver of whatever springs to mind. Gaggles of girls out on the lash in short skirts and high heels, that English idiosyncrasy; but also smartened-up middle-aged women with perms and shoulder pads, pairs of young male students in earnest conversation, here and there a prim and proper pensioner, and as ever, dogs curled up underneath several of the tables. The air reeked of ale, the music was loud, the faces almost unanimously radiant. Some, though, had tipped and become expressionless, as if only a single thought was now possessed, which their minds turned and turned again.

I stood at the bar for some time waiting to be served. I couldn't see Liz. Maybe they'd already gone on somewhere else. I could still have a pint, though.

When at last I'd got one, I took it outside. Liz was sitting with four other girls by the railings in front of the river. I wondered whether to let her notice me or if I should notice her first. The first option would put me on top in a way. I could just sit down somewhere in their vicinity and wait for her to call out my name. The risk though was that she wouldn't notice me at all.

But why think of it as a risk? She was only my excuse to come here, not the reason.

I lingered a moment and looked out across the darkening river and the sky above it, deep blue and unclouded, punctuated by the odd gleaming star. The city shimmered on the opposite bank. The human flesh by which I was surrounded, laughing and chattering on its chairs and stools, teetering to and from the bar, held together by trousers and skirts, shirts and jackets, at once struck me as sloppy and bedraggled in comparison to the stringency of the great universe.

I realised then the impossibility of starting over. The old world could never simply be swept away and a new culture — new art, new architecture, new music — built in its place. The flesh was ever the same. Eyes and noses, bellies and chests, mouths, lips, tongues. Hair and nails. Teeth, intestines, glands.

Mum and all her feelings. Dad and all his expectations. Everyone pulling at each other. Wanting something from each other. Flesh lay with flesh. Flesh begat flesh. Flesh loved the flesh it begat. Flesh died. And new flesh it was which then occupied the chairs and the stools, and drank and laughed with its pudgy face and glassy eyes.

The people at the table next to where Liz was sitting stood up to leave. Before I even contemplated it, I was making a beeline and sat down as if totally unaware of her presence. Subconsciously, I waited to hear my name, but it was not forthcoming. After a while I couldn't help myself and turned to look — a mistake, I immediately discovered, for not only did I find myself looking straight at her, but she also winked at me. What was that supposed to mean? It meant she'd already clocked me ages ago, without letting on. You're not important enough for me to invite you to join us, but then not unimportant enough for me to ignore you either, therefore the wink. I've seen you, but I don't want to acknowledge you while I'm here with my friends. Stay away, sit on your own.

At least I had the presence of mind not to wink back. Instead, I returned her gaze coldly before turning round again to stare once more out across the water to the city on the other side, illuminated now and glittering. I sipped my pint and debated with myself whether or not to go in and buy some more cigarettes. The important thing was to do exactly as I would have done had she not been there.

Would I have had another pint? Bought a packet of cigarettes while I was at it? Or would I have got up and gone home?

My urge to get up and leave was entirely down to her presence, and I couldn't let that decide. So I draped my coat over the chair and went inside to buy some at the bar, ordering another pint while I was at it. The incident with the tramp still clung to every packet I bought, even if it no longer blackened my thoughts as before; now it was just a faint shadow, a barely perceptible sense of dread that momentarily came over me, only in the next instant to be gone, as pint in hand I edged my way through the swell of customers and back outside.

No sooner had I sat down than Liz appeared in front of me. She was a bit unsteady and put a hand on the table for support. She smiled at me for a long moment without saying anything.

'You saw my note, then?' she eventually mustered.

'What note?'

'The one on my door that said we'd be here.'

'I didn't see any note.'

'So you came here to drink on your own?'

'Yes, as a matter of fact I did.'

'Oh. I thought you'd seen the note and come to find me.'

'If I wanted to find you, I could knock on your door any day of the week.'

'I thought maybe you fancied me a bit.'

I didn't know what to say. She stood there looking at me, a smile still stuck on her face. Then, as if nothing had been said, she went back to her mates.

That night I lay awake for some time. It was as if I couldn't sleep until I'd heard her come in and close her door behind her on the landing below. It was stupid, and I wished myself back to the time before I'd had anything to do with her. Not that I had anything to do with her now, exactly, but the fact that we'd visited each other's rooms somehow tied us together — she was no more the anonymous neighbour on the floor below, a person I'd paid no attention to whenever she came and went. But now, without wanting to, I found myself lying in bed waiting for her to come home. It was pathetic, and barely even credible — there was basically nothing at all that connected us.

But if she came home with someone, I wanted to know.

Eventually, I heard the front door. Moments later, her own. No cooing voices, just footsteps, door, bang, silence.

I woke up the next morning with a strong sense of exuberance in my chest. I felt I was close to having my first book ready, and thinking about the Daguerre series contributed too. Perhaps the spring had something to do with it as well, infusing all that was old and dead in the world with new life. The first thing I did was go through the photographs that for the time being made up *The Last Day*. I stood in my underpants with a cigarette stuck to my lip as I ran my eye over the pictures in turn, attentive to even the smallest impulse they triggered in me, it was those first reactions that had to be followed, not the reflections that came afterwards. The minutest waver, the tiniest dissonance — how easy it was to paper over in the mind and convince oneself that it made no odds. Yet it was the gravest error. What did the mind know about photography?

I spent the day in Greenwich Park, finding an outlying spot that was relatively deserted, where I lay down beneath an ancient oak and began reading *Parmenides' Secret* by this Paul Becker who was so worshipped by Vivian and those around her. The main character was journeying by train from Germany to Switzerland, then on to Milan and eventually

Brindisi, from where he went by boat to Athens. Not that any of this was exactly made clear by what he wrote, which for the most part consisted of short, abrupt passages ending with three dots, but nevertheless contained sufficient information for the reader to be able to reconstruct his route. It was evident, though, that he wasn't travelling towards but away from something. To begin with, it was an irritating read: come on, pull yourself together, I'd find myself urging the protagonist, this is nothing to dwell on, no matter what you think, leave it alone and move on — *do* something! But after a while I settled into it, his mode became almost my own, and his thoughts too became almost my own, regardless of how strange they appeared . . .

A man ascended a staircase, he held in his hand a paper bag in which were several oranges, the bag tore open and the fruit rolled down the stairs with the man in pursuit, his arms waving like tentacles. A woman bore sorrow, she was young, her face glowed with concealed joy. A dog in a gateway bared its teeth, a yellow, scabby dog too weakened to follow its instinct to attack . . . They were living, the tall man, the woman and the dog, and yet of everything I saw that day they will not live on in me. A statue will. A young man of stone with a goat draped over his shoulders. Oh, the life in him. What I saw there was life itself captured. And the new. He was new, he was the new — even today, more than two thousand years after he emerged by the chisel from the stone. Even as the electric trolley buses hurtle by in the streets below. Even as the steamships are loaded and unloaded in the ports. Even as the gramophone, the telegraph, the telephone . . .

My thoughts are dirty. Not hungry or lustful as an animal's, but dirty as the wooden floor of a shed at the bottom of a garden is dirty.

The Greeks did not keep journals. This tells us all that is worth knowing about them.

The insight of the Greeks was that there is no mystery. Everything is as it appears, everything lies open, everything is bathed in the light of the eternally blazing sun. Was it perhaps this which prompted Hölderlin to exclaim: 'Come, into the open, friend!'?

Last night I lay awake. Hopelessness gnawed in me like a rat. Sealed in by the darkness, my only refuge was within, in all that I had brought with me from the northern latitudes. Rain and forests, moors and heaths, changing skies, shiftless villages, bustling cities. The people there, whom I knew and had known. The Bird Man — why did I think of him now? He had two ravens tamed, which flew with him wherever he went. If he stood still, they perched on his shoulders. On occasion they would remain there even when he walked. We were afraid of him — everyone was afraid of him, even the grown-ups. But no secrets exist, no hidden language, no forces concealed. There is nothing to be frightened of. Nor indeed anything to hope for.

Jonathan and Vanessa were seated at a table on the terrace when I came down to breakfast. Of course I did not know their names then. I saw two people, a woman and a man, not quite young, though not quite old either. Well dressed they were and appeared cheerful — they wished me a good morning. No one else was there. The sun was already high in the sky. The chirping of the cicadas surrounded the garden like a wall. I ordered coffee and lit a cigarette while studying the couple. They sat next to each other at the table with their backs to me. Knives and forks, spoons, cups and glasses were moved about as if in accordance with a ritual whose performance they had mastered to perfection. She sensed my gaze and turned with a smile.
'It seems we are the only guests,' she said. 'Would you care to join us?'
'Kind of you to ask, but I must beg to decline,' I said. 'I cannot endure other people in the mornings.'
She laughed. He too now turned his head.
'Then we have something in common,' he said.

When I put the book down, a bank of blue-black cloud had gathered in the east. The green of the trees had deepened, and a wind began to gust. Abruptly, the sky cracked above my head. I dropped the book into my rucksack, returned to the bike and made for home. I had been transported into a trance-like state, the mood of the book and the impressions it had already made on me would not let go, and I inhabited simultaneously the book and the world. It was as if the tulips in the flower beds or the branches of the trees with their delicate leaves had become spirited and appealed to me whenever my gaze fell upon them. Oddly, the traffic of cars and buses did not break this illusion, but existed alongside it, as if two ages, two worlds, could hold in parallel.

Liz emerged as I went up the stairs with the bike.

'Hi,' she said. 'How are you doing?'

'Fine,' I said. 'But it's going to start chucking it down in a minute. I'd take an umbrella if I were you.'

She produced one out of her bag, then dropped it back in. I carried on up the stairs.

'I was a bit drunk last night,' she said. 'I hope I wasn't too forward. If I was, I didn't meant to be!'

I shook my head.

'I didn't notice.'

'Anyway, I'm just popping out to rent a film for tonight. You could join me later on, if you want?'

'What film do you have in mind?'

'I don't know yet. What do you fancy?'

'*Blow-Up*,' I said without thinking. 'Or *A Clockwork Orange*.'

'Art movies. I should have guessed. No use trying to entice you with a romantic comedy or two, I suppose?'

'No use at all, no. Anyway, I'm in a bit of a rush here. See you.'

'See you,' she said, and went down the stairs while I lugged the bike up to my own landing. The moment I put it down, the first drops of rain began to drum. I made myself a couple of sandwiches and returned to reading my book. The first-person narrator had now taken ill and was running a feverish temperature, but instead of taking to his bed he struck out into the town and was strangely uplifted, filled with the energy of end-time, rather like a tree in autumn, its final cascade of colour before the leaves are fallen. He was not well, thought everyone was looking at him, even believed he was being followed, and darted down alleys in order to escape. That same evening, he encountered the English couple again and they sat up late, talking in the boarding-house library, the Englishman holding forth on Orpheus and all things Orphic, the Oracles and something he called the philosophy of Night. It was the early Greek philosophers he alluded to, Parmenides, Empedocles and Pythagoras, who he believed to be magi of a kind, knowing life's deepest secrets. During the night, the narrator coughs up blood, a sure sign in any novel that a person is soon to die.

> The philosophy of Night . . . what might it comprise? An eternal interim in anticipation of dawn? At once it struck me that death was dawn. Life was the night, death the day. It was the living who were dead, the dead who were living.

It was a sick thought, and indeed I actually felt nausea as I put the book down. The idea that nothing in life was secret, that everything was found in the open, was a healthy one. The notion that everything had some other, hidden meaning was perverse. So it was fitting that he only came to the conclusion after coming down with a fever and then coughing up blood. No doubt it was the way of the soul to assuage the terrible fate that awaited him. To transmute death into an awakening — only a person at death's door could think such a thing.

I went over to the window and gazed across the rooftops. Almost every colour had seeped away into the grey. Rain ran down the pane, gushed from the drainpipes, streamed in the gutters. Not a soul was out.

Liz was directly beneath the floor I was standing on. Curled up on her sofa watching some stupid film on the video, no doubt. She wasn't a prospect for me in the long run. But right now she was a breath of life, new.

She smiled when she opened the door, in blue jeans and a flowery white top.

'I thought you wouldn't be able to resist the romantic comedies.'

'What if I came for something else instead of watching TV?'

'And what would that be?' she said, meeting my gaze, though her blushing cheeks seemed to indicate that most of all she wanted to look away. 'My fridge is basically empty, if that's what you mean.'

I smiled without replying and she stepped back to let me in.

The television wasn't even switched on, the stereo silent. A book lay splayed open on the arm of the sofa, a mug of greyish-white tea on the floor beneath it.

'So you were messing me about when you said you were going to watch a film?'

'I changed my mind,' she said, picking up her book in a way that was meant to look casual, closing it and putting it down again on the floor next to her tea. 'A bit sad, watching films on your own. Don't you think?'

'Why should it be?'

'Maybe not your art-house stuff. But lighter entertainment's more social, isn't it? I always feel so stupid if I sit laughing on my own. Can I get you something? A cup of tea?'

'Coffee, if you don't mind.'

'Right.'

She sashayed away into the kitchen area while I sat down on the settee. Because she'd so obviously been trying to hide what she was reading, I bent down and picked her book up off the floor. *The Lion, the Witch and the Wardrobe* by C. S. Lewis.

'You're reading "Narnia"?!'

'You weren't supposed to see that.'

'No, I'm sure I wasn't. How old did you say you were?'

'It's my comfort literature. You can put it down now. I'm not exactly proud of it.'

I opened the book and began to read out loud.

'*Once there were four children whose names were Peter, Susan, Edmund and Lucy.*'

'Ha ha,' she said.

'*This story is about what happened to them when they were sent away from London during the war because of the air-raids.*'

'All right, that'll do. Unless you want some arsenic in your coffee?'

'Why are you reading this? Seriously. What do you get out of it?'

'I told you. It's for comfort.'

'What do you need comforting for? And what on earth's so comforting about a kids' book?'

She came over with my coffee, picked up her mug and sat down next to me on the settee, settling back against the opposite arm.

'Haven't you ever yearned for your childhood?'

'Why would I do that?'

'The world was safe then. You were looked after.'

'That was exactly what I didn't like about being a kid. Being at the mercy of others was terrible. I can't imagine anything worse.'

'You're just weird.'

She smiled at me as she said so. I put my hand on her knee. She looked startled. I leaned across to kiss her. She held her mug out of the way and then giggled before putting it down on the floor again. I couldn't stand girls laughing in intimate situations, so I immediately straightened up again.

'Did you just try to kiss me?'

I said nothing.

'Try again!'

The only way I could seduce her was by doing so on impulse, without thinking about it. That moment was definitely gone. But if I shied away now, she'd think I was self-conscious and weak.

The advantage was hers all of a sudden, and the thought was almost unbearable. I had to get back in the driving seat. I curled my hand behind her head and pulled her towards me, while with the other hand I began stroking her thigh. She was soft and compliant and put her arms around me. Within a moment I felt her delicate fingers run through the hair at the nape of my neck.

'Shall we go into the bedroom?' she whispered.

'Can do,' I said, and got to my feet.

The bedroom was small, bright and clean. A window with no curtain. The bed neatly made, with a white bedspread.

She removed her top, arms crossed to pull it over her head. Her hands reached behind her back to unclasp her bra in a quick, practised movement before she unbuttoned and stepped out of her jeans. It was like she was getting changed for sport. Grey light fell on her from the window.

She stood naked in front of me, smiling as she looked into my eyes.

Was she a nudist or something, used to just stripping off?

'Aren't you going to undress?'

I didn't reply, but pressed my body against hers, smoothed my hands up and down her back, her buttocks, between her thighs. She lay down on the bed. I got on top of her, liking the feeling of being fully dressed while she was naked. I pulled my dick out and penetrated her. She winced slightly, eyes closed, then after a moment became wetter and I moved inside her with ease. Opening her eyes now, she gazed up at me as I thrust in and out of her determinedly right until I came.

Afterwards, she snuggled up to me, a leg draped over mine, and stroked my hair.

'My dream prince,' she said. 'Aren't you going to take your clothes off?'

'It's not my bedtime yet.'

'I want to be naked with you.'

'I've got things to do,' I said.

To take the edge off the rebuff, I smoothed her cheek and kissed her before getting up.

'What happens now?' she said.

'How do you mean?'

'Us two.'

'Can't we just enjoy each other's company?'

She smiled.

'Yes, but what sort of status have we got?'

'Do we have to put a label on it?'

'No. No, you're right,' she said. 'You can sleep here though, if you want.'

'I like to sleep alone,' I said, anxious now to get away.

'So it meant nothing?'

'Of course it meant something! I've thought so much about you, Liz.'

'Have you?'

'Yes. Ever since I moved in.'

'Really?'

I nodded.

'But listen, I really do have to get going.'

I cursed myself as I went up the stairs. How stupid could I get? Why did I have to say I'd been *thinking* about her? Her head would be full of ideas now. She'd be difficult to shake off. Her chirpy laughter and gleaming eyes were going to haunt me for weeks. And even if I spelled it out to her and dumped her the hard way, she'd still be living here, and every chance meeting on the staircase or in the street would be excruciating.

Thankfully, she didn't come begging at my door as I thought she might. I lay listening for signs of life down there before I went to sleep, but all was quiet. I imagined her sitting up reading, unless she'd turned in for an early night. Nor was I disturbed the following evening, and I understood then that she had her pride and was reluctant to make any first move. I knew what she wanted, and so what happened next was up to me, I suppose she thought. I respected that. But nonetheless I timed things in the mornings in such a way as to minimise the risk of our bumping into each other. I began coming home late in the evenings. But the fact of her being there was still a distraction, rather like an uncompleted project, almost impossible to get away from. And this was true not least because *she* was remaining passive.

It wouldn't have been hard to stay away. All I had to do was think of her, her nose that was a bit too prominent, her lips that were a bit too thin, her chin that was a bit too round. And though I could picture her, I was still not *seeing* her, and my thoughts would therefore be drawn towards her flat, I'd find myself wondering what she might be doing down there at that moment, all on her own at the sink, at the table, on the settee, in bed, in the shower, standing in front of her wardrobe wondering what to wear. Doubtless she was having the same thoughts about me, speculating as to what I might be doing there on the floor above her ceiling.

When at last I went down and knocked on her door it was Friday, a whole week since our encounter.

The chain rattled, the lock snapped back and there she was, considering me with an inexpressive look.

'Do you fancy going to the theatre?' I said.

She shook her head.

'Not really, no.'

'I've bought tickets,' I said, and produced them from my back pocket. 'One's got your name on it.'

'I'm going home this weekend, an early start in the morning.'

'But that's tomorrow. Come on. The play finishes at nine. You'll be home again by ten. You wouldn't be planning on going to bed before that, surely?'

'No, but I've still got to pack. I was aiming for a quiet night in.'

'OK.'

I slipped the tickets back into my pocket and looked at my watch.

'I'd thought we might go for a drink first — if you were going to come with me, that is. Maybe you could invite me in for a coffee instead? I'll just go on my own afterwards.'

She scrutinised me a moment. I held her gaze until eventually she gave a nod and cheerlessly let me in.

'So, where's home for you?' I said loudly from the hall as I took my coat off.

'Clevedon.'

'Never heard of it.'

'It's a small coastal town, not far from Bristol.'

'Is it nice there?'

I stepped into the living room where she was sitting in the chair facing the settee.

'It is, in that very English sort of way. I couldn't live there now, though.'

'You'll probably move back there one day, don't you think?'

'No.'

I sat down on the settee and pulled my cigarettes out. She got up and fetched an ashtray, put it down on the little table in front of me.

'Did you want some coffee?'

'Whatever's on offer. What are you having?'

She shrugged.

'Tea, I think.'

'The good old cuppa!'

She gave a feeble-looking smile and went over to the kitchen area.

'You haven't asked what play it is yet.'

'No, but I'm not going. I told you.'

I leaned back and propped my elbow on the armrest, inhaled deeply and then blew the smoke out through my nose. The two clouds that puffed before my face in the mirror across the room made me think of Sleipner and our sleigh rides every Christmas Eve — not just him standing snorting in the cold, but also what he actually might have thought about us. I'd never considered it before, he was just always there, observing us the whole time — but what did he make of it all?

Liz reached up and took two mugs from the open cupboard just as the water in the kettle on the worktop beside her began to hiss and hum, like a distant steam train.

'It's *Doctor Faustus*,' I said.

'Oh, the production you were taking the pictures for?' she said without looking at me, unscrewing the lid of a jar of instant coffee.

'Yes. Only they didn't use them, as it turned out.'

Now she looked.

'Really? They were good, though, weren't they?'

'Yes, they were. But I didn't deliver in time.'

'I see. Is it any good?'

'The play?'

'Yes.'

'I imagine so. It wouldn't be so well known if it wasn't.'

'Ha ha.'

She came over and handed me a mug, then sat down next to me with her own.

'It's got some brilliant reviews, anyway. But I thought you didn't want to go?'

'I would actually like to see *Doctor Faustus*. Only not with you.'

She threw me a quick glance, before curling her hands around her mug and craning to take a sip.

'That's frank, at least. Can I ask why?'

'You know why.'

'No, I don't.'

A silence ensued.

'You mean me keeping away since last weekend?'

'Could be.'

'And leaving so quickly afterwards?'

She said nothing.

'Is there a chance you might think I didn't mean anything by it?'

'It's possible, yes. But just so you know, I'm not interested in any excuses. It's OK by me.'

'What is?'

'The whole thing. It's OK as it is. It's fine.'

'Can I be honest with you?'

'I think you should.'

'Very often I think tactically. I know it's not always the best thing to do, but I can't help it. I'm always two steps ahead of myself, if you get what I mean. Anyway . . . I'm really interested in you. I have been since the first time I saw you. But you were with that other guy then. So when eventually we . . . well, when what happened between us last weekend happened, I was over the moon. I've been delirious about it all week. Really, truly happy. Just thinking about you.'

'Then how come you've been avoiding me?'

'I think I got caught up in second-guessing. I was scared it was just a one-off thing, that you weren't really invested. I mean, we're neighbours, aren't we, and maybe it was just because I was around, if you see what I mean. I didn't want to come on like a little puppy, pestering and pining at your door. You'd only have lost interest then. So I think maybe I thought I needed to step back. Let you work out what you felt about me first — if anything at all. So the upshot is that I told myself that if I could just give you some space for a week, then I could come and ask you out to this play. Unfortunately, the plan seems to have backfired.'

'Either you're lying, or you're more stupid than I thought.'

'I'm not lying, I promise. The problem, I think, is that I'm an emotional person. I don't always know how to handle my feelings. I think that's why I take pictures. It's a way of giving structure to it all. Pulling everything together.'

She didn't seem convinced.

'Why would I lie about it, Liz? What would I gain by it?'

'I don't think you are lying.'

'What, then?'

'I don't think you're worth it. The fact that we're sitting here talking the way we are now would seem to suggest you're not.'

'Worth it?'

'Worth my trust.'

'So you don't trust me?'

She shook her head.

'I want things to happen naturally, that's all,' she said. 'Naturally, of their own accord.'

'Aren't they?'

'No. It's all explanations and excuses and analysing already. After hardly anything. That suggests something to me, can't you see?'

It was actually she who wouldn't let things happen naturally. We'd had sex. A week later I'd come down and asked her out. But instead of taking me up on it, she'd dug her heels in, because that wasn't the way she wanted it. In other words, her own demands were what had led us here, to sit and *analyse*. She didn't know me, but wanted to change me nevertheless — while I was perfectly happy for her to be the person she was.

'I only wanted to ask you out to the theatre. It's no big thing.'

'Isn't it about time you got going?'

'Yes, but I'd like you to come, obviously. Can I suggest a plan? We go out to the theatre now, you go home for the weekend tomorrow, then when you get back you come up to mine for dinner Monday night. Yes or no?'

'Perhaps.'

'Perhaps? What sort of an answer's that? Come on, going to a play won't exactly *hurt*, will it? It's one of the best dramas in literary history! And if I'm what's stopping you, you can just pretend I'm not there.'

'That would be impossible.'

'But you'll come, won't you?'

'Yes, all right. I'll come.'

On the way there I told her I'd worked with the director and the stage designer and that I'd seen parts of the play in the making.

'I discussed a lot of the music selections and costumes and stuff with them as they went along. I saw the initial sketches for the set design too. At that point they were still working with three different possibilities. I've no idea which one they chose, so it's all a bit exciting for me. Have you seen much theatre?'

'It's not really my world. I've seen the odd thing or two, though.'

'I imagine you've *read* just about everything.'

'Ha! Nowhere near!'

She'd changed her clothes before going out and was now wearing blue jeans, a white sweater with a pattern featuring some red birds, and white trainers. She looked so incredibly straight, but would have been just about passable had it not been for the red neckerchief she'd added at the last minute.

It was like going out with Bambi, I thought to myself. She hadn't a clue. What's more she was oblivious! It touched me, in the oddest way.

A ghettoblaster powered out Big Audio Dynamite as we passed a small park. Students were sat around it drinking, I noticed, perhaps twenty or so, on a grassy bank.

A row of posters had been strung up on the railings.

THE CLOCK WILL STRIKE

'They only did that because they didn't get my pictures in time,' I said, pointing them out to her. 'They had to go with some graphic art instead. Pretty cool, though, all the same.'

'How did you get involved with them? Was it through your art school?'

'Hans was the first person I met in London. He's the stage designer. I'd only been here a few days when he came up to me in the pub and we got talking. The director's a friend of his. One thing led to another, you could say.'

'Luck, then, in other words.'

'Coincidence, yes. Luck, no. I don't actually like them all that much. It's as if they've no boundaries, in a way. Dope and stuff. But creativity needs to be pure, don't you agree?'

'There it is,' she said with a nod, diverting my attention to the other side of the street.

I'd been expecting the venue to be a disused factory hall or a former bus depot repurposed for the arts, something like that, but the building in front of us looked to be an ordinary old theatre of the classic variety — small and intimate, certainly, but completely without the touch of avant-garde I'd thought Vivian would have brought with her.

Carpeted floors, dark woodwork, a bar, mirrors on the wall behind.

A clock ticked, loud and ponderous above the hum of voices. No music was playing, the ticking was the only sound, intensely amplified.

'We can still get a drink,' I said. 'What'll you have?'

'A glass of white, I think. How about you?'

I shrugged.

'You find a seat, I'll buy.'

Tick. Tock. Tick. Tock.

No one inside appeared to notice the sound. They must have adjusted to it, but to me, standing with my elbows on the counter waiting for the barman's attention, it was resonant and unsettling.

Tick. Tock. Tick. Tock.

She was clever, Vivian.

I looked over my shoulder and located Liz. She'd found room at the long counter in front of the window and stood looking out, a foot resting on the rail underneath.

Tick. Tock. Tick. Tock.

There was no risk of Vivian or Hans being here. They'd have been present at the first night, naturally, but no way they'd be coming to every performance.

Liz could be my provincial cousin for all anyone knew.

I handed her her wine and squeezed in next to her. She glanced up at me. Her eyes betrayed a smile. Her defiance clearly wasn't that deep.

'So what do your parents do there in . . . what was the name of the place, Cleavage?'

'Ha ha, very funny.'

'No, seriously, what's it called again?'

'Clevedon, and my dad's a teacher, my mum's a physiotherapist. What about yours?'

'I grew up on a farm. So my dad's a farmer.'

'Really?'

'Really.'

'You mean, with livestock and everything?'

'That's right.'

'Who'd have thought.'

A bell then began to sound, heavy and solemn. People moved from the bar into the house.

'Sounds like Doomsday,' Liz said.

'It bodes well,' I said, putting the remains of my pint down. 'Shall we go in?'

Our seats, in the stalls, were almost in the middle, upholstered in red velvet and constructed to accommodate small nineteenth-century theatregoers — my knees were nearly touching my chin. For Liz, though, they were as if made to measure.

'I'm actually a bit fazed by you growing up on a farm,' she said.

'I know. A bit more surprising than your own background.'

'In what way?'

'The middle-class parents.'

'Does it bother you?'

'Me? No. I'm against families.'

'How can anyone be against families?'

'Someone has to look after you when you're a kid, I understand that. But why should you have anything to do with them after that? I don't understand it.'

'I like my parents.'

'Good for you! As long as you don't generalise a rule out of it.'

The lights went down, the murmur of voices in the auditorium petered away.

The ticking clock returned, louder now.

We sat for some time in pitch-darkness, listening to it tick. Nothing else happened. After a while, a ripple of unease passed through the audience.

Tick. Tock. Tick. Tock.

A moving image was then suddenly thrown up onto a screen on the left-hand side of the stage. It was an old film, grainy and stuttering. It showed a street, an old, dusty street, narrow and with buildings looming towards each other on each side. Half-timbered, lime-washed structures. They even had thatched roofs. A horse was standing before an elegant carriage, a man was sitting inside it, and some other men came walking past, in strangely high-shafted boots and cloaks. The film lasted perhaps five or six seconds. And then it went dark again.

What was this?

It hadn't lasted long enough to get a handle on it.

The next moment, the same clip was run stage right. Five, six seconds again, and then darkness.

Tick. Tock. Tick. Tock.

It was unsettling.

Something was wrong.

The light in the film was from the sun, shadowy at the edges, though even where it shone there was a murk about the scene. It was an ancient sunlight, I thought. It made everything desolate. Even with the men walking past, the street seemed forsaken.

It could only be Hans's doing. I was reminded of his contact sheets, which looked to be from the same era.

But these were moving images.

Another film came on now, on the same side of the stage. A different street, though quite as narrow as the first. A horse pulling a primitively built cart through the frame in fits and starts. Some men standing outside a house by an open door. A man came out. Looking neither right nor left, he came directly towards the camera. The same high-shafted boots, the same heavy cape. The image froze. For a couple of seconds we stared at his face until it faded into darkness.

Round cheeks that lent him a rather childlike appearance. Bearded, a small mouth, though full-lipped.

Not unlike the portrait of Marlowe.

It was well done.

Prompted by the previous pattern, I turned my gaze to the other side of the stage in anticipation of the face then reappearing there.

But it did not.

Instead, pinpricks of light, hundreds, appeared above the stage, a night sky with stars, while at the same time a spotlight came on and we saw a man seated alone on the stage beneath the firmament, shrouded by darkness. Barefoot, in black jeans and a black T-shirt, trousers turned up above the ankles, shorn hair.

Settle thy studies, Faustus, and begin to sound the depth of that thou wilt profess.

It must have been Hans who'd made the films. He'd recreated the mood of his photographs to perfection. And found an actor who actually looked like Marlowe.

But where had they got the resources to recreate an old-fashioned street like that? Could he have been working on a film set or something? And repurposed material from there?

It wasn't improbable.

But then the actor wouldn't have looked like the portrait. No one could get that lucky.

Terror seized me.

It *was* Marlowe. It *was* sixteenth-century Greenwich.

Yet art thou still but Faustus, and a man. Couldst thou make men to live eternally, or, being dead, raise them to life again . . .

The actor on the stage got to his feet. I folded my arms across my chest and bit into my cheek, gently at first, then harder. This was fear, only fear. The clock and the film, the darkness and the diabolical-looking actor had manipulated my mind. How could I be such an easy prey? It was the oldest trick in the book, the world transformed on a stage.

I breathed deeply, a tremble in my chest, and sensed a glance from Liz. She was sitting with her lips slightly parted, like a child before a magician.

'If we say that we have no sin, we deceive ourselves,' Faustus said from the stage, 'and there is no truth in us. Why, then, belike we must sin, and so consequently die . . .'

He moved downstage, stood and stared at us. The set they'd gone with was quite different from the first sketches Hans had shown to Vivian. Now everything was black. Black backdrop, black stage, and two black cubes, one on each side, against which the moving images had been projected.

'Ay, we must die an everlasting death,' he said, and began to point. 'You. And you. And you. And you.'

Liz felt me looking at her and returned my gaze.

'This is *really* good,' she whispered.

What, that we must die an everlasting death?

Something was wrong. Something was terribly wrong.

It was as if the world was unravelling.

Figures entered the stage. All were in the same black jeans, black

T-shirt, barefoot, hair shorn. But there was no doubt as to which of them formed the focal point, nor as to what was at stake.

Faustus and Mephistophilis, Mephistophilis and Faustus.

The moment of their first encounter, which I had witnessed in its bare beginnings, had been stretched out in time, they stood looking at each other for what seemed like an eternity while the clock ticked.

Homo fuge: *yet shall not Faustus fly.*

Six naked figures entered one by one wearing animal masks and began to dance.

Liz must have sensed my horror, for she took my hand and squeezed it.

*

The next morning I was woken in darkness by the rattle of Liz's alarm clock on the bedside table. She reached to turn it off and then slipped from the bed.

'What time is it?' I said.

'Half past five. Go back to sleep.'

She bent over me and kissed my cheek.

'I'll leave the key on the worktop in the kitchen.'

'OK,' I said, and heard for a while her sounds as she moved about, taking clothes from the wardrobe, going downstairs to the bathroom, coming back into the kitchen, putting the kettle on. I must have fallen asleep again after that, because all of a sudden she was bent over me again.

'Take care, my prince. See you Monday.'

I mumbled a reply — same to you, see you.

When later I woke again, sunlight had filled the room. I lay for some time to get my head together. The unease I'd felt the night before was still inside me. Though not as acute, it was nevertheless there, and without let-up; it was as if something at any moment might come apart. I got up and dressed, wandered around the flat looking at her things, finding them comforting in all their everydayness. On the bottom bookshelf were a couple of photo albums. I took one out and turned a few pages in it just to see, but put it back again almost straight away. I wasn't so interested in her that looking at photos from her childhood was going to do anything for me. I made myself a coffee and lit a cigarette that I smoked while standing at the window. The sky was blue, only a few stringy white clouds dithered high above the rooftops. The people walking along the street looked like normal people with normal lives. No threatening movements, no animal masks, no cracks in time.

I had to see those contact sheets again.

Only not now.

I went upstairs to my own bedsit and got some clean clothes and a towel I took with me to the shower room in the basement. Everything was as normal. The grey, damp stone walls in the passage, the prehistoric shower mixer, old enough surely to be from the days of Empire, the showerhead on its last legs, the tiles streaked with limescale and remnants of shampoo, a clod of hair clinging to the grid, then wafting submissively like seagrass in the running water. The staircase leading through the house, its creaking woodwork underfoot, the banister, the small collections of dust between the balusters. Everything was as normal. It was where my thoughts had to congregate, on what was solid and unchanging in the world. The unease I felt was just an abstract flicker.

I stuffed my dirty washing into the carrier bag under the sink and went and got the contact sheets, holding them with my hand lowered at my side, without looking at them. It felt like the room was infected by whatever it was they had brought with them, that it was part of the same thing, and I decided then to take them back downstairs with me to Liz's flat. I laid them out face down on the coffee table, the magnifying glass on top, and lit a cigarette.

Photographs — what were they?

Light captured on a plate or a sheet of paper.

There was no mysticism involved, no supernatural interference.

They belonged in the world. Photography's every component had existed always. It was only the way they combined that could be dated.

The Romans were familiar with the steam engine — wasn't that what Hans had said?

Hans was the key.

Where had he got these photographs from? The film sequences in the play?

Who *was* he?

I turned the contacts face up and began to study them one by one with the magnifying glass. Now that the idea they were premodern had attached itself, it was impossible to shake off. Nothing in the pictures contradicted it. Quite the opposite. There wasn't a single object of the modern age to be seen. No railway lines, no telegraph wires, no engines or machines. Nothing that was mass-produced. Only dirt roads, more or less churned up, grass growing between wheel ruts; wooden fences, drystone walls, grazed meadows, deciduous woodland; clusters of low-slung houses, wells, the occasional human being such as the shoeless child with the gleaming eyes.

Suppose it's true, I told myself as I got to my feet again and went over to the window. Suppose photographs exist from premodern times. How could it be explained? And how come no one knows about it?

I couldn't get my head around it there, surrounded by Liz's things, it was as if they opposed my every thought — everything I was, in fact.

I gathered the contact sheets together and went back upstairs, returned them to the shelf and stretched out on the bed. It was improbable, but not impossible. Alchemists had conducted loads of chemical experiments in the Middle Ages and Renaissance. The Romans had known the steam engine. It stood to reason that someone could have stumbled on how to capture images. And the alchemists were esoterics. Paracelsus. Agrippa. Magic and science were one and the same thing in those days. Surely someone could have ... but hang on, wasn't there something about this in one of those photography books?

I jumped up and darted to the bookshelf, where I pulled out the book on the origins of photography and sat down with it in the chair, only to get up again immediately — I needed music for this.

Empires and Dance.

With 'I Travel' thumping from the speakers I made myself a coffee, lit a cigarette and plonked myself down again, waiting until I'd finished smoking and crushed the end into the ashtray before opening the book in my lap.

There.

Albertus Magnus discovered silver nitrate. And he lived in the thirteenth century! Georg Fabricius discovered silver chloride in the mid sixteenth century. And someone called Daniele Barbaro had drawn and described the diaphragm in 1568. As if that wasn't enough, the camera obscura, the book said, was invented as far back as the eleventh century, by an Arab called Alhazen.

It actually was not impossible.

Buoyed up by this new insight, I went back to the contact sheets themselves, spread them out on the table and began to scrutinise them again. Fittingly, 'Celebrate' kicked in at the same time. Assuming the photos were from the late 1800s made no sense. The sailing ships on the river were one thing — certainly they'd existed at that time — but the sterns were from another century. Then there were the timber buildings at the riverside. They only added up if you took them to be premodern. And it was possible. Photography's every component was already known in the sixteenth century. Including the lens.

So it was kept under wraps. Why? Well, because they were magicians, esoterics, secretive bastards — it was their livelihood, wasn't it?

But how had Hans tracked them down?

Just then the phone rang and made me jump.

It couldn't be Hans, surely?

That would barely have been believable. But it wasn't impossible!

As I got up to answer it, I realised it would be Liz — pining, wanting to ring and say she'd arrived.

'Hello?' I said.

'Kristian — please don't hang up.'

It was Mum.

I said nothing, but I didn't hang up either.

'It's Liv. It's Liv. She's . . .'

Her voice trailed away and she choked up.

PART THREE

Ever since the first time I landed at JFK I've disliked New York City. The endless chaos at Immigration, the zealous, shouting staff. The mistrustful questioning on presenting one's passport, as if entering the US was something hugely desirable for which anyone would readily lie, steal and deceive. The shoddy terminals, the lack of taste. Granted, the first sight of Manhattan's skyscrapers, rising up illuminated against the night sky, was impressive, and indeed made the hairs stand up on my forearms, but no sooner was I among them and they were looming above me than I found it all rather depressing. The first few times I visited the city I could never understand what it was about the place that lowered my spirits and angered me to such an extent — I was still in my early twenties then, and because so much was happening for me when I was there, so many people wanting to meet me, I simply shoved the feeling aside without further contemplation. That the city filled me with such loathing became in a way a premise, a kind of precondition of my stays there. Whenever my schedule allowed it, I would go back to my hotel and lie reading on the bed. The rooms I would be given then, on my way up, though not quite there yet, were cramped and dark with wall-to-wall carpeting that gave off faint reminders of cooking smells and detergents. If I stepped over to the window to look out, the view would be one of backyards, rooftops, fire escapes, and the constant whirr of the ventilation systems were drowned out only by the wailing sirens of police cars and ambulances that without cessation would be carving their way through traffic wherever in the city one happened to be. Could I locate the source of this feeling and photograph it? I toyed with the idea, but the problem with documentary images was that something romantic always stuck to them, they had such a peculiar tendency to make reality look cool — even the grimmest of them. Garbage containers outside the entrance of a run-down New York building were at once cool New York garbage containers. A fat tourist wearing a cowboy hat and glasses in a tacky diner became if not cool, then at least interesting, and the vulgar aesthetic was endowed with its own peculiar beauty. This was in part photography's curse, and hardly a motif existed that was more accursed than this city. I hated every picture of it, hated the bands from there that consciously or otherwise cultivated its myths, all the Lou Reeds, the Patti Smiths, the Ramoneses, the Tom Verlaines, the Talking Headses, hated its writers and artists — I couldn't think of a single figure in art history whose influence had been more damaging than Andy Warhol's.

What happened when I left my room, took the elevator down and stepped out into the streets?

I became a nobody. I looked up, I looked down, I looked left and looked right, and nowhere did I see a place where the human could find footing.

But were the sidewalks not alive with pedestrians? Were the streets, as wide as rivers, not teeming with vehicles, their drivers and passengers? Was that not human enough for me? What's more, they were forever gabbing, incessantly and unstoppably — if you happened to step into an elevator and stand beside an American, they would immediately open their mouth and say something to you, it didn't seem to matter what; or if you paused a moment to look in a shop window, someone would be standing beside you within seconds, cheeks wobbling with jabber. In the coffee shops and restaurants you couldn't order a glass of water without being bombarded with chat. And everywhere you went, heads blathered at you from their ubiquitous TV screens.

They communicated. They socialised. And it was easy to think they did so at such frenetic pace in order to compensate for their inhuman surroundings, to alleviate the deathly depressing force with which their environment bore down on them. But in actual fact it was two sides of the same coin. Everything went from the inside and out, nothing from the outside and in. Anyone who constructs such a thing as New York City, where the human is unable to find footing, cannot possibly be sensitive to the world, perhaps even is completely *oblivious* to it. And people who spewed out talk without heed to those they were talking to, without differentiating between them, were likewise insensitive, unaware that differentiations were *everything* in human life. For it was diversity that not only made us what we were, but also served us best. They hated communism, but were communists themselves, only with money. Communism too went from the inside and out, treated everyone the same and constructed inhuman buildings. Money was seen as a maker of diversity, establishing divides between rich and poor, but the funny thing about money was that it made everything in the surrounding world the same, so the differences between humans could at any given time be erased; money was not a part of the human sphere, but external to it, all you had to do was reach out, grab some yourself, and hey presto, with a bit of luck you'd be rich too.

They lived a lie, but didn't know it was a lie, and instead were proud of it and everything it represented. They even believed New York to be rather European, and would sometimes brag about it — but much rather some dump in the Midwest that at least only lived *one* lie and didn't strive to raise itself above others by heaping another one on top, as New York did.

At the same time — and it was probably for this reason I wasn't simply disspirited by the place during those first visits, but also in fact irritated by it — New York was an important city. For me there was no getting around it. It was here that everything happened. And if it happened here first, everywhere else would follow suit. After *The Last Day* came out I was invited to take part in a group exhibition along with three other photographers, all European — that was their angle, New European Photography. It was a small exhibition — only six of my photographs were included — but nevertheless it opened doors and led to me getting my own gallerist. Evan, his name was, and he was genuinely impressed by my portfolio. 'I'll make you into a big name, Kristian,' he said. He kept his word too, even if it did take time, though by then I'd outgrown him and soon made the switch into the top 'flight' with the Alfred Burnett Gallery, who continued to represent me. They sucked money out of me, but were good at everything, especially flattery.

It was now more than ten years since my last major exhibition in the city. I'd still been on my way up then, showing at the New Museum. Now MoMA was putting on a retrospective taking in more than eighty works, certainly my most important show to date. It was all basically hung by the time I arrived, but still I made a few changes, among them one that was rather invasive and something of a risk. The curators, Neil Weiss and Tamara Jorgensen, were sceptical, I sensed, even if they didn't say so directly, but it was my exhibition and they had no choice but to accept it. The pictures were hung chronologically, one room per series, not because I was interested in demonstrating any kind of development or maturing process, but because I wanted the audience to enter the final room, far different from those preceding it, only after moving through the others first. The photographs in it were so simple it almost hurt, but that simplicity would only be all the more cathartic if they were viewed last. I'd worked hard through the years at breaking down perspective, notably in a series of images I'd called *Dethroned*, in which a levelling out of the viewpoint was quite as important, if not more so, as the actual subject. I'd been making huge mosaics of pictures showing the same place or the same object, each image with its own perspective. Those hundreds of tiny shifts resulted in a kind of spatial uncertainty. The individual photographs were in themselves clear and unambivalent, but it was the context in which they were placed that unsettled things. Who is seeing? Where are they seeing from? What is a part? What is a whole? What is a space? This last question led me straight into the next series, *Animalia*, in which I inserted photographs of animals into a woodland setting, all more or less out of scale. The pictures were in clear, bright colours and sharp as a knife, and yet they had something unreal about them, they looked a bit like baroque paintings, the same ambivalence in their relation of *trompe l'oeil* realism and highly constructed, meticulous composition. What interested me in that instance was the fact that the retina is two-dimensional and that the space we perceive must therefore be an interpretation, which is to say something added by the brain. It was this aspect of 'self' I was playing around with and seeking to challenge in the *Animalia* pictures. Both of these series, however, were very much controlled by *me*, no matter how much they decentralised the perspective, and from that point on it had been all about relinquishing that control. There were, as I saw it then, two ways I could go. One was about the subject, about giving up control of it and seeking the arbitrary. If you go down that path, you very quickly come up against a wall, where all that is interesting, exciting and dynamic comes to a halt, and everything after that is flat and dead. The question there, in that empty borderland of the arbitrary, is of course whether *that* is in fact the world, and whether our lives take place simply in how we see it. The other path towards giving up control concerned not the subject, but the actual photograph itself. I buried exposed film in the ground and left it there for days before developing the pictures that were on it which I'd taken at the same location, I experimented with the developing process itself, I used all sorts of strange apparatus, from very old cameras to new miscroscope and surveillance cameras, disposable cameras of cardboard and plastic, and I built a mobile camera obscura, primarily to understand what kind of an apparatus it was, but also to photograph the photographs it took. This came together in a series I called *Obscuria*. The technique stemmed of course from before photography had been invented, and the miraculous sense of being able to stand in one place and look at a picture of another is only heightened by the primitive method. We are so used to technology allowing us to do just about anything that we see nothing at all magical any more about photographs or aeroplanes, while the camera obscura with its pre-industrial technology is closer to flint axes and clay pots, perceived as something nigh impossible, a bit like a ten-year-old putting on a pair of wings and flying. The contraption allowed me to throw a surprising light on London and capitalist urbanity, and the contrast, between that sixteenth-century technology and the present day, distressed perceptions of time in much the same way as *Dethroned* and *Animalia* had done with perceptions of space. Since then, I'd explored the same ground, the relationship between the photograph and time, its absolute dependence on the moment. How to escape the moment? It felt a bit like asking how to escape death — so definitive was the connection between the photograph and the now.

But the most recent series, which I had yet to put on show, was radically different. It consisted simply of straightforward photographs of forest. They were big, six by four metres, and in colour. My mother could have taken them. But they were magnificent. They expressed nothing, neither pain nor longing, nor did they ask questions or enquire in any way into our modes of seeing, thinking or being. They aspired neither to art nor even photography — their only intention was to show the forest.

I had arrived in New York late evening and woke up jet-lagged at four the next morning, went for a long walk through the city in order to acclimatise and coax my body into understanding it was now on a different continent, before having breakfast with Mette, my assistant, and then being driven with her to the museum. Mette was Danish and understood me in every way possible, she was loyal and smart, and, importantly, as ugly as sin, so Yelena was quite at ease whenever we were away on one of our trips.

It had started raining, which made the city a touch more human. The dark, caping clouds somehow drew everything that was happening on the streets that bit closer, magnifying its part in reality. Gleaming yellow cabs, wet paving, streaming gutters, pedestrians with faces hidden by vaulting umbrellas, the shining shop windows like grottos that lined the streets. Inside the car, in its sober black interior, hardly a sound could be heard. Mette texted on her phone, while I sat and stared out at the traffic alongside.

'Are we ahead of or behind UK time here?' I said without looking at her. 'I can never remember.'

'We're five hours behind.'

'So it's what, ten past four back home?'

'Yes.'

For a moment I wondered whether to phone and talk to Leo. There wouldn't be much time later in the day.

'When are we going to be there?'

'Not sure. Ten minutes. Fifteen maybe.'

'OK.'

Jacob, my man at the gallery, was standing waiting for us outside the entrance at the back of the museum. I could see it was him even from a distance, his big, blubbery figure unmistakable, as ever dressed in a loose-fitting black suit and black shirt. He'd dispensed with the bootlace tie today — that was mainly for fancier occasions. A woman was standing with him. I'd seen her before, but couldn't quite place her.

'Kristian,' he said, putting his arms out as I stepped from the car.

He was always on the front foot with everything, had a way of making it seem like he was running things.

I placed a hand on each of his shoulders while scrutinising him a moment. His dark lips and the cholesterol deposits under his eyes gave him an unhealthy appearance. It didn't help much that his hair was dyed black — the artificiality of it only took away from everything that was natural about his face.

'Jacob,' I said. 'How are you?'

'Are you kidding me? You've almost a hundred pictures up in there!'

'Is it looking good?'

'It's looking great. You know Sarah, I think?'

So *this* was Sarah.

'Yes, of course,' I said, and accepted her outstretched hand with a smile. 'Thanks for your work on the catalogue.'

'Have you seen it yet?' Jacob said.

I shook my head.

'I have it right here,' Sarah said and held up the black tote she gripped in her hand.

'No hurry,' I said. 'Shall we go inside?'

At the doors leading into the the exhibition rooms, the two curators stood waiting for us. I'd met them in London just a couple of weeks before, as well as quite frequently in the months before that, though they hadn't really opened up, sticking to their professional roles, as I'd stuck to mine.

'Do you mind if I walk through on my own first?' I said after the greetings were over with.

'No, not at all,' said Tamara. 'There's no one in there at the moment.'

Mette handed me a pen and a notepad and I went inside.

The first room contained the work that had made up *The Last Day*, with the big model of London on the floor — the dead cat alongside Liv's empty bed, the young man in Southwark alongside the Chislehurst ruins, the bare trees in the park alongside the illuminated house in the snow. Although I'd seen the pictures a million times and had worked on presenting them again only a few months previously, they once more prompted memories of the time they were from. It was the new surroundings that did it.

They were still good. Powerful.

I stepped over to the model of London. The initials on the flags had been replaced by full names — I didn't want people standing around and having to guess. And I'd included only those with ties to the occult. Cornelius Agrippa. Giordano Bruno. Emanuel Swedenborg. Isaac Newton. Madame Blavatsky. Aleister Crowley. And of course Christopher Marlowe.

It worked well. The mood of the photographs was drawn into the installation, and seeped back the other way.

The photographs themselves were perfectly lit. But the room needed to be darker, heightening the effect of the lighting on the installation.

Or perhaps the other way round? Make the room lighter, lessening the contrast?

The title on the wall didn't work. It would have to go.

The next room contained a series I'd called *Homeless in Utopia*. My derelicts. I spent no more than a couple of minutes with them — I didn't like looking at them and long considered not including them at all. But the curators kept returning to them and eventually I gave in — they were strong images, these too, and anyway they wouldn't be hanging here for my sake, but for the audience's.

I ran my eye over them to see if there was anything that stuck out, but they hung well and I went on into the next room. The photographs there were from my series *The Dead*, my most controversial to date and the one that had elevated me into the echelons of international recognition. Portraits of dead people, seated on chairs or sofas, dressed or assuming postures that suggested they were still alive. They were quite as shocking now as they had been twenty years earlier. The following room logically enough contained *The Night of Orpheus*, pictures of the ancient entrances into the underworld. Caves and volcanos in Greece and on the south coast of Italy, all in colour, flooded with sunlight, here and there blue sea, beachgoers. After that came *London, 1989*. The city photographed using antique equipment whose long exposure time meant that every human, every movement vanished. There lay the city, emptied in image after image. And yet one sensed their presence — there *were* people there, they just couldn't be seen.

Then, *Obscuria*, a natural follow-up to the Daguerre pictures. In the middle of the room a black-painted cube made of wood. Inside it a film was to run, a continuous loop, showing crystals on a glass plate moving towards the light as if they were living. The cube was meant to spark associations to the camera obscura, while the film investigated the boundaries between what was living and what was dead. The monumental images that made up *Dethroned* extended through the next two rooms, then came *Animalia*, including the installation *Car* — an old wreck from the seventies with a boy sitting on its roof — and finally *Forest*. In the last three rooms the pictures were as yet unhung and stood leaned against the walls underneath their designated positions, enough for me to see that the exhibition as a whole was going to be good. But perhaps also a little tame?

It was as if the three installations promised something that remained unfulfilled. *Dethroned* and *Animalia* were both semi-departures from photography, but still, maybe there was too big a gap between picture and installation. And yes, there was a tameness there too.

I went back through the rooms.

Definitely.

I stopped at *Homeless in Utopia*.

It needed to be wilder, more violent.

I closed my eyes.

Not pictures of animals, but real animals. In large numbers.

Heads. A lot of heads.

Here in the tramps' room. On the floor?

No.

In a skip. A yellow skip filled to the brim with animal heads.

Would that work?

Was it kitsch?

A cheap trick?

It connected the forest to the homeless derelicts and reinforced the underlying tone of *Animalia*, where the animals were pictures, objects almost. Here they'd be real, but treated like objects.

It was a possibility.

How would it work?

The audience would have the image of the boiled cat with them as they stepped into the room and saw the skip.

No. It would detract from the photos of the tramps.

Or would it?

After that came the city emptied of life. The underworld. The forest as art image, and then the forest from where the animal heads came.

Good.

I went back out into the hall, where Mette stood waiting.

'Where are the others?'

'In the cafeteria. What do you make of it? Are you satisfied?'

'Not quite.'

No one liked the suggestion.

'It's awesome the way it is, Kristian,' Jacob said. 'I don't think we should be tinkering with it now. And where the hell are we going to get a dumpster full of animal heads inside a week?'

'The city's full of butchers and slaughterhouses. And don't people go hunting in this country?'

'We could probably get hold of, say, a hundred pigs' heads,' Neil said. 'But then how would we preserve them? They can't just lie there and rot.'

'Could we use formaldehyde?' Tamara said.

She at least wasn't opposing the idea.

'No, no,' I said.

My phone vibrated against my chest. I took it from my pocket. It was Yelena.

Leo would probably be there too.

'Sorry, I need to take this.'

His voice came through as I got to my feet:

'Hiya, Pappy!'

He'd called me Pappy ever since he'd started talking. A mix-up of *pappa* and *daddy* that had simply stuck.

'Hi, Leo,' I said. 'What are you up to?'

'Pappy?'

'Yes?'

'I've built a city.'

'A whole city?' I said with surprise in my voice, though nothing could have surprised me less, he basically spent all his time at home building things in Lego.

'Yes, with a river in the middle.'

'That sounds amazing. How are you doing apart from that? All right?'

'Yes. When are you coming home?'

'A week from now.'

'That's a long time.'

'You knew that already, though, didn't you? And it's not really a long time. Seven days, that's all.'

'Seven's a lot.'

'No, it's not. But listen, I've got to get back to work now, OK? So we can buy food — and Lego!'

I glanced back at the little group who sat waiting for me. The table was at the other end of the room, but still they'd be able to hear everything I was saying.

'Leo? Are you there?'

I heard his breathing, his feet as he padded across the floor.

'Leo!'

He was hurt. Seven days *was* a long time.

'It's Daddy,' I heard him say.

'Hello?' Yalena said. 'How are you getting on over there?'

'Fine,' I said. 'A bit jet-lagged, though. Can you tell Leo he can't just ignore me and stop talking to me like that on the phone?'

'He's only six. But yes, I will. Are you at the museum now?'

'Yes.'

'How's it looking?'

'OK, yes. How are you both doing, anyway?'

'Oh, we're having a grand old time! Aren't we, Leo?'

She laughed.

'He's sitting here nodding on the sofa.'

'So what have you been doing today?'

'We've . . . I don't know, what have we been doing, Leo?'

'Nothing,' Leo said in the background.

'We must have done something,' Yalena said. 'Didn't you go to school?'

'No.'

She laughed.

'Ah yes, I remember now,' she said. 'First we didn't get up, then we didn't have our breakfast, then we didn't drive to school. Later, we didn't have our dinner. And now we're not sitting on the sofa.'

'Lovely talking to you both,' I said. 'Must get back, though. I'll try and phone a bit later on, OK? Bye, Leo!'

'No,' he said.

'Good luck with everything,' Yelena said.

'Thanks.'

I hung up, slipped the phone back into my inside pocket and returned to the others.

'Where were we?' I said.

'A dumpster full of animal heads,' said Neil.

'Is it a bad idea?'

'Not at all,' he said. 'I just don't know how necessary it is, if you can follow me?'

'It's fantastic the way it is,' Jacob said.

'If all of you think it's a bad idea, that it messes things up, then we won't do it. Does it mess things up?'

'Not as I see it,' Neil said.

I looked at Tamara. She shook her head.

'Then that's what we'll do,' I said. 'But the skip, the dumpster, has to be yellow. It's important. And it mustn't be new.'

A couple of days later and it was there, a rusty, yellow metal skip with chains at both ends, filled with stuffed animal heads, the kind that you'd often see adorning the walls of country houses or the homes of avid hunters. The fact that it was taxidermy and they were all made ready for display put a fresh layer of culture between them and the natural world of which they'd once been a part. It worked well, too, even if they did lose that raw, savage edge I'd been looking for at first. Animals as trash. Now, though, there was another perspective — animals as decoration. But that was OK. They were still trash.

'Better, don't you think?' I said to Neil and Tamara.

'Absolutely,' said Neil.

'It does take some of the force out of the photographs,' Tamara said. 'But maybe it doesn't matter?'

'That's the problem with photography,' I said. 'It gets pushed aside by everything. If you hang an oil painting up next to a photograph, it almost doesn't matter how bad the painting is, it'll upstage the photograph.'

'So do we take it out again?' Neil said.

I looked at him.

'Why would you do that?'

'Well, if it weakens the photographs . . .'

'Does it matter?'

'Maybe not . . .'

'The dumpster becomes the space. The photographs recede and take a back seat. Is there anything wrong with that?'

'No, not at all.'

'It's not like I *know* or anything. That's why I'm asking. It might be good, or it might not.'

I stepped away into the next room, took in what was in there, and then went back to look afresh at the new installation.

'There's another problem,' I said. 'It's very static. An object and photographs in one room. An object and photographs in the next.'

'And the one after that, and the one after that, too.' Tamara said.

'You're right,' I said with a nod. 'There's a domino effect here. Change one thing and you end up having to change everything. Am I right?'

'I think maybe yes.'

'So, do we add something in here?'

'More photos?' said Neil.

'More objects.'

'Such as?'

'I don't know.'

'Can I say what I'm thinking here?' Neil said.

'Please do.'

'I think we have a perfectly balanced exhibition that pans really well through your entire oeuvre. For me, the dumpster tips it over. Like it's overdoing things a little? It kind of makes the statement too overt in a way, whereas in the other rooms things are communicated more subtly. I think the photographs should be the focus here. *Homeless in Utopia*. The dumpster intrudes on that. I'm just not sure this is the right space to put in something new.'

'Is that what you think too, Tamara?'

'I'd say I'm rather more ambivalent than Neil. But I'm not certain the dumpster adds anything crucial. It's not irreplaceable, let me put it like that.'

'But you don't think it's banal?'

'No, not banal.'

'No, no, definitely not.'

Americans. Either they were all swagger or else they were submissive. They regulated their behaviour according to the prevailing power structures, not what they actually thought.

I went over to the skip and stood for a moment with my hands folded around the lip, the metal a measure cooler than the air in the room. The heads lay this way and that. Their eyes stared out emptily in every direction. It wasn't even death they represented. It was the death of death.

'We leave it in,' I said without turning round. 'But we need something else in here too.'

'OK . . . ?' said Neil.

'I want a big, long wooden box, it doesn't matter if it's knocked together from scratch, so it shouldn't be a problem. Four or five metres in length, a metre high, a metre wide. And we fill it up with used cigarette lighters.'

In the car outside, the driver was absorbed in his phone. I tapped on the window and he gave a start before getting out and opening the back door. Mette got in the other side.

'What do you think?' I said as we turned into the traffic.

'About what? The exhibition?'

'Yes.'

'It's fabulous, Kristian. You haven't a thing to worry about.'

'What about the skip?'

'It's good.'

'You don't think it grabs too much attention?'

'I don't think so, no.'

'You are being honest with me, aren't you?'

'You know I never humour you.'

'I know. I'm a bit nervous about it, that's all. It was so spur of the moment.'

'I understand. But it's not the first time you've taken a chance.'

'True.'

'And you've always pulled it off before. You must trust your gut feeling.'

'You're right.'

I twisted round and looked up at the front of the museum building through the rear window. An enormous banner showing the cat photo hung from the facade with my name across it.

Kristian Pedersen
Animalia
A Retrospective

Smaller banners bearing the same message were fixed to lamp posts along the avenue. Here and there were billboards. It would all have thrilled me when I was twenty, but now it left me cold. All art was about one thing and one thing only: what it meant to be human in the world. The best art was also the simplest, that which came closest to pure existence — but if you followed it there, the need for it fell away, like a scaffolding, superfluous once the building was done. This was why I hoped Leo would not become an artist. I wanted him to be sufficient in himself, to contain all that he needed to live the fullest life. But hardly anybody was, hardly anybody did.

I leaned back into the seat. The lighters were going to be good. Amassed objects of the same kind — piles of shoes, piles of clothes, piles of dentures — were impossible to look at without thinking of the Holocaust. The same would apply to the lighters. But I didn't like it. In fact, it was extremely unpleasant. It touched so closely on what had happened back then. No one would know, of course, but the connection would be there nonetheless, in that space. A mood. I'd sensed it at the time I'd taken the picture. A cigarette lighter, detached from any context, a nondescript, mass-produced object among millions exactly like it. I didn't want it to be manifest that this particular lighter was significant to the photographer. And yet, it could be sensed. Naturally, no one could know in what way it was significant — by dint of that dead man having held it in his hand — but somehow there was a momentous quality about it, a sense of a great many feelings being attached. It was as if those feelings radiated from the simple object itself. From then on, my photographs were permeated by that same sense — it was what made them so good. They were charged with meaning, glowing with significance. Nothing in them was ever simply what it appeared to be.

Until I photographed the forest.

Unless that quality of detachment they possessed had been something in me. It too was a feeling.

The wind talks only about the wind, wrote Alberto Caeiro, a heteronym of that strange Portuguese writer Pessoa, in one of his poems. They were as clear as a day in spring and I read them in one sitting. It was as if in some way I already contained them, as if I was walking through a landscape with which I'd once been familiar and then inexplicably forgotten — until then.

It was after reading those poems that I photographed the forest.

The insight I'd gained was that everything I'd learned, I now had to unlearn. That everything thought, now had to be unthought. But to attain clarity meant first to pass through the blur of opacity — this went by the name of learning. The proposal of putting on a major retrospective was a gift at just the right time. Everything I'd done until then had served this one purpose. Not that I expected anyone to understand it like that — that would have been asking too much; what people understood was up to them, it was a function of whatever cultural currents were prevailing, which is to say that they would basically understand what the critics understood.

'What's happening now?' I said. 'An interview?'

'Yes. In the hotel lounge.'

'Photographer?'

'I'm afraid so.'

'They *always* say the same thing, that taking my picture makes them nervous.'

'That's understandable.'

'But do they have to *say* so? It annoys me. They think nobody's ever said it before.'

Mette shrugged.

'You've nothing after that, though. The rest of the day's free. Maybe that's when you should get Leo his present? There won't be much time otherwise. Unless you leave it until the airport.'

'They won't have anything there. I'd been looking forward to a quiet afternoon, to be honest.'

'Do you want me to find something?'

I looked at her. She smiled half-heartedly. It was tempting. I could just tell her what to buy. But it wouldn't feel right. If I was going to give him a present, it had to be something I'd got him myself.

'No, it's OK, I'll do it. But if you could point me in the right direction, I'd be grateful. Somewhere that's got everything, so I won't have to run around.'

'Let's see. Just a minute.'

She went on her phone and typed something. After a few seconds she turned it towards me so I could see.

FAO Schwarz.

'It's the most well known. On Rockefeller Plaza. They've got everything.'

On my way to the lift after the interview a young man came up to me.

'I love your work, sir,' he said. He made to shake my hand, but I pretended not to notice and pressed the button for the lift, throwing him a quick smile.

'Thank you.'

'Can't wait to see the show.'

I gestured a *what do you want me to say* before stepping into the lift as the doors opened in front of me. That decided it, I told myself as I ascended. I'd drop the shopping trip and spend the afternoon in my room. Or rooms — three of them to be precise, fitted out with the usual items of occasional furniture that no one ever used and which were only to be found in hotels. I threw my jacket over the arm of the narrow, velvety olive-green sofa and went and stood at the window that ran almost from floor to ceiling. It felt like I was standing on a rock ledge, and I pressed the tips of my fingers to the pane to assure my sensory organs that we were in no danger. Manhattan extended before me, a disorderly cityscape with all its different heights. The sky was streaked with greys, lumpy, near-black clouds touched the tops of the tallest skyscrapers. The street lay far below, as if at the bottom of a shaft, the cars moving up and down its length as small and as brightly coloured as M&Ms. I'd tried to describe it all to Leo the day before, but he hadn't been particularly interested. I supposed he found it hard to translate the words into pictures. He knew all about New York, though, and had a book called *Cities of the World* that he often liked to study at bedtime and could also sit and leaf through on his own. I had no idea why it was that he found it so interesting. Kids finding fascination in animals or cars was easy to understand — there was a compelling kind of interplay that arose, they saw a car in the street, a picture of a car in a book, and found satisfaction in the correspondence — the world added up. But Leo liked pictures of things he couldn't see in the real world. Where did that come from? How could he be so spellbound by pictures of Aztec jungle pyramids, a street in Mumbai, St Peter's in Rome, a frozen harbour in northern Norway? What went on inside him then? Was he trying to get a handle on what it was that he saw? To contextualise it in respect of something he knew? Was it because he wanted to go to those places? And if so, why?

He was too young to question his inner workings. No six-year-old boy asks himself why he feels what he feels — he simply does. He didn't possess the tools of self-analysis. And as yet there wasn't that much to analyse. He was very much just a boy, liking the things that boys tend to like. He would run rather than walk, interact with whatever happened to come his way. Happy as the day was long, positive in every circumstance. Easy to lead, easy to form, easy to hold down. There wasn't a sliver of darkness in him. The only vaguely unusual thing was that he could sit still and concentrate on something for hours at a time.

Building with Lego, he disappeared from the world. Where did he go? I imagined a place in which there was nothing, an empty, dark place as wide and as open as the sea at night.

That it was there he went when he played on his own. There, rather on the floor of his room, that his Lego buildings took shape.

I sat down on the edge of the bed and phoned Yelena.

'Hi,' she said, her voice suggesting a smile. 'Are you back at the hotel?'

Leo's voice in the background, sonorous.

'Yes. Are you in the bath, the two of you?'

'He is, yes. Wait a sec, let me dry his hands, then you can talk to him.'

'It's Daddy,' I heard her say. 'Hold out your hands. There we are, that's right.'

'Hello, little fella,' I said. 'Are you having a bath?'

'Yes.'

'Let me guess — you don't want your hair washed?'

'We're leaving it until last,' he said.

'Good idea. What toys have you got in there with you?'

'The ferry.'

'Ah. The big yellow-and-green one?'

'Yes.'

'You're playing with the ferry then, are you?' I said fatuously, it was all that came into my head.

'Pappy?' he said.

'What?'

'Are you still in New York?'

'Yes. But I'll be coming home soon. Three days, then I'll be home.'

'Three days?'

'That's right.'

'On Friday?'

'No, on Saturday. Have you had a good day at school?'

'Yes.'

'What did you do?'

'Nothing. It was rice and chicken today.'

'Wow,' I said. 'Rice *and* chicken?'

'Yes.'

'Leo?'

He didn't answer.

'I miss you. I can't wait to be home again. And do you know what?'

'What?'

'I've got you a present.'

'What is it?'

'I can't tell you that! It's a secret. You'll have to wait until I get back.'

We'd talked for a long time about having a second child. We'd been holding off on it to allow Leo time and space of his own. But if we were going to do anything about it, it would have to be soon — Yelena was forty-one, I was forty-four. It would turn his life completely upside down, of course. Yelena thought it could only ever be a good thing — that it wouldn't be taking anything away from him, but giving him something. Something invaluably precious and for life. She was right about that. My own hesitation was more to do with me than him. I didn't want to share out the feelings I had for him with anyone else. They were for him.

I knew what Yelena would say to that.

'Feelings aren't a limited resource, you know. Your feelings for Leo would be unchanged — and on top of that you'd have new ones for the baby.'

I knew she was right about that as well. But it didn't mean I had to take it into account. So I didn't tell her what I was thinking, and deployed other arguments instead. Like that I was always working, always travelling, and that she, who likewise had a full-time job, would be exhausted looking after two.

The next day, the box had been duly installed on the gallery floor and filled with disposable lighters. The dimensions were spot on, but they'd made it out of new wood, which looked all wrong. Fresh and immaculate planks that should have been grimy and weatherworn. I told Neil and he promised to fix it. He'd have to hurry — the show was opening in less than twenty-four hours.

Apart from that, everything was in place.

To kill time, I walked from the museum back to the hotel. I was thinking of stopping off at the toy store Mette had mentioned, but on the way I happened on a different place altogether and got him something there instead. It was a very small shop, hardly more than a recess, and it sold only one thing — cuddly toys. But there was something unusual about them. These ones appeared to be real quality and seemed somehow to occupy an overlap between toys and real, stuffed animals. I plumped for a wolf — a lot smaller than a real wolf, obviously, and yet there was something genuinely lupine about it. Leo was going to be thrilled. He hadn't yet fully left the infant sphere, there was still a part of him that was four years old and loved a cuddly toy.

The temperature outside dithered a couple of degrees above freezing. The air was raw, the kind of cold that goes to the bone. The traffic was tailed back along the avenue. Exhaust fumes swirled above the asphalt, horns sounded aggressively. I needed to get over to the other side and found a crossing. The light changed to green, I stepped out, and immediately my eyes caught sight of an unmistakable figure moving along the opposite sidewalk. A tall, lanky figure in a long overcoat and trousers that were slightly too short in the leg, a pile of unruly hair.

'Hans!' I shouted, and set into a jog. 'Hans!'

I hadn't seen him since that spring in London more than twenty years earlier.

He didn't hear me. If he did, he didn't react, but strode on purposefully, a white carrier bag in one hand, a cigarette pinched between the first two fingers of the other.

'Hans!' I shouted again. People turned to look at me, but I didn't care about them, for now he was heading down into a subway station. I ran after him, hurtling down the steps. And yet when I reached the low-ceilinged mezzanine I'd lost him. But there was only one way he could have gone, down the escalator — and sure enough, as I stepped onto it I picked him out below. The platforms were clearly far beneath ground level, the plunging escalator steep and long. I hurried down, only to find myself stuck behind a rather corpulent woman in a fur coat, laden with shopping bags in both hands, beside her a girl perhaps ten years old. They ought to have realised they'd be blocking the way of anyone in a hurry to get to the trains, but there they stood.

'Excuse me,' I said.

The woman turned her head.

'I'm sorry,' she said. 'We're almost there.'

I shoved the girl aside and squeezed past. The woman yelled after me as I bounded downwards. Hans had reached the bottom and disappeared from view. With a bit of luck he'd be waiting on the platform, I thought. A train had just pulled away, so the platform was almost deserted, and the long figure I'd been pursuing had sat down on a bench.

He looked up at me and immediately I felt like a fool.

It wasn't Hans. Of course it wasn't. He didn't even look like him. A flaming red face, glassy eyes, cheeks and chin round and ill-defined.

In the hotel room, I poured myself a drink, pulled a chair over to the window and sat down, glass in hand, staring out at the city.

Although I hadn't seen Hans since the eighties — twenty-four years ago, I calculated — I'd occasionally find myself wondering what he might be doing with himself and where he might be living — if indeed he was living at all and wasn't dead. Whenever I had an exhibition opening, I was always a bit nervous in case he turned up. Now that I'd made a name for myself, there was an asymmetry between us — I knew nothing about him, whereas he presumably knew all there was to know about me.

If he was in New York, for example, chances were that he knew all about the exhibition — the banners and ads were everywhere. Wouldn't he be curious? Wouldn't he want to see what his old friend had been doing all these years?

What would he do then? When he saw the occult London installation?

'Ha ha! So, it left an impression on you after all!'

'Aren't you annoyed with me? For borrowing your idea?'

'Why would I be annoyed? I'm flattered!'

Or maybe the opposite:

'I'm going to sue the hell out of you.'

'You inspired me when I was young, I don't mind admitting it. A lot of people inspired me in those days. But any suggestion of plagiarism is ridiculous. I remember exactly where and how I became interested in the occult, and it was long before I ran into you. And because I was going to be living in London I knew just how many of those key figures were connected with the city. The names were there, the places were there, all I had to do was put them together.'

'I've got photographs of my installation from back then.'

'But if I came up with it first, that means you copied me. I didn't *build* it in London, but I did make the drawings then. Maybe I showed them to you? I must have done.'

There was no danger. I was perfectly safe. He couldn't touch me.

He was a nobody. I was Kristian Pedersen.

The lights in the skyscrapers became more and more conspicuous as dusk fell. I hated this bloody city.

I drained my glass and put it down on one of the idiotically spindly tables. I checked my phone for messages. It was basically only Yelena, Mette and a couple of gallerists who had my private number. Separating things that way meant no surprises, but also no need to spend my time and energy replying to people all the time.

Mette had texted.

FT wants a Lunch With . . . interview. If yes, it'll have to be tomorrow. Can you be bothered?

No, I texted back.

Noted, she replied.

To hell with them, I typed.

My plans for the evening extended only to eating alone in my room and going to bed early in order to feel up for it the next day. Although there was nothing special I had to do — the exhibition was set up and the interviews had already been done — openings were always an exhausting affair. In large part, this was down to the pressure that lay in showing one's work to the public, but it was also all the people one had to deflect, the faces who would come up to shake one's hand and congratulate. But after my apparational encounter-that-wasn't with Hans, I found I couldn't sleep. The three or four drinks I ended up having didn't help in the slightest. Instead, I lay awake on the bed long into the night, still in my clothes, reading the online editions of every newspaper whose name I could remember — Norwegian, Swedish, Danish, British and American — even the *Ringsaker Blad*, the local rag from back home in Norway.

Apart from Vivian, who I'd met twice after Hans's disappearance and whose work I occasionally read about in the papers, I hadn't come across any of his friends — neither the Egyptian nor Daniella, nor the other guy whose name I'd forgotten but whose face I still remembered.

It wasn't that surprising — London was a very big place. And yet for a period it felt like I couldn't escape them. It was as if I'd been drawn into a force field: a concentrated space in which active energies collide and combine. It's possible to view society, as I had done for some time, as a myriad of such fields, from the major news broadcasters and educational systems down to the smallest private networks, where information, a form of energy in itself, is exchanged. How much of that information is transmitted to you depends on where you're placed within the system. Let's say you move to a new town — to Tønsberg, for example, if it's Norway — and become integrated there. Before long, in addition to what continuously streams through the national and international channels, a flow of information about local matters will come your way. But you might also come upon someone talking about Rilke, because in every town and village there's always someone who reads Rilke, and in that way, by means of what to the vast majority of people will remain an entirely uninteresting circuit that nevertheless takes in entire societies, eras and generations, the poet's thoughts and the images they give rise to live on. A head lights up, the images have been received, the head begins to talk or write about them, and what it says will be received by another head, which either lights up too or else remains unmoved — in which case the circuit becomes blocked, though not necessarily for good, for in other towns others will perhaps be reading Rilke too.

And only silent death, the wise one, knows what we really are
And what he can get from us in return for what he has lent us.

So he wrote in his *Sonnets to Orpheus*. Rilke's poems, like anyone's poems, are themselves a force field in which energies collide and combine. They were written in order that they might be activated and propel Orpheus onwards through blind circuits leading too from the dead to the living. *Is he bound to a place?* Rilke asks. *No, his ample nature arises from the realms of both life and death.* Thus the entry of Orpheus into Tønsberg, borne by the letters of the alphabet, which is to say a code. I came to Orpheus by another path. I went to London, and there met Hans. Within his sphere I was exposed to names. Christopher Marlowe, Doctor Faustus, the historical Faust, Agrippa and Bruno, Swedenborg and Crowley, Becker, and, by way of him, Orpheus, Parmenides and Pythagoras. Apart perhaps from the speed skaters he talked about the very first time we met, he mentioned no other names. The striking thing about them was that they all led to the same place. It didn't occur to me at the time, because I couldn't yet see my life from the outside. How could I have done? I was in the midst of it. But gradually time extracted me and I was able to see just how striking it was. And no less so than when Hans disappeared.

An epiphany stood out to me. It came in the shower in the house where I rented my bedsit, where it occurred to me that the world was solid, that it was physical. The world was floor tiles, walls, a clod of hair, a metal shower mixer. The abstract didn't actually exist, but was something we stumbled into. It was a way of looking at things, unconnected with what we observed. Hans was a manipulator, he'd got me looking at things in a certain way and was so clever about it that for a brief time I'd thought that the photographs he'd left behind actually stemmed from the late sixteenth century. But he was a manipulator. He made machines appear to come to life. He incorporated technology into biology. And messed around with the fabric of time.

It meant nothing, of course. It was no more than what it was: I met a man who was into the occult and then he disappeared.

That I thought I saw him twenty-four years later on a New York City sidewalk meant only that he was more alive in my subconscious than I'd realised.

The next day I found myself looking out for him nevertheless. Stepping from the lift into the hotel lobby in the morning I was prepared to see Hans sitting on one of the sofas, and when I got out of the car outside the museum a few hours later I was half expecting to see him there among the autistic autograph hunters or lurking a bit further back against the wall behind them. I couldn't shake off the feeling it had sparked in me, to glimpse that ubiquitous carrier bag, the cheap clothes, the mad, unruly mess of hair — it kept returning to me in every situation of the day.

I knew he wouldn't be at the vernissage — it was invitation only — but even then my eyes kept scanning. As if I wasn't tense enough as it was. I always disliked those occasions more than almost anything else. Seeing other people wandering around looking at my work was torturous. How little time they gave to every picture, the casual manner in which they chatted about other things, craning their necks when a celebrity walked in, if they weren't pretending not to care. The hum of voices, the laughter. The wine and champagne that freely flowed, the hideous old faces crimsoning more with every glass. The pretence. And of course the back-slapping. Everyone who felt compelled to come up and say how awesome it all was. The chumminess of people I didn't know was bad enough on its own — how little they understood was even worse.

Like an idiot I stood there in the middle of the first exhibition room and received their congratulations. When after a couple of hours the onslaught of glistening faces eventually began to subside, it was out to the car and downtown for dinner. The entourage that now required feeding was large and around twenty-five people were already seated by the time I arrived, familiar faces mostly, some from way back. Frank, for instance, who had designed most of my books, wild and uproarious in the nineties, now suddenly aged, the energy gone from him, hair greyed, a stooping posture, the leanness that once had given him a lithe, limber air now only making him look as if he'd been hollowed out, enlarging his every feature, so that his nose seemed longer, his eyes sat deeper in their sockets, his cheekbones became even more pronounced. Fifty's nothing, he'd once said to me, but sixty is hell. He was so pedantic that a lot of people found him impossible to work with, the degree of exactness he strove for bordered on the compulsive, but had always suited me, for I had it in me too, even though the power in my work came from abandon not constraint. Frank didn't have that, which was why he wasn't an artist himself. Outside his work, however, his life was full of abandon. A number of my former gallerists were there too — Louis from Rome, Evelyn from London, Björn from Berlin. The team from Alfred Burnett — led by Stephen, the son of the firm's founder, an incompetent whose status resided only in his name — who tonight included a Norwegian woman who worked for them. This clearly was intended as a gesture on their part, though completely misguided — Norway and things Norwegian meant less than nothing to me. Both curators were present too, naturally, with a small delegation from the museum, as well as a few people from the publishing world, the Norwegian ambassador, and the cultural attaché, or whatever was the correct title.

They stood up and applauded as I entered the room. I gave a slight bow and raised a hand to put a stop to it.

'Bravo!' Jacob said.

'Thank you,' I said, and sat down at the head of the table. I'd asked Mette to make sure Frank would be seated on one side of me and she on the other. They were the only people on the guest list I could talk to without feeling like I was at work.

Stephen stood up and said a few words. There was nothing wrong with what he said as such, he just didn't have enough clout. He could say anything at all in any given situation and it would be inconsequential, none of it would stick. It was as if his words weren't lived, as if there was no one behind them. He was the same age as me, slim and fit-looking, with a head that was slightly too big and the kind of puppy-ish face that can come from a life of enormous privilege. His eyes could have belonged to a nineteen-year-old.

'Kristian Pedersen,' he said in conclusion. 'Provocateur, innovator, portraitist of death. How fortunate we are to have you among us.'

There was a small ripple of applause. I gave him a smile and moved my lips in a voiceless *thank you*.

'Aren't you going to say anything?' said Frank.

'Not if I can help it. But you're welcome to say a few words, if you want.'

'Very funny.'

'I've got an interview onstage tomorrow, that'll have to do.'

Twenty years my senior, with all his vast wealth of experience, Frank had been a kind of mentor for me in the early years. He was an alcoholic even then, hands trembling in the mornings until he poured the first beer down his throat and miraculously they stilled. I'd never seen anything like it before. But I learned more in two weeks working with him than I'd learned in my two years at art school. It was Frank who put together *The Last Day*. I'd come to him with what I thought was a print-ready book. He tore it up and started from scratch, asked for more photographs, put it all together again. Made it thirty, forty per cent better. He never explained anything to me — it was from watching him work that I learned from him.

His visual appetite was enormous, though it restricted itself to pictures. He didn't care about trees or people, but was insatiable about pictures of trees, pictures of people. 'Look at these asparagus!' I remembered him saying once, holding up a book to show me a painting of Manet's. 'Aren't they amazing? Unbelievable, don't you think? *No one paints asparagus like Manet!*'

'Does anyone but Manet even try?' I'd replied, so pleased with the quip that it made me smile now, so many years on.

Indeed, it wasn't me but Manet that had brought him to New York this time. He would never have flown over just to see something I'd done, not even if all his expenses had been paid. But there happened to be a major Manet exhibition on in town too, so I talked him into it. We hadn't worked together in a long time. If he'd been offended in any way by that, he certainly hadn't let on. But for my new series I couldn't think of anyone I wanted to work with more.

It was Frank who had introduced me to the work of Eugène Atget. In his opinion, Atget's photographs had never been surpassed. Atget wasn't an art photographer, a reportage photographer, or a portrait photographer, but took on assignments from painters and photographed their subjects for subsequent use in the painting process. His work, in other words, could be classified as applied photography — he didn't put his soul into his pictures, nor did he try to capture the soul of what he was photographing. He just took pictures. Pictures without ambition, without will, without searching, without longing.

Atget's work had been with me ever since, though as a reference, not an ideal. But it was only when I came to Pessoa's Caeiro poems that it fell into place for me. Frank more than anyone would understand where I wanted to go. And his pedantic rigour was exactly what a project of the kind I was envisaging required.

But the time was not yet ripe. I'd prepared the ground — Frank's beloved asparagus were on me, so I could assume he felt a certain amount of gratitude. And he'd seen my trees too.

A waiter came silently up from behind and poured more red wine into my glass. Skipping Frank's, which was still full, he moved on, to the Norwegian woman from the gallery. Her every other sentence so far, I seemed to have overheard, had started with 'In Norway we . . .', and she was impressing no one. But she had a nice figure and a pleasant, bountiful face, and seemed to possess a zest for life that more than compensated for her stupid small talk, I thought as I sipped my wine.

'Have you given up drinking?' I said to Frank, with a nod towards his glass.

'I drank before I came.'

Across the table from him, Mette sat with her knife and fork in a narrow V above her plate while with her eyes on the table and her head slightly tilted she listened to Stephen's prattle. Two places along, Jacob caught my gaze and gave me a fatherly wink.

He was their best man, so if I stopped working with him, I'd have to stop working with the gallery.

It would shake things up. New people, new ideas, new friction.

In which case this was a farewell dinner. It was a good thought.

I lifted my glass towards him and smiled. He smiled back and lifted his.

'Well done,' I heard him say.

Her name was Sonja, it transpired, and she came to the hotel lobby a few hours later. I wasn't sure if she'd cottoned on — I'd only mentioned where I was staying and that I'd probably have a beer in the bar there when I got back — but there she was, with her little crossbody bag, cautious eyes in a glowing face.

'What'll you have?' I said.

'A negroni, I think.'

I signalled to the bartender, who came over while still drying a cocktail shaker with a white tea towel and looked at me lifelessly.

'A negroni and a gin and tonic, please,' I said.

Mette had gone up to her room and there was little chance of her coming back down. I wasn't anonymous, but neither was I so well known that it would get out.

'Are you pleased with the exhibition?' she said. 'Has it turned out the way you wanted?'

'You sound like a journalist.'

'Sorry! Just wondering.'

'What do *you* think of it? If you're honest and ignore the fact that it's your job to flatter me.'

'I think it's amazing, absolutely incredible. It's as if everything you've done so far just comes together in the bigger picture.'

The drinks came and we chinked our glasses together. I enquired a bit about her life, to make her feel I was interested in who she was. No mysteries there. The only unusual thing was that she was half American — her father was from Minneapolis, though he'd been absent when she was growing up with her mother and two brothers in Skien; she'd studied political science in Oslo for a year, before switching to art history and graduating with an MA from Cambridge.

Her eyes became more adventurous, she held my gaze more than once, and when we went up to my room she kicked off her shoes and stepped up close, her head thrown back, her face laid bare now that she'd dropped her guard.

I kissed her and led her over to the bed. She was warm and soft and willing, closed her eyes and opened her mouth as I entered her. Her lips fell back to expose her teeth, and to my dismay her face seemed then to change, as if mutating into another form. And no sooner had it assumed this new form than it mutated again into another. I found it deeply unsettling. The room was dark, only the light from outside shone on us faintly. She tossed her head to one side, tensed and arced her body underneath me, moaning. I understood that it was somehow in me that these transformations were happening, that I couldn't keep hold of what I was seeing, and I looked away.

Afterwards she snuggled up to me and wanted to remain there. I studied her, everything was as before, her face the same as it had been during the dinner and in the hotel bar. What I'd seen had of course only been in my mind.

I didn't want her lying there like that, as if she was my girlfriend. What made her think it was OK?

I got up and went to the bathroom, where I turned the shower on in the dark. When I came back into the room with a towel wrapped around my waist, she'd propped herself up with pillows and sat looking at me.

'Have you washed me away?' she said.

'I've showered, yes,' I said. I wanted to put on some clean underwear, but not with her watching.

'Do you want me to go?'

'That would probably be a good idea.'

'What if I refuse?'

I looked at her. She was smiling, but was she joking?

I hoped she wasn't a lunatic.

'Why would you do that?' I said.

'Are you going to shove me out into the corridor and throw my clothes after me?'

I gave her my most astonished look.

'Because I'm not leaving,' she said.

'I see,' I said. 'And why not?'

'I'm not expendable.'

'I never thought you were. It's more of a practical issue. I've an event to do tomorrow and a breakfast appointment with my head of studio.'

'I'll go before then.'

'OK.'

Why she insisted on staying when it was so obvious I didn't want her to was beyond me. But I couldn't run the risk of throwing her out now. For all I knew, she could start kicking up a fuss, screaming and shouting.

I bent over my suitcase and unzipped it with one hand, the other clutching my towel, took out a pair of underpants and a T-shirt and went to the bathroom again. *I'll go before then*, she'd said, which indicated a measure of reason, at least. Provided, of course, she could be trusted.

She lifted the duvet and made room for me in the bed when I came back, as if it was the two of us now and no one else, and snuggled up again with her hand on my chest.

'How fine you are,' she said, propping her head in her hand and gazing at me. 'Have you any brothers or sisters? Or are you an only child? No, let me guess – you're an only child.'

'Two sisters.'

'Oh yes, now I remember. One of them died, didn't she?'

I fixed my eyes on her without replying. Her face was firm now, and she gave a faint smile.

'I read it on Wikipedia,' she said. 'You don't have to talk about it, if you don't want to.'

Who did she think she was?

I contained my sudden anger and lay unmoving, staring up at the ceiling.

She ran her fingers through my hair, then leaned forward and kissed the pit of my neck.

'You want to sleep. It's OK. Goodnight.'

'Goodnight,' I said, and turned onto my side and closed my eyes. She cuddled up, her arm across my chest.

I was woken by the sound of a phone ringing and sat up in confusion before reality slotted back into place. She was still lying next to me in the bed. The sound was coming from the floor, from the inside pocket of my suit jacket that was dumped in a crumpled heap.

It was Yelena. I let it ring.

Behind me, Sonja stirred.

'Would that be your wife, by any chance?' she said with a yawn, stretching an arm vertically into the air while holding the duvet in place with her other hand.

I said nothing. A text chimed in.

Why aren't you answering?

No need to panic.

I was asleep. Late night last night.

'I've got that breakfast meeting now,' I said. 'After that I'll be checking out, then straight to the airport after my event. You can stay here, if you want, but any longer than twelve and you'll have to pay for the room yourself, I'm afraid.'

She smiled sarcastically, sitting up now.

'I'll go,' she said. 'Don't worry.'

The fear I'd felt the night before, that she'd turn out to be unstable and try to drag me into her destructive vortex, had let go of me. She'd probably been a bit drunk, that was all. But she was still annoying.

I took a pair of jeans and a shirt and went to the bathroom. Normally, I liked to spend time figuring out what to wear for an event, but with her in the room it was out of the question.

She was sitting on the edge of the bed fastening her bra when I came back in.

'I'll be in the audience later,' she said. 'So I'll see you then.'

'Fine.'

She stood up and stepped into her skirt, pulled on her top and then gathered her hair in both hands behind her neck, untangling it as she gave a shake or two of her head.

'Right. You can be rid of me now.'

I knew I ought to say something to the effect that I didn't want her to go, offer a compliment, but I was afraid she'd believe me, so I said nothing and instead showed her to the door. She looked up at me there. It was an unfriendly look.

'Thanks for a nice time,' I said, and leaned forward to give her a kiss, but she turned her head away, opened the door and stepped out without a word. I closed it behind her, found my phone and called Yelena as I went over to the window and looked out over the city, grey and dull in the rain.

'What's happening over there?' she said. 'What have you been doing?'

'Nothing, nothing at all. It all went on until late last night, so I've only just woken up.'

'You could have phoned after the vernissage. Texted, at least.'

'Yes, I should have. It was all so hectic, I hardly had a minute. You know what these things are like. So many people. And all wanting to talk to me.'

Suddenly, someone was hammering on the door.

'Kristian!' Sonja shouted. 'Kristian!'

'What's going on?' Yelena said. 'Who's that shouting?'

I darted towards the bathroom.

'I've no idea,' I said. 'There's been a hell of a lot of noise all night. Kids partying, or something.'

I closed the bathroom door behind me. She was quiet at the other end.

'How are you two getting on, anyway?' I said. 'Is Leo there with you?'

'He's at Luke's birthday party.'

'Ah yes, I forgot. Was he excited?'

'Yes, he was.'

'What's wrong?'

'What do you mean, what's wrong?'

'You seem a bit stand-offish. A bit hostile.'

She didn't answer.

'Anyway,' I said, 'I've got to have breakfast with Mette now before we get off to the event.'

'All right.'

'Aren't you going to ask how it went yesterday?'

'Why did you go into the bathroom?'

'I didn't. What are you talking about?'

A text message came in.

'Someone was banging on the door shouting your name and you went into the bathroom. Do you think I'm stupid? The acoustics are completely different.'

I sighed.

'I'm not in the bathroom, I'm standing at the window looking out over New York. I don't know what you mean about the acoustics. Maybe it's the phone.'

She said nothing. She couldn't prove anything, not without firm evidence, all she had was a vague sense of altered acoustics. She wouldn't get far with that.

'Will you phone Leo this evening?' she said eventually.

'If I can, I will. I'll try. What time will he be back?'

'I'm fetching him in half an hour.'

'OK. But I'll see you tomorrow, anyway.'

The text was from Sonja, I saw after I hung up.

Why won't you open the door? My watch is on the bedside table. Waiting now in reception.

Who'd given her my number? Not the gallery, surely? Were they really that bungling? If they were, this was reason enough on its own to leave them.

Now I remembered.

I'd given it to her myself.

I must have been drunker than I'd thought.

I couldn't allow her to have my number, that was for sure. I'd have to get a new one as soon as I got home.

Her watch was on the table like she said. I took it with me downstairs and found her sitting on a sofa in the lobby, legs crossed, jiggling her free foot while speaking to someone opposite who was facing away from me, but I could see who it was straight away. It was Mette.

'Hi, Mette,' I said. 'What a good night it was last night. Are you on your way out?'

She nodded, fingering the umbrella she held in her hand.

'I thought I'd buy a couple of presents before we have to go.'

'Sounds like a good idea,' I said, and turned then to Sonja, took the watch from my pocket and handed it to her.

'Here it is.'

'Thanks,' she said, and put it on. 'And thanks for a lovely night!'

She stood up with a smile on her face. I smiled back.

'Which way are you going?' she said to Mette.

'Downtown,' Mette said.

'Me too,' Sonja said.

She fixed her gaze on me.

'No breakfast meeting?' she said.

I glanced at Mette.

'Shall we meet back here at two?' I said.

Mette nodded, and she and Sonja went down the steps and out through the door. I watched her put her umbrella up and offer to share it before I turned and took the lift up to my room again. I lay down on the bed and began reading the reviews. They were brilliant, without exception.

*

Entering the green room I saw that my interviewer was there already. Gordon Grenham had his mouth full of peanuts and on seeing me hurriedly tried to wash them down with a swig of mineral water straight from the bottle. He stood up and put out his hand. In his late forties, short in stature, he wore round glasses, his curly hair rather cropped. A film of perspiration glistened on his brow.

'Honoured,' he said.

'Nice to meet you,' I said as I sat down. He said hello to Mette, who took a seat opposite us at the other side of the low table. The stage manager, who'd collected us outside, hung back over by the wall. She was almost as tall as me, with impure skin and a steely gaze.

'Just waiting for Amy now, then,' Gordon said.

'She's on her way,' the stage manager said. 'She'll be here in a couple of minutes.'

A monitor in the corner showed the house. It wasn't even half full yet, but people were filtering in all the time and finding their seats, edging along the rows.

'A sellout in four minutes, so I'm told,' said Gordon.

I smiled.

He was in a dark suit with a white shirt underneath. The perfect contrast to my own informal attire. It meant I was free, I could say and do whatever I wanted, whereas he was bound by convention, the institution and all attendant expectations.

He picked up a small stack of cue cards from the table in front of him.

'I thought I'd start off with the exhibition, obviously, and from there go wherever it takes us basically.'

'I'd rather not know what you're going to ask me. It'll be better that way. More authentic.'

'Sounds good to me. Is there anything you *don't* want to be asked?'

'No. Just do your thing.'

'Good!'

He put his cue cards back down on the table and rubbed his hands together.

'I'm looking forward to this,' he said.

'Do you want a coffee, Kristian?' Mette said.

I nodded and she poured me a cup from the vacuum jug in front of us. A woman, she too late forties, came in through the door. Blonde hair and a face like a horse, in blue jeans and knee-high suede boots.

'Amazing to meet you!' she said. 'I'm Amy.'

'Nice to meet you, Amy,' I said.

She held my gaze a moment while smiling, as if at long last she'd found a peer among deadbeats. Or as if she wanted to fuck me.

A technician appeared with two headsets.

'I use the onstage mic, right?' Amy said. 'The one on the lectern?'

'Right,' said the technician and gave me a wink. I stood up, lowered my head slightly so he could put the headset on me, and dropped the transmitter into my inside pocket. The monitor showed a full house. Twelve hundred capacity, I'd been told.

'Have I got time to go to the bathroom?' I said.

'Sure, we won't start without you!' Gordon said with a laugh.

The stage manager showed me out into the corridor and pointed to a red door at the far end. I forced a few dribbles into the toilet bowl and stood washing my hands for some time while staring at myself in the mirror. At first I saw me, but then, as always happened when I stared at my mirror image for long enough, my face slowly morphed into another. A handsome chap, with short dark hair, a chinful of stubble and regular features. Nothing that stole attention from anything else, only perhaps the eyes, the intense gaze. He leaned forward, propping himself on his hands that were planted flat against the sink unit, in order to scrutinise me, then stepped back without releasing me from his gaze. If he looked away when I did, I would never know.

I turned off the tap and held my hands under the dryer. It kicked in with its apocalyptic racket, which always frightened the life out of Leo and for a time made him blankly refuse to visit any public covenience.

I turned round and cast a final glance at the mirror man, who now like me was standing in the doorway. Where did he go when I went out? Perhaps there were rooms and corridors, houses and streets in his world too?

'Ah, there we are,' Gordon said when I returned. 'Ready to go?'

'I'm ready,' I said. I followed him and Amy and a couple of other people through a labyrinth of corridors and passages until we arrived behind the stage, where another technician sat at a mixing desk, a monitor showing the empty stage. It was strange to see Amy go up the steps in the room in which I stood and then appear on the screen, as if she'd crossed the threshold into another dimension. Strange too that the applause that ensued came not from the monitor, but from the adjoining space.

'The man we're about to meet needs no introduction,' Amy said. 'That's something of a cliché, but once in a while it happens to be true. His art has drawn attention and admiration wherever it has been shown. Some of his works are iconic. Some are controversial. And some are just damned good.'

Laughter rippled.

'It is no exaggeration to say that his pictures have become a part of our collective visual consciousness. I am of course talking about Kristian Pedersen, whose major retrospective exhibition has just opened at MoMA. Pedersen was born in Norway in 1965, but has lived and worked in London for more than twenty years. His work has been put on show almost everywhere — let me name as examples the Guggenheim Museum Bilbao, the Tel Aviv Museum of Art, the Royal Academy of Art in London, the Sezon Museum of Art in Tokyo, as well as the New Musuem here in New York City. Throughout his career, Pedersen has relentlessly explored the medium of photography, pushing back its boundaries, and often transcending them. His pictures question our ways of seeing. More importantly, perhaps, they question the ways in which photography mediates between the world and our perceptions — and the ways in which it affects us all. In our hypervisual, hypercapitalist societies, these are indeed compelling themes. Another major theme in Pedersen's work is death. Or more precisely, our perceptions of death. I vividly remember the first time I saw the exhibition *The Dead*. Not just the pictures themselves, but the emotions they stirred. Rarely has an exhibition made such an impression on me. I was shaken to the core of my soul. You've all seen those pictures. They're as simple as can be: a woman or a man sitting at a table in a room somewhere. All are dead, and yet they're sitting there in their clothes as if they were alive. It was inflammatory, it was unethical, but it was also completely unique.

'It's therefore a great pleasure for me to be able to welcome the man behind those photographs. Kristian Pedersen will be interviewed by Gordon Grenham, art critic and author among other books of *Echo and Narcissus* and *Time and its Counterpart*. Ladies and gentlemen, please welcome Kristian Pedersen!'

Applause rang out as I entered the stage. I took Amy's hand in acknowledgement, bowed to the audience a couple of times and then sat down on the chair that stood ready and waiting behind me as Gordon shuffled his cue cards.

I folded my arms across my chest so he wouldn't think he was in for an easy ride, and crossed my legs.

'Kristian, great to have you here,' he said. 'First of all, congratulations on the new show!'

'Thank you.'

'So why don't we start there? What does it mean to you to put your work on show?'

'In what way?'

'Well, there are artists who make art for their own sakes and who would be producing pictures even if nobody ever saw them. And then there are artists who want to be seen. How important is it to you to be seen? To have your pictures seen by an audience?'

'I don't believe any artist wants to make art nobody sees.'

'You don't?'

'Absolutely not. They may say so, but it wouldn't be true.'

'You seem pretty certain about that.'

'That's because I am. But it's not necessarily about being *seen* in the sense of being validated, even if for many artists that can be a driving force. Art basically is about communication. Every work of art is an expression of something. But in order for the work to actually convey anything at all, in order for it to actually *exist*, then clearly it has to be seen. So, no work of art in fact exists until it's seen. Without an audience, it remains meaningless.'

'Does that imply that for a work of art to become meaningful it needs only to be seen by one person?'

'It certainly does, yes. But the more the merrier, of course.'

'The more popular a work of art, the better it becomes?'

'No, no. It's got nothing to do with quality. But if you think of a work, any work at all . . . I don't know, you choose . . .'

'OK, how about *The Scream* by Edvard Munch? Just to keep things between compatriots.'

There were some chuckles.

'Good example.'

'Yes, I think it's safe to say that's a work that's been seen by quite a few people.'

Laughter.

'It is, yes. But there was a time when nobody had seen it. There was a time when it simply didn't exist in the world. And then one day Munch decided to paint something. Perhaps he even had a clear idea of what it could be. Perhaps he had a certain feeling. Or most certainly he did. He felt anxiety and he wanted to paint it. But when he painted it, it wasn't like the painting became the idea. The painting became something of its own, something in its own right, something external to him. An object. This object was an expression of something. But as long as the object wasn't seen by anyone it *expressed* nothing, conveyed nothing. It was only when someone looked at it that it came to life. And only then did it become art. Before that it was just an object, like a teacup or an umbrella. The significant thing about a work of art is that it's untranslatable. The meaning of any work of art is bound to the work in question. To tap into the meaning, you have to see the work. I hope I'm making it plain — that since a work of art releases meaning only insofar as it is beheld, and hinges thereby entirely on every single person who looks at it, its meaning lives *only* in the beholder. And because people are different, then obviously the work of art will be different in every case. Which is why I said the more the merrier — the work is enriched by every new beholder.'

'Your own pictures are then rich indeed.'

Laughter.

'Kristian, this exhibition spans your whole career so far. It's also been put up chronologically, so that we begin with your first pictures and end with the most recent. How do you relate today to those first photographs, the ones you took when you were in your twenties?'

'We still get on quite well together.'

Laughter.

'The first picture many people connect with you is the dead cat. It's an image that has become nothing short of iconic. What was the genesis of that picture? Can you share something about that?'

'I can, yes. It's rather a long time ago now, but I remember it very well indeed. I think probably in the life of every artist there comes a moment when what you're doing is suddenly on another level. I was just reading about Pessoa —'

'The Portuguese poet?'

'Fernando Pessoa, exactly. He puts an exact date on the day he first wrote a poem as Caeiro — one of his heteronyms. I think he even says somewhere that it was the greatest day of his life. It came quite unexpectedly: all of a sudden there was something completely new on the page. Now, I felt something similar to that when I took the photograph. It was just so much better than everything I'd done up until that point.'

'In what way?'

'I don't know,' I said with a shrug.

Laughter.

'That's interesting,' Gordon said. 'That something so good can just appear out of nowhere like that. If you were to reflect a little, what do you think quality actually is? A lot of us here today take pictures, I'm sure, but not so many of us are familiar with what it is you're describing, about suddenly finding yourself on another level.'

The laughter rang out. How little it took to coax it out at events like these. Things that wouldn't arouse a smile in private made an audience burst out laughing. But it was good, I became a Midas, and everything I said turned to gold.

'Let me put it this way: I know quality when I see it, but I don't know where it comes from. It's something to do with the expressive power of a work, wouldn't you say? That there's something there that we find compelling in some way. Something that speaks to us personally.'

'How does a dead cat speak to us?'

Laughter.

'But that's just the point. You can't rationalise it, you can't think it. I had no idea myself what I was doing.'

'But something happened anyway.'

'Something happened, yes. But I was trying out all sorts of things at the time.'

'OK, so getting the idea is one thing. Another thing is, how did you get hold of the cat?'

'You're asking me how I got hold of the cat?'

'Yes, let's stay with that picture, and let's try to be as specific as possible. So, first: how did you get the idea? And then, what happened from there?'

'OK. I moved to London when I was twenty to go to art school and study photography. I would cycle all over the place taking pictures of whatever I found interesting. So one day in winter I was photographing trees. Bare, leafless trees, you know? That gave me an idea about taking pictures of skeletons. Frameworks. Structures that hold things together. So I was thinking, fishbones, animal skeletons like in the museums — but not just organic material, I was interested in scaffolding as well, for example, like in front of buildings.'

'And that gave you the idea of photographing a dead cat?'

'Yes.'

'How did you lay hands on it?'

'You're not letting go of this, are you?'

Laughter.

'Well, I'll tell you about that cat. I stole it.'

'You stole the cat?'

'Yes. I mean, it was dead and everything . . .'

Laughter.

'I cycled over to a veterinary clinic near where I was living, thinking they were bound to have a bin somewhere full of dead animals.'

As soon as the words left my mouth, it was as if the mood of the audience changed. Now they weren't sure.

'You know, before they're incinerated. I mean, they were dead, no one owned them any more, so I figured I could just take one. Hey, I was twenty years old. Reckless and stupid. Anyway, I got rumbled and they came after me. I had to run for it with the cat in my backpack. I remember jumping on my bike with this angry vet on my heels.'

Laughter.

Thank goodness.

'And then what?'

'Then I boiled it, at home in my flat. But you know, it was dead and it was going to be incinerated anyway. So it wasn't actually this huge transgressive thing.'

'And then you took pictures.'

'Yes. Not very many, as a matter of fact. But when I developed the film I could see right away that there was something about it. Others saw it too. At that time I was actually held in poor regard at the school because I just wasn't very good.'

Laughter.

'I think everyone was as astounded as I was myself.'

'When you look at that picture today, what is it that you see? Why do you think that particular photograph was the one that gave you your breakthrough?'

'I see what's left of a dead cat.'

Chuckles.

'And I see how amazing it is. That life could produce something like that, something as magnificent as that framework of bones. Something as beautiful and at the same time as functional. How is it possible that something like that comes into being? So what I see is the mystery. And that it's physical. That's probably the most important thing. The mystery is flesh and blood and bone. And I see too how death claims it as its own and destroys it. So yes: life's unfathomable beauty and brutality.'

The more gullible audience members clapped. Gordon smiled.

'So, although you stole the cat, which of course is a crime, this is a picture that has never been seen as controversial. But we can't talk to you without also talking about controversy. Going back to your series depicting homeless people, when that came out there was a lot of discussion about whether you — or I should say, your pictures — were according those people dignity or the opposite — taking away their dignity and exploiting them. Likewise with your photographs of dead people, which Amy mentioned in her introduction — when they were put on show all hell broke out, if you'll pardon the expression. Are you drawn towards the controversial, would you say? And if so, why?'

'You mean, do I enjoy getting people's backs up just for the sake of it? You don't really expect me to say yes to that, do you?'

'But you photographed dead bodies as if they were living people. You must have known all along that was going to be inflammatory?'

'Indeed, yes.'

'So why did you do it?'

I paused a moment to think. Sometimes a straight and honest answer was liberating. An audience would often not be expecting it in a stream of overinflated art talk. But it didn't always work. Could I say that I would cut off my right hand in order to produce a significant work of art? That art was more important than any moral consideration? Could I say that I was willing to tramp on the dead if only it would lead to good art — just to beat him to the draw, in anticipation that he was getting ready to use such a tawdry image?

'It was said at the time that I was tramping on the dead for the sake of those pictures. Firstly, that's a rather tasteless metaphor. And secondly, it shows scant understanding of the artistic process.'

'Explain that process to us. What was your point of departure there? What were your thoughts?'

'Well, the first thing to say is that I never do anything in order to get a *reaction*. What I do, I do in order to explore something. To discover something.'

'So you do it for your own sake?'

'You want me to contradict myself? No, it's not *me* that does the exploring, it's the *picture*. The picture has its own life, over which I have no control.'

'But you could have photographed anything at all. And yet you chose dead people. Human corpses.'

'Yes. What fascinated me was that something always stays behind after a person dies. The soul departs, but the body does not. The body is still here. If not forever, then at least for a long time after death has occurred. But what is it that disappears? What disappears is what we cannot see. And it is what we cannot see that makes us human. So those photographs are actually photographs of *that*. If you follow my drift?'

'Photographs of what makes us human, you mean?'

'Yes, exactly. It's not there, and that's when we see it. If I'd photographed living people in those poses, we wouldn't have seen anything, because then it's in plain sight. But as soon as it's not there, we see it.'

He nodded. The audience were quiet, as audiences are when someone on a stage says something they think to be weighty and consequential.

'But those pictures are also a meditation on photography as form,' I went on. 'A photograph has no soul either, it's just dead matter. The soul is in the moment the picture's taken, but it doesn't exist in the photograph. So in a way we might consider that the photograph is the moment's dead body.'

'How many people would you guess thought all this when they saw those pictures for the first time?'

A scattering of laughter.

A faint warmth flushed through me. I picked up the glass in front of me and drank some water, fixing Gordon with a smile as I put it down again, to show him I was in control and knew what I was doing. But what I'd said had been too lofty, too abstract.

I needed to reel in again. Say something more concrete.

'Probably none,' I said. 'That's just the way it is, and so be it. A picture evokes feelings. Reflection comes later. But the feeling is more important than the reflection. Always.'

'Is it the same for you as the artist? That you first feel something and then reflect afterwards, when the picture is done?'

'Yes.'

'What about your other controversial series, the one with the homeless people in London? Presumably, you didn't just feel like taking pictures of them, there was a clear thought behind it, right?'

'Yes. But still I'd call it a concrete feeling, rather than a thought. Those pictures are of course to a large extent a piece of social criticism. But that wasn't what motivated them. It was more personal than that. You know, when I started taking pictures seriously I moved to London and went to art school there. And as I said earlier, I would cycle around photographing all sorts of different things. Anyway, one night I got myself into an altercation with a homeless person. It wasn't my fault. He bummed a cigarette off me and wouldn't give me my lighter back.

And when I tried to take it from him he resisted. He hit his head against a stone wall and was gone, you know.'

'What do you mean? What happened?'

'Well, he died. It wasn't my fault. He resisted when he should have given me the lighter back. There wasn't much force behind it, so I can only assume he was already in poor health. But still, after that I started *seeing* those destitutes. From being anonymous lives I never really noticed, they became individuals. And *that* was what I was trying to show with those pictures.'

'Wait a minute, what is it you're actually saying here?'

Gordon was staring at me in disbelief. A murmur went up among the audience.

I'd completely miscalculated.

'How do you mean?' I said to win time.

'Are you saying that you actually killed a homeless person? Tell me I'm misunderstanding something here, Kristian.'

'No, no, no, no, no, that's not what I'm saying *at all*,' I said with a laugh. 'You've got the wrong end of the stick. I *did* get into an altercation with a homeless man. But that wasn't what killed him, of course not. I looked him up, much later, and found out *then* that he was dead. He'd lived a hard life, apparently.'

Gordon didn't respond.

'Anyway, that incident was a personal involvement and that's when I decided to photograph people who were sleeping rough. To show their lives the way they were. I wanted it to be a wake-up call, make people see the way society treats these people.'

'So what you're telling us is you were in a fight with a homeless man when you were twenty years old —'

'Not a fight, a scuffle.'

'But then you said he died and that it wasn't your fault. How is that meant to be understood?'

'Well, that it wasn't my fault that there was a scuffle. And that later he died.'

The audience were completely silent.

'And that's why you decided to photograph homeless people.'

'If we're to put it simply, yes.'

He leaned forward and sipped some water from his glass, then shifted his weight on the chair, straightened his posture. He shuffled his cue cards, and when finally he looked at me again, he did not look me in the eye.

'What we haven't talked about yet, or not that much, is *form*,' he said. 'I know this is something that interests you a lot.'

'It does, yes.'

'You've experimented with form quite a lot over the years. I'm thinking for instance of the *Dethroned* series with all those tiny shifts in perspective.'

A figure rose from the audience and edged towards the exit. Others followed.

'*Dethroned*, yes,' I said, trying not to look. 'It's perspective itself, of course, that is dethroned in that work. The notion that it's always one person seeing, from a single point of view.'

No one was listening. Those closest to the stage were turning round to see what was happening. Even Gordon seemed to be more attentive to the audience now than to me.

'Please, go on,' he said when I fell silent. 'One person seeing, from a single point of view?'

'Yes, I wanted to break that down.'

He hesitated, as if suddenly he was unwilling to help me out, his eyes vacantly fixing on his cue cards. His whole being exuded discomfort.

'But we have to be careful not to overtheorise,' I said. 'People should be able to look at the pictures and have their own thoughts about them.'

'Indeed,' he said. 'I think that's as good a place as any to conclude our talk. Thank you so much for being here. Kristian Pedersen, ladies and gentlemen.'

He got to his feet and put out his hand.

A smattering of applause quickly died. Half the audience were already on their way out.

The mood in the green room was likewise tense. No one said anything, no one smiled, no one congratulated me. I removed the headset and pulled the transmitter out of my pocket, handing it to the technician, who received it without acknowledgement.

'Well,' Gordon said, opening a bottle of mineral water from which he drank while remaining standing.

'What did you think?' I said to Mette. She was leaning forward where she sat, head tilted towards her phone.

'It was good,' she said. 'At least it was until you got to that story about the homeless person.'

'I know, what the hell happened there?' I said. 'How come *that* was such an issue? Are we not supposed to talk about reality, is that it? People get so self-righteous when they sit down together like that.'

'I don't know,' she said. 'But it's getting shared on the internet already.'

'What is?'

'What you said.'

'I hardly said anything.'

She performed a sharp intake of breath and gave a grimace that made her look even uglier.

'You said you were involved in a scuffle with a homeless person and that he died, but it wasn't your fault. A lot of people are going to interpret that in the worst possible way.'

'They can interpret all they want.'

I took my own phone out. No shitstorm there, as far as I could see. But then hardly anyone had my number.

A text from Yelena.

What was that all about?

What? I typed back.

That homeless person, she replied. She must have been sitting with her phone in her hand waiting for me to respond. I checked when she'd texted. Fifteen minutes ago.

Were you watching?

Yes.

'Was this webcast?' I said, turning to Mette.

'I'm afraid so.'

'Oh well.'

I put the phone to sleep and dropped it back into my inside pocket. I could give her a ring on the way to the airport.

When we came out, Jacob was standing waiting by the car.

'Interesting talk,' he said. 'Though it did take rather an unfortunate turn. You should think about putting a denial out there.'

'A denial? Of what? Getting into an argument with someone when I was twenty? Who's never had an argument in their life?'

Again, a whistling intake of breath between the teeth, again a grimace, small and yet so out of place.

'There's a video clip circulating already. In which you *appear* to be saying you killed someone. I know, I know, but that's what it sounds like. This could stick to you, stick to your name. We don't want that, do we?'

'Of course not.'

'OK. You get out to the airport and make your flight. We'll talk once you get back. OK?'

'Yes, fine.'

It was a relief to leave New York behind. But I wasn't able to savour it, mainly because of Mette who sat staring at the illuminated screen of her phone the whole time, now and then with tapping thumbs, now and then a swiping index finger, continuously, and conspicuously, on edge. I knew of course what it was she was following, and I didn't like it.

'Can't you leave it alone? At least until we get home? There's nothing we can do about it before then anyway.'

'It's becoming a topic now, Kristian. It's not looking good. I think it'd be best if I put a statement out from you.'

'What, now?'

'Yes. A few sentences, that's all.'

'Saying what?'

'That you were trying to be funny, which you now deeply regret. Or it was all just a performance — whatever. Something that takes the edge off what you said.'

'Listen. I said what I said. And there was nothing wrong with it. I can't help it if people put two and two together and come up with five. Can't you put that thing down now? I'm exhausted, it's stressing me out just looking at it.'

'I'm only doing my job.'

'And who did you say your employer was again?'

407

She gave a sigh and dropped the phone into her bag, shuffled away from me on the seat and stared out the window on her side.

After checking in and negotiating security, we took a light meal in the lounge before parting company in the boarding queue — she to find her seat at the rear, me to find mine up front. She'd been uncommunicative ever since our disagreement in the car, which annoyed me, so it was a relief to finally be on my own. I declined the champagne and sat with my earphones on listening to Sibelius's piano pieces while gazing out at the work that went on around the aircraft. Men in hi-vis vests, overalls and ear defenders, flitting around on their little vehicles. An impersonal PA was fine, but antipathy wouldn't do. In movies, celebrities were always surrounded by yes-people, which was presented as something negative, a sign of poor judgement and egomania, but of course it wasn't that simple in the real world, at least not for creatives, who needed a no-tension zone, a space without conflict, loaded with the belief that everything was possible — a space where the answer was yes, yes, and never no. No came later, no came all in good time, no came always at some point, no matter what. So yes-people were necessary. At least at the closest quarters.

When you worked as closely with someone as Mette did with me, you saw everything, including the unvarnished bits. All my bad habits, the aspects of my personality that were anything but winning. Implicit in that relationship was trust. It was a trust that had to be earned. A personal assistant had to understand that a human is a complicated being, that a human is all things, that creativity and talent exist side by side with impatience and irascibility, often manifesting as petty-mindedness.

Mette saw all that. Recently I'd suspected that she didn't care for it, that she was averse to it, averse to *me*, and was doing her best to hide the fact.

Thoughts like that never came out of nowhere, were never entirely without foundation. Instinct was rarely, if ever, wrong.

So bye-bye, Mette.

I'd made the decision.

Or had I?

I didn't feel the usual lift in such a step, the liberating feeling I expected it to give. Did that mean it was a wrong decision? Should I hang on to her anyway?

That was instinct too.

We pushed slowly back from the gate. I closed my eyes. The answer would deliver itself when I woke in the morning. I'd know then.

Even as the aircraft — big, heavy, cumbersome — accelerated down the runway, I was drifting into sleep, and when we rose into the air it was as if in a dream, before the gates of the world closed and left me shut out from it.

The lights came on and an announcement said we'd be landing in London in an hour. I stirred, stiff and cold, disgruntled that I hadn't availed myself of the facilities and reclined the seat into the sleeping position, instead having sat upright the whole way as if I was a backpacking tourist.

Mette got started as soon as she was off the plane.

'Jacob's suggesting you do an interview with one of the major newspapers instead of just sending out a press release. I agree with him. Perhaps as early as this afternoon?'

'Did you get any sleep?'

'Yes, thank you, I did,' she said, and pressed her lips together into a smile.

'Today's for my family. I haven't seen them in nearly two weeks.'

She nodded.

'It's important we do this as soon as possible,' she said. 'It'll take an hour at the most.'

'Tomorrow.'

'OK.'

She'd ordered a car from Addison Lee that was waiting for us when we came out. It dropped her off in Hammersmith, where she lived with her mediocre art historian husband, before carrying on to our house in Islington. Given that I hadn't called her after the event as I'd promised, I was half expecting Yelena to be standing in the doorway waiting for my explanation when the car pulled up, but she wasn't. I let myself in, put my suitcase down in the hall and went through.

'Hello? Yelena?' I called.

Faintly, I heard her voice reply from upstairs. I went up and along the corridor to her office that faced the garden at the back.

She was working at her desk and turned her head towards me after I opened the door.

'Hi,' she said.

'Hi,' I said. 'Are you working or do you want a coffee?'

'Coffee sounds good.'

She got up and we went back down into the kitchen, directly underneath her office.

'Is he at school?' I asked, unscrewing the top of the espresso maker. Yelena nodded. She was standing at the worktop, her hands flat against its surface, as if she was about to hoist herself up onto it at any moment. I filled the bottom of the pot with water, spooned coffee into the aluminium funnel, and put the top and bottom together again before placing the pot on the hob.

'I'm sorry I didn't phone,' I said.

'I imagine you had enough on your plate. Have you looked on the internet?'

'Why, should I?'

'You're everywhere. It looks bad.'

I said nothing. The coffee pot hissed and spat. I pressed it down on the hob, as if it would boil any quicker.

'What actually happened back then? The incident you were talking about. What did you do?'

'I didn't kill anyone, if that's what you're thinking.'

'But it's what you said.'

'No, it wasn't. If you'd listened properly, if the world had listened properly, you'd know that what I said was that I got myself into a slight altercation. Which is true. I took pity on this tramp, gave him a couple of fags, and he repaid me by thinking he could steal my lighter. When I tried to get it back, he put up a fight. That's all that happened. Then when I was doing the series on the homeless, I tried to find him again, seeing as how there'd been this personal contact between us, but it turned out he was dead.'

I looked at her and held her gaze. She nodded a couple of times, then stared into the garden. A text message chimed in my pocket. I got my phone out to look at it. It was from Sonja.

Murderer.

'Who was it?' Yelena asked as I slipped it back into my pocket.

My eyes fixed on hers.

'What are you asking me that for? Do I ask who's texting you?'

'There's no need to get worked up about it. I was just wondering, that's all.'

'It was from Jacob. He wants me to do an interview and get this thing sorted out.'

'Is that what you're going to do?'

'I haven't much choice by the sounds of it.'

The coffee had begun to rise up through the narrow cylinder into the top chamber. How bedeviled could I get? An unstable woman, on top of everything else. I'd have to get a new number. And hope she wasn't crazy enough to come looking for me.

The coffee bubbled. I took the pot off the heat, a couple of cups from the cupboard, and poured for us both. The thick liquid, as black as oil, swirled against the white insides of the china.

'There you go,' I said, handing her hers and blowing on the surface of mine, taking a sip as we sat down facing each other at the table.

'Aren't you going to answer him?' she said, her piercingly blue eyes latching onto mine.

'I'd rather talk to you.'

'I don't mind.'

'I'll do it later.'

Fatigue welled in me. Not slowly, not serenely as it normally did, but abruptly, aggressively almost. It was always the case after flying back in that direction. The trick was to stay awake as long as possible.

'Why haven't you ever told me about what happened with that homeless man?'

'Because there's nothing to tell. It's just something that happened a very long time ago. If I had to tell you everything from before we met, I'd still be at it.'

'OK.'

'OK what?'

'It's OK that you didn't tell me. It was such a small thing. I understand.'
'Do you?'
'Yes.'
'Good.'

We sat a while without speaking. She drained her coffee and got to her feet.

'Are you going?'
'Yes. I've got work to do.'
'How's it coming along? The thesis.'
'Hard to say. OK, I suppose.'
'That too?'

She smiled back at me as she left the room and I heard her go up the stairs and along the corridor.

The strange thing about Yelena was that even now, after seven years, she remained a stranger to me. In principle we shared everything — house, bed, our lives — and besides that we also had a child together. Yet often I got the feeling I didn't know her. I'd never thought I'd find myself wanting more closeness from another person in my life, since most people were all over me as soon as they got the chance, and I loathed it. But with Yelena it was different. She was completely autonomous, which I found unusual. Everyone else wanted something. I appreciated her independence, it was a good quality and it gave space. But sometimes, when I saw her sitting on the sofa reading or watching TV, or if she even just came into the kitchen with a carrier bag of groceries in each hand, I could find myself thinking that her autonomy meant also that she didn't need me, that she might simply walk away whenever she felt like it and go and read on a different sofa, put her groceries down in a different kitchen, exchange glances with a different partner. These were moments of weakness, not of truth, for the life I gave her was something she'd be hard pressed to find elsewhere, with another man.

I'd held little in the way of expectations the night we met. It was early December, London was grey, cold and raw, and I'd been invited over to Jenny Olsson's studio in Bethnal Green where together with the Norwegian investor Emil Stray she was holding a pre-Christmas drinks party. Stray had been buying my pictures almost from the start, and

Jenny did good work, so I felt I at least ought to show my face. The cab driver went up and down the same bit of road without being able to locate the number I'd given him, until I looked at the invitation again and could direct him into a car park at the rear of a warehouse. Flames flickered from garden torches, while a pair of tight-suited bouncers, bearded and muscle-bound, stood guard on either side of the entrance. The building looked to have been a garage at one point, or perhaps a small factory of some sort. As I stepped from the cab, two other vehicles rolled up, black with tinted windows, and it dawned on me that I'd got it wrong — this obviously wasn't going to be just a small gathering of friends and acquaintances of Stray and Olsson. Inside the entrance, a woman in a black dress and high heels welcomed the arriving guests, while another stood ready to receive coats and other items for the cloakroom. Classical music drifted from the space further inside, and when I entered I saw a live string quartet playing to a room already buzzing with well-dressed individuals, most either overweight or filled with Botox. Serving staff wove among them bearing trays of canapés or drinks. Champagne, red wine — and something else that may have been margaritas. I went over and took a glass from the nearest minion. Sure enough, a strong, tangy cocktail with a crust of salt around the rim of the glass.

I spotted a few museum directors, from Norway as well as the UK, a scattering of journalists, the odd actor, a celebrity author, and a couple of television faces I recognised, one of them a famous talk-show host. Among the other guests I saw no one I knew, but without exception they reeked of too much money and too little taste.

Stray himself stood chatting with two bulging women in their sixties. He was in a red blazer, white shirt and blue jeans, probably the worst-dressed person in the room. His eyes were darting and as soon as he saw me he excused himself from their company and came striding towards me.

'Kristian,' he said. 'Have you found yourself a drink?'

I held up my glass.

'What sort of a nightmare is this?' I said. 'I'd never have come if I'd known it was going to be this awful.'

That was when I saw Yelena. Standing with her back to me in the middle of the room in a red dress, tall and slender as a reed, her dark hair set up, presenting a delicate neck.

'Who's that?' I asked, with a nod. 'Over there.'

'That's my son Egil,' he said. 'But you've met him before, haven't you?'

I didn't correct him and say it was the woman his son was talking to I meant. Instead I shook my head.

'I thought your sons were called Harald and Gunnar.'

'You've met them, then?'

'Yes, I have.'

'Well, Egil's the third. He lives in Norway. That'll be why you haven't met him.'

'Not only have I not met him, I had no idea he even existed.'

'Then let me introduce you. Come on.'

She turned her head towards us as we stepped up, smiled at Emil's son and walked away in the opposite direction before we got to introductions.

'Egil, you must meet Kristian,' Emil said.

For a brief second, Egil's gaze brushed mine before he looked down. It would turn out that he was in the habit of only *almost* looking at the person he was talking to at any given time. It was as if he was peering up out of a well, only for the lip to then obscure his line of vision.

'I make documentary films,' he said when I asked him what he did.

'Oh yes?' I said. 'About what? What are you working on at the moment?'

'Smith's Friends. Have you heard of them?' he said, and *almost* looked at me. It was unsettling. I felt an urge to yell, Look at me, man!

'That sect where the women have very long hair and are only allowed to wear dresses?' I said instead.

'That's them, yes. They're literalists, you know. So they actually believe that God created the world in six days and that Adam and Eve were the first humans. Not to mention the Flood and Noah's Ark. That's interesting in itself, I think. That these *pockets* of ancient belief can exist in our modern culture. The most interesting thing about them though is their conception of Jesus. They believe that Jesus was born an ordinary individual, but that he was without sin and could do only God's will, and that *that* was what made him divine and able in the end to rise up from the dead. The Resurrection is thereby framed as proof that he acted righteously.'

From his father's body language I inferred that he was eager for this meeting to conclude, his gaze sweeping conspicuously about the room as he shifted his weight uneasily from one foot to another.

'But of course no person could ever be capable of that, could they?' Egil went on, continuing his mumbling monologue, punctuated by the occasional glance over the lip of the well, as if to make sure we were still listening. 'We sin, and do not as God would wish — whereas Jesus was unique in that as a human he did *not* sin and indeed followed the will of God in every respect. Extraordinary, wouldn't you say? In other words, we can subjugate our human nature to God's will and thereby *become* God. Or rather, Jesus could. But if Jesus could, then perhaps others can too?'

His father touched my arm.

'You must say hello to Mathias,' he said. 'You have met him, haven't you?'

'Nice to meet you, Egil,' I said and followed his father towards a small group standing beside a low wall on which various items of ceramic art were displayed. After saying hello, I excused myself and went away in the direction of the entrance, took another margarita and stood there scanning the room. I was most inclined to leave, but I was curious about the woman in the red dress and now I picked her out, again with her back to me and in conversation with a male guest, her tall, erect posture, the curve of her spine, the fingers of both hands around the stem of her glass. It didn't look as if she knew him that well — it was something in the way she held her head, slightly tilted, her posture not soft and compliant-looking as it would be if they shared each other's confidence, but stiff, as if self-conscious. The man himself was rather small, not someone I would regard as competition in any way.

A waiter paused where I was standing and wiped some perspiration from his brow with the back of his hand. His other hand held an empty tray at his side.

It was as if we belonged to two different species. The black-clad serving staff belonged to one, the festively dressed guests to another. The latter were not unlike birds: extravagant, preening bodies, hideous turkey-throated faces and thrusting chests, cackling voices, their senseless strutting hither and thither. Some undoubtedly possessed at least a degree of self-insight, but on the whole none of them out there knew who they were. Birds stuck together because they were of the same feather, albeit they were unaware of the fact. So it was here too.

The man she was talking to pointed upwards. She turned and looked, nodded, and both then came towards me. I stared blankly into space as they passed, feeling little need to make myself known to her, since she'd already seen me when Stray had dragged me over to meet his son. They went up the stairs behind me. I waited a couple of minutes before wandering the same way.

There was a library up there, I discovered, a metre-high interior wall at the far end separating the space from the room below. She was sitting in an armchair in front of a low table, while he browsed the bookshelves.

She had high cheekbones and rather narrow eyes, and her upper lip arched markedly towards the philtrum, it too rather conspicuous — could she once have had a cleft lip?

I went over and surveyed the party below, my forearms resting on the wall. I'd liked the son more than I liked the father, which wasn't saying much. Emil Stray was the archetypal self-made man, the sort with two settings only — greedy pursuit of material goods and self-aggrandisement. The son at least seemed to be cut from a different cloth, though seriously socially inhibited — most likely on account of his father.

'Do you like Ruscha?' the man said. I turned my head to look. He'd pulled out a heavy art book to show her.

'No,' she said. 'Do you?'

'Not really,' he said.

I smiled. She looked at me.

'I think he does,' I said.

Both ignored me. He because he felt threatened, she to be loyal.

'I'm sorry,' I said. 'I couldn't stop myself. I'm Kristian.'

'Matthew,' he said.

I looked at her.

'Do *you* like Ruscha?' she asked me.

'I can't bear him. He goes against everything I stand for. As in everything.'

'And what would that be?' he said.

I gave him a wide, benevolent smile, though without answering, and turned again to the woman he was with.

'You didn't tell me your name.'

'Yelena.'

'That's a Russian name, isn't it?'

'Yes,' she said, and then rose to her feet, throwing a glance at her short suitor who immediately came to her aid to accompany her from the room and go back down the stairs.

There aren't many people I give a second thought to after meeting them. Most I simply forget, nothing about them makes an impression, and if I see them again it's as if for the first time. Some do leave at least something behind, if only a vague, blurry recollection in need of a concrete trigger in order to become activated, and then the memory of them comes as if from nowhere. Oh yes, I think I met this person once. And then there are the very few people I not only remember well, but occasionally find myself thinking about after having met them. Why it happens, and what it is about them that does it, I have no idea. I'd only exchanged a few short words with Yelena, and nothing out of the ordinary had been said. She was beautiful, yes, but a lot of other women were too.

Two days later I phoned Stray to find out who she was. He didn't know offhand, he said, but shortly afterwards sent me an email with her various particulars. Her name was Yelena Meyer and she worked for something called Argus Capital Management. I thought about calling her, but didn't. I was already involved with someone and not at that point prepared to manage a relationship on the side, or indeed to wrap up the one I was in.

But destiny decreed otherwise. Or Yelena did. A couple of days later, as I sat smoking in my studio, I saw her through the window entering the rear courtyard, where she paused a moment while looking for a doorbell to ring.

'Hello,' she said when I opened the door.

'Hello,' I said, and stepped back to let her in. She walked slowly around and absorbed the place, while I sat down again and lit another cigarette. Now and then she looked at me and smiled.

'Do you want some lunch?' I said. 'There's a place round the corner I go to. A small French bistro.'

'I'd like that, yes,' she said.

It was a completely new experience to me, as if everything was already decided. I wasn't the sort of person to just drop what I had in my hands, but that was what I did. We met up again the next day, at a pub after she'd finished work. Even though nothing happened and no promises had been made on either side, I told Claire that same evening that I'd met someone else. She was preparing dinner, placing chicken legs in an ovenproof dish with slices of lemon in between, and turned towards me with a smile when I stepped into the kitchen. We need to talk, I said, and a shadow fell over her face. At first she wept, then she was angry, then she wept again. I sat up in the living room all night, listening to her sobs from the bedroom. It would take a couple of days, perhaps a week, and then it would be over, at least the emotional slush would. Aloofness was easier by far to deal with — anyone thinking they could punish me by being aloof didn't know what they were doing.

Yelena wasn't Russian, but German with a Russian mother. She'd grown up in Leipzig and when she was eighteen she moved to Berlin to go to university, before moving over here and carrying on her studies in Cambridge. She'd been in the UK ever since. Her English was almost without trace of an accent. She was the type of person that inspired other people's trust — it wasn't uncommon that people she hardly knew confided in her, or said more than they would normally have said. When out among people, she would laugh a lot, and her laughter was then almost a language in itself — everything she said would be modulated by a giggle, pauses in conversation would be punctuated in the same way, so it had nothing to do with finding things funny. Nor was it of nervous or neurotic character. What it expressed above anything was a sociable nature. At home with only Leo and me it would be absent. The same if she was with her parents or her sister, Katja. Eventually, I realised it never surfaced at all when she spoke German. In other words, the part of her personality that was tied to home and origins was different from that she stepped into as soon as she was out among people.

I was present when she gave birth to Leo, and how bizarre it was to see a human being come out of another. It was like a sick, Gothic fever-dream, something the dying crew of a seventeenth-century merchant schooner in the Far East could have seen present itself before their eyes as they trembled and sweated with sickness and fear. And yet it was real. The small human slid from the large one in a cocoon of slime, birth fluids and blood. It took a year before I could have sex with her again, and even then the grotesque vision was there in my mind. Yet she was able to let go of it all as if shedding a skin. No sooner was it over than her undivided care and attention was his. I had no place there, where everything was driven by instinct and I had none. I was a spectator. Nothing was changed in me. I was the same after as I was before.

While on parental leave with Leo she began studying again. At first simply in order to keep her mind ticking over, but then after a while more seriously, until she ended up packing in her job altogether. Now she was writing her doctoral dissertation on the subject of 'place' in history. How is the notion of place established, and how is it maintained? These were the questions she posed. Place was to her the result of a dynamic process constrained by physical, cognitive and cultural factors. The seed of her interest was of course the transformation and subsequent loss of the country in which she'd grown up. It's one thing to move away from the land of one's childhood, quite another when that country disappears off the map — not least when its buildings, squares and streets, its rivers, plains and forests remain. The place she was writing about was Leipzig, an apposite example — Bach lived and worked there for many years, in the same church where Wagner would later be christened. Leibniz was born there, Napoleon lost his biggest battle there, and Auerbach's Cellar, where Faust and Mephistophilis sat and drank, still existed. The big book fair, visited in their heydays by Schiller, Schelling and the Schlegel brothers, continued to this day.

She didn't know yet what she would turn to when her thesis was done. While not consciously putting off its completion, she wasn't exactly hastening either, so it was taking its time. As far as I was concerned she could do what she wanted, we didn't see much of each other any more anyway, which was fine. She still looked good, and most people we met found her interesting, so I couldn't complain.

I took a shower to fend off the jet lag and for a while it worked — going back down into the living room in a clean shirt and a clean pair of trousers I actually felt refreshed. But then fatigue returned and since I still had four hours before I could pick Leo up from school and there was nothing else I could do in the meantime that wouldn't send me to sleep anyway, I capitulated and went for a lie-down.

I woke up to someone saying my name. In the depths of a dream it was Mum, and it was Mum too who then put her hand on my shoulder, but when I opened my eyes it was Yelena standing there. She was holding her mobile up in front of me, showing me the screen.

'Have you seen this?' she said. 'In the *Mail*?'

I sat up to look, but it was too much to take in so close to sleep.

'What? What is it?'

'It says you were wanted by the police in connection with a murder in 1986.'

'What? But that's ludicrous.'

'But that's what it says.'

I took the phone from her hand.

'Go,' I said. 'I can't concentrate if you're hanging over me like that.'

She didn't move. Her eyes were filled with terror.

'Go, I said!'

Eventually, she did as I asked.

It appeared they'd dug up the newspaper articles from back then, the ones detailing the body's discovery, as well as the blurred CCTV image the police had put out when they'd appealed to the public.

Famous artist sought for murder in 1986 – admits onstage 24 years on.

That wasn't what fucking happened.

The malicious bastards.

I hadn't admitted anything. What's more, I'd done nothing to admit. I'd gone to the police and been questioned, and they'd let me go without charge, completely exonerated.

Fucking journalists, concocting the worst imaginable lies and presenting them as truth.

I found Yelena standing outside the door and handed her phone back.

'There's nothing in it,' I said. 'It's absolute bollocks. They've fabricated the whole story. I can sue the bloody hell out of them.'

'You were wanted for murder, Kristian. I've read the article. I've seen the picture.'

'No! It's a bloody lie! I was wanted as a *witness*. I went to the police myself and gave a statement, and then I walked home again. That's all there was to it.'

I went into the kitchen and picked my phone up off the table. I'd received forty-six text messages. A lot were from Mette, a lot were from the madwoman. I blocked her and then switched it off.

Yelena came after me.

'You said onstage yesterday that you'd been in a fight with a tramp and that he'd died. Then you said he hadn't died until a long time after that. Only now it comes out that you were wanted by the police in connection with his death. I don't understand.'

'That's what I'm saying — they wanted to speak to me as a *witness*.'

'But if he didn't die until much later, why would they be looking for you as a witness? It doesn't add up, Kristian.'

'Look, I only said that he died much later so as to avoid exactly this kind of idiotic conspiracy talk, all right? It's true that I had a run-in with this person before he died, and that's why the police wanted to talk to me. But nothing happened, I didn't fucking kill anyone, OK?'

'But this scuffle, this altercation?'

'It was nothing. I took my lighter from him. That was it.'

'OK.'

'What do you mean, OK? You mean you don't believe me, is that it?'

'I don't know what to believe.'

'Yelena. This is absurd. I didn't *kill* anyone, of course I didn't. It's the media, cooking up a story. You're not going to believe the gutter press over your own husband, surely? The *Daily Mail*? Come on. It's important to me that you, at least, believe me. It's absurd, Yelena, can't you see? Laughable, even, if it wasn't for the fact that people out there are actually going to fall for it.'

'What will you do?'

'I don't know. A major interview to a serious outlet, probably. I need to call Mette now and hear what she's thinking. Knowing her, she'll probably have a plan ready.'

Yelena sat down and ran her hands over her face.

'What about Leo?' she said.

'Leo? He's got nothing to do with this.'

'His teachers, the other parents, they'll read about it too.'

'Let them! As long as I've done nothing wrong it doesn't matter what people *think*. People are idiots anyway. They can think what they want.'

I looked up at the clock on the wall. Twenty to three.

'It's quarter past three today, isn't it?'

She nodded.

'Yes, but you're not picking him up today. I'll do it.'

An enormous rage rose like a wall inside me. I stepped right up to her and leaned into her face.

'*I'm* picking him up. Understand?'

'Calm down.'

'Don't you fucking tell ME to calm down.'

'You don't need to shout,' she said. Her head was lowered, her gaze fixed to the floor. I took hold of her chin and lifted it.

'*I'm* picking him up.'

She stared at me without speaking. I released her and marched out into the hall, put my shoes and jacket on and went through into the garage, slamming the door behind me as I went. Who did she think she was, thinking she could rule me like that? I hadn't seen the boy in two weeks, and now she was trying to stop me? Climbing up onto her high horse, assuming the moral high ground. Not a word of support, not even a suggestion of help. She couldn't even say she believed me. That was the least a person could expect. Believe me, and don't go telling me when I can see my son and when I can't.

I opened the garage door, got in the car and reversed out. The school was only a few minutes away, so I had plenty of time. I parked in the street outside and phoned Mette.

'Thank goodness,' she said. 'I've been trying to get hold of you.'

'So I noticed.'

'Listen, this thing. It's escalated.'

'You're telling me.'

'You've read it, then?'

'Yes. Unbelievable what they can spin out of some half-truths and a pack of lies.'

'It's not looking good.'

'It's pigswill.'

'I know, but we're going to have to do something about it, nevertheless. Can you come in for a meeting tomorrow morning?'

'Who with?'

'There's a PR bureau who've agreed to help us, and Alfred Burnett's lawyer, James Haigh, will be there too.'

'Oh, come on. A PR bureau?'

She didn't respond.

'But there's nothing in it. It's all invention. Can't we just sit tight and let it blow over?'

'It's too big for that, Kristian. If they're able to run a picture of you that's linked with that case, then … well, you've no option but to explain yourself.'

'And if I don't?'

'You must.'

'OK, I'll do it. But listen, can you get me a new phone? With a new number?'

'Yes.'

'Bring it with you tomorrow, then.'

I hung up and climbed out. Parents were arriving on both sides of the street. Most of the faces I recognised, but I'd never spoken to any of them. I locked the car and dropped the key into my jacket pocket. It was overcast and a cold wind pressed through the corridor between the buildings. To the west, the sky was ragged, torn open to now show patches of blue. I could take him for an ice cream or something. I couldn't be bothered with Yelena just yet.

How incredibly unempathetic she was. I hadn't seen the boy in two weeks, and she still wanted to pick him up.

A man across the street stared and turned his head away as I met his gaze. I knew his face, a tired visage of gaping pores, a long nose, hair dyed bright red. He never wore anything but the same baggy green cargo pants and black T-shirts with heavy metal band logos on the front. A total loser, in other words.

He got his phone out and started typing. No doubt something about me.

Looks were sent my way too as I came to the gate. Middle-class parents with nothing better to do. They knew they shouldn't look, but still it was too much of a temptation for them, a little glance and they'd have something to talk about to their unremarkable friends for weeks ahead. What pathetic little lives they led. Sorry bastards.

His class was already lined up in the playground. Leo stood out in his yellow coat, leaning back against the wall, thumbs hooked around the straps of his satchel. He hadn't seen me yet among the flock of sheep, and I exploited the opportunity to observe him, to see what he was like when he was with his schoolmates. Two boys darted out of line, one in pursuit of the other. It sparked a commotion of whoops and cries. Leo looked on, but was clearly uninvolved. I'd seen it before. The other kids belonged together, in pairs, in threes. They were connected. When one of them did something, the others were on board too, egging on from the side or actively joining in.

It was always a stab in the heart to see him left out. But it was only a phase, there was nothing wrong with him, nothing at all, he was a happy little chap, spirited and funny. His challenge was to bring that side of him out at school too, not just at home.

The caretaker, wearing shorts and a puffer jacket, came striding across the playground, pulling a bunch of keys from his pocket and finding the right one as he went. He opened the gate with a measured movement and the sheep poured in. It was as if Leo detached from the wall as soon as he saw me. He came running, zigzagging a path between the other children, and I kneeled, threw my arms around him and lifted him high into the air.

'Pappy!' he said.

'I've missed you, you little rascal,' I said.

He pressed his cheek to mine. I ran my hand up and down his back, and tears welled in me.

PART FOUR

There comes a moment in everyone's life when we understand what death is. I can't remember that moment myself, it's as if I've always known. But I was there when that understanding suddenly came to Leo. It was a terrible moment. We were upstairs in his room reading at bedtime. He was three or four years old and was snuggled in my lap. The book contained a passage in which the main character was thinking about his grandmother, who was no longer alive. I'd read the same book to him a number of times before without him having reacted to the passage in question. But now he asked.

'Where is she?'

'Who?'

'His grandmother.'

'She's dead.'

'But where is she?'

'When you're dead you're nowhere any more. You no longer exist.'

'Why?'

'I don't know. Shall we read on?'

'Yes.'

I read on. But I sensed he wasn't really following. Something was stirring in him.

'Why is she dead?' he said after a while.

'I suppose she was old and not very well.'

'When will she be coming back?'

'She won't be coming back. When we die, it's forever.'

He said nothing and so I carried on reading. But he wasn't listening.

'Does everyone have to die?'

He sat quite still and stared out in front of him, as if willing the answer he wanted.

'Yes,' I said.

'Why?'

'I don't know. But everything living has to die. That's how it is, Leo.'

'Is my bed going to die?'

'Your bed isn't, no! Not unless it's alive!'

He chuckled and shifted his weight on my lap.

'Is the wall going to die?'

'No!'

'Is the carpet going to die?'

'No!'

'Is the car going to die?'

'No, only what's living can die. Plants and trees and animals and people.'

I hugged him tightly and we sat a moment without speaking.

'When will you die?' he said all of a sudden.

'Me?'

'Yes.'

He was as motionless now as before, his whole body concentrated on what I was going to say.

'I don't know. Not for a long, long time.'

'When you're old?'

'Yes. But that's not for a very long time yet.'

'Is Mummy going to die as well?'

'Yes. But not for a long, long time.'

That was when he understood. He turned his head and looked up at me.

'Will *I* die too, Pappy?'

I smoothed his hair and nodded.

'But not for a very, very, very long time yet. You don't even have to think about it.'

'How long will I be dead?'

'For ever and ever.'

'Will I not come back?'

'No. When we die, it's for good. Come on, time to brush your teeth.'

He climbed down, then tried to divert things onto a more light-hearted track.

'Will the lamp die?' he said.

'No, you little rascal!' I said. 'The lamp's not alive!'

I went after him as he scurried towards the bathroom, where he turned the tap on and wet his toothbrush before squeezing out some toothpaste. He could barely reach the sink, in his blue-and-white-checked flannel pyjamas, his glasses that he so often pushed back onto the bridge of his nose with his forefinger. I so much wished that he could live without knowing that life would end.

He handed me the toothbrush and I brushed his teeth. Returning to his room, he placed his glasses on the bedside table and climbed under the duvet, while I sat down in the chair next to the bed to sing him one of the nursery songs and lullabies my mother had sung to me when I was his age. 'Little Peter Spider', 'The Elephant's Lullaby', 'Master Jakob', 'Sleep Tight, Little Child'. Danish mostly, but Norwegian too. 'The Bear's Asleep', 'Bah, Bah, Little Lamb', 'Little Song Thrush', 'Mikkel the Fox', 'The Crow's Song'. Songs from a bygone age, a time of forests and animals, and I often wondered how he related to them, what pictures were conjured in his mind when he listened to the words I sang. Presumably it was the ritual that meant most to him, the repetition, the feeling of security that was instilled. When he was five and started school he hid his glasses. The first time it happened we thought he'd mislaid them. When it happened again, we realised it was on purpose. He wanted to be like all the other children, and to look like them too. He'd always enjoyed playing on his own, no doubt because he was an only child, but also because like me he was wired that way. At preschool he'd kept to himself much of the time, though without adverse effect − it was the way he wanted it. He cracked the reading code soon after his fourth birthday, which further enhanced his sense of independence. He enjoyed being close to Yelena and me, while keeping others at arm's length. But when he showed a person his trust, it would be boundless. He had inherited my facial shape, Yelena's features. An inquisitive child who couldn't help but ask questions − it was as if he wanted to know everything that could be known.

It took time for me to fully appreciate him. The first year of infancy I could barely relate to him, a baby with undiminishing demands, unable to give anything back. We could just as well have had a dog instead. The second year wasn't much better. OK, so he learned to walk and could often be adorable, but I found it hard to handle the wreckage he left behind everywhere in his wake, the constant onslaught of nappies, the bedtime battles — when he was at his worst, it would be two hours before he fell asleep. He was a bundle of energy, though unable yet to articulate.

It changed when he started talking. And perhaps he'd sensed I needed to be won over, because he was forever climbing onto my lap, demanding my attention and refusing to give up until he got it.

That eventually he sorted that situation out for himself, fixed what needed fixing in order for him to thrive, made me secure in the thought that life would work out for him. Perhaps he would go through a few difficult years, but then he would be seen, and liked.

The worst of the storm following my comments in New York died down after a few weeks. I gave two major interviews in which I made clear what had happened, that the incident with the homeless man in London all those years ago, when I'd been interviewed by the police, had left such a mark on me that I'd produced a series of photographs about it, and that the experience had taken on increasing significance for me. But like many artists, I contained decidedly mythomaniacal tendencies, which I'd be the first to admit — and in the interview onstage in New York I'd blurred the boundaries between reality and imagination. But of course there had been no physical altercation at all, what had occurred had simply been a verbal dispute centred on something as trivial as the return of a borrowed cigarette lighter. The CCTV image that had surfaced in the newspapers at the time indeed showed me, but once the police had interviewed me they were in no doubt and eliminated me immediately from their inquiries.

Although the matter was thereby to a degree straightened out, it nevertheless clung to my name and would no doubt continue to do so. The invitations with which I'd always been inundated basically stopped coming. It didn't matter much, given that I'd normally turned down ninety-nine per cent of them anyway. Besides, we had exhibitions planned for several years to come, which, as long as there was patently no substance to the so-called scandal, as long as it so clearly was nothing but words and innuendo, no one dared cancel. If anyone did, they risked being sued to pieces.

No, the worst thing was that I lost my urge to work. The joy of artistic creativity vanished from me completely, and in such circumstances it was meaningless to even try. For the first time since my teenage years, my days lay empty before me. I made Leo his breakfast and took him to school, and nothing else would happen that day until I went to pick him up again — and every other day, when it was Yelena's turn, I didn't even do that.

I wasn't made to be idle and was miserable for months. I couldn't surface again — the mind was willing, but the body heavy and recalcitrant. Art was about doing, it wasn't enough to just want. I was still getting ideas, but the urgency required to implement them was absent. One such idea was for a series of pictures in which I would try to reconstruct the past exactly — a certain year, 1986 let's say — in such meticulous detail that no one would be able to detect, or even suspect, that they'd been taken now and not then. It was an idea I'd got from one of Borges's short stories, the one where a writer rewrites *Don Quixote*. Writing *Don Quixote* surely hadn't been easy in the first place, but of course had nevertheless been possible: Cervantes had everything he required at hand — what he saw when he looked around him, what he heard and was told about, what he thought and felt, what he'd experienced — to write the novel was then merely a matter of hoisting the sails of his imagination and plotting a course towards a specific point, and everything he needed in order to get there would appear of its own accord during the voyage. But to rewrite *Don Quixote* required something quite different and in essence impossible, because that which *came* to Cervantes had to be *fetched* by the new author, and under completely different circumstances, in a world that was now another. There were two things I hoped my pictures would be able to show. To reconstruct the time in question I was thinking of building a room in the studio, for simplicity's sake the bedsit in which I'd lived in 1986, with the same wallpaper, the same furniture, the same posters, the same records, the same kitchen utensils, and perhaps also two people in it, dressed in the same clothes and wearing their hair in the same style as then, while in the street outside, visible through the window, there could be two or three cars, models typical of the day, and perhaps also a bicycle. If I did this painstakingly enough, the picture would be indistinguishable from pictures that had actually been taken at that time, and then the viewer would be able to see that time, rather than existing independently, in fact was a product of culture. That without culture everything would be the same, week after week, month after month, year after year. This notion was scientifically supported, for in the physical world there was simply no such thing as time. That we didn't see it that way was simply down to a defect in how we were wired to perceive the world. Yet, I suspected, no matter how carefully I reconstructed that bedsit in time, anyone who looked at the resulting photograph would sense immediately that it was a copy. In fact I was certain that would be the case. And therein lay the pith, the essential tension. For why was that so? If everything in the photograph, as well as the equipment I used to take it, was authentic, from 1986, and if time was nothing but a product of culture, how come the beholder would sense right away that the picture was a fake?

My job was to raise questions, not answer them. Besides, this one couldn't be answered. What is time? Was it what separated one moment from the next? But time wasn't anything objective, it was a function of where one stood, the locus from which one's world was observed. This meant that determining when something occurred was impossible, since it depended on the relationship between event and point of observation and was therefore variable. In principle it meant that a day in 1986 could take place now — not in my perception, but in that of someone else who was sufficiently removed. The present was what you were close to, constrained by the body. There was *my* time, and when we shared it there was *ours*. And *that* was what changed, because *we* changed. A reconstruction couldn't capture this sense of closeness, which was time's very core. The fetishisation of history, the enormous warehousing of the past and cultivation of what once was, all the digging in the soil for remains of prehistoric cultures, the tourism connected with castles and palaces and ancient towns, bound time and in that way gave to it an existence. But there were other ways of relating to history. The ancient temples of Japan were not in fact ancient at all — every now and again they were torn down and rebuilt. What was old about them was thus not fetishised, but removed. And why not? Age was confused with depth, past time with substance. We were like Orpheus, unable to stop ourselves from looking back, and when we did we lost what was most important.

I was in no doubt that it would make a good project. But nothing burned in me when I thought about it. Still, shouldn't I have been able to carry it through regardless? I still had the bike on which I'd cycled around London, I could get it fixed up, dig out the cameras I'd used at the time and for inspiration look up all the old haunts south of the river, then set about building a room in the studio. But the mere thought of venturing into the basement to even *look* at the bike filled me with loathing. And who even cared anyway if time was a cultural construct? What relevance did it have to anything? What would come of it? Even the most recent series I'd been working on, the direct, straightforward presentation of the world around us, repelled me. It was deception, overthought and pretentious.

I wondered if I'd burned out. The big retrospective, the idiotic and yet wide-reaching backlash, must have drained me more than I'd realised, sucked the marrow out of me. But I couldn't have burned out in the usual, everyday sense — I went running every other day, for instance, and had no problem with that. I wasn't depressed either. No, it was to do with my work only, my pictures. I *could* work, there was nothing physical that was stopping me, there just wasn't a spark, there was no *go* in me. I didn't see the point any more, everything just seemed to fade into futility. I'd never felt like that before. Which frightened me, because what if it was permanent? What would I do then? Rest on my laurels? At my age?

Yelena didn't think it was the slightest bit surprising, I'd been going full pelt for so many years and the shitstorm I'd suddenly wound up in had in her view worked like an emergency stop. 'We're not machines, we can't go on producing year after year,' she said. 'Be patient. There's no rush. We've plenty of money and you've already created a lifework. It'll be good for Leo to have you around the house a bit more. And for me too, perhaps, don't you think?'

'Are you saying I've neglected him?'

'Oh, Kristian, Kristian.'

Being at home during the daytime was humiliating. The triviality of the everyday shrank my thoughts so they too became trivial. Plant pots, rugs and teacups, the little hand-held vacuum cleaner — who could find anything of value in such things? Oh yes, this was the stuff of real life, one could argue, and therefore where the true meaning of it lay. But that was just something that was said so that people wouldn't feel they lived the pointless, empty lives they in fact did. Otherwise they might revolt against it all and chaos would result. Besides, a hand-held vacuum cleaner was a very useful thing when we left crumbs in places where a big vacuum cleaner was impractical, on the kitchen worktop for instance, or we might make just a small mess somewhere, perhaps we'd spill thirty or forty grains of rice onto the floor when we tipped the bag, and who would go to the cupboard to get the big vacuum cleaner then, which had to be lifted and carried, plugged in and switched on? No, it was much easier to turn to the small one that sat so snugly in the hand and was always at the ready. I lived in the age of hand-held vacuum cleaners, but it didn't mean I had to bow down to them, just as Giordano Bruno in his day had felt unobliged to bow down to the Catholic Church. And so I continued going to the studio every morning, not to work but to read. I returned to Shakespeare, picking up where I'd left off when I was twenty years old. That I'd dismissed his plays back then seemed unfathomable to me now that the hubris of youth had long since departed me. His genius was to carve out a space in time — shaped and performed on the stage — a space where everything was open and nothing was fixed, which allowed an audience or reader to pursue now one theme, now another, depending on who they were and the way they thought. The space was constrained, just a tiny section of the world, but what happened in it possessed a near-infinite sense-making power. *Hamlet* in particular was a play that gave me so much. It was utterly morbid, seething with rotting corpses, death's wriggling maggots and bare white skulls, and it was filled too with disgust for everything that had to do with the body and its functions, especially food and sex. Hamlet's intellect was extraordinary, an instrument he used to try to break free of all that pulled him down towards the soil, where copulation, death and putrification eternally neutralised each other, but found only meaninglessness and indifference, and the play of course ended in him going to his death very much of his own accord. Hamlet was a supreme soul incapable of life. His father, the dead king, who appears to him as a ghost, was the opposite — a hero, a man of action, who took care of people, who protected his family and his country, and overcame his enemies. As such, Hamlet is a classic son. His only way of separating himself from his father, of stepping from his shadow so as not forever to remain a miniature, is to forge his own path and live as he sees fit. But his father returns and demands of Hamlet that he avenge his death. In other words, he must step into his father's place — he must become his father. He doesn't want to, but the matter is by no means clear-cut, for in another way he *wants* to become his father, which is in relation to his mother Gertrude, the queen. Had Hamlet really been like his father he would have chosen Ophelia. It would have been a spirited, vigorous choice, and daringly counter-current. But he will not, cannot, for his feelings are directed towards his father's wife, his own mother. It's depraved, sexuality as denial of life, a closed circle, a locked room. Hamlet's conflict is irresolvable, not least because his father is dead and thereby it is the past that is playing out in him, invisible to all, including himself. Shakespeare was a master of the word, and nowhere is he better than here, in his utterly equilibristic soliloquies on life and death. At the same time, it is hard to imagine, based on what we know about him, a person as far removed from the Hamlet figure than William Shakespeare. Shakespeare was orderly, conscientious in money matters, occasionally pedantic, circumspect, generally of pleasant disposition and well liked. Apart from a few years of school, he was uneducated and did not hail from a scholarly or book-loving home, his father a glovemaker in a provincial market town. So how did he come to create a character so feral and reckless, so luminously intellectual as Hamlet? How did he manage to give such life to him and make him so credible? It was a question that ignited a little spark in me, for I remembered how we'd talked about Marlowe and *Doctor Faustus* when I first moved to London and hung out with Hans and Vivian. And Faustus was very much reminiscent of Hamlet. He too possessed a superior intellect that saw through everything with never a hindrance, tense, electric and nihilistic. He too was reckless with his life, loved no one and nothing. And, like Hamlet, he studied at the university in Wittenberg. The differences between them were of course also great — Faustus had no mother or father, so his conflict was simpler, purer. But there was little doubt that Shakespeare had an eye to Faustus when he created Hamlet. At least that was what I thought until I realised that Faustus was merely a decoy — it was Christopher Marlowe *himself*, his brilliant yet destructive intellect, his supreme, impetuous character, his absence of belief in anything, Marlowe himself who was Hamlet! They knew each other, of course, Shakespeare and Marlowe, they were born in the same year and wrote plays in the same city. Marlowe was already a star in his early twenties, he renewed the medium of theatre, bringing to it a vital, reality-near force, absorbing into his being the violence and power, the dreams and ideas, the desires and emotions of the age in which he lived, which was raw, incomplete, wide open, brutal — an age in which he would be killed at twenty-nine, stabbed through the eye. Hamlet was Marlowe. Of course he was.

The other possibility, though more far-fetched, was that it was Marlowe who had written *Hamlet* — as Hans too had suggested. He'd rejected the theory out of hand, but the mere fact that he'd mentioned it meant surely that the idea had appealed to him and that he hadn't completely closed the door on it. Whatever, it was a fact that Shakespeare's first dramas were ordinary, not bad as such, but then not very good either. The fact was too that they improved radically after Marlowe's death. The most plausible explanation was that Marlowe left behind him a gaping space for a dazzling, innovative new writer, a space Shakespeare not only filled, but gradually expanded. Marlowe had shown the way, but had been unable to follow the path himself, and then Shakespeare did. But then there was the complete absence of connectivity between Shakespeare's life and his work as a writer. The estate disposed of in his will included no books, no library, no manuscripts and no instructions as to what should happen to his own works. It's odd too that his daughter was unable to write — what sort of a writer would not teach his child that skill? If, furthermore, one believes that imagination and empathy are insufficient aptitudes on their own to create rich and credible depictions of foreign countries, times, environments and characters, then the notion that Shakespeare could not have written the plays himself but merely lent out his name gains credence.

And if that is likely, then it is no less likely that Marlowe was in such dire straits that he faked his own death and fled from it all, to Scotland, the realm of Macbeth, where he could continue doing what he did best, which was writing dramas for the stage. It is commonly established that throughout Shakespeare's works one here and there finds reference to Marlowe's, and the question then is basically whether it was Marlowe himself who scattered these traces for amusement or whether Shakespeare was simply tipping his hat to a deceased rival.

The final part of the mystery is the fact that Shakespeare stopped writing so suddenly and lived out his last years attending to his business matters and properties. It's possible that he just came up against a brick wall, so to speak, that he ran out of energy, desire, joy. But it's conceivable too that the wellhead of dramas suddenly ran dry when their real writer died.

I was by no means unaware of the possibility that the problem that characterised both Hamlet and Faustus — their lack of connection with anything or anyone in their respective environments — was mine too, albeit to a lesser degree. I'd had girlfriends who had accused me of being incapable of loving anyone. Not true, was my reply, I'm only incapable of loving you. But there was a grain of truth in what they said, because at some point I would invariably stop caring about them, they could think and feel whatever they liked about me. Once they realised this, they became filled with despair, and what they did in their despair was try to ramp up the intimacy in the relationship, as if somehow I'd start caring the cosier we got, and then it was never long before it was over. I'd never 'loved' my parents — what a horrendous word to use about one's family! I never had much against my father, and there were sides of my mother that I appreciated, the same being pretty much true when it came to my sisters. We lived and grew up in the same house, the five of us together, and had to get along with each other in order for it to work. Strong feelings make strong bonds, and bonds — well, what do they do? They bind. If people want to be bound, then fine. I for my part have always wanted to be free. Not that it was ever a conscious decision, it's just the way I've always been. The imperative of intimacy and closeness is everywhere and allowed to go unchallenged, accepted as nothing but good. But listen to the word: love. There's something ingratiating about it, dishonest and treacherous. Slippery, slimy, snake-like, slavish. To be loved by someone is never merely a gift but comes always with conditions. The same is true of loving someone. Naturally, I have nothing against people loving each other, as far as I'm concerned they can love each other until it comes out of their ears, what irritates me is that they believe so blindly in the great illusion of love around which society and our entire culture revolves, that they do so without understanding, or else actively ignoring, what goes on in its hallowed name. Love is the facade before which we halt, never to dare or even wish to investigate what might be going on inside the building.

Was it possible to love another supremely?

No, was the answer Shakespeare gave in *Hamlet*. The supreme human loves not.

I could not have thought so clearly without having read. It was what the best literature offered: from books I drew thoughts which otherwise would have been unavailable to me; from me they drew thoughts which otherwise would have been unavailable to them; these thoughts would be drawn out onto a table between us, there to be scrutinised and considered. But it was a fatiguing business, this too. I could read only for a couple of hours at most before having to yield. The rest of the day I would lie on the sofa in the studio or go to a nearby cafe or restaurant and sit there. It is reasonable to say that I clung to books. Without them my days would have been quite empty and utterly without meaning. At the same time, they led to nothing — nothing came of my reading, apart that is from these thoughts, and what use did I have of them?

Spring came, an eruption of chlorophyl. A green canopy stretched across the city, and on sunny days, when the brickwork gave off its golden light, even the greyest and grimmest of London streets became resplendent. Meeting Leo from school on days such as these, I would take him often to the park. There was a pleasant little cafe there with tables outside where he would sit with an ice cream while I sipped an americano and smoked a cigarette. A path ran by, and beyond it was a great expanse of grass, always populated in fine weather by kids kicking footballs or throwing frisbees, families picnicking, couples in love unable to keep their hands and lips from each other, and by people on their own, lying reading on the lawns, standing around at the edges, working out or performing stretches. Further away was a pond whose water we saw glitter through the leaves of the trees. The colours appeared almost to be fluid, as if detached from the objects to which they belonged. On the big, unicoloured lawns the opposite seemed to be true, the colours there appearing concentrated and localised. Even the slightest fleck of red came to the fore. But in our immediate vicinity, under the big, near-flat parasols of grey canvas, colours were as if neutralised, perhaps because we were so close to them that they could not be separated from their objects, and because they were dampened by the shade.

Leo would say nothing while eating his ice cream. I suppose he wanted to savour it, to maximise the pleasure. His mouth would be rimmed, a near-unbroken oval of ice cream and melted chocolate, his eyes open, though he seemed not to be seeing anything. The inner experience of devouring an ice cream shoved everything else aside. I wondered if there was any food I could enjoy in the same way. Something I really looked forward to eating and which absorbed me completely while I was doing so. But I couldn't think of anything. I had to go back to my childhood, when a bag of sweets was crammed with meaning. After that, food was food, drink was drink.

He put the wooden stick down on top of the wrapper and wiped his mouth. I raised my eyebrows, indicating first the little heap in front of him, then the rubbish bin that hung from the wall. He stood up and ran his sticky hands over his T-shirt before gathering up his debris.

'Not on your T-shirt!'

He looked down at himself and seemed surprised to find he was even wearing one.

'Sorry,' he said.

'You don't need to say sorry. But go to the loo and wash your hands. You can put your rubbish in the bin on the way.'

When he returned, he came up to me and pressed his cheek to my chest before sitting down again. I lit another cigarette.

'Pappy?'

'Yes?'

'Was ancient history *here* as well?'

'In the park, you mean?'

He nodded.

'Yes, it was everywhere,' I said. 'But there was no park here then.'

'What was there instead?'

'I don't know. But once there was ice everywhere. Snow and ice, and it was terribly cold.'

'Was it a long time ago?'

'Yes. And do you know what? Before that, Britain wasn't an island. It was joined to the Continent.'

'Why?'

'There wasn't as much sea then, so there was more land. You could walk from France to England, and nearly all the way to Norway. They call it Doggerland.'

'Doggerland.'

'Yes. Now it's at the bottom of the sea. But things can be fished up from it. The sea is very deep, but sometimes things turn up.'

'What sort of things?'

'Wood and skeletons, perhaps. Doggerland would have had forests.'

'Hmm.'

He sat with his head propped in his heads, swinging a leg back and forth under the table. It was as if he viewed the world through a prism of questions, with a fundamental uncertainty, but also pervaded by a sense of belief, for he clearly believed there to be an answer to everything.

'So the fish are swimming in forests?'

'You could say that.'

'And if the sea got bigger, would they be swimming here in the park?'

'I'm sure they would, yes.'

'And in the streets?'

'Yes, certainly.'

He wasn't lacking imagination. But I got the same feeling as I sometimes had when I was reading — that it led to nothing. Or even, that it *was* nothing. Just a kind of dream-reality he was able to step into and hide when the world became too complicated.

'What was school like today?'

'It was all right.'

'Who did you play with?'

'Different kids.'

'Like who?'

He shrugged and looked uncomfortable.

'I don't know.'

'You don't *know*?'

'A bit with Luke. Damon, maybe.'

'Maybe?'

He shrugged again.

'I don't like it when you don't look at me when we're talking, Leo.'

'No,' he said, and glanced up, before immediately looking down again. I reached across the table and ruffled his hair.

'Shall we get going? Mum'll be waiting for us, I'm sure.'

He took my hand as we went along the path, which was rather busy. A pair of pushchairs came rolling past, two small boys on scooters rather faster, and then there were the ubiquitous dog owners that filled up the park daily, walking their pooches. Leo suddenly pressed against me with his whole body, an expression of affection he'd been using ever since he'd learned to walk.

'All right, steady on,' I said, squeezing his hand at the same time and smiling at him so that he wouldn't think I was cross.

Leaving the park, I released his hand to check my phone. Mette had forwarded a message, but that was all.

Hi! Trying to get hold of Kristian, but he must have changed his number. Can you send this text on to him?

Hi, Uncle Kristian! Arriving London next week. Hotel until Friday, but thinking of staying the weekend too. Can you put me up? Would love to see little Leo again. You and Yelena too, of course! Ane

'Wait a minute,' I said to Leo, and stopped to text Mette back.

Mette, don't forward stuff to me, it doesn't matter what. OK?

I shouldn't have had to tell her. I'd told her a thousand times already. What was it she didn't understand? If I'd asked her to use her discretion, then obviously I could have expected her to pass this one on. But not when I'd told her *never*.

It wasn't that I didn't care for Ane. There was grit in her. But that didn't mean I wanted her in my house.

Maybe dinner in town somewhere.

OK, Mette texted back. *Sorry*. I dropped the phone back in my pocket and carried on walking. Leo slipped to my side again.

'Let's walk separately for a bit now,' I said.

'Why?'

'Because you're nearly seven years old. You walk on your own when you're seven.'

He didn't respond. I saw him push his glasses up with the tip of his finger as he stopped at the kerb of the street we had to cross, just as a car was coming. I ran my hand over his back a couple of times. He looked up at me and smiled.

'Shall we ask Luke if he wants to come for a sleepover at the weekend?' I said.

'Can do.'

'Or don't you want to?'

'Yes.'

'But not that bothered?'

Though it didn't have to, the car stopped and the driver waved us across.

Leo didn't answer.

'Why not?'

'I don't think he will.'

'Of course he will! It'll be great, you'll see. We'll buy some sweets and you can watch a film together.'

'All right,' he said.

'You have to make an effort to make friends, you know. Everyone does. You could build something in Lego, the two of you.'

'Luke doesn't like Lego.'

'What does he like, then?'

'Football.'

'Is that all?'

He shrugged.

'You like football as well, though, don't you?'

'A bit.'

'You're my son, you know, Leo. And I've never been interested in football.'

'I know.'

'So we won't ask Luke to come?'

'No.'

He walked for a while at my side without saying anything. Eventually we turned into our street.

'Shall we do something together, then? On Saturday?' I said.

'Yes,' he said, a bit happier-sounding all of a sudden, though still without looking at me.

'What would you like to do?'

'Go into town, maybe?'

'Just that? Not the Science Museum? Or the Transport Museum?'

'Can we go to the cinema?'

'Not when the weather's this nice, surely?'

He opened the gate and we walked up to the front door.

'Let's talk about it later,' I said. 'OK?'

He nodded.

Stepping into the hall, we were met by a smell of fried onions. The radio was on loud. German voices. Leo twisted out of his shoes and went to his room.

Yelena was standing with a spatula in one hand, the other on her hip. The kitchen was drenched in the strong sunshine of afternoon. A couple of flies zigzagged about. The patio door was open.

'What are you making?' I said.

'Lasagne.'

'In this weather?'

'Perhaps you'd like to make dinner instead.'

'What's got your back up?'

'Nothing. Until now.'

'No need to get annoyed. It's hot outside. Something a bit lighter might have been more appropriate, that's all.'

I took my socks off, hung them over the handrail on the decking and stepped down into the garden, walking across the grass to the table and chairs on the raised deck in the shade of the old apple trees in the corner. Nothing here suggested I was in London. The garden stretched back so surprisingly it felt almost like a park, and beyond the wall at the bottom were other gardens quite as large. The house, far too big for us, resembled a country hall. This was the irony of the city: the further away it felt, the more expensive it was to live there. As if the whole point of being in the place was to get away from it.

Anyone knowing where I came from, where I'd started out, would never have guessed I could have ended up here. It was against all odds.

The strange thing about families was that people expected lifelong affiliation, regular contact and unflagging interest. But I had nothing in common with mine, nothing as in zero, so why should I have anything to do with them? And even worse, why should I ever return to the house I grew up in, where it would only be expected of me that I step back into the same role as before? It was no less rational to think that *they* should be the ones to change when they had a son like me. But no, they were the norm, I was the deviant.

Look at this house! Look at this garden! Read the articles about me, for Christ's sake — or the books! Was that what it was to be a *deviant*?

They found it heartless of me not to have attended Liv's funeral. I understood that, she was their daughter and they were distraught, it wasn't how they'd envisaged her life turning out when she'd been born. But that was their business. Mum's and Dad's. I didn't try to tell them what they should be feeling and what they should do. It was up to them. But that didn't apply the other way round. Although I was a grown man they wanted to steer me, to tell me what I should do and what I should feel. If I could have been the only one there, I would have gone to the funeral. I had many fond recollections of Liv from my childhood. But the very fact of my attendance would have been taken as an act of atonement, of reconciliation. That was what they didn't understand. They couldn't see themselves, tangled up as they were in their net of conventions.

Ane wanted away from them too, and so she'd picked me out as someone to identify with. Clearly, she felt she had something in common with me. She wanted to be a writer and had gone to writing schools in both Sweden and Norway, and she was welcome to it, she could spit out all the mediocre poetry collections she liked as far as I was concerned, it just wasn't anything to do with me — where was the relevance in her being my sister's daughter?

On the other hand I liked the thought that she was so different from Helene. While she might not have been turning her back on her exactly, she was at least doing something of which Helene had absolutely no understanding. How long before the cracks appeared in that family over a Sunday lunch?

A movement at the edge of my field of vision made me turn my head. It was Donat, our Albanian gardener. For quite some time Leo had thought his name was Doughnut, which we laughed about after we found out. He lifted his hand in a wave, I did likewise and then immediately turned away so as not to encourage him to come over for a chat.

Little did it help, for a moment later he was on his way over the lawn, gloves clutched in one hand, in his shorts and a T-shirt, a pair of dark brown wellingtons. He was rather bandy-legged, his thighs thin and pale, and had the kind of mouth that always seemed to be curled in a smile.

'Good afternoon, my lord,' he said.

He found amusement in such irony, making fun of his own status in order to rise above it. We were in fact equals, he seemed to be saying.

'Nice to see you, Donat. Everything all right?'

'Oh yes. I've fixed the sprinkling system for you. In exactly —' he lifted his forearm and looked at his watch — 'one minute from now, the water will come trickling right there.'

He indicated the flower bed next to me with a nod.

'Very good.'

'And I've trimmed the hedge facing the street. Did you notice?'

'I did, yes.'

'You still have a problem with slugs, though. Would you like me to deal with it?'

'Yes, do.'

He stood for a moment, motionless, his eyes fixed on the flower bed. It was impossible not to do likewise. We humans are rather simple in that respect — when something's about to happen, we'll wait for it expectantly.

The water began to seep soundlessly from a hole in the black hose, before the pressure mounted sufficiently for it to fan into the air and sprinkle.

'What did I tell you!' Donat said.

'Thanks a lot,' I said. 'Will you be here as usual next week?'

'Unless someone tells me otherwise.'

A shadow passed behind the shrubs. A second later a fox leapt up onto the wall, turned its head and stared at us a moment before jumping down to the other side.

'You should get rid of them too,' Donat said. 'If you want, I can take care of it.'

'I like them being here.'

He shook his head to himself, presumably at my stupidity.

'Then if the master will allow, I'll call it a day.'

I gave an ironic salute, a hand peaking my brow. He waddled back in the direction of the shed and I lit a cigarette. One of the first things I'd mentioned to him was that I'd met his prime minister in Tirana. I suppose I'd thought it would impress him. It didn't. Instead, he'd kicked off with all this fawning lord-and-master business. Not that it was that big a problem — I wasn't normally at home when he was at work.

A fox's gaze was more unfathomable than a dog's. Stranger to us. Its depths, I mused, lay in the unknown.

The door opened. I'd expected Yelena, but was glad to see Leo step out. In his socks.

'Bare feet or shoes!' I called out to him. 'Not your socks!'

He sat down on the edge of the decking and pulled them off before coming over. As he stopped in front of me, I saw there were tears in his eyes.

'What's the matter?'

'My tongue's all yellow.'

'Let me see.'

He opened his mouth and extended his tongue. Sure enough, it was coated.

'Have you eaten something that was yellow?'

He shook his head and looked at me with frightened eyes.

'It's nothing to worry about,' I said.

'But what *is* it?'

'You've got a coating on your tongue, that's all. Go and brush it with your toothbrush.'

'Is it cancer?'

'Cancer? Of course not, don't be silly. It's nothing.'

'But isn't it dangerous?'

He was sobbing now.

'Leo. Come on, pull yourself together. Go to the bathroom and brush your tongue with your toothbrush.'

He gave a nod, his mouth twisted, and went back towards the house.

I didn't like it. Being afraid of something that was nothing to be afraid of like that. It was anxiety. Leo had always been so happy-go-lucky. Healthy and normal.

I had to make sure he stayed that way.

Yelena had set the table in the dining room. She'd opened a bottle of wine too. The lack of any explanation was reason enough for me to understand that she wanted me to ask. I sat down without comment. I didn't like being dictated to, no matter how subtly. But Leo came to her rescue.

'Why are we eating in here?' he said when he came in.

'Because Mum's finished her thesis,' Yelena said, and looked at me with a smile.

'Well,' I said, 'there's a surprise.'

'Not to me.'

'Is it submitted?'

'Mm-hmm.'

She poured wine into our glasses and I raised mine in a toast.

'Congratulations,' I said.

'Thank you,' she said. 'Cheers!'

Leo wanted to join in too and raised his own glass high in the air. The sun was descending beyond the trees outside, and the rays that slanted in through the window behind Leo and Yelena were full and yet diffused in such a way that some things on the table glowed while others remained matt. The strange thing about the sun in the evening was that darkness seemed already to be present in even its strongest beams. I'd always sensed it, and now the thought occurred to me again. The ambient light in the room was indirect and weaker, but contained no darkness, which existed only in those saturated rays of sunlight — they struck a fork and it was aglow; they struck the edge of a plate, the stainless steel of a candlestick, a gleaming glass.

'Congratulations, Mummy!' Leo said. I wasn't sure he understood what it meant that her thesis was now done, but he seemed at least to have overcome the terror he'd felt at his tongue turning yellow.

Yelena cut out a slab of lasagne and put it on his plate. She was wearing a white shirt and blue jeans, and her hair was up. It wasn't hard to see that he was her son when they were sitting next to each other like that. Their mouths, eyes and cheeks were of the same mould. He looked up at her and smiled. He had endless reserves of joy.

'Mmm,' he said. 'Lasagne's the best.'

'That's why I made it,' Yelena said. 'Here, let me give you some salad, too.'

She put a small heap of greens and reds, glistening with transparent dressing, onto his plate.

'No need, I'll serve myself,' I said when she turned to me with an exploratory glance.

'It's delicious, Mummy,' Leo said.

'That's good,' Yelena said. 'What was school like today, anyway? I've hardly seen you since you came home.'

'We went to a church.'

'Oh yes, that was today.'

'You didn't tell me you'd been to church,' I said.

'I forgot.'

'Was it interesting?' Yelena said.

He nodded.

'There were a lot of steps! I was tired out when we got to the top.'

'What was the name of this church?' I said.

'It was St Paul's,' Yelena said. 'Wasn't it?'

'Yes.'

Whenever I'd heard the name or had driven past, I couldn't help but think about what Hans had said that time about it standing in a certain relation to other notable buildings in central London, an obscure

Kabbalist system whereby the location in itself was significant. But in what way it was significant was something I'd never grasped.

'There was this man there,' Leo said.

'I expect there were a lot of men there, weren't there?' I said.

'Yes, but he looked at me.'

'Perhaps you reminded him of someone he knew,' Yelena said with a smile.

He must have stared at him quite intently for Leo to feel the need to tell us.

'He didn't follow you around, did he?' I said.

'I don't know.'

'You don't know? Did he look at you more than once?'

He nodded and swallowed his food, took a gulp of his Fanta and appeared not to want to pursue the matter.

'Did you see him anywhere else?'

'He was there when we got there. And he was in the dome when we went up. And he was standing at the bottom of the steps when we came down.'

'Did he look at you each time you saw him?'

'Yes.'

Yelena and I exchanged glances. She didn't like what she was hearing either.

'Did you tell your teachers?' she said.

He shook his head.

'Can't we talk about something else now?'

'Yes, of course we can,' Yelena said. 'What do you want to talk about?'

'I don't know. What do you want to talk about?'

It was still light outside when Leo went for his bath before bedtime. The sun was completely hidden behind the trees, but the sky above held a faint orange blush. Through the open window, sounds of the city drifted from afar. Now and again, as if by an adjustment of focus, something was brought to the fore, a neighbour's door slamming shut, a car starting, a sudden cry. Leo lay on the floor playing, his hair still wet, in a pair of pyjamas that were already too small for him. His head lay resting on his outstretched arm as he moved his figures and cars around his

Lego town in patterns whose logic was known only to himself. I sat on the chest in which his toys were kept and watched him absently. He'd been allowed ten minutes more, but I could tell that sleep was circling in on him. He could barely open his eyes again whenever he blinked.

I got my phone out. Jacob had just sent me an email, which I opened.

Christ. The fucking idiots.

MoMA were closing the exhibition ahead of schedule. Jacob was most apologetic, they'd done everything they could, he wrote, but after a comprehensive review the museum had decided not to exploit the full period. The explanation they were giving was low ticket sales. But the real reason was hardly a secret. They were cowing to outside pressure.

'Pappy?' said Leo.

'Yes?' I said without looking up.

'Are we going to read?'

'In a minute. Let me do this first.'

'I'm tired.'

'Don't pester. It won't take long.'

I wrote back to say I couldn't accept it. Didn't we have a contract with the dates in black and white? If they stood by their decision, we'd sue them. Our association, I added, would be over if they didn't get this fixed.

I tapped to send and put the phone back in my pocket. When I looked up, Leo's head was slack where he lay and his eyes were closed.

'Are you asleep?'

He didn't answer. I stood up and leaned over him.

'Fooled you!' he shouted, and giggled.

I lifted him up. He nuzzled his cheek into the pit of my neck and his body relaxed and went limp.

'You're tired,' I said.

'Yes,' he said.

'Do you want to go to sleep and give reading a miss tonight?'

'No.'

'OK.'

He leaned up against me on the toy chest as we turned the pages of his favourite book. It was one he'd been given for his birthday in April and he'd been reading it every night since. It was about the world and all its continents and countries, richly illustrated with photographs of cities and towns, countryside and wilderness. He liked the Asian countries the best, perhaps because they appeared the most exotic. A picture of a teeming harbour in Vietnam, so packed with boats, barges and canoes that it looked more like a market than a harbour. A picture of a forest-clad mountain in China, a monastery and a pavilion at its foot. And then Japan — a Tokyo street with giant video hoardings, neon signs, a train crossing a bridge where another temple nestled amid trees. Thailand, a wide boulevard milling with cyclists who had boxes balanced on their luggage racks, mopeds and a myriad of small cars.

'Can we go to Vietnam sometime?' he said, as he always did when we looked at the pictures from there.

'Yes, we can. We could go to Vietnam *and* Japan, if you want?'

'And China.'

'Yes. I have a friend who said that if you want to see China, you must do it now, before everything has changed. There's such a lot happening there now, you see.'

'Like what?'

'They're building everywhere. Great big cities. Factories and roads, all sorts of things.'

'Can we go this summer?'

'No, it's such a long way to go, we'd need to plan well ahead. Next summer, perhaps.'

'Next summer?'

'Yes. Would you like that?'

'Yes.'

'But what time is it now, do you think?'

'Bedtime?'

'Bedtime, yes.'

When I came back into the living room Yelena had taken the bottle of wine and was sitting outside. I went and got my glass and joined her. She was barefoot and sat with her legs stretched out and crossed. She'd let her hair down, which changed her. It was as if she became shorter when her neck was no longer visible, and there seemed to be a bit more of her somehow as well. She looked younger for it too in a way. Strange how so little could alter so much.

'Is it a good feeling?' I said, sitting down at the other side of the table.

She nodded, cupping the glass in her hand, swirling the small amount of wine at the bottom.

'How come you didn't tell me you were nearly finished?'

'You had enough on your plate.'

The roar of a plane abruptly reached our ears. It was a phenomenon I liked, the way the sound didn't just start quietly in the distance and then gradually increase, but was suddenly just there, as if it had broken through from the beyond.

I looked up to find it. The sky was still blue, with that very particular depth to the colour that came as the light was leaving it. The plane, with its protruding nose, angled into view in the east. A yellow-and-green tail fin. What company was it now that had those colours? A Brazilian one, perhaps. Or one from the African countries.

Yelena looked at me.

'Are you happy, then?' I said. 'Is it as good as you'd hoped?'

'Is anything ever?'

'Are you in a bad mood about something?'

'No.'

'Good! Because I'm *really* happy for you. But yes, there *has* been a lot going on of late.'

'Yes.'

'MoMA want to close the exhibition early.'

'Oh, how stupid.'

'Stupid's not the word. Bloody scandalous is what it is.'

'Can you do anything?'

'I can threaten them.'

'Is that going to be help?'

'I shouldn't think so. It'll make me feel a bit better though. I don't care to let other people ride roughshod over me.'

She gazed out at the lawn. It was still green, though the colour seemed to be releasing its hold, giving way to grey, while over by the fence, beneath the plants and shrubs, the ground had already submitted to grey-black. It was as though darkness stood impatient in the wings, waiting for its cue.

'Can I read it *now*, then?' I said.

She gave me a smile.

'I'm not sure I'm up to it.'

'Of course you are! I'll read it tomorrow, if you want. I haven't exactly got much else to do, as you know.'

She nodded.

Another rumble, another plane to the east.

'Leo wants to go to China,' I said.

'So it was China tonight, was it?' she said with a laugh. 'Last night it was Singapore.'

'I told him we could go next summer.'

'You promised him?'

'Not promised exactly. I said it was a possibility.'

'He'll be over the moon.'

'Yes, he will. No reason we can't take him there.'

'No, why not.'

'Yes, why not.'

She leaned forward and picked up the bottle, poured some wine into her glass and looked at me to see if I wanted any. I nodded and held out my own. The few drops that were left barely covered the bottom.

'Shall we open another?' she said.

'Yes, let's do that,' I said.

She got up and crossed the lawn. I could hear someone moving around on the other side of the fence, then a gentle hiss. The neighbour, our nocturnal garden-waterer, had in other words turned on his sprinkler. It made me think of Donat. His bandy-legged gait when he came waddling with a full watering can in each hand. His legs were so hairy they made him look like an insect. A two-legged spider.

I thought about his prime minister. How he'd made us stand around for nearly an hour in a tiny anteroom without windows before receiving us in his office. The way he'd then completely dominated the conversation. We were pawns, present only in order that he could be seen to run the show and bask in positive media coverage. He wanted only to talk about superintelligence and singularity. And then we were ushered out. I'd been seething, but what could I do?

Yelena appeared again, holding the bottle by its neck, making it look like a cudgel. She handed it to me along with the corkscrew.

'Who do you suppose might have been staring at Leo like that? Or was he imagining things perhaps?'

I threaded the metal spiral into the cork, which it penetrated with a squeaking sound.

'Someone probably did look at him, but then the rest was his own embellishment, don't you think?'

'It wouldn't be unlike him. Not that he makes things up, but he does immerse himself in things. And he does embellish.'

'Exactly, he's not short on imagination.'

I pulled out the cork with a pop and replenished our glasses.

The next morning Yelena told him we'd decided to go to China. I could see how it lit a light in him. A year was an eternity in the life of a six-year-old, but the energy in looking forward was more positive than it was in impatience, especially when the wait was long.

'Can I tell Luke?' he said.

'You can tell whoever you like,' I said.

'Then we're definitely going?'

'It's as sure as money in the bank.'

'Perhaps not the most apposite of similes,' Yelena said, standing with Leo's bowl, in which two or three soggy cornflakes floated in what he'd left of his milk.

'You'd know more about that than me.'

She raised her eyebrows and gave me a partly superior, partly fatigued look before picking up her own plate and going over to the worktop with it.

'What are your plans for today?' I said.

'I'm on holiday,' she said.

'And what might that involve?'

'I'm having lunch with Katie.'

'Sounds more like work to me.'

'After that, the hairdresser.'

'Who's coming to pick me up?' said Leo.

'I am,' I said.

'Can I have an ice cream in the park?'

'We'll see,' I said as I left the table. 'But get your shoes on now, it's time to go.'

'Are you going to the studio afterwards?' Yelena said, on her way out into the hall to say goodbye to him.

'Yes.'

'Can you get something for dinner tonight?'

'No, I want to get some work done before I pick him up.'

'Well, *I* can't.'

'Pappy? Are we going?' he called out from the hall.

She bent down and kissed him on the cheek as I appeared from the kitchen. He wrapped his arms around her hips.

'I love you, Mummy,' he said.

'I love you, too,' she said and couldn't resist a smirk in my direction: who was it he said he loved? Not you, *Pappy*.

'Come on then,' I said, and stepped out into bright sunlight.

The week that followed brought little cheer. An exhibition in Milan that was to open in February was cancelled. Louisiana in Denmark pulled out just as suddenly from one that was in the planning stages. MoMA's decision was irrevocable, I was told, and Burnett's lawyers advised strongly against legal action.

As if that wasn't enough, Mette left me. She quit, just like that. After twelve years of unbroken success, she chose to leave the minute the going got tough.

I'd thought she was better than that. She didn't even quit to my face, but sent me an email, a long spiel taking in both 'seeking new challenges' and 'I've come to a stage in life where change feels right', while thanking me for our 'incredibly rich and stimulating time together'. She was a newspeaking rat abandoning what she thought was a sinking ship.

But she could do as she liked. It was no use getting anxious when circumstances changed, for the displacement that followed invariably meant that new opportunities would present themselves, opportunities that wouldn't otherwise have arisen, and if moreover the circumstances that changed were fundamental, then in some instances you could end up in places completely different and previously unimagined.

Perhaps Mette's resignation was a sign, perhaps it indicated a new direction for me to go. I'd been thinking about ending my association with Alfred Burnett and moving on to another gallerist. But what if I didn't move on? What if I severed all ties without committing anywhere else? A year or two on my own. No exhibitions, no interviews, no sales. Just me alone in the studio. Like it had been in the beginning.

I wrote a formal letter to Jacob informing him that I no longer wished to be represented by the gallery. I decided I would change my email addresses and phone numbers and began looking around for a different studio. If I'd been able to move house, I'd have done that too. Far too many people knew where I lived, but it would be too big an operation, the consequences would be too great — Leo had lived there all his life and knew nothing else.

I said nothing to Yelena. She was in a transitional phase herself, not knowing what she was going to do now that she'd finished her dissertation. I still hadn't read it, it was on the table next to the sofa in the studio, a 400-page stack that called for will and commitment that I didn't have. She was probably waiting for my response, but didn't want to push me.

With all this going on, I freed myself from every point of contact with the world. I switched off my phone in the studio and left my laptop well alone — I was expecting Jacob to ring or email in order to convince me to stay, and that Mette would be unsettled by my lack of response and want to get hold of me. I didn't want to talk to Yelena either while I was there. What I wanted was a sense of being at the bottom of the sea, where the world and all its industrial hue and cry existed only at a great distance, if not in another dimension, then at least in another element than the one I inhabited. I had a few hundred books, I had tubes full of oil colours, I had brushes and canvas, stacks of old films, a darkroom; I had notebooks, sketchpads, and paper in every size; and I had my cameras, from the premodern models to state-of-the-art digital. Now and then I slept, I wandered about, I jotted down ideas, and slept again. A Shakespeare drama required only a few hours to read, and in the course of that week I completed the project I'd started twenty-five years earlier, which was to read everything he'd ever written, in chronological order. The only play that wasn't unduly tainted by the age in which he wrote, the only one that still retained its relevance, was *Hamlet*. Perhaps *Macbeth* too, the way it descended into night and blood. Night and blood were unchanged, night and blood had been with us always. On the Friday, I returned to Becker, beginning with the poems, which I found oddly moving. Suns setting over forests, strange horsemen, tormented souls and pale moons, but also clear, babbling brooks, flashing trout, blackberry thickets and sun-warmed earth, a place where time was blurred, for the sun, he wrote, was ancient, and where birdsong from one moment to the next could be filled with fate and become an omen of ruin.

To step out into the streets of London after being near to Becker's time and soul was an alienating experience. It was as if his words had swelled in me, expelling everything that they were not. I unlocked the car, turned out onto the road, followed the abrupt rhythms of traffic with all its stops and starts at traffic lights that came at such short intervals on both sides of the bridge. What was only a few kilometres as the crow flies took nearly an hour by car. By the time I arrived at the school I was therefore fully acclimatised, surrounded in other words by entities and forms so familiar as to appear almost shadow-like. I was lucky and found a space to park right by the gate, which opened as I got out, allowing the flock of parents to filter through.

I couldn't see Leo. I scanned the faces again where his class was standing. The teacher, a fresh-faced young man, with glasses and a curly mop of hair, noticed me and came over.

'Leo's gone home,' he informed me. 'His mum came and picked him up.'

'Oh? Why was that?'

'He had a headache, so we phoned home.'

'OK. That was all, a headache?'

'Yes,' he said, and was already moving on to whatever it was he had to do next.

Why hadn't Yelena told me?

Of course, I'd switched my phone off.

I switched it on again as I returned to the car. Five missed calls from Yelena, and three texts. Quite a number from Jacob too, but nothing from Mette. She probably didn't give a toss any more.

I got in the car and phoned Yelena.

'Hello?'

'Hi, it's me. I'm at the school. Leo isn't here, they told me.'

'No, I had to pick him up. He's got a migraine.'

'Migraine?'

'Yes, quite a bad one, it seems. I was trying to get hold of you. You can't have your phone switched off like that.'

I said nothing.

'Can you get him something for it on your way back? I can't leave him on his own, or else I'd do it myself.'

'Won't an aspirin do?'

'No, it's not powerful enough. They sell migraine tablets over the counter. Ask for the strongest they've got for a child.'

'OK,' I said with a sigh.

'There's a pharmacy by the station.'

'I know. See you soon.'

A headache had been no reason to come home from school in my day. And not exactly something my parents would have been particularly bothered about either. But then again, Yelena didn't tend to be overly anxious when it came to illness, so I could only assume it was severe enough. On the other hand, it was impossible to measure pain, you couldn't gauge the extent of a headache. Maybe he was enjoying the attention and exploiting the situation for all he could get.

Yelena didn't appear in the hall as I'd been half expecting when I came in, but was sitting out in the garden with the patio door open.

'Did you get those tablets?' she said.

I held up the packet.

'Good. Thanks. He's asleep now. He can have one when he wakes up.'

I turned to go back in.

'Aren't you going to sit here a bit?'

'I thought I'd look in on him.'

'All right. He's in our bed.'

She'd pulled down the blinds, so the room was rather dark. Leo was lying on his back on top of the covers, with one arm stretched out behind him, the other resting on his tummy. He looked calm and peaceful.

As I went to leave the room he stirred.

'Pappy?'

I turned and he sat up and gently shook his head.

'I haven't got a headache any more,' he said with bemusement.

'That's good.'

'What are we having for dinner?'

'I've no idea. Why don't you come with me, and we'll ask Mummy!'

It turned out to be entrecôte with baked potato wedges, broccoli salad and a home-made béarnaise sauce. We ate in the garden. Leo was refreshed and in fine fettle. We asked him tentatively about his headache, but all he could say was that it had hurt a lot, as if there'd been something that had tightened inside his skull. He hadn't had anything like it before, he told us. Yelena didn't have any migraine in her family as far as she knew, and I hadn't in mine, so it was all a bit of a mystery. Still, he ate with good appetite and stayed at the table to chat with us a while after we'd finished eating, the way he usually did, before going to his room, leaving Yelena and me to sit with our wine.

'He cried,' she said.

'You told me.'

'The school wouldn't normally ring for no reason.'

'Why do you say that? It sounds like you think I don't believe there was anything the matter with him.'

'No, it's not that. It was just so awful seeing him in pain.'

'So you want to talk about it?'

'Yes.'

'Go on then. Talk to me about pain.'

'Kristian.'

'What? Did I say something wrong?'

'You don't have to be so aggressive.'

'Aggressive?'

'Yes.'

'You know what I think about being reduced like that, don't you? You make it sound like it's all I am, *aggressive*.'

'You're not being very nice, if that's any better for you.'

'Don't you think I'm affected as much as you if he feels pain?'

She looked at me with what seemed to be genuine astonishment.

'Of course I do,' she said. 'Have I ever said anything like that? I haven't even thought it!'

'What's the *even* supposed to mean?'

'Kristian, you're obviously looking for an argument, but you'll have to look somewhere else, I'm afraid.'

She got up and went back into the house.

I stayed at the table. Often, I didn't realise what I was feeling until I hurt someone. So being aggressive was as much news to me as it was to Yelena. But it was hardly surprising. I had plenty to be angry about. The hypocritical wankers who wanted to boycott me, for a start. For what reason? A ridiculous piece of banter, that had taken up ten seconds of my life and theirs. But then they had to go and get on their high horses and make a big issue of it — why? So they could feel better about themselves. Because *they* of course wouldn't ever make light of a thing like that. *I*, on the other hand, was not only a bad person because of it, everything I did was bad too.

But I'd left it all behind. Severed every bond. And where I was now, or where I was going, no one could ever get to me with their stupid, insulting insinuations. Their words didn't matter there, they hadn't the slightest significance.

Cunts. What had they ever created? What had they ever achieved?

Nothing. They were completely without value. But when they ganged up, one worthless loser after another, they discovered themselves to be powerful and could drag other people down. It was the only way they could make themselves seen in the landscape, by bringing down everything of splendour around them.

It was deeply human. Perhaps the basest human instinct of all. People became smaller with others. The more there were, the smaller they became.

Yelena understood this, at least. If she hadn't been so broad-minded, I wouldn't have been able to stay with her.

A window opened. Leo leaned out, bare-chested.

'Hi, Pappy!' he shouted.

'Hi, Leo! Are you going for your bath?'

'Yes!'

He vanished inside again. The next twenty minutes I heard their voices come faintly from the bathroom. His laughter, unstoppable more than once, hers then too.

Not much of a headache there.

It was Friday, so he was allowed to stay up an hour longer, time he devoted to television and crisps. Yelena and I sat on either side of him. There was nothing he liked better than that. Just as there was no one I liked better than him, the enthusiastic little damp-haired boy in pyjamas next to me, his eyelids slowly drooping towards sleep. His quiet intervals grew long, and eventually he succumbed.

Yelena looked at me and smiled.

'Will you carry him up to bed?' she said softly.

'Let him sleep a bit first. If he wakes up now, he'll only be full of beans again.'

She nodded.

I felt an urge to say something good to her.

'I've read the first fifty pages, by the way,' I said. I hadn't, but I'd cast an eye over them, noted a few names, so she wouldn't catch me out if she wanted to go into detail. 'Impressive,' I added. 'Really, really good.'

She gave me another smile.

'Do you think so?'

'Yes, I'm only sorry I haven't had time to read on yet. There's been such a lot happening. All that trouble.'

'I know.'

'I'll try to make time tomorrow, though.'

'Aren't you taking Leo into town? He's been looking forward to it.'

'Oh, yes. Tomorrow afternoon, then. No, wait a minute, I've left it at the studio.'

'I'll print another copy, it's no trouble.'

'Right.'

'I think you can take him upstairs now. He's very tired.'

'Yes, why is that? He slept this afternoon.'

She gave a shrug. Leo lay with his head tipped back and his mouth open, emitting a faint little rasping sound with every breath.

Yelena smiled.

'He takes after his dad.'

'What do you mean?'

'The snoring.'

I made a face — *ha ha, very funny* — before getting to my feet and picking him up. Like a sack of flour he lay in my arms, his head on my shoulder. As I tucked him into bed, he opened his eyes and sat up without looking at me. I smoothed his cheek and told him everything was all right, and he lay back down and turned onto his side. I spread the thin duvet over his body and stayed with him. Only when he began to snore again did I leave the room.

The next morning I woke early. The light outside was weak and brittle, the low-slanting rays seemed as delicate as butterfly wings, quite without the dense immovability of mid-afternoon sun. I went outside with a mug of coffee, lit a cigarette and listened to the birds, their dawn chorus almost undisturbed by any human element. There were parrots too, the descendants of long-escaped pets, among crows and starlings, sparrows and blackbirds. My new plan, to work alone, without connection to the art world, still seemed good after three days, which meant that in all likelihood it *was* good. It certainly wouldn't harm, not now.

It was true as well what Yelena said, that I would have more time for Leo. Not that my conscience wasn't clear about the time I'd spent away from him — that was a part of life he had to learn. No, it was more for my sake than his.

The question was, what were we going to do today?

Fortunately, he didn't require anything out of the ordinary to make him happy. He'd be excited if we went to the Natural History Museum or something similar, but just as glad if we went into Covent Garden and ambled around a bit there and then found a good place to have lunch. Maybe we could go to the cinema, he'd mentioned that. Or maybe not, in this heat.

We'd go to the big new Lego shop and buy him some Lego. Then have some lunch in Soho.

It was a good plan.

I had another coffee before going upstairs to wake him. He was lying on his side with the cover bunched up and clutched to his chest. I opened the curtains and light flooded the room without him reacting.

'Leo?' I said softly. 'Are you awake?'

I touched his shoulder. He opened his eyes and looked up at me. There was no bleary-eyed blinking, no veil of sleep, all of a sudden he was just there.

He looked frightened.

'Pappy?'

'Are you ready for a new day? We're going into town, remember?'

'I'm going to die today.'

'What kind of a thing is that to say? Don't be silly! You mustn't say such a thing.'

I bent forward and ruffled his hair.

'It's a beautiful day. The sun's shining and you and I are going into town together.'

He just stared at me.

'Are you still thinking about that yellow tongue? Or is it the headache you had yesterday? There's nothing to be afraid of, whatever it is. I promise. Come on, let's go downstairs and have some breakfast, eh?'

I went to the door. He sat up and slithered out of bed, until his feet were on the floor.

'You can have your breakfast in your pyjamas, if you want.'

He nodded. I put my arms around him when he came towards me.

'Did you have a bad dream?'

He nodded again.

'It wasn't about that, though.'

'About what?'

'About dying today.'

'That's enough, do you hear? Enough. You're not going to die, Leo, don't be silly. What you're feeling has a name. It's called anxiety. It's when you're scared, but you don't know what of. It's very common, though, a lot of people get it. What you have to do is tell yourself it's silly. Nothing's going to happen. Do you understand?'

'Yes.'

'All right, we'll have our breakfast now, shall we? And let's not talk about it any more.'

'OK.'

He sat down at the table in the kitchen while I went to the cupboard. I took pains not to look at him or pay him any special attention in case he was angling for it. If I made a fuss of him now, it would only encourage him to hold on to the idea.

'What do you want, cornflakes, muesli, baguette or toast?' I said.

'I don't know.'

'Well, that's all there is. Cornflakes, muesli, baguette or toast?'

'Toast.'

'Right, and what do you want on it?'

'Butter and . . .'

'Cheese? Ham? Jam? Or there's Nutella, I think.'

'Just butter.'

'No, come on. Cheese? Ham?'

'Ham.'

'Now you're talking!'

I put two slices of bread in the toaster and took the ham out of the fridge, glanced at him and saw that he was just sitting there watching me. I said nothing, took a carton of juice out too, and a glass from the cupboard, poured him some, then poured myself some more coffee.

'Shall we sit outside?'

'Can do.'

It wasn't like him to be so detached, so listless. I'd have to put some life into him, or else going into town wouldn't be much fun for either of us. I wasn't going to tell him about the Lego shop until we got there, but if it could inject some enthusiasm into him now, there was no point in keeping it for later.

The toast popped up out of the toaster and I removed the two slices using my fingertips and put them down on the breadboard. They were nice and golden.

'There's butter on it,' I said putting it onto a plate for him. 'It's melted into the bread, that's all.'

'Mm.'

I put the plate and his glass of juice onto a tray along with my coffee and took it out into the garden with Leo following along behind me.

He sat down and nibbled his toast. His back was to the sun. Its light seemed almost to swirl around his head.

'Leo?'

'Yes?' he said, and looked up at me.

'How about we buy some new Lego today?'

'Can do.'

'Can do? Don't you want to?'

'I suppose so.'

'All right, we won't.'

'But I want to.'

'Are you sure?'

'Yes.'

I leaned back in my chair, crossed my legs and lit a cigarette. He didn't like the smoke, especially when he was eating, but we were outside now with billions of cubic metres of fresh air all around us.

'Where's Mummy?'

'She's asleep.'

'Can I go and wake her?'

'Let's wait a bit, shall we? She likes to have a lie-in in the mornings.'

'OK.'

'And, Leo? You mustn't say anything to Mummy about what you said to me, all right?'

'Why not?'

'It'll make her upset. There's nothing to be scared of, so it makes no sense to tell her anyway. Don't you agree?'

'Yes.'

He'd liven up as soon as we got into town. As soon as he could *see* the Lego in the shop — and could choose what he wanted.

'It's shorts weather today,' I said. 'You can wear your cap as well. That'll look good!'

'Are you going to wear shorts?'

At last, some life.

'Me? Shorts? Have you ever seen me in a pair of shorts?'

He shook his head.

'Once, though, on the beach in Italy.'

'Those were swimming shorts, dafty. I could hardly go swimming in long trousers, now, could I? But apart from that, you'll never catch me wearing shorts.'

'Why do I have to, then?'

'You don't *have* to. But you like wearing shorts in summer, don't you?'

'Yes.'

'Well, there you are. Come on, let's get your togs on.'

He traipsed back across the lawn. I followed him with the tray, put the glass and plate in the dishwasher, went and got the newspapers from outside the front door and then dumped them on the table in the living room, picked out the arts sections and leafed through to see if there was anything more about me. There wasn't. It all had to blow over at some point — perhaps that point was now.

Yelena was sitting up in bed when I went in to change my shirt. Leo was standing at the bedside.

'I thought I said you weren't to wake her?'

'It's all right,' Yelena said. 'I was awake already.'

She almost certainly hadn't been. I didn't like her lying to Leo just to make him feel better.

I picked a shirt out of the wardrobe and unbuttoned the one I had on, the clean one draped over my arm.

'Leo says he doesn't really want to go into town today.'

'Oh, so that's what he says now, is it?'

I threaded my arm through the sleeve and turned towards him.

'How come you didn't tell me?'

'I don't know.'

'No way. We've planned to go into town, so that's what we'll do. Unless you're not well, that is. Are you ill?'

He shook his head.

'Then go and put your shoes on. And cheer up. It's not as if you're going to be tortured with Lego, pizza and ice cream, is it?'

'No.'

Yelena looked at me with disapproval, but said nothing. I buttoned my shirt and then ran a hand through my hair while checking myself in the mirror on the inside of the wardrobe door.

Outside in the sun-drenched street I curled my arm around his shoulder.

'That's better, isn't it?'

'A bit.'

'If something's troubling you, Leo, or if you feel sad or frightened about something, do you know what the worst thing you can do is?'

'No.'

'It's to do nothing. To stay at home and mope. Because everything will only stay the same then. Do you understand? But if you do something, if you go out like we're doing now into town, for example, then you're doing something that can make you feel better, and very often you *will* feel better. Do you follow?'

'Yes.'

'Good. Now, we'll take the Tube and go to the big Lego shop first, then we can see what we'd like to do after that. Does that sound like a good plan?'

'Yes.'

It was still early, but the sun had gained considerably in strength, the air felt hot, and the street we now walked along was already busy with traffic. Towering red double-deckers, black beetle-like cabs, small, spirited family cars, and then, in the distance at first, but very quickly approaching, two unmarked police cars with blue lights flashing and sirens blaring. Leo stopped as soon as he heard them, his eyes following them as they threaded their way towards us.

'What do you think has happened?' he said.

'I don't know. Something serious. A murder, perhaps. Or a robbery.'

'But why haven't they got proper police cars?'

'Because they're operating undercover, so the criminals won't know they're police.'

'So they can surprise them?'

'That's right, yes.'

'I want to be a policeman.'

'Do you? It's a very good job. But I thought you wanted to be a bin man?'

'That was when I was little.'

He looked up at me and smiled, then tucked his hand into mine.

The buildings stood wall to wall now, there were no more gaps between them, and a couple of minutes later we approached the station, where all the shops and cafes stood crammed together along the street. I bought Leo an iced tea and myself a cappuccino, and we took them down with us into the Underground. Both escalators were packed, as they would be the rest of the day. It was remarkable, I always thought, how people were willing to let themselves be transported so fearlessly into the depths of the earth. The escalators were steep, the corridors long, leading us further and further down, until at last we were perhaps fifty, perhaps seventy, perhaps ninety metres under the ground. We could do so of course only because such great efforts had been made to hide the reality of it. We could have been inside a shopping centre, with artificial light and advertising, and never a hint of where we actually were, what was behind and beneath the passages and platforms. Had the escalators plunged through narrow shafts blasted out of grimy rock that dripped with moisture, and had the corridors leading to the platforms patently presented themselves as the mined tunnels they were, illuminated only faintly by the occasional burning torch, people would surely have thought twice before venturing to take the Tube.

Leo looked up at me and held out his bottle of iced tea.

'Can you open it for me?'

'Wait until we get to the platform.'

He didn't say anything, but instead tried to open it himself before we came to the bottom of the escalator and stepped on towards the next.

Nor did we give it a thought when walking on the pavements overground, that rolling trains rattled incessantly through holes in the bedrock far beneath our feet. They'd been doing so in this city for nearly a hundred and fifty years and yet it barely ever occurred to us. The notion of trains passing through the ground underneath us was as if alien to our mind, still somehow a vision of the future that one day perhaps would become reality, but which for now remained rooted in the world of science fiction.

'Let me,' I said as he struggled to twist off the lid. He smiled gratefully and then gulped a mouthful while standing against the wall where we'd stepped aside so as not to be in the way.

'Ahh,' he said exaggeratedly. There was no trace in him now of the morning's gloom, whatever it had all been about. He put the lid back on and took my hand.

'Left or right?' I said as the corridor divided in front of us.

'Left.'

'Sure?'

'Of course. I've been this way a thousand times before.'

At the same moment, a train left the platform — I heard its rising, rumbling lament and felt the suck of air it dragged with it into the tunnel.

The next was in three minutes, so it didn't matter.

I sat down on one of the benches. Leo looked around, inquisitive as ever. He stepped to the edge and leaned forward to look along the tracks.

'Leo!'

He turned and looked at me.

'Back behind the yellow line, please. You should know well enough by now.'

He nodded and came back to look at some of the posters on the platform wall, pausing to study a Tube map.

It was the strangest thing to say, that he was going to die today, a disturbing thought to think. It could only be tied to the concern he'd felt at his yellow tongue, perhaps also to his headache the day before. Perhaps it had to do too with the fear that had gripped him the first time he'd understood that he would one day die. It had lurked there all this time, somewhere in the folds of his brain, waiting to attach to a passing thought.

He stood now at the yellow line, peering into the tunnel again, as the rumble of an approaching train gained in force. He loved to see the lights in the darkness.

I stood up and stepped quickly towards him, put a hand on each of his shoulders.

'You've got to be careful down here,' I said.

'I know, Pappy.'

'Good.'

When eventually we emerged into the open air again, the streets outside the Tube station were teeming with people. Heads in their hundreds bobbing along the pavements. Looking down a side street was like a window being opened on a phenomenon of nature, a population of seals on an expanse of rock, a great flock of sheep in a narrow valley, only here it was people instead.

'Where do they come from, Leo, all these people?' I said as we waited for the green man at a crossing.

'They come from all over the world,' he said, sounding far too grown up for his age.

'But what are they doing here?'

'They're shopping.'

'They are, yes. And that's what we're going to do now as well. Do you know what you want?'

The traffic stopped on both sides and the crowd set in motion seconds before the red man actually turned to green. Leo shook his head and held my hand again.

'When I moved here,' I said, 'in the eighties —'

'When was the eighties?'

'A long time ago. I was only twenty years old. But there weren't nearly as many people in the streets then.'

'Was London smaller?'

'No, not at all. London was a gigantic city then too.'

'So why weren't there as many people?'

'I'm not sure,' I said, walking into the shadow of the buildings. 'But people didn't travel as much in those days. It wasn't as common to fly, for example.'

'But there were planes, weren't there?'

I looked at him and smiled.

'Of course there were planes.'

The street opened out and delivered us into a bigger public space of cinemas and tourist traps, entertainers with small tentative audiences who had gathered around to watch their performances, whether they were climbing ladders no one held, juggling knives or singing well-known songs. Outside the Lego shop on the other side, there was a queue. But at least it was moving.

The people in front of us, a family of four, spoke Spanish. I heard Swedish further along, and behind us a moment later came a pair of Germans, a couple my own age, the man wearing a Germany football shirt. I hoped for their sake they were there to buy a present and not something for themselves. You never could tell — the Tube and the buses were filled with grown adults playing video games on their phones, so it wouldn't have surprised me if people in their forties played with Lego too.

'Do you know what you want when we get in?' I said to Leo, who was still holding my hand even though we were basically standing still, looking in through the window.

'Star Wars, maybe.'

'Isn't that for older kids?'

'I'm good at building Lego.'

'I know you are.'

'Can I decide on my own?'

'Of course you can. As long as it's nothing unreasonable.'

Somehow, I got the feeling someone was watching me and I looked around, my eyes scanning.

A homeless man was standing across the road staring right at me. He was dressed in a long, shabby overcoat, unbuttoned, shorts and a T-shirt underneath. His hair was long and unkempt, and his face — his face looked like Hans's.

It *was* Hans.

The moment our eyes met, he bent down and picked up a rucksack he then slung over his shoulder, before disappearing into the street behind him.

I put a hand on Leo's shoulder.

'Can you stay here on your own a minute?'

'On my own?'

His eyes filled with apprehension.

'Yes. Two minutes, that's all. I've just seen someone I used to know and I'd like to say hello to them, if I can. OK?'

He didn't reply.

'Just move along with the queue. And if you get in before I'm back, you can go round the shop by yourself and look for something you want. I'll find you soon enough. OK?'

He nodded reluctantly and I hurried across the square. No more than a minute had passed and Hans, tall as he was, would be easy to spot in a crowd, but in the narrow street I couldn't see him anywhere. I cantered on, up into Chinatown and the manic throngs there.

He must have ducked into a shop or some other building.

I turned and went back, glancing in all the windows, poking my head inside a door here and there, but he was nowhere to be seen.

Why had he made off like that?

Perhaps he felt embarrassed.

Of course he'd feel embarrassed.

Everything indicated that life hadn't worked out for him. And then all of a sudden he claps eyes on me, one of the most prominent artists in the world, whose pictures went for ridiculous sums of money. It was hardly surprising he wanted to avoid me.

This time I'd seen his face and was in no doubt. It wasn't some phantom of my subconscious mind, it was Hans.

Had he been in London all this time?

Only when I came to the square again and saw the flagship store ahead of me on the corner did I remember that Leo was waiting there.

Not that it was any disaster if he'd had to go in on his own. The place would be like a paradise to him.

I jumped the queue and went straight to the entrance. A security guard stopped me bluntly and told me to wait my turn like everyone else.

'My son's inside. We were standing in line together, only I had to go to the loo,' I explained.

'OK,' he said, and let me in.

I looked behind me and scanned the square one last time in case Hans had returned, but of course he hadn't, and I resigned to giving my full attention to Leo.

He wasn't to be seen anywhere on the ground floor, so I went up to the first and found him in front of a display with flowers made entirely of Lego.

'You've been ages,' he said. 'Couldn't you find them?'

'No, but it doesn't matter.'

'Who was it?'

'An old friend called Hans, who I haven't seen for many years.'

'Was it in the eighties?'

'It was, yes! In the eighties. Anyway, what's all this? Flowers? Is that what you want?'

'No. I was only looking at them. I want something from over there.'

He pointed to a display shelf at the other side of the room.

'The police station?'

'Yes. Or the bank robbery. Which one do you think?'

We stood and looked at them for a while. I tried to imagine I was him. The police station was good, it had a helicopter with a landing pad, a van and a car, a few police officers and a dog. There was not much happening in it, but maybe that was what he was looking for, maybe it made him feel secure. Whereas the bank robbery was different altogether, all action, with police and robbers, police cars and escape vehicles, money and guns. Would it be too unsettling for him? No, come on. Nothing dangerous happened in his life, he was completely safe in every respect, so the bank robbery was perfect, it allowed him to live out some excitement.

'I'd have the bank robbery.'

'But there's no helicopter.'

'You've decided, then?'

'No.'

'You want the helicopter, and the helicopter only comes with the police station. That settles it, doesn't it?'

'But there's no robbers in the police station.'

He reached out and placed a hand on each box.

'Can I have them both?'

'Both? You're joking, aren't you?'

'If I never ask for Lego again?'

'I think you're pushing your luck a bit there, Leo. Mind it doesn't run out or you'll end up with nothing. One or the other, so make up your mind.'

'Can I think about it and come back later?'

It was something he had from his mother. Think about it? No way.

'No, we're not coming back today. We're going to have some lunch and then we're going home.'

'Oh.'

'Come on, which one do you want?'

'But I don't know.'

'Leo.'

'I don't know!'

'I thought you'd be over the moon with some new Lego. Instead you're whining. I don't like that. What's the point in buying you anything if you're only going to whine?'

He went quiet. It seemed for a moment that he was going to choose the bank robbery — there was a slight movement of his hand, which then he halted.

'Can't I just think about it a bit, Pappy?'

'You can decide now. I'll count to three and then you choose. One . . .'

'No! Don't count!'

'Two . . .'

'But, Pappy, I don't know!'

'Three. Have you decided now?'

He shook his head.

'Then you'll have to do without.'

I turned towards the stairs and sensed him immediately pick up a box from the shelf. Sure enough, he was coming now as I glanced back, the police station set in his hands.

'Well done, Leo,' I said. 'Now let's find the till so we can pay. And I want no sulking, do you understand? That's a very expensive present I'm giving you.'

He nodded, his eyes moist.

I sighed and joined the queue.

Passing through the narrow streets and lanes of Soho I looked out for Hans, though of course he was nowhere to be seen. He was probably looking out for me too, but for the opposite reason, to avoid me. Leo had cheered up again and walked at my side with his big yellow Lego bag dangling from his hand. He wanted sushi, he said, which was all right by me, so we went up towards Carnaby Street where I was sure I remembered a sushi restaurant from one time or another. The streets were teeming with people and the pavement cafes we passed were all fully occupied. There was a lot of bare female skin on display — bare stomachs, bare arms, bare calves, bare thighs, and, in sandals, bare feet. That so many men too went around with bare legs, some as hirsute as apes, was perhaps a result of the movement towards equality, what did I know, but to me it looked most of all like an upsurge of the infantile. Shorts were for children, trousers were for men. Short skirts were for young women, and the older a woman got the longer her dress should get too. These days, mature women dressed like fourteen-year-olds, full-grown men as twelve-year-olds. It wasn't my problem, people could do as they liked. If they wanted to look like simpletons, it could only be because they were.

The sushi restaurant wasn't where I thought it was. It wasn't in the street that ran parallel either.

'Does it have to be sushi?'

'No.'

'How about pizza? We just passed an Italian place.'

'Will they have pasta?'

'They're bound to. Shall we try there?'

'Mmm.

The tables outside were all taken, but there was plenty of room in the dim interior. The head waiter, if the shabby-looking bearded man with yellowed teeth and a tongue that kept flicking out from between his lips could be given such a fine title, showed us for some reason to a table next to the toilets and was clearly dissatisfied when I said we preferred to sit somewhere else, but with so many tables available he could hardly have refused.

'Will here do?' I said to Leo as we sat down.

He nodded and took the kids' menu the waiter handed him, thanked him politely, and even smiled at him.

'Can we have a Coke and a pint of lager to start off with, please?'

'Certainly, sir.'

I opened the menu. I wasn't particularly hungry, doubtless it was the heat, but I hadn't had breakfast either, so I decided on the spaghetti carbonara, which I reasoned even the poorest Italian restaurant would be able to throw together fairly well.

'What do you fancy?' I said, looking across the table at him as with a forefinger tracing the words he spelled his way through the options. 'Don't say you can't decide again!'

There was a startled look in his eyes as he met my gaze. Or maybe I was imagining things.

'A pizza.'

'I thought you wanted pasta? There's no rush, so take your time.'

I didn't like the thought of him saying something just to please me. He had to learn to stand up for himself and speak his mind, regardless of what others around him might think.

'I'll have a pizza, please.'

'OK. Which one?'

'Margaret.'

'Margherita!

'Yes, Margherita.'

A server came with our drinks, a young woman, twenty at the most, with big upper arms and chubby cheeks, and took our food order as well.

Leo dipped his fingers into his Coke and fished out an ice cube. I let it pass — I couldn't be on his back all the time. He balanced the ice cube on the tips of his fingers, which he'd bunched together like a bouquet, leaned forward and popped it into his mouth with a slurping sound. His eyes widened, either because of the sudden cold shock or because he was trying to be funny.

I swallowed a couple of mouthfuls of my beer.

The server, who was pretty enormous across the hips too, I noticed now, appeared again at our table, clutching a handful of crayons.

'Would you like to use these?' she said to Leo.

He nodded, and crunched his ice cube.

'You can colour the back of the menu,' she said, turning it over for him to see. 'Or you can draw on the table covering too, if you like.'

'Can I?'

'It's only paper,' she said with a smile, and went away again.

Some peaceful minutes followed. Leo immersed himself in his drawing and I felt liberated. Not from him, but from the attention I gave him, which drained me imperceptibly, so it was a relief to let go.

I looked through the room and out at the busy street while drinking my beer and wishing I could smoke. When the food arrived I ordered another, but regretted it immediately, I might have finished eating by the time it came, in which case I'd have to drink with Leo waiting impatiently.

He tried to tear off a slice of his pizza as if it was paper.

'Haven't they sliced it for you?'

'Yes, but not enough.'

'Here, let me help you,' I said and leaned across to cut fully through the existing slits until half his pizza was separated into slices.

He took one in his hand and blew on it. I pricked a hole in the egg yolk, which ran yellow into the pale, black-peppered spaghetti.

'Do you want some ice cream for afters?' I said, pleased with myself for suddenly having hit upon a solution that would satisfy us both.

He nodded and smiled.

'Is the pizza too hot?'

'Yes.'

'Then wait a bit. Pizzas cool quickly, because they're so thin. At least the proper Italian ones are.'

I twirled my fork a few times until winding up enough spaghetti to put it in my mouth.

'Leo?' I said.

'Yes?'

'You know what you get when you can't choose?'

'No, what?'

'Nothing. In fact, it's better to make the wrong choice and take the consequences. Then at least you've got something. So you shouldn't be afraid of choices. Choose one thing and stick with it. Do you understand what I mean?'

He nodded and picked up his slice of pizza again.

'Is it cooler now?'

'I think so.'

We ate a while without speaking, interrupted only by the female server who against all odds appeared with my beer only five minutes after I'd ordered it.

Leo was soon full and shoved his plate away across the table after three slices. It didn't matter, since I was already wiping the last of my carbonara sauce off my own plate with a piece of bread.

I ordered the ice-cream dessert for him, with two scoops of vanilla, and a coffee for myself.

The server ruffled Leo's hair as we were leaving and he smiled at her sheepishly, though warmly too. Outside, I lit a cigarette and stood back against the wall a bit further along from the restaurant while Leo waited on the pavement with his Lego bag in his hand. I'd never liked walking and smoking at the same time, there was something about it that felt wrong in a way. Not that standing around smoking was much better, but better somehow, nevertheless.

'Aren't you going to buy something for yourself, Pappy?' Leo said, squinting at me.

'Why are you asking me that? Do you want to stay in town a bit longer?'

'No. I just thought you should have something too.'

'I've already got everything I need.'

I dropped my cigarette end onto the pavement and stepped on it.

'Shall we go?'

He slid close to my side and took my hand. It was a fair way yet to the Tube station and I didn't want to hold his hand all the way, but a couple of hundred metres wouldn't hurt.

The sun was almost directly above us, its shadows short, the still air hot and sticky.

'Shall we fill the paddling pool when we get home?' I said.

'Yes!' he beamed back.

'Shall we ask Mummy to give Luke's parents a ring and ask if he can come over too?'

'I don't think he'll want to.'

'We won't know until we've asked.'

'OK.'

We'd left Soho when my phone chimed in my pocket. I let go of his hand to see what it was. A text from Yelena.

A woman was here. She said she knew you well and would come back later when you got home. Her name was Sonja. Who is she?

Oh, fuck. The stupid bloody cow.

It couldn't be true.

Had she come to the house? My home?

'What is it?' Leo said.

'Nothing,' I said, and dropped the phone back into my pocket. I'd have to come up with a good answer. I could say I had no idea who she was, that she must be some kind of a stalker. Or maybe it was better to stay as close to the truth as possible. Someone I met in New York who worked at the gallery. Nice enough. We chatted a few times and I may have said she was welcome to look us up if she was ever in London. I can't remember exactly, but you know the sort of thing you say to people.

Unless she'd told Yelena what happened.

Why else would she come to the house? What did she want? There could be no other reason than to ruin things for me, to destroy my life.

I halted at a busy pedestrian crossing. A crowd of people stood waiting for the light to change while cars and buses thundered past. Leo bent down, his shoelace had come undone.

He wasn't very good at tying his laces yet, it always took him an age.

'Do you want me to help you?'

He shook his head.

It was good that he wanted to do things himself.

I took my phone out and read the text again.

A woman was here. She said she knew you well and would come back later when you got home. Her name was Sonja. Who is she?

Clearly, Yelena knew nothing. The question was tinged with suspicion, yes. But so far all she had on me was that a woman I'd never mentioned had come to the door and asked if she could speak to me. There could be any number of reasonable explanations.

Sonja's from Norway and works as a journalist, I met her in New York, a very nice woman.

No, that wouldn't do, I realised, pausing and then deleting it.

I think she's someone new at Burnett who I met in New York. A pushy type, but I didn't think she'd go this far. Did you get rid of her?

I hesitated. This was risking it a bit more.

The pedestrian light changed back to red, but there was always a leeway before the traffic light went green and so I scurried across the two lanes to the island in the middle.

Only then did I think of Leo, and turned to see where he was. He ran out after me.

'No, Leo!' I yelled.

A double-decker hit him. It wasn't going very fast, but it knocked him to the ground and he went in underneath it.

It stopped.

People screamed. The traffic ground to a halt. Someone blew their horn.

I saw his legs sticking out, the blue shoes on his feet. He wasn't moving.

The only thing I saw were the legs of my little boy, and his blue shoes.

The bus door opened and the driver bundled out.

And then I was kneeling in front of the bus. Everything else was a shadow-world, a flickering, insubstantial blur.

'Leo?' I said, and touched his lower leg. It felt warm in the sun.

'He just ran out,' the driver said behind me. 'I hadn't a chance. Not a chance. It wasn't my fault. He just ran out. Right in front of me.'

I found myself gently pulling Leo towards me.

'No, don't do that,' a woman's voice said. 'I'm a nurse. We need to wait until the ambulance gets here. Is it your child?'

She crouched down beside me and gripped my arm.

I wrenched free and kept pulling.

His hip felt soft, a mushy consistency, and his shorts were wet with blood.

His eyes were open. There was some blood at the corner of his mouth, but apart from that his head looked undamaged.

'Leo?' I said. 'Leo, can you hear me?'

'You mustn't move him. There's nothing we can do until the ambulance comes. They'll be here any minute.'

She was right. I heard sirens.

I knew as well as she that you had to be careful with an injured person in the event of such an accident. So I slid my hand under the back of his head, as I'd done when he'd still been a baby, and picked him up as cautiously as I could. I clutched him to my body and got to my feet.

He was warm and soft.

'Oh, my little boy, my little boy. Oh, my little boy.'

Everything was white inside me, as if everything had been burned away. The sirens were louder, closer now, until suddenly they stopped. I pressed my cheek to his.

Two paramedics bustled towards me with a stretcher trolley and dumped their bags. I handed Leo over to them. They laid him down on the stretcher and set to work on him.

'He's alive, isn't he?' I said.

'Are you the father?' one of them said.

'Yes.'

'He just ran out, I hadn't a chance,' the driver was saying to a policeman I hadn't noticed until then.

'We're taking him in now. Come with us.'

'But he's alive. That's what you're telling me, yes?'

'His heart's not beating. We're trying to get it started again.'

'We're going to China together,' I said.

My eye saw something yellow underneath the bus. It was his new Lego. I kneeled down and reached in to retrieve it. The paramedics rolled the trolley to the ambulance. I followed them. The Lego box was quite intact.

'You can sit in the back here,' I was told. I climbed in and sat down with the bag on my knees.

The siren came on. Two policemen cleared the way, the driver mounted the kerb, passed the bus, then pulled away onto the road at sudden speed. I leaned forward and puked between my legs. A spew of carbonara all over the floor. The female paramedic stroked a hand up and down my back a couple of times, barely taking an eye from the equipment she was monitoring.

They always got the heart going again after an accident. They had equipment that shot electricity into it. And his chest hadn't been damaged. It was his hip.

I closed my eyes and folded my hands.

Please God. Let him live. Please let him live.

I felt her hand on my back again.

'Leave me alone,' I said.

She took her hand away. We were outside the hospital. The driver went down a ramp into an underground drop-off zone. Staff were ready waiting. As soon as we stopped, the rear doors were flung open. I stayed rooted to my seat as Leo was rushed away.

'Come with me and I'll show you where you can wait,' the paramedic said.

Yelena.

Yelena.

I got out and took out my phone.

'Are you ringing to explain?' she said.

'It's Leo. There's been an accident. He's at the hospital.'

'What are you saying? What's happened?'

'He's been run over.'

'Is it serious? Is he injured?'

'Yes. I'm sorry.'

My voice cracked.

'Are you at the hospital now?'

'Yes.'

'I'm on my way. Which hospital?'

I told her which one and hung up. The paramedic, who had stepped away while I'd spoken to Yelena, now appeared again.

'Come with me,' she said.

I followed her down a corridor.

When Yelena got there forty-five minutes later, Leo was dead. She realised the moment she saw me. Her face drained before my eyes.

'Tell me it's not true,' she said. 'Tell me Leo's alive. Tell me, Kristian. Tell me. Tell me.'

I couldn't speak. I couldn't look at her.

'Is Leo dead? Our little boy?'

I nodded.

She sank to her knees.

'It's not true. Say it's not true.'

She buried her face in her hands and expelled a long, tortured sound.

We wouldn't get through this. We'd never get over it.

She didn't cry. She yelled out her pain.

'I want to see him,' she said and scrambled to her feet. 'Where is he?'

'I don't know.'

I went out into the corridor and stopped a nurse, asked her for the doctor who'd told me Leo was dead. But the doctor was busy, she said.

'We want to see our son.'

'What's his name?'

'He's dead.'

A grave expression came to her face as she realised. Behind us, Yelena came out of the room where I'd sat waiting.

'Just give me a second,' the nurse said, and disappeared into an office diagonally opposite.

'What happened, Kristian?' Yelena said, suddenly composed.

'He ran out into the road without looking and was run over.'

'But where were you?'

'I was there.'

The nurse appeared and jerked her head for us to come with her, and we followed her to the room where Leo lay.

They'd closed his eyes and cleaned away the trickle of blood from his mouth, and covered him with a blanket.

He looked like he always did.

Yelena bent forward and put her arms around him, she pressed her cheek to his, and kissed his brow, over and over.

'Come back, Leo,' she whispered. 'Come back to me.'

Her shoulders trembled and she began to sob.

I felt nothing. I was completely empty inside.

But Yelena had no means of withstanding, she was completely in the grip of grief, unable to leave him, even when the nurse cautiously suggested it was time, unable simply to leave the room in which he lay.

'Come, Yelena,' I said, and put my arm around her.

'But we can't just leave him.'

'He's not here.'

'How can you say that?' she said and bent over him again, ran her fingers through his hair, kissed his brow.

She looked at me with eyes so full of despair that I had to look away.

'There's some information here and a phone number if you feel you need to talk to someone,' the nurse said quietly, handing me a leaflet.

I put it in my pocket.

I couldn't bring myself to say: Are you coming? I couldn't bring myself to say: Shall we get a taxi home?

'Yelena . . . ?' I said.

'Come here,' she said.

I stepped towards her.

'We have to say goodbye,' she said.

She took his hand and held it in hers. I understood that she wanted me to do the same.

I felt how cold his fingers were between hers, which were so much warmer.

He looked like he was asleep.

I thought she was about to say something, but she broke down and began sobbing again uncontrollably. Gently, I lowered her hand to the bed, she let go of Leo's, and I held her tight. I glanced towards the nurse, who looked down at the floor, and then I led her slowly from the room.

We had nowhere to go. We had nothing we could do.

We were lost.

There were taxis outside. We got into one. I gave the driver our address. No one spoke until we got there.

She broke down again as soon as we were inside the door, and sank to the floor.

There were his shoes. There were his coats.

I knew what she was thinking.

I went into the living room and sat down on the sofa. I heard her go up the stairs. Her footsteps on the bedroom floor. From the light outside I judged the time to be somewhere between three and four. My eyes found the clock on the kitchen wall.

He'd been alive that morning. Now it was twenty past three and he was dead.

I had to have him back.

I had to bring him home.

Oh, my lovely little boy.

He looked up from where he lay in my mind's eye, playing with his Lego, smiling warmly and full of trust.

I went into the kitchen, stuck my fingers down my throat and bent over the sink. I retched, but nothing came up.

I went back to the sofa and sat down again, slouched against the arm. I tipped my head back and closed my eyes. An image came to me of the pond in the forest back home. An early morning, one of those endless days in summer when the surface mirrored the sky and the air was filled with light and dancing insects. The soft mud into which the feet would sink, its little clouding whirls. The way the water had different temperatures at different levels, gauged by the body that swam towards the bottom. The taste of metal and earth. And in autumn, when the sun was behind the hill, when the water was as black as oil and the forest all around was aglow with vivid colours. The sky a deeper blue than it ever was in summer. The thinnest veneer of ice in early morning, gone well before midday. Winter, the snow falling wet and thick, a landscape in grey and white, and everything indistinguishable.

Sensing these images become harder to sustain, I saw then the fields below the house. Golden and abundant in summer, when the days were open-ended and lazy swells of light drifted through them. The cars that drove past unnoticed on the road. The clusters of green trees, islands in all the yellow, among which were the red roofs of the various farms. The clouds of dust from the combine harvesters, and the stubble they left behind to the rain of autumn, when darkness was no longer merely a veil, like smoke in the summer night, but dense as a wall.

I had to find him and bring him back.

Above me, footsteps. She appeared a moment later and sat down without looking at me.

'I want to know everything you did together today,' she said after a long while.

'I don't think I can, Yelena.'

'I was looking forward to him coming home and telling me what you'd done today.'

She looked at me.

'Was he happy?'

'Yes, he was happy.'

'He didn't want to go to town. Why did you make him? If you hadn't, he'd still be alive.'

I didn't answer.

'Kristian?'

'It's no use, Yelena.'

'Where did you have lunch? What did he eat?'

'Please.'

'You can't keep it from me.'

'We found an Italian restaurant. He had pizza.'

'What did you talk about?'

'Yelena.'

'He was happy, you say?'

'Yes. He wanted me to buy something for myself.'

Her eyes filled with tears. She laid her head on my lap. I smoothed her hair. But it felt wrong. She was too big. My body expected *him*. It should have been him.

I made to stand up. She pulled herself straight, and I got to my feet.

'Where are you going?'

'Outside.'

'I'm coming with you.'

I took my cigarettes from my jacket pocket, and we sat down facing each other across the table. The only thought in my head was that he wasn't there. He wasn't in his room, he wasn't in the living room, he wasn't in the kitchen. He wasn't anywhere. There was only us.

'You have to tell me what happened.'

I looked back at the house. The window from where he'd called to me yesterday before his bath. The door he'd come through when he came to tell me his tongue was yellow.

'It just makes it worse.'

'You think it can get worse?'

'No.'

'How did he die, Kristian?'

'He ran out onto the road.'

'Why? Why did he run? Where were you?'

'I was there.'

'Beside him?'

'Yes.'

'Then why did he run? It's so unlike him.'

'I don't know. He'd been tying his shoelace. And then he ran right out.'

She looked at me for a long time.

Then suddenly her face crumpled. Her upper lip twisted, her shoulders began to tremble. The sounds she emitted were so full of torment they no longer seemed human, it was as if they came from the pit of her soul, and her soul was an animal soul. She leaned forward and put her face in her hands.

I saw her, but could not contain her.

I couldn't bear her grief.

I waited until she was finished before I got up.

'Where are you going?'

'I'm going for a drive.'

'You can't leave me.'

'I'm coming back.'

'Kristian, don't go. Stay with me.'

'I won't be long.'

I took the car key from the hook in the passage and opened the garage door. Only when I stepped into the cool air there did it occur to me how hot it was outside. I started the car, nice and cool, it too, and waited with impatience for the garage door to open. As I turned my head in order to reverse out, I saw that he'd left a thin jacket and a sweatshirt on the back seat, a cap too. I threw the gear lever back into neutral, put the handbrake on and got out, opened the rear door, snatched up the forgotten items and took them outside, where I threw them in the bin. There were other things in the back that belonged to him too — a couple of books, some old toys, some sheets of paper from school. I gathered them up and sent them the same way as his clothes before getting back in the car and reversing out. The gravel crunched underneath the wheels, a sound I'd always liked, though not now, it reminded me that he was no longer with us. The sun that burned in the sky, the blue sky, everything was contaminated and filled me with disgust. The trees in the park, the shadows they threw, the people milling there.

Would Leo never see the park again?

It was *teeming* with kids. There were *hundreds* of them there.

Why could he not be one of them?

I was seething with rage as I parked outside the supermarket, because I realised too that going there had been a mistake — everyone in the place behaved as if nothing had happened, oblivious to how privileged they were as they shuffled and waddled behind their shopping trolleys.

Why were *they* allowed to live?

I took some rolls of bin liners from a shelf, paid for them and drove home while trying to keep the worst thoughts at bay, the ones that wanted only to say that Leo would never again see this or this or this, the ones that wanted to tell me again that he was no more. That his warmth, his devotion, his trustfulness were no more. That he would never be a teenager, never go to university, never know a lover or a significant other, never be allowed to live his life. But if I could fend off such thoughts, the underlying feeling they represented was unrelenting. There was no getting away from it.

Yelena was not in the garden when I got back, nor was she in the living room. I stood a few seconds without moving in the hall, listening out, but there wasn't a sound from anywhere. I reasoned that she was upstairs in the bedroom and went and smoked a cigarette in the garden as I summoned up the courage to do what I had to do.

Whenever a respite came, four or five seconds in which I didn't think about him, I would be punished fourfold, because it was like finding out again: Leo is dead.

Oh no. Oh no, no, no.

Oh no, no.

Leo, my little boy, what have you done?

I got to my feet and took the bin liners with me up to his room. Everything was still as it was when he'd woken up that morning. But I couldn't think about that. What I needed to do, shutting out all thoughts of him, was to gather together all his things — every toy, every book, every poster, every picture, every pair of trousers, every T-shirt — put them into bin liners and take them out with me to the garage when they were full. His Lego buildings would be just Lego buildings, his tractor just a tractor, the little doctor's bag he still liked to play with just a hard plastic doctor's bag. It all had to go, his room had to be emptied. Everything was going in the garage, and tomorrow I would phone someone and get them to come and take it all away. Nothing could be saved. I didn't want anything left.

I started with his clothes. It was the worst part. Every single shirt, every pair of shorts, every jumper was like seeing him. But they were clothes. Cotton and nylon, wool and acrylic. I wept as I binned. Heaps of clothes, I stuffed them into black bin liners. And when one was filled I put it aside, against the wall under the window, and began to fill another.

'What are you doing?' Yelena said from the doorway.

'Clearing his room,' I said without looking at her.

'Are you mad? You can't do that!'

'It's all got to go.'

I was holding a pile of his underwear between my hands as I looked up at her.

Then the doorbell rang. Yelena jumped. I went to the window and squinted down at the front doorstep.

It was Ane standing there, in a short black dress and a white T-shirt, a bag hanging from her shoulder. She was peering in through the living-room window.

'It's Ane,' I said quietly.

'I can't talk to anyone,' Yelena said.

I shook my head. The doorbell rang again. As it died away into the silent house, I realised Leo wasn't there to go and see who it was.

The gravel crunched again as she went away.

'I want his room left the way it is,' Yelena said. 'Please, Kristian.'

'You want a museum?'

'I want a place where . . .'

She started crying again.

I stepped past her and went downstairs into the living room where I slouched again against the arm of the sofa. She came down after me and sat at the other end.

It was so quiet I could hear the clock ticking in the kitchen.

'I can't just sit here,' I said. 'It hurts too much. I need to do something.'

I got up.

'You're not throwing his things out,' Yelena said. 'If you do that, we lose everything.'

'We've *already* lost everything. He's *dead*. Do you understand? Dead! His things only make it worse. They're meaningless when he's no longer here.'

'If you need to do something,' she said, 'there's the funeral to arrange.'

I looked at her. It hadn't even occurred to me. And I didn't want to think about it.

I went into the garden again. The air was hot and still, the sun burned on my skin. A pair of bumblebees hummed among the flowers over by the wall, whose brickwork in the powerful sun was a reddish glow. I followed its line towards the bottom of the garden. Blue, white, yellow and red flowers stood out in all the green. I went over to the table, sat down and lit a cigarette.

The funeral would be just Yelena and me. Our last time with him. No tributes, no music, no people.

She wouldn't accept that either. She'd want her parents there, her sister, her friends. She'd want to wallow in other people's pity.

I couldn't bear it. I went inside to the bathroom, opened the mirror cabinet and took out a packet of sleeping pills. I swallowed two with some water directly from the tap, took the packet with me into the bedroom just in case, thinking I could take another if they didn't work, pulled the curtains shut, undressed and climbed into bed under the thin blanket. I wondered whether to take the third pill straight away so I'd be sure to fall sleep, and did.

I was standing at the kitchen sink filling a glass with water when Leo came up behind me. Blood was running from the corner of his mouth and his hip was crushed, his eyes stiff and staring.

'It's just an apparition,' Yelena said. 'It's not him. He's somewhere else.'

'Where is he, then?'

'He's behind the mirrors.'

I woke at that same moment with a good feeling in me, for everything had seemed so natural, and he *was* somewhere after all — but it was a feeling reality then ripped to pieces in a split second.

I heard Yelena howling somewhere in the house.

I took two more sleeping pills and turned onto my side, and was asleep before she could come back in.

I told her I didn't want anyone else at the funeral as we sat in the taxi on our way to the undertaker. As I'd expected, she wouldn't hear of it. She said Leo wasn't ours alone. It turned into a quarrel, which ended in her saying the only person I cared about was myself, that I even thought more about myself than I thought about Leo.

'I'm never going to forgive you for saying that, Yelena,' I said. 'I'll remember it till the day you die.'

I didn't say anything else after that.

'Do we have to decide everything now, or can we think about it?' Yelena said to the funeral director, who of course said that we could think about it, and then gave us some brochures and documents Yelena took home with her, even though they were all online too.

She would be on the phone to her parents and her sister, it was to them she went now when she needed to cry, pacing back and forth in the garden or sitting on the edge of the bed. She ignored me. After she rang off, the house would be still again and she would lie silently in bed or sit silently on the sofa, depending on where I was or what I was doing.

I woke in the night and she was lying beside me, and I put my arms around her and held her tight. She said nothing, but did not stiffen as she often would when we'd been arguing. After a while she took my hand in hers.

'What are we going to do?' she said. 'What are we going to do?'

'I don't know,' I said.

Everything was about getting through the days. In the mornings everything seemed impossible, everything was unbearable, a minute was like an eternity. But then evening would come, as evening came always. I took my sleeping pills. God knows what Yelena did, perhaps she was awake day and night. She wasn't eating, whatever she was doing.

It was good to feel her body against mine when we lay in bed. There was comfort in it.

'Yelena?' I said on the third night.

'Yes?' she said.

'We could start anew. We could have another baby.'

Her body tensed. But she said nothing.

'It's not too late,' I said. 'We could have another baby.'

Still she said nothing.

After a short time she got up and went to the bathroom. When she came back I sat up.

'Did you hear what I said?'

She nodded.

'Then what do you think?'

'Don't ask me about it, Kristian.'

'Why not?'

'Just don't. Now's not the time.'

'No, of course not. I don't mean now. But soon.'

She lay down again, with her back to me.

'Yelena?'

'I don't want a child with you.'

'What?'

'I don't want a child with you.'

'You mean, never?'

'Never.'

I got up and gathered my clothes, then went downstairs. She said nothing, didn't ask where I was going, didn't ask me to stay.

I would make her pay.

By the time morning came I knew what I was going to do. I was filled with the same restless energy I was familiar with from my work, when I could hardly wait to carry through an idea. It would require surprisingly little preparation, so little that in a way it was as if subconsciously I'd been readying myself all along. I kept some boxes of old stuff in the studio, stuff that Yelena had never seen. I drove down there and picked out a couple of hoodies from sometime in the nineties, some trousers, a small backpack and two or three caps, all of which I stuffed into a bin liner and chucked in the boot of the car before driving back. Money wasn't a problem either. Before we got married, I'd transferred, with the help of a professional adviser, a certain amount of funds to a so-called tax haven, where no one could get their hands on them but me. I'd also had an account with a Norwegian bank ever since my youth. I was fairly sure I'd never mentioned it to her. There was money there too, not a huge amount, but certainly not an inconsiderable sum.

I told her she could have the funeral exactly as she wanted. The news seemed not to gladden her, it was as if it didn't mean anything to her after all. I couldn't have cared less, though a nod of acknowledgement wouldn't have been amiss.

No, it wasn't important one way or another. The funeral itself wasn't important either. Nothing was important. Death and emptiness were all there was.

She went upstairs to bed around nine that evening. I waited a while in the living room before going out to the garage. I wanted her to still be awake so that she'd hear me leave. I started the car and reversed out. The sky was dark blue, and the sun was touching the tops of the trees and buildings. Everything was quiet, the way only evenings in summer could be quiet. The wheels spun in the gravel when I threw the car into gear and accelerated away. The gate had already opened. I imagined her listening to the sound of the engine as I turned left onto the road, hearing it melt into the traffic a few seconds later. Leaving the house in the evening without saying where I was going would disquieten her. And her concern would only be heightened when after a few hours I still hadn't returned as she no doubt expected, not to mention when morning came.

I drove out of London and took the M4 towards Bristol. The traffic was light and I kept my foot down. Turning off at some services to get myself a coffee, I found pleasure in the thought of someone later identifying me on the CCTV footage, my figure seen diagonally from above as I went towards the counter, ordered, paid, picked up my coffee, left the shop, and then, from another camera, crossed the forecourt, got back in the car and drove off.

Approaching Bristol an hour or so later, I headed south from the outskirts of the city, to a nature reserve I'd visited several times with

Liz in a distant past. It was a place she'd loved. Exmoor National Park. Close to the Bristol Channel, I turned off the main road and followed a gravel track that led into the woods. After a few hundred metres I parked the car between some trees. Left my phone and wallet containing my Norwegian credit cards in the glove compartment, the key in the ignition, closed the door without locking the vehicle and lit a cigarette as I leaned back against the wing. It was still dark and would be for another couple of hours. There were no cars on the roads here, and I was hardly likely to wake anyone in the few houses that lay scattered about.

I hadn't thought about Leo once in half an hour. It felt like a betrayal, and when the longing for him returned it only hurt more than ever.

I dropped the cigarette end onto the ground and crushed it under my shoe. It would be days before the car was found, weeks even, but when it was discovered and they found out who it belonged to, everything would speak for itself.

Taking the old clothes out of the boot, I changed, bagged the ones I'd been wearing and put them in the backpack before threading my arms through the straps. I took one last look at the car, which from that moment on would be the suicide's vehicle, noted that it appeared convincingly abandoned, and began walking. For a few kilometres I kept away from the roads and encountered not a soul. I tired rather quickly, unused to walking any great distance, certainly not in such rugged terrain. But it was necessary to put time and distance between me and the car. It was the middle of the night, the roads as good as deserted, and anyone that did happen to be out probably wouldn't see me at all, but it would be stupid to run the risk.

It took me nearly six hours to get to Barnstaple. In case they at some point checked the CCTV, I stayed away from the station until the train arrived and I could get straight on, in clothes Yelena had never seen. In London, between Paddington and St Pancras, my resolve came close to collapse, home being only a short Tube ride away, but the thought of Leo came to my rescue. He wasn't there, nothing was there, nothing but emptiness and death, emptiness and death. So I followed my plan and took the train to Dover, the ferry to Calais, then trains again, to Copenhagen, where I dumped my former clothes in a bin. From Copenhagen I took the train along the coast of Sweden to Oslo, from there the sleeper to Bergen, then the hydrofoil to Florø. There I bought myself a big new rucksack, which I filled with clothes and food before taking a bus the last part of the way to the ferry.

*

Now only night remains.

My mind is clear. The world outside seems to be readying itself too. For so long, the owner of the house had been unaware that anyone was here. For so long, no one had recognised me. But now my days are numbered. Yesterday in the store a young man came up to me, while his embarrassed girlfriend hovered in the background, pretending to be preoccupied.

'Excuse me, but aren't you Kristian Pedersen?' he said in English, with what I took to be a German accent.

'No, thank goodness,' I said. 'But I've been told before that I look like him.'

He held my gaze a second and then smiled. I don't think he believed me.

'In that case, I hope you'll excuse me,' he said. 'The likeness is just so very . . .'

'As far as I know, Kristian Pedersen's dead,' I said. 'So it's a bit bizarre to ask, don't you think?'

'Yes, I realise that. But of course his body was never found, and there's been a lot of speculation, so when I saw you, well . . .'

I wanted to tell him to fuck off. But the only sensible thing was to play down the situation, so I simply smiled and shook my head, told him I'd lived there all my life, and wished him a nice holiday.

As if that wasn't enough, the neighbour, Einar, has just been here. I sensed something might be amiss as soon as he knocked on the door — he hadn't done so since my first day in the house. If there was anything he needed to convey, which was basically never, he would send Viggo.

'Hello there,' he said.

'Hello,' I said. 'How's things?'

'I just got a phone call from Stray's son. I believe Egil is his name. He says he'll be staying here a month or so over the summer.'

'Oh?'

'It turns out he didn't know you were here. He hadn't heard about anyone borrowing the place. Which I thought was a bit strange.'

'No, not at all. I squared it with his father, Emil, quite some time ago. He probably forgot. Or else Egil didn't check in with him first.'

He arched an eyebrow. Or maybe I was imagining things.

'When did Egil say he was coming exactly?'

'This weekend, he said.'

'I see.'

'Why they didn't tell you is a bit beyond me. How long had you said you'd be staying?'

'I didn't, it's more open-ended. I met Stray — Emil, that is — at a reception and he told me about the house here when I said I was looking for somewhere out of the way where I could write. He said I could borrow the place, all I had to do was get here, the key was underneath the front steps — which it was!'

He nodded a couple of times.

'It's a shame. For you, I mean. Getting thrown out like this.'

'Well, all good things come to an end.'

'It's usually the way.'

'It is, yes.'

'Won't you come over for a cup of coffee before you go — or something stronger, perhaps?'

'I will, thank you.'

He nodded, turned and went away.

It's Wednesday today. Two days left, in other words.

All I need is two minutes, so it'll be all right.

I went for a walk, as I do every night, along the rocks at the shore below the house and around the island, to the far side and the open sea. Normally I'd have the fishing rod with me, but not tonight. The sun put flame to the sky, the horizon looked like it was on fire. The sea was a millpond. I haven't seen that out here before.

I sat down on an outcrop of rock and stared at the water a few metres below, where long strands of flat, brown seaweed lay floating on the surface. The water was not warm, I knew, even though it looked to be. I guessed it was fourteen or fifteen degrees at most.

Leo would never see this.

I would never see Leo.

The absence I felt was no use fighting. Absence was the shadow of death, and death was insurmountable — nothing compelled more than its void. No sun, no galaxy, not even life itself.

For a while, it's enough to wake to one's self in the morning, as the birds and the otters wake to their own selves. For a while, it's enough to have a place in the world. You feel nothing, you know you are going to die, but it doesn't matter, for death is not now, and you are only now.

Then absence comes, and with it the longing for that which is not and never can be, the distaste for what is. The contempt of the self and one's life. Absence is not mild, absence is not something fine that lends to existence a mere tinge of melancholy. Absence is aversion, disdain, nausea, anger, hopelessness. The only relief from absence is to pit it against the void. To fight fire with fire.

I sat down at the desk in front of the window upstairs where I had sat almost every day since the previous autumn the year before. I had written what I wanted to write. The sun was setting, but the sky would not become dark, for the nights here were light and delicate. To the east, the fells hovered magically, as if unconnected to stone, earth, weight, sleep, death.

The sun's low-angled rays deceived the eye and created a strong sense of day, which the rest of the body, in the thrall of its biological clock, opposed — something was awry, and a sense of foreboding arose, since the only conclusion was that the light in fact was darkness.

No sooner had I written these words than something caught my eye in the distance. A small movement on the water, something white — the hydrofoil on its final tour of the day. When there were no passengers to alight here it would curve around the island and head back towards the mainland where it moored until the next morning. But if there was anyone wanting to come here, it would continue in a straight line.

Which now it did.

Who would be coming here now?

Everyone living on the island was at home.

A visitor, then. Perhaps more than one. Tourists.

I only hoped it wasn't Egil already.

It couldn't be ruled out. He must have been unsettled when Einar said there was someone in the house. No, it couldn't be ruled out at all.

But it had only been a few hours since they'd spoken. He couldn't possibly get here so quickly.

The boat cut through the tranquil surface, trailing a white V in its wake. I could pick out details now. The red stripe along the hull, the eyelike windows at the front, the radar or whatever it was, slowly turning. The green deck, the gunwales.

No one had emerged from any of the houses, no one had gone down to receive any visitor.

It didn't mean it had to be Egil.

A hundred metres perhaps from the jetty now. The ferry slowed abruptly, its bow sank back into the water.

The skipper knew his craft, he must have performed the same manoeuvre thousands of times before, and within a moment the hydrofoil was alongside and the gangway lowered.

A man stepped ashore. His feet had barely touched land before the gangway was raised and the ferry set out once more.

He stood clutching a carrier bag in one hand, the other peaked his brow against the low sun as his eyes found the house in which I sat.

There was something familiar about him.

He started walking. Tall, loose-limbed, a brisk swing of the hand.

It was Hans.

I got to my feet and went downstairs to the kitchen where I was spooning coffee into the filter bag when he knocked on the outer door. I went to let him in.

He winked at me as if time had never separated us. Stood there, in a rather shabby army jacket and grey jeans. The carrier bag was from Rema 1000.

'Hans,' I said. 'It's been a while.'

'A while indeed,' he said. 'Mind if I come in?'

'Have I got a choice?'

He smiled, and I stepped aside.

'Do I have to take my shoes off?'

'Preferably. The owner's coming soon and I was thinking I'd leave the place clean for him.'

He bent down and undid the laces of his trainers.

'Do you want coffee?'

'Please. If you're having, that is. No need for my sake alone.'

'I got some on the go when I saw you get off the boat.'

He went through into the living room, which was filled with light from the low-hanging sun.

'Nice place,' he said as he looked around.

'It's served its purpose. Sit down and I'll bring the coffee.'

I poured two cups in the kitchen. When I went back in he was sitting on the sofa, bent forwards with his arms on his knees, the way I remembered him from his garage studio in London that first night.

He didn't look a day older.

'You seem to be keeping well,' I said, handing him his cup.

'Thanks,' he said.

I sat down on the armchair opposite him.

'Have you come to collect me?'

'What makes you think that?'

'Hell awaits.'

He laughed.

'Kristian. Haven't you understood? Hell is here.'

I looked at him without replying.

It made sense.

'You got everything you asked for, Kristian. But there's always a price.'

'Which is?'

He reached into his coat pocket and took out a packet of cigarettes, then delved again to retrieve a lighter from the same place. He curled his hand, shielding the flame even though we were indoors, then took a long drag. Held his breath a moment, before exhaling the smoke and fixing me in his gaze.

'That you no longer get what you ask for.'

'I'm not asking for anything. There's nothing I want.'

'You don't want Leo back?'

I felt sick all of a sudden, the way I always did when I thought about Leo.

'I know I can't.'

'And you don't want to die?'

I returned his gaze.

'What do you mean?'

'You say there's nothing you want. But I don't think that's true. I think you want to die. Am I wrong?'

'No.'

He nodded.

'There, you see. There's always something a person wants.'

He stood up.

'Welcome to Hell, Kristian.'

It could have been one of his witty comments, but he didn't smile, and his voice was solemn. He stepped up to the window and looked out in the direction of the harbour, then lifted a hand and scratched the pane with the nail of his forefinger to see if the mark he saw was inside or out.

'Do you want to see Leo again?'

I didn't answer.

He turned and looked at me kindly.

'Do you?'

I couldn't muster a word, but nodded.

'Then come with me,' he said. 'The bathroom's out here, yes?'

I went with him. He closed the door behind us and stood in front of the mirror.

'Stand here beside me.'

I did as he said.

A bathroom with white tiles, a shower cabinet with a white curtain, a white wooden door. Hans and I, staring at ourselves.

'Leo?' he said in a low voice. 'Leo?'

In the mirror, the door opened and Leo came in.

My little boy. Oh, my little boy.

He stared at me with his dark eyes.

I turned round. The door behind us was closed.

Leo stepped forward to the mirror and without taking his eyes from me placed the palms of his hands flat against the glass.

He looked like he did the day he died.

'I'm so sorry, Leo. I'm so, so sorry.'

'He can't hear you,' Hans said, and put his hand on my shoulder.

The distinction between life and literature has been much discussed in recent years, and is a complicated issue, since if a boundary does exist between the two domains, it is porous and osmotic, the traffic in both directions considerable, even at night, when outright bands of smugglers, unbeknown to anyone but themselves, set to work. In practical terms, however, for me as a writer, the matter is simpler: literature happens inside my study, whereas life is what happens when I open its door and emerge into the company of those I love, Michal and the children — Vanja, Kaia, Heidi, Evie, John, Anne and Tom. They make every day meaningful and without their light I would never have been able to withstand the darkness of this novel. One of the people who read it while it was still taking shape asked me who the main character was modelled upon. I replied, truthfully: no one. As a character, Kristian Hadeland has no basis in reality. It's an important point for me to make when thanking, as I do now, two friends who both happen to be photographers — and brilliant ones at that! — for all our inspiring discussions over the years, about photography, art and life: Thomas Wågström and Stephen Gill. Thomas also read and commented on the manuscript, as did Monika Fagerholm, Martin Aitken, Greger Ulf Nilsson, Karin Mamma Andersson, Bjørnar Lia, Bjørn Arild og Kari Ersland, Yngve Knausgård, Eirik Riis Mossefinn and Christian Hieronymus Heyerdahl: thank you all for your insightful and utterly crucial feedback. Karin and Greger also for their fantastic pictures and design! Moreover: thanks to Andrew Wylie, Charles Buchan, and everyone at Forlaget Oktober, not least Kjersti Instefjord and Øyvind Lysebo Ekelund. And Geir Gulliksen: had a word of thanks been enough for his indispensable contribution to this novel, it would have come here.

Karl Ove Knausgaard's My Struggle cycle has been heralded as a masterpiece all over the world. From *A Death in the Family* to *The End*, the novels move through childhood into adulthood and, together, form an enthralling portrait of human life. Knausgaard has been awarded the Norwegian Critics Prize for Literature, the Brage Prize and the Jerusalem Prize. His work has been published in thirty-six languages. His most recent novels — *The Morning Star*, *The Wolves of Eternity*, *The Third Realm* and *The School of Night* — form the spine-tingling and critically acclaimed Morning Star sequence.

Martin Aitken's translations of Scandinavian literature number some thirty-five books. His work has appeared on the shortlists of the International Dublin Literary Award (2017) and the US National Book Awards (2018), as well as the 2021 International Booker Prize. He received the PEN America Translation Prize in 2019.